Praise for

Monica Burns

"Burns doesn't disappoint!"
— **RTBOOKreviews**

Monica Burns writes with sensitivity and panache.
— **Sabrina Jeffries, NYT bestselling author**

"powerfully done…the scenes between Tobias and Jane mesmerized me. I loved it."
— **Joey W. Hill**

"No one sets fire to the page like Monica Burns."
— **eCataromance**

"Definitely recommended reading."
— **The Romance Studio**

"Ms. Burns is masterful at escalating the sexual tension and suspense with her characters."
— **Coffeetime Romance**

The Rogue's Offer

Monica Burns

Cover Design: Viviana Izzo, Enchantress Design & Promo
Copyeditor: Rosie Murphy

Publishing History
Digital 1.0 edition / 2019
Print 1.0 edition / 2019
Print 1.1 edition / 2021 Updates

ISBN: 978-1-948505-03-1

Acknowledgements

With warm thanks and gratitude to Laura Polito McEleney, Debbie Samson-Fitts, and Viviana Izzo.

Thank you ladies for always giving me feedback when I'm stumped.

Contents

Chapter 1

Ophelia Fullerton, Viscountess Havenstock, studied the tall man on the opposite side of the Melton House ballroom and wrinkled her brow in puzzlement. He was much younger than she expected, and he looked nothing like the debauched brute she'd imagined.

Where was the monster her father had described? The reply in the back of her head wasn't one she wanted to hear. Attempting to cool her skin in the stifling heat of the room, she waved the peacock-feathered fan she held in front of her to create a gentle breeze. She'd bought the fan less than a week ago. It was the type of luxury that would no longer be affordable unless she was able to secure the return of Marymont. Ophelia tipped her head in her sister's direction.

"Lizzie, are you certain this is the man? He looks nothing like the disreputable scoundrel Father described." The dubious note in her voice prompted Ophelia's sister to bristle like a hen ruffling her feathers.

"Of course, I'm certain. Everyone knows who the Earl of Thornbury is."

"And exactly *when* were you introduced to the earl?"

Ophelia arched an eyebrow at her much younger sister, Lizzie, who had made her debut last year under Ophelia's watchful eye. The one thing Ophelia was meticulous about when it came to her sister was ensuring Lizzie never received an introduction to men of the earl's ilk.

Lizzie was good-hearted, but far too trusting when it came to people. She always thought the best of everyone, with the exception of individuals Lizzie thought had harmed her family. Then Lizzie became a tigress, intent on protecting her cubs.

Ever since Lizzie's debut, Ophelia had hoped her sister would find a nice young man to marry and enjoy the happiness denied Ophelia. That hope had become even more fervent than ever before, given their current change in finances.

"Well…we've not actually been introduced." Elizabeth Sheffield tilted her head haughtily, clearly affronted that her identification of the earl had been called into question. "Lady Alice pointed him out to me the other day during our walk near the Serpentine. But he's definitely the man who stole Marymont from Papa, and if we don't do something soon, we'll have nowhere to go."

There was the touch of the dramatic in her sister's words. It was a trait she'd inherited from their father, who had a flair for exaggeration. Unfortunately, this was one instance where her sister's woeful tone was more than appropriate. They were definitely in dire straits thanks to their father's love of wine and cards. A familiar bitterness rolled through her.

"Naturally, Father is completely blameless in this entire debacle," Ophelia bit out as she sent her sister a scathing look. "Perhaps you've forgotten he's the one who wagered our home and lost."

"No, I've not forgotten, but you know Papa is far too polite to refuse someone's offer of hospitality. Papa said the earl kept plying him with wine. It's obvious the man took advantage of him."

"Oh, of course, Father would *never* turn down a drink." Her caustic remark emphasized her belief that the baron's lack of judgement carried the largest burden of guilt. Even if she were wrong in her assumption as to their father's behavior, the baron still held some responsibility for their current situation.

"You are too hard on him, Ophelia. He's been desolate since Mama's death." The note of sorrow in her sister's voice tugged at her heart. Almost eight years younger than her, Lizzie had been happily planning her debut with their mother when the baroness had become ill, never to recover.

"It has been three years since her death, Lizzie. We miss her as much as Father does, but look where his folly has taken us," Ophelia said quietly. "Where Mama always found a way to keep him from indulging in his vices, I have failed."

"You've done your best, Ophelia. We both have." Lizzie's voice held a forlorn note, and Ophelia quickly squeezed her sister's hand.

"We shall find a way out of this quandary, dearest. I promise you that. At least we have the annual stipend George left me. It might not be much, but we will not starve."

Despite Ophelia's lack of confidence in her statement, Lizzie's dejection vanished, and she nodded her belief in her older sister's ability to save them from destitution. A polite cough made her turn around to see Paul Nickens standing behind them. Tall and dark-haired, the young man was of modest means but was good-natured and had a promising future as a solicitor.

Ophelia had liked him from the moment she and Lizzie had been introduced to him. Deep inside, she hoped the young man would offer for her sister and that Lizzie would accept. Under the current circumstances, she was all the more eager to encourage the man's attentions to Lizzie.

"Good evening, Mr. Nickens," she said with a welcoming smile.

"Lady Havenstock. Miss Sheffield." Paul Nickens bowed his greeting with a smile at both of them before he quickly fixated his attention on Lizzie. "I was hoping I might persuade you to let me claim several dances on your card, Miss Sheffield."

"I would be honored for you to do so, sir," her sister said in a breathless voice as her cheek grew pink with pleasure. She handed the young man a stiff rectangular dance card, and he proceeded to draw a line down more than half of Lizzie's card and dashed off his name in bold fashion.

"There, now. I believe this will ensure that several of my rivals will find themselves suitably disappointed this evening," Mr. Nickens said with a grin. "Perhaps you will allow me to claim my first dance now."

"I would find that most enjoyable." Lizzie flashed a brilliant smile at the young man, then accepted his outstretched hand and allowed him to lead her out onto the dance floor.

Satisfied her sister was in good company, Ophelia resumed her assessment of the earl. Despite the loathing she felt for him, the man's appearance underscored one of the reasons he'd earned his reputation as a master of seduction. He was a picture of masculine strength and beauty. It was impossible not to think of the powerful tigers she'd seen pacing in their cages at the Regents Zoo. The earl displayed the same relaxed, yet powerful, sinewy strength in his movements. It epitomized an image of raw power.

The dark hair falling casually over his brow gave him a sinfully wicked look. Everything about the man's appearance was a far cry from the decadent libertine her father had labeled him. Clean-shaven, the earl had chosen to eschew the large mutton chops she'd found so distasteful on her husband. His profile was sharply defined, and his jaw was square and strong-looking. It surprised her that she found him so fascinating when she was incapable of passion. A fact her husband had repeated every time he'd left her bedchamber in the short time they'd been married.

Less than two years after their wedding, George's death had been a relief from the constant bombardment of his criticism. But their brief marriage had convinced her of one thing. She'd failed in her duties as a wife, and she would never possess the ability to seduce a man or find pleasure in the bedroom. It was a conviction that was at distinct odds with her reaction to the earl, and it confused her.

Despite his reputation, there was an almost angelic look about him, which masked the dangerous predator she knew lay beneath the surface. The woman at his side said something that made him laugh, and he bowed slightly as she departed. Enthralled, Ophelia watched the earl take a glass of champagne off the tray one of the footmen carried. Before she could turn her head away, the man looked directly at her and lifted the flute of sparkling liquid in her direction. She couldn't discern the color of his eyes, but the sensual curve of his lips made her mouth go dry.

Dear God, how long had he been aware she was watching him. The air in Ophelia's lungs disappeared, and her chest tightened until she could barely breathe. Frozen in place, she remained pinned beneath his gaze as a small frisson skimmed its way across her skin. Mesmerized, she watched him drink from the crystal glass. As he lowered the flute, a small tipped one corner of his mouth. Long fingers stroked the fragile neck of the glass, invoking the powerful image of his hand trailing down the side of her throat. A raw sensation spiraled through her. It was unlike anything she'd experienced before. Butterflies swirled in her stomach as his tongue flicked out to erase a droplet of wine from his lips. She had no doubt it was a deliberate act on his part, and it sent a shiver skimming down the back of her spine.

In a split second, her nipples grew stiff beneath her corset until they pressed against her chemise. The soft linen roughened the hard peaks until a pleasure that was almost painful in its intensity assaulted her senses. It aroused something unfamiliar inside her that was as startling as it was unexpected.

Another tiny shudder sped through her. It traveled downward to settle between her legs and made her sex ache. It created a need for his hand to caress her as intimately as he did his glass. Disoriented by the sensations flowing through her, Ophelia jerked her gaze away. What in heaven's name was wrong with her? As she fought to regain her faculties, a light touch on her arm made her jump.

"*Ophelia*, how lovely to see you this evening."

The quiet greeting was a welcome distraction, and she quickly turned to see the youngest member of the Rockwood family standing in front of her. Dressed in a dark mauve-colored gown, the only other color Viscountess Westbrook wore was the Stewart plaid in a sash over her breast.

Despite Louisa's somewhat austere appearance, Ophelia thought her friend was even more beautiful than when they'd both been girls riding across the fields of Melton Park. It had been almost a year since they'd last seen each other, and she greeted her friend with an affectionate kiss on the cheek.

"Louisa, oh, it's wonderful to see you. Our paths never seem to cross anymore."

"The season holds little interest for me anymore, and I seldom come to London. Aunt Matilda and I brought the children from Scotland last month for Sebastian's and Helen's tenth-anniversary celebration. Everyone pressed me to stay for a bit longer, although I confess I'm eager to return to the solitude of the countryside." A sorrowful look darkened her friend's hazel eyes as her mouth curved in a small smile. "I find Callendar Abbey suits me far better. The boys do well in the fresh air, and Aunt Matilda loves having company."

"How is your aunt?"

"She's quite well, and she has a suitor. Although, I don't think she's willing to admit it. She grumbles about his arrogance."

The laugh that parted Louisa's lips reminded Ophelia of a time when her friend had been happy and carefree. The death of her husband and her brother in a tragic fire more than two years ago had changed her friend. The tragedy had changed all the Rockwoods. Their impulsive natures were enhanced by their clear determination to live life to its fullest. Even Sebastian, who as the eldest had always been the least impulsive of the Rockwoods, had become less rigid in manner. Ophelia was certain his marriage to the countess was the primary reason many in the Marlborough Set saw him as less staid.

"And the boys?"

"They're sprouting up like weeds. Charles is six now and has become enamored with botany. I wouldn't mind so much if he didn't bring half the earth with him wherever he goes." Louisa smiled with motherly exasperation, yet more than a hint of pride. "And Willie is becoming increasingly precocious. Just last week, he demanded we begin addressing him as Wills since he is no longer a baby. He has taken an intense dislike to being called Willie."

"It sounds as though he's a great deal like his mother." Ophelia smiled as eyed her friend with an arched look. "I remember a time when you were equally determined to be taken seriously. As I recall, Sebastian's look was one of abject horror."

"Good heavens," Louisa gasped with surprised amusement. "Are you referring to the time I told Sebastian I would unscrew the wires in his piano if he didn't stop calling me Weezie?"

"Yes." Ophelia nodded with a laugh. "I have never forgotten how horror stricken he looked."

"My threat worked, though. He never called me Weezie again," Louisa sighed softly. "We were so young back then."

"I'm sorry life has been so terribly difficult for you, Louisa. I truly am," Ophelia said as she touched her friend's arm. A haunted look flitted across Louisa's features before her mouth curved in a smile reminiscent of earlier days, and she patted Ophelia's hand.

"Thank you, Ophelia. It's kind of you—" Louisa suddenly gripped Ophelia's hand tightly. "You're in trouble."

"What?" she choked out in a soft gasp, staring at her friend in surprise.

"Do not deny it, Ophelia. The *an dara sealladh* doesn't come to me as often as the rest of my siblings, but I *do* possess the family gift," Louisa said in a stern voice as she squeezed

Ophelia's hand and shut her eyes. "There's a man. He has something that belongs to you. Letters? No, there's only one, but it's very important to you. You know him, but…"

As her friend's words trailed off into silence, a chill skimmed over Ophelia's skin. Although the Marlborough Set knew of the Rockwoods' gift of sight, it was always discussed with great discretion. As children, she'd been accustomed to Louisa's ability to know things others didn't. But this was the first time her friend had seen something about her. Louisa's eyes flew open, and she stared at Ophelia with a worried frown furrowing her brow.

"You must tell me what's wrong, Ophelia. I trust the *an dara sealladh*, even when the images are confusing and make little sense."

"There's nothing wrong," she prevaricated with as much aplomb as she could muster. "Father lost an important paper the other day, and we've been trying to find it. Perhaps that's what you're seeing."

"No, I don't think so," Louisa murmured as she studied Ophelia closely. "I couldn't see the man's face, but he was much younger than your father."

"Then perhaps you're seeing someone I've yet to meet." Her lips curved in a placating smile, Ophelia struggled to hide how close to the truth Louisa's words were.

"Perhaps…" Louisa said with a look of concentration before a smile of pleasure suddenly curved her lips. "*Mathias*, you came. Percy said you might be here tonight. Why haven't you joined us for dinner recently? I know he's invited you to several occasions, but you keep avoiding us."

"I would never willingly avoid dinner with the Rockwoods," a deep voice filtered its way past her shoulder as a tall figure stopped at Ophelia's side and bent to kiss Louisa's hand. "I've simply been extremely busy."

As she turned her head, Ophelia immediately recognized the owner of the hypnotic voice, and her heart stopped beating for a full second before it resumed again at a faster pace. The most intense jade-colored eyes she'd ever seen locked with hers, and the way he was looking at her made her feel as if he could see the darkest secrets she possessed.

"Ophelia, are you acquainted with—"

"Viscountess Havenstock," the earl said in a voice that was as silky and sinful as one of the rich chocolate truffles she indulged in far too frequently. "I had hoped you would be here this evening."

Speechless that he knew her name, she trembled and slowly extended her hand in a silent greeting. She'd forgone wearing gloves this evening, and his mouth singed her skin in a way that sent a shock wave through her. Dear Lord, what was wrong with her? She'd never experienced this type of reaction to a man before, and it left her feeling completely out of control. The earl raised his head, his gaze never leaving hers.

"Louisa, I hope you don't mind, but Lady Havenstock promised me a dance, and I am here to collect."

"But of course, Mathias," Louisa said with a surprised smile as she looked at Ophelia with avid curiosity.

Still unable to utter a word, Ophelia found her hand clasped in the earl's firm hand as he guided her out onto the dance floor. Her brain sluggish, she didn't even have the wherewithal to protest as he swung her into her arms. The soft, subtle scent of spice and pine swept across her senses, causing her heart to pound a fierce rhythm in her ears. It was a reaction that set her on edge.

She and Lizzie rarely moved in the same exalted circles as the Earl of Thornbury, but tonight had proven an exception. The moment Ophelia had learned the earl might be in attendance, she'd braced herself to do whatever was necessary to capture the man's attention. But her determination had not prepared her for the earl's magnetic presence or the way it affected her equilibrium.

A pulse of panic threaded its way through her. Now that she'd managed to capture the man's attention, every plea she'd rehearsed had fled her brain. Ophelia looked away and remained silent as the earl danced her around the floor.

A low laugh whispered its way past her ear. She immediately glanced up to see green eyes flickering with amusement, and the wicked smile twisting his lips caused her to stumble slightly. The powerful strength she'd noted earlier allowed him to pull her tight against him. Heat suffused her skin the instant her body pressed even more intimately into his chest, and he skillfully whirled her around the dance floor as if she'd not faltered at all.

"Shall I confess something, my lady?" The deep melodious sound of his voice held her spellbound.

"Confess?" she replied breathlessly. Ophelia swallowed hard as she stared up at him. Amusement mixed with something far more dangerous glittered in his gaze.

"You intrigue me."

"Intrigue you?"

"Yes," he said with another soft laugh. "I think I surprised you when I asked you to dance with me."

"Asked me?" she snapped as she remembered her inability to speak one word to the man. "You didn't give me the opportunity to say no."

"You object?" Curiosity echoed in his voice as he arrogantly arched his eyebrows. "From our silent exchange earlier, I was under the impression you wouldn't reject my offer of attention."

"I did not...I was..." Ophelia's voice trailed off at the abrupt tension filling the air between them. Her disdain irritated him, which jeopardized the possibility of Marymont being returned. "Objecting isn't an option for me where you're concerned."

"Once again, I'm intrigued," he said as he whirled her around several quick turns to dodge another couple, and Ophelia experienced a pleasant yet slightly dizzy sensation. "Explain."

"I'm uncertain how to broach the subject."

"Intrigued is becoming an overused word where you're concerned, my lady. Fascinated seems far more appropriate."

The scintillating flash of humor that crossed his face unnerved her. She hadn't expected to find the man devastating to her senses. But then she'd not anticipated feeling anything at all. All she'd ever experienced where men were concerned was either antipathy or friendship. A knot formed in her throat. Perhaps the bargain she'd thought to strike with this man was a foolish one.

It unnerved her to think he might actually be able to awaken something inside her, contrary to established fact. Ophelia quickly dismissed the thought. She was incapable of passion or stirring a similar sensation in a man. George had taught her that. The question was how far she was willing to go to save her childhood home. She'd never been able to bear George touching her. Suddenly, she wasn't sure if she was capable of bartering herself. In the back of her head, a small voice taunted her with the fact that she'd chosen her path the moment she'd looked at the earl from across the ballroom floor. She drew in a shallow breath.

"You have something that belongs to me, or rather my family, Lord Thornbury."

"Indeed," he murmured with an odd look. "What might that be?

"My home."

"*Your home*," he exclaimed softly and his brow wrinkled in puzzlement.

"Marymont. My father lost it in a wager to you several nights ago," she said, as her voice dropped slightly. "I would like it back, and I am willing…I think I have something to offer in exchange."

"And the currency you're referring to?" A glitter of cold calculation darkened the jade eyes narrowing on her.

"Me."

"Ahh, a proposition of the intimate kind." Boredom tugged at his sensual mouth, but his eyes had hardened with something approaching contempt or pity. She was unable to discern which, and it heightened her sense of desperation.

"I do not offer myself up lightly, my lord," she choked out with great effort. "But I believe I am unique enough that I would be unlike other…other women with whom you enter liaisons."

"And tell me, what is this unique quality you possess that makes you think I would be willing to trade a valuable piece of property for it," he murmured with what she was certain was a sneer.

"I…I am incapable of passion," she finished her stumbling statement in a rush.

This time it was the earl's chance to stumble slightly. The awkwardness of the moment was highlighted by his amazement. As the dance music ended with a resounding flourish, he quickly guided her off the dance floor. His sensual mouth was a hard, thin line as he firmly, yet discreetly, maneuvered her through the crowd out into a long hallway that ran the length of the ballroom itself.

Although the corridor wasn't empty, it was significantly less crowded. To anyone else in the hall, his grip on her elbow no doubt appeared solicitous, but his firm grasp indicated he had no intention of letting her escape. He seemed completely certain where he was going, and for the second time in the space of minutes, she was too startled by his behavior to protest. The earl stopped at a door and opened it at the same time he glanced back at a couple who had passed them seconds before.

Satisfied the pair had not turned their heads, he none too gently pulled Ophelia into a darkened room. Firelight created soft shadows against the walls, and as he closed the door behind them, she heard the key turn in the lock. Trepidation spiraled through her, and she quickly put several feet between them. As he turned away from the door, he held up the key.

"To ensure we're not interrupted," he said tersely.

For some reason, she had expected him to be surprised, but he actually appeared angry. Arms folded over his chest, his eyebrows arched upward arrogantly.

"A moment ago I stated I was intrigued and then fascinated, Lady Havenstock. However, I am now attempting to determine precisely what you expect to achieve with your confession." The contempt in his voice sent a chill sliding through her, and Ophelia shook her head.

"It was not a confession, my lord," she bit out in a crisp tone as she stared at him without looking away. "It is a fact. I am incapable of inciting passion in a man or feeling it myself."

"I see," he said in a voice devoid of emotion. "Do you seriously expect me to believe not one of your lovers since Havenstock has failed to arouse you?"

"I've not shared a bed with any man other than my husband."

"None?" The earl snorted with disbelief. "Forgive me, Lady Havenstock, but I find it difficult to believe you've not had at least one lover since you became a widow."

"I am not a liar." Ophelia tilted her chin upward. She resented the insinuation that she was lying. If either of them was deserving of contempt, his disreputable behavior had earned him that distinction.

"Very well, let us put aside the question of your experience," he said as he studied her as a collector might when assessing the value of an antique. "Explain why you believe yourself incapable of arousing a man to passion or experiencing pleasure."

"Because my husband repeatedly stated I was cold and unfeeling in the performance of my wifely duties," she said in a tight voice, remembering George's angry denouncements of her inability to arouse a man.

It had been horrible enough knowing her father had insisted she marry George simply because the viscount had agreed to cover her father's outstanding debts. But knowing she was incapable of inspiring passion in her husband had made her avoid any liaisons in the ten years since George's death.

"Good god," the earl muttered beneath his breath, a frown creasing his forehead as he studied her. Ophelia looked down to fiddle with the ostrich feathers of her fan.

"I realize my proposition is unusual, but your reputation is such that I thought you might…might find me a challenge," she choked out as humiliation swept through her. "I have nothing else with which to barter for the return of my home."

"Havenstock was clearly a fool," the earl bit out as he slowly closed the distance between them.

The way earl was studying made her skin grow hot as he took his time observing her from top to bottom It was as if he were disrobing her in his mind, and the effect it had on her made her senses reel. Her heart racing, she forced herself not to look away from him as he approached her. With each step he took toward her, Ophelia experienced the urge to take two back, but she held her ground.

The man was doing things to her senses that didn't just alarm her—they made her long to possess the ability to entice and seduce him. The moment the thought flitted through her head, she struggled not to race toward the door. Dear Lord, what was she thinking? The earl halted inches away from her, then tipped her chin upward with his finger and forced her to look at him.

"Let me be the first to assure you, Ophelia, that you are more than capable of enchanting a man." His voice was a soft caress across her senses. Even the way her name rolled off his lips it was an invitation to join him in sin. "I've been captivated from the first moment I saw you this evening."

The silky note of seduction in his voice made Ophelia's heart slam into her breast as he lowered his head and brushed his mouth against hers. Fire singed her lips at the light caress, and the air left her lungs. A slight tremor skimmed over skin at the unfamiliar sensation assaulting her senses he lifted his head to study her intently. Gold flecks glittered in his green eyes as the firelight cast half of his profile in relief, while shadows darkened the other half. The earlier angelic impression she'd had of him returned, but this time it was a dark angel she saw. Ophelia swallowed hard as she looked at him.

"Am I to understand that you have decided to accept my proposition, my lord?"

"Perhaps," he murmured. "I wonder if you've considered the ramifications of your decision."

"If you're suggesting I mean to trick you into returning Marymont to me, I have only my word that I shall honor our bargain."

"It's not a question as to whether you'll honor any agreement between us. The question is how quickly you learn."

"I don't understand," she said as she eyed him warily. "It sounds as though you are proposing an extended arrangement."

"Do you think one night is sufficient payment for what must be a valuable piece of property given your willingness to offer yourself up to me so blatantly?"

The harsh note in his voice made Ophelia drag in a sharp breath. It was precisely what she'd thought. She shook her head as trepidation slid through her, followed by a throb of excitement that made her blood race.

"I did not consider the details of any arrangement we might make."

"Then I suggest we come to an agreement on terms that are agreeable to both of us."

His voice echoed with a hint of satisfaction that set off an alarm in Ophelia's mind. The man was clever, and she would need to be equally so if she was to emerge from this bargain with Marymont in her possession.

"Name your terms," she said quietly as he narrowed his eyes at her.

"In exchange for your home, you will give me one month," he said as he folded his arms over his chest. "At the end of our month together, your home will be returned to you."

"And how do I know you'll return Marymont to me after I surrender myself to your instruction?" At her question, he grew rigid.

"Are you suggesting I won't honor our agreement, my lady?"

The sharp note in his voice indicated she'd angered him by implying he might fail to respect the bargain they were negotiating. Whether she did or didn't believe he'd honor any agreement they committed to, it was of no consequence. If she wanted Marymont returned to her, she had little choice but to trust he would uphold his end of the bargain. With a sharp nod, she agreed to his terms.

"One month." The moment she replied, the earl's mouth curled in a wicked smile.

"Then let us begin," the earl said smoothly.

"Here? Now?" she gasped as the distance between them became almost non-existent.

"I think you will find the threat of discovery heightens the senses *and* the pleasure."

"You cannot possibly be serious." With a vehement shake of her head, Ophelia took a quick step backward to open up space between them. He closed it just as quickly.

"Pleasure always involves the senses, my lady, but there are many forms of pleasure." He laughed softly. It was a warm whisper across her mouth as he leaned into her. "Anticipation itself can be quite pleasurable."

"I don't understand," she choked out as his head dipped toward her. Her heart skipped a beat as his mouth bypassed her lips to brush across her cheek.

"Tonight, when you're alone in your bedroom, Ophelia, you're to undress slowly," he murmured as his teeth lightly nipped at her ear lobe. "I want you to imagine I'm there watching you. When you're wearing only your chemise, I want you to touch your nipples."

"Oh dear lord," she choked out, unable to look away from him. In a lazy stroke, his finger traced a path along the edge of her bodice. The light touch made Ophelia tremble, and a small smile curved his mouth.

"When you touch your nipples, I want you to imagine I'm there sucking on them. My tongue swirling on your stiff, rigid peaks." Barely able to breathe, it was impossible to look away from him. His smile became even more wicked.

"Please…this is…"

"You're experiencing pleasure right now, aren't you, Ophelia?" The laughter in his voice was mixed with something sinful and tantalizing, and she flicked her tongue out to lick her dry lips.

"Yes." She barely breathed the word.

"Yes, Mathias."

"Yes…Mathias."

"Good," he said softly as his mouth lightly touched hers, lingering for a brief second. "I want you to experience the ache, the need, the desire for my touch. I want you to imagine my mouth on your skin, licking and sucking on you until you shatter in my arms."

"Oh, God." It was little more than a breath of sound as fire spread its way through her body. She swayed slightly, and his hands gripped her waist to steady her.

"I think you are more than capable of passion, Ophelia," he murmured in a slightly thick voice.

There was a fire burning in his eyes that warmed her from the inside out as he stepped back from her. A shiver of excitement streaked down her back as his gaze remained locked with hers. She should have been appalled she'd even suggested their bargain to him. But it was the fact he excited her that alarmed her the most.

Chapter 2

Lust unlike anything he'd ever felt before, slammed into Mathias's chest as he struggled not to pull Ophelia into his arms. Brown eyes, large and wide, shimmered with gold flecks in the firelight. Desire had softened her countenance, and her full mouth was parted slightly. The tip of her tongue flicked out to wet her lips, and Mathias swallowed the dark groan rumbling up in his throat.

The woman had no idea how tempting she looked at this precise moment. A small shudder rippled through her as he gripped her waist to steady her. He would enjoy making Ophelia see herself as the sensual creature she was. A vivid image of her lying beneath him with her lustrous chestnut hair spilling across her bare shoulders made his cock stir in his trousers.

In a split instant, Mathias's lust vanished as if he'd been doused in icy water. He stiffened and took a quick step back from her. What the hell was wrong with him? He'd just said he wasn't a liar, and yet here he was pretending to be Charles. Worse, he'd even gone so far as to negotiate terms for her audacious proposition without divulging who he really was.

Self-loathing twisted his gut into a vicious knot. What in God's name had he been thinking to let the interlude progress this far? The immediate answer that came to mind was a perfunctory one. He was doing what he'd done for years. He was protecting his brother from scandal. Mathias almost snorted with disgust. As the Earl of Thornbury, his brother was a family scoundrel when it came to his dalliances. But even Charles would have arched his eyebrows in disapproval at Mathias's behavior.

He cleared his throat, his body hardening as he Ophelia's sultry look of desire. Christ Jesus, he wanted to explore every inch of her right here and now. The images flying through his head made his muscles grow taut with a need he'd not experienced in a long time. It was a tension and desire that would be unfulfilled because the minute he told her the truth, she'd flee.

It wasn't the first time he'd been mistaken for his brother. Despite the small gap in their ages, they'd both inherited the same dark hair and features of their father. The only difference was the color of their eyes. The fact they were easily mistaken for one another had proven helpful in his efforts to save Charles from female entrapment and a hellish marriage. But for the first time in his life, he found himself wishing he really was the Earl of Thornbury. Mathias took two quick steps back from Ophelia.

"I'm afraid, my lady, we've both made a grievous error." Mathias deliberately kept his voice devoid of emotion as he watched her. Confusion made her brows furrow as if she were lost trying to find her way out of a maze. His jaw tightened painfully with regret.

"An error?" She shook her head slightly.

"Regrettably, I am *not* the Earl of Thornbury." The words hung in the air for a long moment as she stared at him in bewilderment.

"I don't understand."

"My brother holds the Thornbury title," he said quietly. Mathias's gut twisted into a hard knot at her dazed look. He was truly a bastard for having toyed with the woman. It wasn't a pleasant sensation.

"You're not...but you said—"

"No. You *assumed* I was the earl," he grounded out between clenched teeth. Furious with himself for allowing things to become out of hand, his tone was harsher than he meant it to be.

Slowly, Ophelia's confusion became one of mortified shock and horror. The fact he was responsible for her humiliation made his muscles knot with tension. His regret only underscored what a bastard he was. He'd known Ophelia had mistaken him for Charles when she'd addressed him so formally on the dance floor, but he'd deliberately chosen not to correct her.

Over the years, he'd perfected his role of protecting his brother from women seeking nothing more than a title and access to Charles's vast holdings. Unlike other titled peers whose fortunes had been decimated over many decades of excessive spending and poor investments, the Thornbury fortune was still intact. Through the decades, the Gilchrist family members had used their innate financial skills to keep their coffers from being drained. Mathias and Charles were no different when it came to their financial acumen. Between the two of them, the Thornbury finances were sound for many years to come.

It was one of the many reasons women vied for the Countess of Thornbury title. An image of Miriam flitted through his head. When the memory of her betrayal tried to secure a place in his thoughts, he discarded it. Instead, a new image was being seared into his memory as he saw the color drain from Ophelia's cheeks. Humiliation and shame caused her mouth to work slowly as she tried to speak. Her efforts deepened his self-loathing.

Even when Ophelia had made her outrageous proposal, he'd failed to have the decency to reveal his true identity. The idea he'd been looking out for Charles's best interests didn't excuse his demeaning the woman. Disgusted by his behavior, he tried to form a coherent and sincere apology in his head.

The problem was he was failing to come up with anything sufficient to make amends for his behavior. Perhaps the situation could be salvaged by returning Ophelia's home to her without any ties. That might go a long way toward atoning for his sins. Silence stretched out between them as he considered how best to extend his broken olive branch. When she didn't speak, he cleared his throat.

"Naturally, I have no expectations of you choosing to move forward with our agreement, but I—"

"Not move—*you bastard.*" The sharp, brittle words made Mathias tense as he prepared himself for the outrage about to be inflicted on him. Her fury was slowly taking shape, and it was easy to see it would be scathing in its intensity. even in her anger, she was lovely. "You *allowed* me to humiliate myself—offer my body in exchange for something you cannot give."

"No, I didn't promise something I couldn't give," he bit out between clenched teeth. "As my brother's business and estate manager. I have complete autonomy in managing his affairs and properties."

"Do you *honestly* expect me to believe you would have returned Marymont to me?"

"I do not expect you to do so, but it is the truth."

"The *truth?*" she exclaimed with bitterness. "The truth is that your brother displayed no moral compass when he stole Marymont from a drunken, old fool. But *you,* sir, are worse. You are beyond contempt."

Mathias went rigid. Despite knowing his original intent had been to protect his brother, he deserved Ophelia's brutal condemnation. He was more than worthy of her insult, but his brother was not. While Charles had many flaws, his brother was a good man at heart.

It was one of the reasons Mathias quietly investigated every new paramour his brother became involved with. But somewhere in the middle of his efforts to protect his brother, he'd lost sight of everything except Ophelia. Angered by the realization and his responsibility in fortifying Ophelia's poor opinion of Charles, his jaw clenched painfully.

"I will not quarrel with your judgement of me, even though it wasn't my intent to humiliate you." A voice in his head, snorted with disgust. No, he'd simply chosen to ignore how difficult it had been for her to offer herself in exchange for her home. "That said, I'm the wall that stands between my brother and any woman who seeks to become the next Countess of Thornbury through less than honorable means."

Ophelia's head jerked backward as if he'd slapped her. Guilt crashed through him. *Christ Jesus*, this wasn't how to apologize to the woman. He'd simply added insult to injury. Intense dislike darkened her eyes as she stared at him with such loathing that if she'd been holding a weapon, she would have mortally wounded him.

"I have *never* had any designs on your brother *or* his title," she bit out in an acerbic tone. "I have no intention of tying myself to any man ever again."

"Perhaps not, but my brother is not always discreet in his liaisons. It's my responsibility to ensure the women he indulges himself with are not in pursuit of a title." Bloody hell, what was the matter with him, trying to defend his actions. He might be telling her the truth, but it was clearly only making things worse.

"I want nothing more from your brother than for him to return my childhood home to me. And I was willing to pay in the only currency I possess. Unfortunately, I underestimated the depths of your family's depravity."

Pale with humiliation and outrage, Ophelia's brown eyes flashed with gold sparks of anger as she quickly stepped around him and headed for the door. He matched her pace and held up the key he'd pulled from his pocket.

"I will escort you back to the ballroom, my lady."

"*No.* You will *not*," Ophelia snapped as she tugged the key from his grasp and unlocked the door.

With a sharp movement, she jerked open the door and allowed it to fly open. Caught off guard by her action, Mathias didn't move fast enough to avoid the door hitting him. An oath escaped him as he released a low cry of pain. Preoccupied with his injury, Mathias failed to halt Ophelia's flight from the room. One hand pressed to his nose, he felt a warm trickle of blood touch his lips.

"Damn it to hell."

Mathias pulled his handkerchief out of his pocket and pressed it against his nose to staunch the bleeding. After several moments, he straightened his head while gently wiping the last bit of blood from above his upper lip.

He deserved every bit of Ophelia's anger. There was no doubt in his mind that her outrageous proposal had been born of desperation. He'd been so blinded by his preconceived notions as to her motives, he'd failed to see the humiliation layered beneath her initial proposal. No, not failed to see it, he'd chosen to believe the worst of her without any evidence. She was a friend of Louisa's. That should have been enough for him to know she was not the kind of woman to play games like women of Miriam's ilk.

His failure was compounded by his inability to control the lust she'd aroused in him. Not only had Mathias allowed her to believe he was his brother, but he'd also negotiated an agreement with her. There was no doubt in his mind that Charles would find his behavior worthy of Ophelia's contempt. He grimaced at the thought.

This was the first time since he was a boy that he'd done something less than circumspect, not to mention dishonorable. Generally, it was Charles who chafed at the constraints of society, thereby being prone to actions that were not always in his best interest. Mathias bit down on the inside of his cheek. As much as he loved his brother, he knew Charles was far removed from a saint. Even when they were children, Charles had always walked the fine line between acceptable behavior and outright defiance of social conventions.

Tonight, Mathias had been the one to cross the line. The fact he'd not attempted to quickly correct Ophelia's mistaken belief as to his identity was reprehensible. It illustrated how jaded Mathias had become since first taking on the task of guarding Charles's reputation. Protecting his brother from scandal was a duty he'd performed ever since their father had died ten years ago.

From the moment Charles had inherited the Thornbury title, Mathias had served as his brother's confidant and estate manager as well as the wall any woman intent on becoming the next Countess of Thornbury would have to breach. But none of that excused his conduct in bartering with Ophelia and accepting what she'd offered in exchange for the return of her home. He deserved every bit of her contempt, particularly when he considered his base reaction to her.

Reluctantly, he admitted it had been difficult not to be fascinated by her proposition. His admission that she intrigued him was true. When she'd shared Havenstock's opinion of her wifely duties, he'd been outraged the man had convinced Ophelia she was incapable of passion. The idea that she thought herself incapable of feeling passion or arousing a man's desire would have been laughable if he'd not seen the look of humiliation in her brown eyes.

Everything about her reaction to him illustrated she was more than capable of great passion, but it was obvious she believed what Havenstock had told her. In all likelihood, the old bastard hadn't been able to raise his cock and blamed his wife. Mathias had only spoken with Havenstock a few times, but he had never really cared for the man. Havenstock had been a bombastic, pompous ass. Ophelia was better off a widow.

With a grunt of frustrated disgust, Mathias strode out into the corridor and headed back to the ballroom. He was far too preoccupied with the woman. He'd done what he'd needed to do to—protect Charles. It was a poor attempt on his part to explain away his behavior tonight, which was inexcusable. The thought made him feel even worse. He muttered a harsh oath beneath his breath. He'd allowed matters to get out of hand to the point he'd failed to apologize or reassure her that he would see to it her home was returned to her. As he entered the ballroom, he saw two of the Rockwood family members conversing with Ophelia. Both Percy and Louisa laughed at something Ophelia said, and he debated whether or not to approach the three of them.

Almost as if she sensed his presence, Ophelia turned her head and their gazes met. Revulsion flashed across her features before she quickly looked away. That answered that question. Mathias bit down on the inside of his cheek. She was right. He was a bastard. The question now was how to make her understand he wasn't the man she believed him to be. The instant the thought filled his head, Mathias went rigid. And he'd been worried about Charles becoming infatuated with Ophelia. He uttered another oath beneath his breath as he spun around on his heel and left the ballroom. Tomorrow Viscountess Havenstock would have her home back, and he'd be able to apologize.

Mathias stepped out of the hack onto the sidewalk in front of the small, plain townhouse. When he'd seen Percy at the club earlier this morning, he'd managed to subtly secure Ophelia's address. Now, as he stood in front of the nondescript residence, he frowned slightly. By all accounts, Havenstock had been quite well off. Surely Ophelia could afford something more in keeping with her title.

He quickly strode up the three steps and grabbed the knocker to rap firmly on the door. The door was answered almost immediately by an elderly gentleman who arched his eyebrows at him. The look evoked a childhood memory of being the focus of his stern school master, and Mathias bit back a smile.

"Mr. Mathias Gilchrist to see Viscountess Havenstock. I believe I'm expected." The small fabrication made the butler open the door wide to give him access to the narrow entryway.

"Who is it, Taggert?" The voice echoing out of a room on his left made Mathias turn his head as a younger version of Ophelia emerged from what he assumed was a parlor. *"Lord Thornbury."*

"Actually, I'm Mathias Gilchrist, his brother." At his brief reply, the young woman's eyes widened in surprise before she recovered her wits and smiled.

"Good morning, Mr. Gilchrist. I'm Elizabeth Sheffield."

"A pleasure," he murmured as he stepped forward to kiss the young lady's hand. A blush crested over her cheeks as she quickly pulled her hand from his and gestured toward the doorway behind her.

"Won't you come in? Taggert, please inform Lady Havenstock we have a caller and ask Mrs. Barstow to bring us some tea." Elizabeth Sheffield led the way into a modest salon. She pointed to a chair beside the fireplace and a small fire burning in the grate. "Please, Mr. Gilchrist, have a seat."

"Thank you," he said quietly as his looked around the room. There was barely room for the couch and two chairs that filled the parlor while the small piano against the wall took up what little space remained.

"Please forgive my staring, Mr. Gilchrist. Your resemblance to the earl is quite striking."

"We're often mistaken for one another," he said with a smile. "And sometimes it's most inconvenient."

"Since we've not met before, I can only assume you are here to call on my sister."

"If you're referring to Lady Havenstock, then yes. We met last night at Melton House."

"Oh, I didn't realize she'd actually met you—" Elizabeth uttered a gasp of horror and covered her mouth. "Good heavens. No wonder Ophelia barely said two words to me on the way home last night. She must have thought you—"

"Lizzie, would you please go check on father? He's suffering from another of his headaches." At the sound of Ophelia's voice, Mathias immediately stood up and turned toward the parlor doorway.

"It was delightful to meet you, Mr. Gilchrist," Elizabeth said as she stood up and curtsied in his direction. Despite the furtive look she shot in her sister's direction, there was a cheerfulness to her voice that made him smile.

"And I, you, Miss Sheffield. Perhaps you'll save a dance for me when next we meet."

"That would be—"

"*Lizzie. Now*, please." Ophelia's command was quiet, but there was a raw edge to it that made the younger woman flinch.

"Yes, Ophelia."

With one last smile in his direction, Elizabeth Sheffield hurried past her sister and left the parlor. As her sister disappeared from view, Ophelia moved to stand in the center of the room. The look she directed at him was one of cold fury, and the silence filling the space between them was riddled with tension. As the sound of her sister's footsteps faded up the stairs, Ophelia narrowed her gaze at him.

"Why are you here?" A winter day could not have been colder than her voice.

"I've brought you a gift."

"I want nothing from you, Mr. Gilchrist, except to see the back of you as you walk out of this house."

Mathias ignored her icy reply and reached into his coat to pull out a small packet of documents from his inside breast pocket. Without a word, he offered her the papers. Ophelia studied him warily for a moment before she cautiously stepped forward to accept the paperwork from him. Papers in hand, Ophelia quickly put space between them again. The soft crackle of parchment echoed in the air as she reviewed the documents he'd given her. After a brief moment, she jerked her head up to stare at him in amazement.

"This is the deed to Marymont."

"Yes. I told you it was within my power to return it to you," Mathias said quietly.

"And I presume you will require my signature on another document in exchange for your generosity." The bitter sarcasm in her reply made his jaw tighten until it hurt.

"There are no conditions tied to the deed."

"Do you actually expect me to believe your largess comes with no ties at all, Mr. Gilchrist?"

"I do," he said with an abrupt nod. Irritated by the question, Mathias clenched his teeth in anger. How was she to think otherwise? He clasped his hands behind his back and fisted his hands. "You were right to hold me in contempt last night. My behavior was less than gentlemanly. I had resolved to visit my brother's solicitor first thing this morning to arrange for the return of your property without stipulations as an apology for my behavior. My brother, however, circumvented my efforts."

"What are you saying?" Trepidation made her draw in a sharp breath, and he saw her fingers tighten around the paperwork she held.

"While it had been my intent to be the one responsible for restoring your home to you, that honor belongs to my brother. Charles, *who*, according to you, has no moral compass, had already left instructions for our solicitor to transfer the property into your name and return it to you this week. I am simply the bearer of good tidings."

Mathias held himself stiffly as he watched the varied emotions flitting across Ophelia's features. Damn Charles for stealing his ability to fully redeem himself and advance his cause with her. The thought made Mathias's entire body harden with tension as a voice in the back of his head shouted a cry of surprise and alarm.

What the devil had he hoped to achieve by restoring her home to her? The answer only made his body grow more rigid. He should have simply written a note of apology and sent it with the solicitor and the deed as opposed to coming here in person. Christ, he'd made a mess out of this entire situation. Eager to be done with the matter, Mathias cleared his throat.

"As I said, I deeply regret my behavior last night. Now that your home has been returned to you, I shall bid you a good day, Lady Havenstock."

With a sharp, perfunctory bow, Mathias turned and strode out of the room. Once he put distance between them, he'd soon forget the temptation the woman presented. Wild laughter exploded in his head at the lie. Ophelia was not a woman one could easily forget.

Chapter 3

Stunned by the earl's generous gesture, Ophelia stared after Mathias's tall figure as he walked out of the room. Marymont was theirs again. They would not be homeless when their lease ended here in town. Relief and gratitude propelled her forward. As she reached the parlor doorway, she saw Mathias, hat in hand, opening the front door.

"*Stop*. Please." At her sharp command, he slowly turned around. The hard set of his jaw and impassive expression made her bite down on her lip, and Ophelia drew in a deep breath.

"I don't understand," she whispered. "Why would you…why would your brother do such a thing?"

"While my brother has a scandalous reputation, Charles is incapable of leaving anyone destitute." Mathias's voice held the ring of cold steel. The icy words made her wince as she remembered her condemning his brother's integrity last night.

"Then I…I owe him…and you… an apology." The quiet words hung in the stillness between them as he studied her in silence for a long moment. With a grimace, he shook his head in obvious regret.

"You do not owe me any apologies, my lady. I presumed the worst of you last night, and I regret adding insult to injury with my treatment of you. I'll bid you a good day, my lady."

"*No*, wait. Please…I…"

At a loss for words, Ophelia's voice died away. She had no inkling why she'd stopped him a second time. A mocking laugh echoed through her head as she bit down on her lip and met his penetrating look. Again the silence stretched taut between them before he took a step forward.

"Perhaps I might have that cup of tea your sister offered me."

"Yes. Yes, of course," Ophelia exclaimed softly as she gratefully accepted the olive branch he'd extended to her. "I'm sure tea will be here momentarily."

Not waiting for his reply, Ophelia led the way back into the parlor. A frisson skimmed its way down her spine as she sensed his commanding presence following her. She gestured toward the chair he'd been seated in earlier and sank down into a love seat opposite him. The parlor was a small room, and Mathias made it feel even smaller as he settled his muscular body into the chair across from her.

What in heaven's name had possessed her to ask him to stay? Marymont had been returned to her family. She had no need to continue her acquaintance with Mathias Gilchrist. She was mad to entertain the man after their exchange last night. Her throat tightened slightly as she tried to think of some small pleasantry to break the silence between them. The sudden rattle of china announced she'd been given a small reprieve. Relieved to have something to distract her from the tension in the room, Ophelia sprang to her feet to greet their cook as the woman entered the parlor.

"Thank you, Mrs. Barstow. Please set it here," Ophelia said, pointing to the short, oval table between the love seat and Mathias's chair.

As the servant left the room, Ophelia poured their tea. The porcelain rattled slightly as she offered him a cup and saucer. Dismayed by the tremor that shook her hand, she hastily turned her attention to pouring her own cup of tea.

"Tell me, how do you know the Rockwoods?" he asked. The tension that had gripped Ophelia for the past several moments eased as his question brought back thoughts of her childhood. She smiled.

"Marymont was my grandmother's home before she died. It's a short distance from Melton Park, and I spent most of my summers with my grandmother. Louisa and I became great friends and did almost everything together. They were happy times."

A warm nostalgia swept through her as she remembered the warm, lazy days that had been such joyous ones. She doubted she would ever be so carefree or happy again. Ophelia winced as she saw Mathias's curiosity. There was an air about him that made her think he could see straight into her heart. It was an alarming possibility.

"And how long have *you* been acquainted with the Rockwoods?" she asked as she took a sip of her tea and studied him over the rim of her cup.

"Charles and Percy were roommates at Eton. When I arrived at school, the two of them would often allow me to tag along wherever they went." Mathias set his tea cup on the table, and when she leaned forward to pour him another, he waved her silent offer aside.

"They are an indomitable family, and they've always made me feel as though I were a member of their family. Louisa, for obvious reasons, is quite dear to me," Ophelia said quietly as she silently compared her own state of widowhood to her friend's.

Louisa had loved her husband. Ophelia had not. Despite the annual pittance she received as George's widow, she was still grateful to be free of her husband. She shook her head slightly at the tragedies that had befallen her friend.

"When I think of the loss they suffered as children, and more recently with the fire at Westbrook…I can only admire their fortitude. Their reputation for being reckless is not a fair one."

"I agree. I find them more impulsive than reckless."

"Yes, that is much better and accurate description. They're always so passionate about living life to the fullest, even more so now."

"You possess a passionate nature as well." The quiet response startled her.

"*Me?*" Ophelia shook her head as an ugly memory of George berating her filled her head. A sense of irony made her smile at his observation. "No, I will never be a creature of passion."

"That's Havenstock talking. I believe you're far more capable of deep emotions than you think. I've seen the fire in you, Ophelia."

The conviction in his quiet words made her draw in a sharp breath as an unexpected heat engulfed her. It bore the same strength of the firestorm that had swept through her last night when he'd brushed his lips over hers. Ophelia's cheeks grew hot at the memory, and as their eyes met, she quickly jerked her gaze away. Unable to prevent it, a small shudder rippled through her. Dismayed by her reaction to him, she swallowed hard.

"You're wrong, Mr. Gilchrist. The woman you saw last night was desperate to save her home."

"And now that you have it back, are you still going to allow Havenstock to control you from the grave?"

"I don't know what you mean."

"Last night, you challenged me to teach you how to feel passion and how to arouse it in a man." The blunt statement took her by surprise, and she gasped.

"That was a mistake." Her tea cup rattled violently on its saucer as she set it down on the table with a small clatter.

"No. Your mistake is that you believe your husband's lies." Mathias slowly leaned forward in his chair. The intensity of his look hypnotized Ophelia as the man studied her as though she were a butterfly on an entomologist's board. "Tell me, Ophelia, despite my abysmal behavior, did you do as I told you when you were alone in your bedroom last night?"

"*No*, I did *not*," she gasped.

Hot color flooded Ophelia's cheeks as she quickly denied the truth. She *had* done as he instructed, and it had been the most hedonistic thing she'd ever done in her life. Not because she'd never touched herself before in the privacy of her own bed, but because she'd done as he'd ordered. She'd imagined he was with her. Touching her—caressing her. Her heart thudded a fast beat in her breast as she tried to school her expression into one of serene denial. A small smile tilted his lips, and her mouth went dry at the way he was looking at her.

"Why do I think you're lying?"

"You may think what you like," she huffed as she regained some of her composure, her chin tipped upward slightly at a haughty angle.

"Then let me tell you *what* I think. I believe you long to feel passion, Ophelia. Your husband was wrong, and I would like to prove it to you."

Mathias's words made her draw in a sharp breath of surprise. How could he possibly know what she'd only just acknowledged last night in the dark? It had been scandalous enough to offer herself in exchange for Marymont, but to consider his current proposition was reckless.

But she couldn't deny the way her body had reacted when his mouth had briefly caressed hers or the wild imaginings that had filled her dreams. Now, as she considered his suggestion, she found herself wavering between dismay, alarm, as well as a heady excitement that sent her pulse skittering along at a frantic pace.

"Are you suggesting…we have a…liaison?" she stammered.

"More a relationship between student and teacher. Allow me to prove Havenstock knew nothing about women, especially his wife."

"I don't…"

"Fear, Ophelia?" The mockery in his voice angered her.

"I am *not* afraid of you," she snapped. She narrowed her eyes at Mathias as she stiffened and straightened in her seat.

"Then let me transform you into a swan every man in London will be eager to come to blows over."

The comment made her stare at him in surprise for a moment before she laughed. Her feet were firmly rooted on the ground when it came to her effect on men. Even if George had not convinced her of her inability to incite a man's passion, she had never been under the illusion that she was anything more than passably attractive.

"It is highly unlikely any man would be willing to fight over me," she said as she eyed him with amusement. His green eyes narrowed as he studied her for a long moment before a sinfully wicked smile curved his firm lips.

"As your tutor, I'll show you just *how likely* such a possibility is," he said. Mathias leaned forward, and he had the appearance of a man not about to accept no for an answer. "Unless, of course, it's not me you're afraid of, but yourself."

"The only thing I've ever been afraid of is losing my home, Mr. Gilchrist," she said with irritation.

"Then say yes."

"Very well, I agree to be your student for one week." Exasperated by his persistence, she agreed to his proposal with an abrupt nod.

"No, that's hardly enough time." Mathias shook his head. "I can work miracles, but not in a week. I shall require at least a month."

"A month then," she murmured in agreement. The look of triumph on Mathias's handsome profile immediately stirred trepidation inside her. But he didn't give her the opportunity to retract her acquiescence.

"If you are to learn the art of seduction, you need to arm yourself accordingly. The first place to start is your wardrobe." Mathias waved his hand at her gown in a dismissive gesture. "I believe the answer to that problem is a visit to Sabine Marchand's shop."

"*Madame Sabine?*" Ophelia gasped with a shake of her head. "My finances do not allow me to even *enter* her dress shop."

"Sabine is a personal friend. I will ask her to give you every consideration where you're concerned," he replied.

As Mathias glanced around the room, she straightened her back at the sudden comprehension that crossed his features. Ophelia's mouth tightened resolving not to let him take advantage of her the financial situation.

"If you think I will allow you—I did *not* agree to be your mistress."

"Lesson number one, Ophelia," he murmured. "Be agreeable. Use honey when dealing with the opposite sex. You need not surrender your independence, but if you must protest, do so in a manner that assures the gentleman in question understands you're grateful for his thoughtfulness. As I said, Sabine is a friend."

Ophelia studied him for a long moment, debating whether she'd made a terrible mistake. Of course, she'd made a mistake. Mathias Gilchrist was a man used to getting his way. She'd already allowed him to persuade her to engage in this madcap adventure. He arched his eyebrows at her, and she winced at her inability to retract her agreement. Doing so would make her look like a coward, and she was anything but that. Liar. A small voice whispered the accusation in her head.

"I shall accept your offer of introduction and nothing more." At her firmly worded reply, Mathias narrowed his gaze at her before he accepted her reply with a slight tilt of his head.

"I shall leave instructions with Sabine to receive you this afternoon. I have no doubt she'll find something suitable for you to wear this evening when we attend the opera."

"The opera," she said with a grimace.

"You dislike Puccini?" Amusement made his mouth twitch as he arched an eyebrow at her.

"I can think of other things that are far more enjoyable."

"As can I," he murmured in a silky voice as a slight smile curved his lips. "However, if you're to have the men of the Marlborough Set vying for your company, there will be times when putting aside your distaste for certain entertainments will endear you to the male sex."

Ophelia eyed him with a wary expression then acquiesced with a sigh. With a look of satisfaction, he stood up, and before she could rise to her feet as well, he closed the space between them. Heat instantly enveloped her skin as Mathias bent toward her. With great effort, Ophelia managed not to shrink back into the cushions of the small couch as he took her hand in his.

"Shall we practice?"

"Practice what?" Confused, a small tremor spiraled through her at how little space there was between them and the warmth suffusing her hand.

"Make me believe you'll enjoy attending the opera this evening."

"But I won't," she said with a sniff of derision.

"I can see you intend to be a difficult student," he said in a wry voice.

With a quick tug, he pulled her to her feet without letting go of her hand. The distance between them was mere inches, and Ophelia swallowed hard at the way her pulse was racing out of control. His forefinger tapped her mouth lightly.

"Now then, convince me you're looking forward to attending the opera tonight, not because you like opera, but because you'll be in *my* company."

The stern, autocratic look of a school master darkened his face as he arched his eyebrows as if it were a royal command. Ophelia frowned and shook her head slightly in puzzled contemplation. Flirtations came so easily to others, but she'd never developed a talent or taste for it. She bit down on her bottom lip and glanced away from him.

"I'm looking forward to this evening, Mr. Gilchrist."

"That sounds like a debutante fresh out of the schoolroom, Ophelia. Make me believe you're a woman counting the hours until we see each other again this evening."

The soft command was more of a caress than an order. It created an odd fluttering sensation in her belly. Confused by her body's response to him, Ophelia jerked her head up and look at him. Wicked amusement darkened his green eyes, and she quickly fought back against her body's reaction to him.

When she remained silent, he cocked his head at a slight angle, his sensual mouth tipped upward in an arrogant challenge. It signaled his belief he held the upper hand, and she didn't like it. She didn't like it one bit. The man was supposed to be teaching her, not irritating her. Eager to suppress the way he was affecting her, Ophelia took refuge behind her growing irritation at his autocratic manner and glared at him.

Completely unphased by her scowl, Ophelia frowned as she tried to think of a way to level the playing field between them. Out of all the thoughts careening through her head, one in particular, pushed its way to the front. Honey. He'd said she should use honey when dealing with a suitor. It was a game she'd agreed to play, and suddenly it was important that she prove she would be a worthy pupil.

"I read once that Oscar Wilde believes there are only two tragedies in life, Mr. Gilchrist. One is when we fail to get what we want, and the other is when we do." She allowed a small smile to curve her lips as she looked up at him. "At long last, I understand what he meant."

"I see," he murmured. "And I trust you will enlighten me as to your revelation?"

"Anticipation." She tipped her head to one side to appear as if she was considering a deep philosophical question

"Anticipation?" He chuckled.

"As you said last night, it can be quite…pleasurable." A shiver skimmed its way down her spine as she breathed in the warm, spicy male smell of him. "The more we long for something—ache for it, the more intense the pleasure. So I shall enjoy the anticipation between now and this evening."

Without realizing she'd done so, Ophelia lowered her voice so that her final words were little more than a husky whisper. As their gazes locked, she saw fire flare in his eyes. Slowly, he raised her hand and brushed his mouth across the tips of her fingers. A second later, he turned her hand over and kissed the inside of her wrist.

The intimacy of the gesture tugged a sharp gasp from her as fire streaked through her body. Instinctively, she tried to tug free of his hold. Mathias thwarted her effort, and she was certain his mouth deliberately lingered in retaliation for what she knew had been a provocative reply.

"Brava," he said softly as he lifted his head. There was a flare of something wicked in his gaze as he studied her. "That was enough to stir the blood in any able-bodied male. Perhaps a week would have been enough time to transform the swan."

"Then we can—"

"I said perhaps, Ophelia. I'm not about to relinquish my claim on your time so easily." The low laugh that parted his firm lips made her heart race even faster. Mathias released her and took a step back. "Until this evening, my lady."

With a quick bow, he turned around and left her standing in the parlor staring after him.

Ophelia studied her reflection in the full-length mirror. This afternoon at Madame Sabine's dress shop, she'd been overwhelmed with the selection of gowns the modiste had offered up for inspection. Although she'd tried to select only two new gowns, the woman had insisted she choose three times that many. The dressmaker had reassured her the bill would be reasonable as Mathias had informed her that Ophelia was a close friend.

She'd always considered herself reasonably attractive, but never pretty. Now, as she stared at the woman in front of her, Ophelia realized why Madame Sabine had insisted on such vivid colors for her. The jewel-toned, green gown drew out the chestnut highlights in her brown hair and made her pale complexion take on a soft peach hue. Pleasure swept through her as she marveled at the way a change of color could enhance her appearance.

A knock on her bedroom door made her turn around as she called for her visitor to enter. Lizzie poked her head into the room before pushing the door open wide to step into the room.

"Ophelia, you look *beautiful*," Lizzie exclaimed. At her sister's compliment, Ophelia smiled. Looking downward, she brushed her hands over the blue-green silk of the gown's skirt.

"Thank you. It is a lovely gown, isn't it?"

"It's magnificent. I don't know why Mrs. Smithers hasn't suggested a color like this for you before now."

Ophelia almost said she'd not gone to their usual dressmaker, but caught herself in time and turned around to look at her reflection again. She'd not yet had the chance to tell her sister that the earl had returned Marymont to them. If Lizzie were to discover that Mathias had arranged for her to visit Madame Sabine, her sister's imagination would run wild. Not that Lizzie's imaginings would be that far from the actual truth.

"You went out earlier before I could ask what Mr. Gilchrist wanted," Lizzie said as their eyes met in the mirror. Ophelia turned to her sister.

"He came to return Marymont to us."

"*What?*" Lizzie's stared at Ophelia in stunned amazement before tears suddenly spilled down her cheeks. Appalled, Ophelia quickly retrieved a handkerchief from her dressing table and closed the distance between them. She offered the small square of linen to her sister and wrapped her arm around the younger girl.

"Good heavens, dearest, why are you crying? This is good news."

"Not if you have to become the earl's mistress," Lizzie blubbered as she shook her head. Horrified her sister had deduced her original intent to give herself to the earl in exchange for Marymont, Ophelia caught her sister by the shoulders and shook her slightly.

"*What on earth* have I said or done to make you think such a thing?" she exclaimed, knowing full well her own words and behavior had led Lizzie to suspect Ophelia's intentions.

"Lord Thornbury's reputation as a scoundrel. I thought he would expect…" Her sister hiccupped as she brushed the dampness off her tear-stained cheeks. "…would expect you to be his mistress if he returned Marymont to us."

"I am *not* going to be Lord Thornbury's or anyone's mistress," Ophelia said with a sharp shake of her head. In the back of her head, mocking laughter protested her words, but she ignored the silent taunt of amusement. "Mr. Gilchrist explained last night that his brother had made arrangements for Marymont to be returned to us shortly after his card game with Father."

"Oh, thank God," Lizzie said softly as her tears slowly ebbed away to become soft hiccups. Ophelia squeezed her sister's hand in a comforting gesture.

"Apparently, the scandalous Earl of Thornbury has a heart after all. One he's managed to hide from the Set. The earl even had the forethought to place the deed in my name, so Father cannot wager it again."

"We must find a way to thank his lordship, Ophelia," her sister said fervently.

"I sent the earl a note earlier today expressing our thanks."

"Will that be enough?" Lizzie frowned as if contemplating further action.

"I think Lord Thornbury is the type of man who will not take kindly to any overt displays of gratitude. My letter will be sufficient." When Lizzie's frown didn't fade, Ophelia eyed her sternly. "*Lizzie.*"

"Oh, all right, but if I see the man, I shall discreetly express my thanks."

"It is unlikely you will set eyes on the earl as we both know we do not move in the same social circles."

"I am simply saying what I shall do if I'm afforded the opportunity." Lizzie shrugged as she tipped her head to one side, an inquisitive look on her sweet face. "Lady Alice and her aunt will be here shortly to take me to the Witherspoons for the evening. I thought you said you didn't want to go with us."

Ophelia turned away from her sister and moved back to her dressing table. In an effort to avoid looking at Lizzie, she pretended to rummage through her small jewelry box for her pearl earrings.

"Actually, since I knew you had plans, I accepted an invitation to attend the opera this evening."

"*The opera,*" Lizzie exclaimed. Her mouth falling open in astonishment, Lizzie stared at Ophelia in the dressing-table mirror. "You loathe the opera. Who on earth convinced you to go?"

The accusation made Ophelia wince, before she quickly looked away from her sister. Fingers fumbling, she adjusted her earrings, then pulled a simple strand of pearls from her jewelry box.

"Mr. Gilchrist," she murmured.

"Mr. Gilchrist."

Her sister's voice rose in pitch as she squeaked out Mathias's name in a squeal of excitement. Ophelia looked into the mirror and winced at her sister's sly contemplation. Quickly twisting around on the dressing table stool, Ophelia eyed the younger woman sternly.

"It is simply one invitation. I felt obligated to accept since Mr. Gilchrist made such a concerted effort to deliver the deed to Marymont this morning."

"Of course, you did," Lizzie said with a knowing smile.

"Do not read more into it than there is, Elizabeth Sheffield."

"But it's romantic."

"It's nothing of the sort," Ophelia retorted.

"Yes, it is, and I think it's wonderful that you finally have a suitor."

"*Good heavens.* Mr. Gilchrist is *not* a suitor." Ophelia held up her pearls in a silent demand that Lizzie help to secure them around her neck. Her sister quickly hurried forward to fasten the necklace around Ophelia's neck. When she'd finished, Lizzie placed her hands on Ophelia's shoulders and met her gaze in the mirror.

"You deserve to be happy, Ophelia," her sister said softly. Patting Lizzie's hand, she smiled.

"I *am* happy. Marymont's been returned to us, and I believe Mr. Nickens is quite taken with you. Both of those things make me very happy."

"No. I mean truly happy. You should be married with children."

"You are a hopeless romantic, Lizzie Sheffield." She smiled gently at her sister. The one thing Ophelia was certain of was that the happiness her sister described would never be hers.

"Perhaps, but I know I'm right," her sister replied with a confidence that demonstrated a maturity Ophelia hadn't seen before now. The front doorbell clanged softly in the corridor, and Lizzie turned her head toward the sound. "I'm certain that's Lady Alice. It's not even the top of the hour, but her aunt insists on punctuality. I must go. Have a lovely time this evening, Ophelia."

With a quick kiss to Ophelia's cheek, Lizzie hurried from the room. Left alone with only her reflection, she stared at the woman in front of her. Large brown eyes stared back at her from inside the mirror. Pink color flushed her cheeks, while her mouth was a darker pink. Her outward appearance was one of cool composure, and she looked every bit the ice maiden George had accused her of being. A woman incapable of feeling passion or stirring it in a man.

Ophelia closed her eyes at the thought. Was it possible Mathias was correct? Did she really possess a fire and passion buried deep inside her? She sniffed a sound of disgust. The agreement they had would prove her right and him wrong. Resigned to her fate, Ophelia sighed softly. Tonight was an unknown quantity, and she was uncertain whether she should be excited or nervous.

The jangle of the front doorbell echoed softly in the corridor, and Ophelia quickly gathered her things, then proceeded downstairs. As she reached the foot of the stairs, she heard male voices in the parlor. Squire Sheffield's voice sounded slightly slurred, and Ophelia's heart sank.

Her father had been drinking again, which meant he was apt to be indiscreet. If he inquired about Marymont, Mathias might reveal he'd returned the property to her. Although her father was fond of drink, he wasn't a fool. He would most likely assume, as Lizzie had, that she'd made an agreement with Mathias in exchange for the return of Marymont.

The squire would not be as easy to put off as Lizzie had been. She'd already decided to tell her father she'd taken some of her investments to purchase their home back from the earl. It was a plausible explanation, and Ophelia was confident her father would believe it of her. But she would need Mathias's help in convincing her father should he question her explanation.

"So…do you know if Thornbury intends to sell the property?" Horrified by her father's question, Ophelia hurried forward.

The moment she stepped through the doorway, her eyes were immediately drawn to Mathias, who looked splendid in evening dress. His angular profile was sharply defined, and her heart skipped a beat at the sight of him. A split second later, it began to race wildly as her blood flowed hot through her veins. It had been a mistake to agree to his proposal. She had Marymont back, and that was all that mattered.

A second later, Mathias turned his head toward her, and a delicious tension and anticipation spiraled through her. Once more, she realized she should never have accepted his challenge. Mathias Gilchrist was a wolf who could easily devour her before she even realized what was happening. A small shiver skated down her spine as he smiled at her. It was as if he could tell precisely what she was thinking. Oh, she was definitely mad.

Chapter 4

Mathias smiled at Baron Sheffield as the man offered him a glass of wine. The baron was a tall, burly man, and his daughters looked nothing like him other than Ophelia possessed some of her father's height. As he accepted the snifter of brandy from Sheffield, the baron cleared his throat.

"So you're here to escort Ophelia to the opera."

"I am. La Bohème is at the Lyceum."

"Odd, she doesn't like the opera," Sheffield said with a frown.

"Then I'll take it as a compliment that she believes she'll enjoy my company enough to endure an evening of Puccini."

Mathias bit back a grin as he remembered Ophelia making her distaste for opera quite clear earlier in the day. The baron gulped down the rest of his drink, then returned to the sideboard. Narrowing his eyes as he watched the man, Mathias noted how the baron swayed slightly as he poured himself another glass of wine. Although he'd not had the opportunity to speak with his brother, Mathias had already seen enough of the baron to guess the man had been drunk when he'd wagered Marymont in his game of chance with Charles. As if he'd read Mathias's mind, the baron turned back to him, his ruddy complexion darkening with a look of assessment.

"Your brother is an exceptional card player."

"That he is, sir. Charles seems to have the luck of the devil on most occasions. I've seldom seen him lose." Mathias nodded.

"I lost a sizeable piece of property to him recently." The baron looked down into his brandy for a moment before lifting his head with a hopeful glance at Mathias. "I don't suppose you would be in any position to convince your brother to let the property to me."

"I believe that would be Marymont you're referring to."

"How the devil did you know that," Sheffield sputtered in amazement.

"I manage my brother's finances and estate. I actually reviewed the property's paperwork this morning." Mathias took a drink of his brandy as he watched the baron struggle with his surprise.

"I see." Baron Sheffield cleared his throat. "So…do you know if Thornbury intends to sell the property?"

The sound of silk rustling outside the parlor caught Mathias's attention, and he turned his head toward the room's open doorway. As Ophelia entered the room, the air left his lungs with an unexpected strength that startled him. If someone had asked him to describe her before this moment, he would have said she was attractive. But Sabine had done her work well. Tonight, she looked magnificent.

"Ophelia, you look enchanting, my dear," the baron said jovially as he greeted her with a salute of his glass before downing the rest of his brandy.

"Thank you, father." Her voice was soft, but Mathias saw anger flash in her large brown eyes as she silently noted the just emptied glass in the man's hand. Either the baron didn't see his daughter's irritation, or he ignored it. He smiled broadly and gestured toward Mathias.

"As you can see, Mr. Gilchrist has been patiently awaiting your appearance."

"Indeed, I have, and my patience has been handsomely rewarded. You look exquisite this evening," Mathias murmured as he stepped forward to take Ophelia's hand in his.

A slight tremor vibrated through her fingers into his as he kissed her hand. The scent of citrus and strawberries wafted off her, and an urge to pull her close tightened his muscles. Color crested over her high cheekbones, and he smiled at the pleasure he saw brighten her brown eyes.

"I hope I've not kept you waiting too long," she said quietly. There was a breathless quality to her voice betrayed her cool composure. It was a serenity Mathias wanted to strip away. He wanted to find the real woman beneath that serenity.

"I thought perhaps you were regretting your agreement to attend the opera with me. Your father tells me you don't care for it," Mathias said with a chuckle. Ophelia hesitated for a split second before she smiled. The impact it had on his senses was as if one of his sparring partners at the club had landed a hard blow to his gut.

"I have decided to rely on the recommendation of an acquaintance who stated I should consider the company I am in and not the entertainment when it comes to whether or not I enjoy my evening."

"Then I shall endeavor to ensure you enjoy my company immensely this evening." Mathias glanced over at the baron to see the man watching the two of them closely.

"Speaking of Ophelia being in your company, Gilchrist, I've been remiss in my fatherly duties." The baron said as he pinned his gaze on Mathias. "Exactly what are your intentions where my daughter is concerned, sir?"

Caught off guard by the man's question in front of his daughter, Mathias arched his eyebrows in surprise at the man's poor social skills. A loud gasp escaped Ophelia as a dark pink flooded her cheeks.

"Forget my father's poor manners, Mr. Gilchrist." Ophelia glared at the baron, who had the good sense to look ashamed. With a slight shrug, Sheffield looked at Mathias.

"Please understand I'm simply looking out for my daughter's best interests, Gilchrist."

"Of course," Mathias murmured as saw the humiliation that had broken through Ophelia's serene composure. Eager to ease her discomfort, he smiled at her. "I think we will be late if we don't leave now. Shall we, my lady?"

Relief swept across Ophelia's face as he spoke, and she agreed with a sharp jerk of her head. The baron, having recovered from his gaffe, stepped forward to kiss Ophelia's cheek. She immediately recoiled, and Sheffield grimaced as if realizing for the first time how upset his daughter was. Mathias quickly stepped forward to solicitously capture Ophelia's elbow with his fingers.

"Shall we?" he said quietly.

Ophelia nodded again and allowed Mathias to guide her out of the house to the carriage waiting for them. When they were settled in their seats, Mathias rapped on the small window behind him as a signal to the driver to move on. The carriage rolled forward with a small jerk, and Mathias focused his attention on Ophelia. She was staring out the window in an obvious effort to avoid looking at him.

There was still a hint of color in her cheeks, indicating her deep embarrassment at her father's ill-timed remark. A sudden desire to console her swept through him. He wanted to pull her into his arms to comfort her as one might a child. He quickly dismissed the fanciful notion. When had he become so sentimental? He'd entered this bargain simply for the pleasure of awakening the fire he was convinced laid beneath Ophelia's calm demeanor.

Mathias leaned forward to peer out the window as well. The soft scent of citrus and vanilla filled his nostrils, and without thinking, he brushed his lips across her exposed shoulder. Silky smooth against his lips, the sweet taste of her shot a bolt of desire clean through him. It possessed the same strength as his earlier reaction when she'd entered the parlor.

A small tremor rippled through her at the caress. Her response only reinforced Mathias's conviction that she was capable of great passion. It was simply a matter of persuading Ophelia that she wasn't the cold creature her husband had declared her to be. She looked delectable enough to eat at the moment, and a twinge of regret tugged at him as he imagined the stir she was bound to cause at the Lyceum.

No doubt there would be half a dozen men showing up at the Thornbury box, under one pretext or another, this evening simply to receive an introduction to Ophelia. The sudden image of another man tasting her sweetly curved neck filled his head. The thought was far from pleasing. Instantly, his muscles knotted with tension, and he quickly reclined into his leather-padded seat. What the devil did it matter if another man kissed her? It was the purpose of his instruction.

Despite her tranquil expression, Ophelia's brown eyes flickered with something that convinced him she'd found his caress pleasurable. Pink lips parted slightly as if surprised, she drew in a soft breath, which only enhanced his desire to pull her into his arms. Mathias' muscles tightened further as he studied her in silence. Her lovely eyes narrowed on him when he didn't speak.

"Have I misunderstood the nature of our agreement, Mr. Gilchrist? I thought our relationship was to be that of student and teacher."

"No, you didn't misunderstand. However, given your fascination with the scenery, the caress seemed to be the easiest way to remind you that you aren't the only occupant in the carriage." Mathias' shoulders rolled in a small shrug. "You can hardly expect to hold a man's attention if you fail to focus on him alone."

"Am I to assume that in order to enthrall and intrigue a man, I must fawn over him?" Irritation became gold fire in the depths of her beautiful eyes as she shot a haughty look in his direction.

"Good God, no," he exclaimed in disgust as he remembered one of his brother's first paramours. "In fact, if I catch you simpering like a silly school girl at *any* point in time, I shall devise a suitable punishment to ensure you never do it again."

"Clearly, you have little fondness for women who simper." Her mouth twitched slightly as if she was trying not to laugh.

"An intelligent woman is far more likely to keep the interest of a suitor than a woman who has the mind of a simpleton."

"I think you're mistaken in your belief that men will choose an intelligent woman over a beautiful one." There was a hint of ironic resignation in her voice as she smiled with obvious amusement. "But let me ease your fears, Mr. Gilchrist. I *never* simper."

"Call me by my first name, Ophelia," he said softly. Her throat worked nervously as their gazes locked.

"Mathias." His name was little more than a whisper, but it did things to his insides that tugged the air from his lungs. Clearing his throat, he nodded.

"I expect you to call me Mathias from now on."

"But—"

"Formality during a moment of passion would seem a bit absurd, don't you think?"

"Yes, but *we* are *not* in a liaison."

"True, but you can hardly expect me to transform you into a swan without some instruction as to what passion is." The image of her lying beneath him filled his head, and the muscles in his body that had relaxed became stiff again.

"So you are changing the rules of our agreement." Anger tightened her lips as she stared at him with a look of disdain.

"It's not my intent to trick you, Ophelia," he replied with a shake of his head. "I think perhaps I'm going about this all wrong."

"What do you mean?" Suspicion threaded its way through her voice as she shook her head in confusion.

"I propose you attempt to *seduce* me into kissing you." His answer heightened her look of doubt as she bobbed her head with understanding.

"Very well." The clipped, pragmatic response made Mathias laugh.

"I didn't say to kiss me, Ophelia. I said *entice* me to kiss you." The thought of tasting her lips again made his blood run hot. "The first step in capturing a man's attention is to make him believe he's the only man you're aware of. Second, you must make him believe his kiss is something you long for, crave even."

Ophelia stared at him for a moment with a contemplative frown furrowing her forehead. She nodded slowly as a look of comprehension dawned in her eyes. She remained still for a long moment, then slowly leaned forward to smooth the lapel of his jacket. Her gaze locked with his as her lips curved upward slightly as if amused by her thoughts.

"I think you've undertaken a hopeless cause, Mathias. It's not possible to make a silk purse from a sow's ear." There was a self-deprecating note in her soft voice, which caused him to disagree with a shake of his head.

"You underestimate yourself, Ophelia. I'm convinced you'll easily stir the blood of any man you wish."

"Even you?"

Mischief darkened her eyes as she smiled at him. His lungs constricted at her light-hearted teasing. *Christ Jesus*, the woman had no idea as to the magnitude of the power she possessed when it came to holding a man hostage with her alluring smile and sultry voice. He'd ordered her to entice him, and she'd done so with little effort at all.

If he wasn't careful, he'd be even more enthralled than he already was. The instant the thought entered his head, Mathias dismissed it. He wasn't a schoolboy susceptible to falling under the spell of a woman. The last time he'd done so had taught him a painful lesson he'd never forgotten. Mathias shoved the old memories aside and smiled.

"I believe that was the point of the exercise," he said as he lightly tapped the tip of her nose. She eyed him with annoyance.

"You are being *far* from helpful."

"There is no better way to learn than if one is pushed into a body of water and forced to swim."

"I see." She stared at him with annoyed disgust, and Mathias was forced to bite back a laugh at her reaction. As if aware of his amusement, she suddenly relaxed. "And if I were any other woman, what would you expect me to say right now?"

There was a beguiling quality to her voice that he'd not heard before, and his heart slammed into his chest. Desire, stark and fierce, crashed through Mathias, knotting his muscles with tension. Had he made a mistake in offering to instruct her on how to feel passion? When he didn't answer, Ophelia tipped her head to one side as a questioning look softened her mouth in a way that made him ache to explore the sweet taste of her. With great effort, he suppressed the hunger gripping every muscle in his body.

"At the moment, I can't think of any other woman except you."

Color flushed her cheeks as she jerked backward and stared down at her lap. Mathias immediately leaned forward and one finger pressed against her jaw, he forced her to look at him. Ophelia flinched and shrank back into her seat and turned her head to stare out of the carriage window once more.

"I do not enjoy being mocked, Mr. Gilchrist." The humiliation in her voice aroused a need to comfort her once more. Leaning forward, he caught her hand in his and squeezed it gently as he silently encouraged her to look at him.

"I am not mocking you, Ophelia."

"Then you are far more skilled at this game than I am." Her stilted reply made him gently caress her cheek as he forced her to look at him again.

"It doesn't take skill to speak the truth." He grimaced at her inability to believe him. Havenstock had to have been even more of a bastard than he thought. "I'm beginning to realize it's not that you are incapable of passion but that you lack confidence."

"And I think you're delusional." She quickly disagreed with a shake of her head.

"Simply by objecting, you make yourself desirable."

"I don't see how." This time she laughed. He was reminded once more how much he liked the sound.

"Simply put, you're a challenge. That cool exterior of yours makes a man long to see if there's heat beneath that icy surface." His thumb rubbed over her bottom lip as he stared into her wide-eyed gaze. "And I'm convinced there's fire there."

Ophelia turned her head away from him as color flooded her cheeks while her fingers nervously tugged at the beaded purse lying in her lap. Slowly retreating from her, Mathias leaned back in the cushions of his seat and studied her in silence. She didn't move for a moment before she drew in a deep breath, and he saw the vulnerability in her that she tried behind a smile.

"It appears you were correct this morning when you suggested I would be a difficult student," she said softly. "So perhaps I should try once more to do as you instructed."

"Practice does make perfect," he said with a low laugh as he saw her arch her dainty eyebrows at him.

An undefinable emotion flitted across her face before a small smile curved her lips. It was a soft, bewitching look that suggested she had a secret. Instantly, Mathias experienced a visceral twist inside his body as his muscles grew taut in reaction. Ophelia leaned forward again, and her warm breath blew across his cheek as her lips caressed his ear.

"Will you forgive me?"

"Forgive you?" he choked out as her teeth lightly grazed his ear lobe, and he struggled to loosen the knot in his throat.

"I've been remiss in saying how handsome you look. I shall be the envy of every woman tonight."

Her lips brushed across his jaw, and without thinking, Mathias turned his head to kiss her. In a quick movement, she retreated, her lips still curved in a secretive smile. She shook her head slightly in a silent reprimand.

"I believe you said I was to *entice* you to kiss me, not allow you to kiss me."

"So I did," he growled softly as he fought the urge to kiss her soundly. "And you did not disappoint, Ophelia. I said you *had* the ability to incite passion in a man, and you succeeded."

A flash of pleasure crossed her lovely features before the serene composure he was growing accustomed to returned. Mathias didn't tell her how well she'd accomplished the task he'd assigned her. He couldn't remember the last time a woman had ignited desire inside him with the simple sound of her voice and the lightest caress of her lips. He was beginning to think he'd miscalculated badly where she was concerned.

The carriage rolled to a halt, and he leaned forward to capture her hand in his. He turned it over and pressed a lingering kiss against her palm. In the next breath, he swirled his tongue around her finger, then took it into his mouth. The sharp breath she drew in filled him with satisfaction as he released her hand. Lips parted slightly, she stared at him in mute surprise, and with another emotion she quickly concealed behind her mask of composure.

"That is to remind you that when you entice a man, the outcome might not end so sedately as my response."

"I'd hardly call such a…decadent caress…sedate."

"No?" he grinned. "Then imagine how epicurean you'll feel when I really do allow you to kiss me."

"*Allow…*" Ophelia gasped as she glared at him.

The carriage door opened, and Mathias quickly exited the vehicle, then turned and offered Ophelia his hand. Although she looked as if nothing unseemly had transpired between them, her brown eyes flashed with gold fire as their eyes met. Still grinning, he arched his eyebrow at her and waited for her to accept his hand. Hesitation and annoyance tightened her lovely mouth before she placed her hand in his and joined him on the sidewalk.

Mathias tucked her arm through his as he escorted her up the steps to the theater. They reached the interior of the Lyceum fairly quickly, and there was a large crush of people in the main lobby. Many people turned their heads to look at them as they made their way through the crowd. The slight tremor that vibrated off of Ophelia made him bend his head toward her.

"They're looking because you look exquisite, and they're trying to understand how I managed to capture your attention for the evening," he murmured in her ear.

"I think you're mistaken," she said with a note of resignation in her voice. "I'm certain they're thinking something entirely different."

"Then, by the end of the evening, I'll enjoy telling you how wrong you were."

Ophelia sniffed with skepticism, but didn't reply. Biting back a smile at her refusal to believe him, Mathias guided her through the crowd and up to the second floor. As they entered the Thornbury box, he could feel the tension radiating off her the moment people in the audience below looked up to stare at them. In silence, he gently urged her to take a seat, then sat down next to her. Program in hand, Ophelia opened it to study the contents. There was a quiet strength about her, but a vulnerability as well. As if aware he was watching her, she directed a questioning look at him.

"Is something wrong?"

"Not at all. I was simply wondering how Havenstock could have been such a fool not to see how lovely you are." His reply sent a rush of color flooding through her cheeks, and she bowed her head beneath his admiring look.

"Thank you." The quiet response made him smile.

"So you're not quite the hopeless student you professed to be."

"Thank you, again," she said with a laugh. Mathias enjoyed the sound, and he leaned toward her. Before he could speak, the box door behind them swished open. He glanced over his shoulder to see Ralph Merrick entering the box. They were barely passable acquaintances, which meant the man was here for one reason only—Ophelia. In the back of his head, a voice strongly protested introducing the man to her. Merrick was likable enough, but certainly not stimulating company. He forced a polite smile to his lips and rose to greet the man.

"Merrick," he murmured with a slight bow. Beside him, Ophelia turned her head toward their unexpected visitor.

"Gilchrist." The man returned Mathias's bow, then focused his attention on Ophelia. "It's been a while since we last saw one another, and I thought I would stop by to say hello."

"Indeed," Mathias murmured as he cast a mocking look in the other man's direction. "Allow me to present the Viscountess Havenstock. Ophelia, Mr. Ralph Merrick."

"Lady Havenstock," the man said warmly as he stepped forward to kiss Ophelia's hand with a look of admiration. "It's a pleasure."

"How do you do, Mr. Merrick."

"Quite well, now that I've made your acquaintance," Merrick said with a cheerful smile. "I don't know how we've not met before, my lady. Do you come to the theater often?"

"Ophelia isn't all that fond of the opera." Mathias experienced a twinge of irritation at the man's blatant interest in Ophelia.

"Then we should do everything we can to find an entertainment that suits her." Merrick smiled broadly as he leaned in closer to Ophelia. "We can't allow ourselves to be denied such an enchanting creature merely on the occasional off-note of a singer."

"You flatter me, Mr. Merrick, but I don't see myself as enchanting." Ophelia laughed as a flush of color crested in her cheeks at Merrick's compliment.

"The very fact that you don't see yourself as such only makes you all the more bewitching." Merrick stared at

Ophelia with absolute admiration, and a small bolt of satisfaction sailed through Mathias as he arched his eyebrow at her over the man's head. Her eyes flashed with amused disgust as their gazes met before she turned her attention back to Merrick and smiled at the other man.

"I surmise you enjoy attending the opera, Mr. Merrick?"

"I do. In fact, La Bohème has become a new favorite. Has Gilchrist explained the story to you?"

"I think convincing me to accompany him this evening proved challenging enough." The mischievous note in her voice as she glanced in his direction made Mathias's gut twist, and tension tightened his entire body. The woman had no idea that Merrick had spoken correctly. She *was* enchanting.

"Despite its sad ending, Puccini's compositions are masterful."

"Then perhaps I won't regret coming after all," she said with another smile at Merrick. Again, Mathias's muscles knotted into hard cords of something he didn't like.

"I, for one, am exceedingly glad Gilchrist persuaded you to do so."

As the man smiled at Ophelia, Mathias resisted the urge to throw Merrick out of the box. Tension lashed through him. What the devil did it matter that Merrick was expressing such a blatant interest in Ophelia?

Mathias was doing precisely what he'd told Ophelia he would do. He would transform her into a swan, then walk away without a backward glance. He knew all too well the folly of becoming too deeply involved with any woman. A voice in the back of his head reminded him that Ophelia wasn't like other women. He quickly dismissed the thought, despite the mocking laughter in the dark recesses of his brain.

Chapter 5

The sound of the door opening behind them caught Ophelia's attention, and Mr. Merrick turned his head as well. Both Mathias and Merrick frowned as two men entered the opera box.

"Margate. Chelmsford," Mathias said with an abrupt bow before his lips twisted in a cynical smile. "I take it you're here to meet Lady Havenstock?"

The mockery in his voice made Ophelia experience a twinge of discomfort as she suddenly felt as though she were goods on display.

"Gilchrist," the taller of the two newcomers bowed slightly in greeting with a humorous twist of his lips. "You know me well enough to know I won't insult your intelligence."

"Naturally." The sardonic note in Mathias's voice made the man arch his eyebrow upward as his eyes narrowed. Not waiting for a reply, Mathias turned toward her with a smile on his lips, but the warmth and amusement she'd seen in his eyes just a few moments ago had disappeared.

"Ophelia, allow me to present the Earl of Chelmsford. And this fellow here is Viscount Margate. My lords, Lady Havenstock."

"Lady Havenstock, a pleasure. How is it we've not met before?" The earl's warm smile made her smile in return as he took her hand and brushed his lips across her fingers. There was the hint of a rogue about him that said he had a trail of broken hearts behind him.

"I would imagine because I lead a fairly quiet life. I wouldn't be here this evening if Mathias hadn't convinced me to come." Ophelia looked at Mathias, and her smile faltered strong, impassive angles of his profile.

"Then we must rectify the situation," Chelmsford said with the authoritarian tone of a man accustomed to being obeyed. "I'm hosting a small dinner party tomorrow evening, and I insist you come."

"I'm not sure—"

"I won't take no for an answer, my lady. I'm sure Gilchrist won't mind accompanying you."

"And if Gilchrist isn't available, I'm happy to stand in his stead," Viscount Margate exclaimed as he stepped forward to take Ophelia's hand and bow in front of her. "I'm delighted to make your acquaintance, Lady Havenstock, and it would be an honor to escort you to Chelmsford's dinner party."

His youthful enthusiasm made Ophelia laugh. He appeared to be the same age as Lizzie's suitor, Mr. Nickens, and far too young for her.

"You're both too kind, but I cannot—"

"What Ophelia is trying to say is that she's already agreed to attend the Markham affair with me tomorrow night."

Although Mathias's mouth was curved in a slight smile, his expression was unreadable as he looked at the two men towering over Ophelia. For a second time in less than five minutes, she experienced the sensation of being little more than an object of fascination. Irritated by Mathias's cursory tone, Ophelia smiled at the young Viscount, who was looking decidedly crestfallen.

"We do have to eat, and I'm certain Mathias wouldn't mind if we begin our evening at Lord Chelmsford's dinner party."

"Excellent," the earl said with a charming smile in her direction. "I'm delighted you agreed to join my guests and me."

"As I recall, you did say you wouldn't take no for an answer, my lord."

Ophelia arched her eyebrows, and the earl's eyes widened slightly at the implication she'd been coerced. Satisfied that her teasing had taken him by surprise, she smiled up at him mischievously. Instantly, the man threw back his head and laughed heartily.

"So I did, and it bodes well for our friendship that you understand I usually get my way."

"I would expect nothing less from a man of your stature." At her cheerfully irreverent response, the earl laughed again. The sound sent a rush of exhilaration through her. She was enjoying the relaxed banter between the two of them. The earl caught her hand in his, and she experienced a sense of power as he studied her with obvious admiration before he caressed her bare knuckles.

"I cannot begin to express how happy I am that you have agreed to dine with me tomorrow night, my lady." The earl's voice was husky and held a distinct note of seduction. Ophelia shook her head slightly.

"I think you mean you're happy I agreed to be one of your guests. I would never agree to dine alone with a man I've just met," she murmured. The surprise on the earl's face was quickly replaced by a seductive smile. Before he could speak, she shook her head and laughed. "And if you dare to say you're counting the hours, I shall disappoint you and not come at "

"Then I shall simply say that I look forward to seeing you tomorrow evening, Lady Havenstock." The earl kissed her hand again, his lips lingering on her skin in a caress that would have made another woman's heart flutter. Ophelia felt nothing. "And I should warn you that I intend to see much more of you in the weeks to come."

There was a sinful invitation in his gray eyes that made her cheeks grow hot as she wondered if he was implying something much more intimate. The performance warning bell rang out in the theater, and Chelmsford and Margate quickly made their goodbyes, but Merrick remained seated in the chair next to her. Ophelia glanced in Mathias's direction, then back to the man at her side.

"Mr. Merrick, is there anyone who might miss you?" She smiled politely at the young man, who flushed at her question.

"Forgive me, my lady. I confess to being so enthralled with you I forgot I'd left my mother and sister conversing with friends. They are probably wondering where I am." Slightly uncomfortable with Merrick's obsequious manner, Ophelia frowned slightly as she found herself wishing the man would just leave.

"Then you mustn't let us keep you from seeing they enjoy the rest of their evening."

"Yes. Yes, of course. How remiss of me." Merrick quickly scrambled to his feet and bent over her hand. "I hope you will allow me to call on you tomorrow, my lady."

"That's most kind of you, sir, but I'm uncertain I'll be home."

"The day after tomorrow then," Merrick said with persistence. The last thing she wanted was to entertain Merrick. There was something off-putting about the man. It seemed an unkind judgment to make, but his fawning manner did little to endear her to the man.

"Forgive me, Mr. Merrick, but I believe they're about to start." She tipped her head in the direction of the orchestra, which was in the process of tuning its instruments.

"Yes, of course." Merrick nodded, clearly reluctant to leave. "Until our next meeting then, my dear Lady Havenstock."

The kiss he placed on her hand was far more fervent than she liked. It reminded her of George's son, Edgar. The memory of the past and her son by marriage sent a small tremor of repugnance through her. Ophelia forced a smile to her lips as the man straightened, and with a brief nod toward Mathias, left the opera box.

The man's behavior only emphasized her feelings of being placed on display, as if she were available to the highest bidder. Logically, she knew she had no one to blame for her current situation but herself. She'd allowed Mathias to goad her into accepting his proposal. She could have said no, but a part of her had objected with vehemence.

For the first time, she recalled how aloof Mathias had been the entire time the other men had been present. He'd pushed her into the water and left her to drown or swim. The thought angered Ophelia, despite knowing the terms of their agreement.

As the house lights dimmed, Mathias sank down into the seat Merrick had vacated seconds before. Music swirled up into the air, and Ophelia realized how much she was coming to regret having agreed to Mathias's proposal. It only heightened the tension that connected her to him. A soft chuckle floated into her ear as Mathias's warm breath brushed across her cheek.

"You look as though you are about to be thrown to the lions." The teasing comment made her frown. It was precisely how she felt. But not because she was about to endure several hours of singing. She slowly turned her head to look at him with disappointment.

"That's precisely what happened just a few moments ago, only they were wolves."

Not bothering to wait for his reaction, she turned away to stare at the stage as the curtain drew back and the opera began. For the next hour, she barely heard the music or the singing filling the theatre. Mathias believed there was no better way to learn other than being thrust into a body of water without warning or skill. But the water he'd thrown her into had left her feeling alone and uncertain.

It was a sensation she'd not experienced since her father had sold her into a marriage that had been one of constant humiliation. The music rose to a loud conclusion, pulling Ophelia out of her thoughts. The sudden touch of Mathias's hand on hers made her jump. She jerked her head toward him as he carried her hand up to his mouth and warmed her skin with a kiss.

"I'm a heartless brute for having thrown you to the wolves, as you so aptly stated. I'll not do it again," Mathias said softly as his mouth caressed her skin. The regret in his voice warmed Ophelia in a way that made her heart race. Her mouth suddenly dry, she acknowledged his apology with a sharp nod and pulled her hand from his.

"Thank you."

"However, you should be proud of the way you acquitted yourself. Chelmsford was quite taken with you, and he's not a man who gives his admiration easily." The odd note of irritation in his voice startled her, but he projected nothing more than self-satisfaction as he smiled at her.

"I found Lord Chelmsford quite charming, although a bit intimidating."

"I predict the man will be completely enthralled with you within a week." At his declaration, Ophelia laughed.

"A premature assumption, I think."

"Not if you continue to excel at your lessons as you did earlier this evening."

Mathias lowered his voice as he leaned into her. The warmth of him enveloped Ophelia, and her breathing hitched at the mere inches between them. A warm aroma of spice and leather filled her senses. It was a pleasing smell that emphasized the raw potency of him.

Mathias was no less charming than the earl was, but he was far more dangerous to her state of mind. Chelmsford didn't make her body feel as though it were on fire. A fire that could consume her. In the back of her mind, she found herself wishing she could seduce him. The audacious thought warmed her cheeks, and she bowed her head.

"My lessons, as you call them, will be sorely tested when it comes to enticing the Earl of Chelmsford."

"As I said previously, what you lack is confidence, not the ability to stir passion in a man or feel it."

"And I'm not convinced," she said as she stared out at the audience.

"Then I shall have to do my very best to prove you wrong. A task that will give me great pleasure."

The soft promise sent a shiver of anticipation skimming its way down her back. The thought of his mouth on hers made her pulse throb violently through her veins. She knew how dangerous it was too long for his kiss, but it didn't stop her from craving to experience his touch. Desperate to hide the direction of her thoughts, she arched an eyebrow and eyed him with disapproval.

"Surely, any attempt to convince me as to the validity of your theory would involve an intimacy we both agree does not exist."

"Touché," he said with an almost boyish grin, and she found it impossible not to smile in return. Behind them, the door to the opera box opened to reveal Louisa, then Rhea, and Percy Rockwood.

"Good evening Mathias, Ophelia. Louisa saw the two of you during the middle of the first act and insisted we come say hello," Percy said cheerfully, which prompted his wife to rebuke him with a playful smack on his arm with her fan.

"That's not completely true, Percy Rockwood, and you know it."

"It's partly true," Louisa said while directing an amused look of sisterly disgust in her brother's direction. "I *did* see the two of you, but Percy was the one who insisted we come to say hello."

Louisa kissed Mathias on both cheeks, then stepped aside to let Rhea and Percy greet their friend. As Percy was shaking Mathias's hand, Louisa turned to Ophelia with a smile of delight.

"How exquisite you look this evening, Ophelia."

"I agree," Rhea said with a smile as she greeted Ophelia. "The color suits you well."

"And it appears Mathias thinks so too. The man barely took his eyes off you during the entire first act," Louisa murmured as Percy greeted Ophelia and complimented her as well.

She nodded her thanks to Percy and deliberately ignored her friend's teasing comment. The Louisa she remembered from her childhood suddenly appeared as the youngest Rockwood cast a sideways glance at Mathias, who was now engaged in conversation with Percy.

"I see you and Mathias were able to work out your differences from last night."

Louisa's eyes twinkled with mischief as she studied Ophelia with interest. The heat that had subsided from her cheeks at their complimentary remarks returned as she saw her friend's avid curiosity. Last night Louisa had noted Ophelia's distraught manner when she'd returned to the ballroom. Although she'd put off her friend's questions as to the source of her discomfort, Louisa had witnessed the silent exchange between Ophelia and Mathias when he'd returned to the ballroom. Rhea released a long-suffering sigh of amusement.

"My sister-in-law is on a fishing expedition, my lady. You mustn't indulge her *or* Percy's curiosity." At Rhea's warning, Louisa gasped with mock indignation.

"How can you say that, Rhea?" she exclaimed.

"Because it's true," Ophelia said with a laugh. "You've never been able *not* to meddle. None of you have, although Sebastian will most certainly deny the charge."

"You're absolutely right, Ophelia. My dear brother does like to interfere more often than he realizes. In fact, he almost prevented Devin…"

Louisa's voice trailed off into silence as a haunted look flashed in her hazel eyes. Quickly grasping her friend's hands, Ophelia squeezed them in silent sympathy. A bittersweet smile curved the young widow's mouth while Rhea looked on in dismayed concern. The smile on her lips brightened as Louisa looked at them in a chiding manner.

"What dour faces," she exclaimed with a smile. With a gentle, reassuring pat on Ophelia's hand, Louisa pulled free of her grasp. "One would think I was about to leave for the farthest corners of the earth in a few days instead of Scotland."

"You're returning to Callendar? I thought you had planned to stay in town a little longer." Ophelia eyed her friend in surprise.

"I've grown weary of navigating the gossip of the Set. I plan to leave some time at the end of the week or first of next," Louisa said with a nod of determination. "The boys will remain here until Aunt Matilda brings them back to Callendar just before Christmas."

"You're going alone?" Ophelia's eyes widened with surprise at her friend's plans.

"That was the family's reaction as well," Rhea said quietly.

"I need the solitude. Devin would be angry with me for mourning him for so long." Louisa smiled at them, but Ophelia heard something more than grief in her friend's voice, although she couldn't define it. "He always thought the Queen's constant state of mourning for Prince Albert didn't serve her or the country well."

"The fresh air will do you good," Ophelia said matter-of-factly, determined to support the decision her friend made. A glimmer of the Louisa she'd known in childhood suddenly returned as her friend eyed her mischievously.

"So tell me, how long have you known Mathias?"

"Not long," Ophelia said vaguely as she wasn't about to reveal the shortness of their acquaintance.

"He seems quite taken with you," Rhea said with a smile, her gaze shifting toward the two men so deep in conversation.

"I'm sure you're mistaken."

"No, I would have to agree with Louisa's earlier observation. The man finds it difficult to take his eyes off of you," Rhea murmured softly as she arched an eyebrow at first Ophelia and then Louisa.

Quickly rejecting the woman's assertion with a shake of her head, Ophelia couldn't help darting a glance at Mathias.

The instant she did so, he looked in her direction, and their gazes locked. Startled, her cheeks grew hot, and her heart skipped a beat at the intensity of his stare. She quickly turned back to Louisa and Rhea. Both women were studying her with amusement, and the heat in her cheeks skimmed its way throughout the rest of her body. Louisa's mouth was tilted upward in a complacent smile, and Ophelia shook her head.

"I assure you there's nothing between us other than friendship."

"I'm not—" Louisa's words were interrupted by the performance warning bell. Disappointment made her friend's mouth twist with a wry smile, while her hazel eyes twinkled with mischief. "I'm not convinced, and I shall call on you before I leave for Scotland. I'm eager to hear more about this friendship as Mathias's attentions suit you well. I don't think I've ever seen you looking lovelier."

All too aware of Louisa's tenacious nature, Ophelia laughed in an effort to allay the younger woman's unfounded suspicions.

"And my response will not change."

"Rhea, Louisa, we should return to our box," Percy said as he turned toward them.

He smiled at the three of them before looking at his wife. The adoration on his handsome features caused a rosy blush to fill Rhea's cheeks as she stepped forward to entwine her arm with Percy's.

The special look that passed between the couple spoke volumes as to their feelings for one another. Percy had married for love, and Ophelia was happy for her childhood friend. But deep inside, she experienced a twinge of envy.

The warning bell rang a second time, and in a flurry of goodbyes, the Rockwoods left the box. With a reluctant twist of her lips, Ophelia took her seat again, all too aware of Mathias as he sat down next to her.

"Percy tells me Louisa intends to return to Scotland this week. Alone." The troubled note in his voice made her glance in his direction. He was staring at the dark red carpet beneath their feet with a look of deep concern.

"I think she realizes it's time to rejoin the living, and she wants to say goodbye to Devin in her own way."

"Percy said essentially the same thing, but he's worried about her, as am I." The frown creasing his brow made Ophelia wince slightly. What would it be like to have someone worried about her as Mathias was Louisa? Irritated that she'd even considered the thought, Ophelia stiffened in her seat.

"Louisa, like most women, is not a delicate flower that needs constant tending." It hadn't been her intention to speak so sharply, but her words caused Mathias to jerk his head up in surprise. She quickly averted her gaze. "What I mean is that Louisa is not a child. She's quite capable of managing her life *without* anyone's help."

Music signaling the start of the next act rose from the orchestra pit, and Ophelia deliberately pretended to give her full attention to the stage below to avoid any further conversation. As the musical entertainment progressed, Ophelia found herself studying the people in the theater than the performance on stage. In the far curve of the opera house's balcony, she caught sight of her stepson.

Antipathy swept through. Referring to him as her stepson was ludicrous given the fact she was only five years older than Edgar. His head was bent toward the woman at his side who was smiling at him. George's son shifted in his chair, and Ophelia jerked backward into her chair to avoid being seen. She had no intention of being caught, even acknowledging the man's presence. Although she seldom encountered Edgar in public, she made every possible effort to avoid him whenever she did. The man had always made her uncomfortable, but George's death had made him unbearable.

At the reading of George's will, she'd been stunned to learn the bulk of her husband's estate had been placed in Edgar's hands to manage while she'd been given only a small annual stipend. Even the house had fallen under Edgar's purview. Her stepson had been an almost daily caller throughout the mourning period, unlike when his father had been alive. When he'd delivered the ultimatum that she become his mistress or leave the house, Ophelia had packed the few possessions she owned and returned to Marymont. Far from pleased, Edgar had threatened to reduce her stipend, but the solicitor had informed him the monies were solely in Ophelia's control.

Raucous laughter on the stage penetrated her morose thoughts. Her attention returned to the stage that had been transformed into a small café. Although she knew very little Italian, the music itself was passionate and compelling. Without realizing it, she leaned forward in her seat to watch the performance. With each passing moment, the music drew her into the story until she was blinking away tears at Mimi's death as the opera ended. A handkerchief was suddenly waved in front of her, but she rejected the offer with a shake of her head.

"No, thank you. It's unnecessary."

"You're a stubborn woman, Lady Havenstock," Mathias growled with amused, almost tender exasperation. Ophelia blinked the rest of her tears away as she turned her head toward him.

"And you, Mr. Gilchrist, can be quite annoying."

Her words sparked a glint of laughter in his eyes that said he agreed with her. But his only response was a nonchalant shrug of his shoulders. Rising to his feet, he waited for her to stand, then ushered her out into the crowded corridor.

"I thought perhaps we'd have supper at Rules."

"I'd like that," she said with a smile. "I've not eaten since breakfast."

"Is it your habit to starve yourself like other women I know?" The question created an image of Mathias flirting with other women in her head. The moment the picture popped in her head, a sharp, strange sensation streaked through her. Her heart sank. She could ill afford to become enamored with this man. It would be disastrous to her heart and soul. Ophelia forced a smile to her lips.

"I was simply too busy to find the time to eat. I can assure you my appetite is far more robust than deemed respectable."

When they reached the sidewalk outside the Opera house, Mathias cupped her elbow with his hand and guided her toward the Strand. They'd almost reached the end of the city block when she saw Mathias's driver waiting patiently for them beside the carriage. As Mathias sank down into the seat opposite her, Ophelia turned her head to study the heavy carriage traffic resulting from the opera's conclusion.

"Despite what you led me to believe, I think you enjoyed Puccini's work." The light-hearted teasing made her sniff with irritation at his words.

"If you expect me to say the evening was intolerable, I shall have to disappoint you."

"Then you didn't find my company without its charm."

"Actually, I was thinking about the last half of the performance. I found it quite pleasing." Not about to admit how much she enjoyed his company, she shook her head.

"You've forgotten lesson number two, Ophelia. A man likes to know *he's* the reason you're finding the evening so enjoyable."

"But you're simply my tutor. I'm not supposed to seduce you," she said with a smile. A low growl rolled out of him before he laughed.

"You enjoyed putting me in my place, didn't you?"

"I did." She laughed and nodded with satisfaction. "I must take my small triumphs where I can."

"Again, you underestimate yourself, Ophelia. Have you forgotten Margate and Merrick are already at your feet? And I'm certain Chelmsford will follow in relatively short order."

"You're impossible." She scoffed at him with a skeptical smile. He appeared to contemplate her response for a long moment before he shook his head.

"And you, my sweet Ophelia, are absolutely enchanting."

The sincerity in his voice took her by surprise, and she stared at him in amazement. A slow smile curled his lips, and her mouth went dry at the way he was watching her. It was a wickedly sinful look that caused an unfamiliar ache to twist her insides as a strange lethargy slid through her. Unable to think of a response, Ophelia looked out the window.

"Merrick was right. The fact you don't believe yourself enchanting makes you all the more desirable."

"Don't be ridiculous." Her efforts to sound pragmatic and indifferent to his compliment failed miserably. Instead, her voice was little more than a breathless rasp. Mathias leaned forward, and the male scent of him filled her senses.

"I think perhaps another lesson is in order."

"Another lesson?" She swallowed hard at his words.

"It *is* what we agreed to." An unreadable emotion darkened his eyes, and a shiver raced down her spine.

"Very well, what pearl of wisdom do you wish to enlighten me with," she breathed as she struggled to regain some of her equilibrium.

"I believe you could benefit from another session practicing your skills of seduction."

"As I recall, you said I passed my last lesson quite admirably."

Ophelia tipped her chin upward slightly in an attempt to hide her trepidation at the thought of obeying his command. At her obvious reluctance to obey his command, Mathias folded his arms across his chest. One eyebrow arching upward, he smiled with amusement.

"Naturally, if you're not feeling up to the task—"

"That's not the first time you've accused me of being a coward," she snapped as she glared at him.

"I have never labeled you a coward, Ophelia. But you cannot deny you're afraid to believe in yourself." As she glared at him, Mathias leaned back further into the seat cushions and, with a small shrug, silently challenged her to do as he'd instructed.

Ophelia's irritation grew as she saw a slight twitch at the corner of his mouth. The man was clearly amused by her outrage. Her annoyance grew as she imagined inflicting all manners of harm on him. When she ran out of potential punishments, she realized the only penalty she could inflict was to beat the man at his own game.

She needed to do as he'd ordered—arouse his desire. The daunting thought made her stomach lurch. The sight of his mouth curved in the slightest of smiles sent determination speeding through her. Without looking away from him, Ophelia slowly reached out and drew the shades down over first one window and then the other. The small candle, fluttering in its glass globe on the side of the carriage wall, barely illuminated the interior and threw Mathias's features into the shadows.

He was no longer trying to hide a smile, and she leaned forward to lightly press her forefinger against his lips. His teeth nipped at her flesh, and an odd flutter assaulted her insides. Despite her instinct to draw back, Ophelia pressed her palms against his chest.

"I find you quite..." She deliberately hesitated before releasing a sigh. "...exasperating, Mathias Gilchrest."

"Do you indeed."

His chuckle rose up from his chest and vibrated against her hands. There was something exciting about the sensation. She studied the black tie around his neck and experienced the urge to loosen it. In an idle gesture, she played with the endings of the black material and looked upward. Mathias was still smiling, something in his mood had changed. It was if the balance of power had shifted between them.

"Yes, but I wonder what you think about me." She frowned as if considering her words when what she was really doing was questioning her sanity.

"I believe I've already told you I find you enchanting."

"Does that mean you thought of me last night lying alone in your bed?" The question was more for lack of inspiration than anything else. But the moment Mathias stiffened against her palms, she knew it had been the right one to ask.

"Possibly." The one-word response was quiet, but his smile had faded.

"Did you imagine I was doing as you'd ordered?" Ophelia marveled at her audaciousness, but she was determined to win this battle between them. Her question was met with a long pause, and she saw his throat bob as he swallowed hard.

"Yes."

This time, it was clearly an effort for him to respond. Ophelia slowly slid her hands under the lapels of his coat until her palms rested on his chest. Beneath his shirt, his nipples were rigid against her fingertips. In a slow, methodical fashion, she began to draw small circles around one of his nipples with her forefinger.

"It felt quite wicked to do as you instructed, but it was definitely pleasurable." Her words caused a dark sound to rumble in his chest, and she smiled. "Should I repeat the exercise again tonight, or should I wait?"

"*Wait?*"

It was a hoarse, choked-out sound that sent a wave of triumph cresting through her. She didn't fully understand how, but she had no doubt he was aroused by her words.

"Yes," she whispered as she brushed her mouth against his cheek. "I would not want you to experience any discomfort because of me."

"I'm *already* experiencing discomfort," Mathias rasped as his hand wrapped around the back of her neck to tug her forward and capture her mouth in a hard kiss. .

Chapter 6

Desire pounded its way through Mathias as he tasted the sweetness of Ophelia's lips. It had been years since a woman had tempted him the way Ophelia did. Inside his trousers, his cock was hard and tight with arousal. At the moment, the exercise he'd commanded of her was wreaking havoc with every part of him. With a tug he pulled her closer. She came willingly, her body pliant against his.

As her lips parted slightly in a soft mewl, he took advantage of the fact to tangle his tongue with hers. Honey had never tasted as sweet. Her response to his kiss was tentative at first, but the instant he deepened their caress, she responded eagerly. The subtle scent of strawberries filled his nostrils as she pressed her body deeper into his. His mouth slid away from hers to caress its way down her neck to the base of her throat.

The soft sigh whispering out of her silently gave him permission to continue downward until his mouth encountered the edge of her bodice. A primitive urge to rip the material aside and give him access to her full breasts fired his blood. Instead, he restrained the savage sensation and focused his attention on her neck, nibbling at the spot where her pulse fluttered wildly. Without any actual presence of mind, he roughly caught her hand and pressed it against the hardness of his erection. She gasped as he forced her hand to slide over his hard length and his teeth gently bit her sweetly curved ear lobe.

"For a woman who doesn't believe she can arouse a man's passion, I think this proves otherwise." Mathias heard the harsh note in his voice as he dragged in a deep breath in an attempt to quash the desire raging through his limbs.

Their eyes met, and there was a sultry look about her that made him wish he'd ordered Jacobs to drive them to Thornberry Place instead of the restaurant. He wanted to quench his need for her until he could easily let her walk away into another man's arms. The sudden image of Chelmsford pushed its way into his thoughts while, simultaneously, an oddly familiar emotion snaked through him.

"Mathias?"

The sound of his name passing from her lips sounded more like a soft prayer than a question as her mouth brushed against his. The light, tentative caress of her fingers against his thigh made him stiffen. *Christ Almighty*, what the hell was he thinking? He wasn't a wet-behind-the-ears school boy. He'd promised to transform her into a creature desired by men, not to become one of them prostrating at her feet. The last time he'd been foolish enough to do such a thing, it had crushed not only his heart, but his pride as well.

In an abrupt move, Mathias lifted her off his lap and set her back on the seat opposite him. He quickly suppressed the need to pull her back into his arms. Refusing to act on the urge, he quickly raised the shades over the carriage windows. The action did nothing to alleviate the disappointment crashing through him. Despite his best intentions, he was finding her far more enticing than he wanted to. Clearing his throat, he looked at her confused expression then quickly raised the window shades.

"Forgive me, Ophelia. I used you badly just now. I said I wouldn't throw you to the wolves again, only to act like one myself."

If he hadn't been watching her so closely, he would have missed the way she flinched at his statement. Before he could speak, she assumed a look of self-deprecating amusement.

"But your tutoring is clearly proving to be successful. We've now confirmed I'm more than able to make a man desire me physically."

"But?" He eyed her closely as she looked away from him.

"I doubt I'm capable of indulging in a frivolous affair." Her words triggered the memory of the past and how Miriam had said something similar.

"So it's a husband you want," he said with disillusion. No sooner were the words out of his mouth than her eyes widened with horror.

"*Dear Lord, no,*" she exclaimed before her features became solemn and unreadable. "I will *never* marry again."

"Never?" He eyed her with a touch of cynicism. "It's hard to believe any woman would reject the proposal from the right man."

"I am not like other women. I have no intention of ever becoming a possession again." Ophelia's lips had thinned with inflexible determination. "My home has been returned to me, and I have a small stipend Edgar cannot touch. I will never sacrifice my independence again for a husband."

His thoughts flashed back to the few minutes he'd spent with her father. The man had clearly been seeking to pin Mathias down as to the possibility of a match between them. The baron would no doubt expect something in return for handing his daughter over to another man. Disgusted by the way the men in Ophelia's life had treated her, remorse gnawed at him. Was he really any better than her husband or father? The answer didn't please him. Unwilling to examine his own complicity in the manner of her treatment, he shook his head.

"Not all men are like Havenstock. And for that matter, not all fathers use their daughters as collateral to clear their debts." His observation made her jerk slightly as her body straightened and pressed rigidly against the carriage cushions.

"Perhaps, but I've never met a man willing to give his wife control of her own destiny."

"I disagree. You know at least two men of that ilk. I happen to know full well that the Rockwood men treat their wives as partners, not subjects under their control. In fact, I've also seen Lord Lyndham defer to Constance in matters that affect them both. He asks her opinion."

"Three men out of thousands does little to fortify your argument," she said in a cool, detached fashion. "If anything, it supports mine because the Rockwoods have always been a law unto themselves."

The obstinate note in her voice told Mathias it was pointless to argue with her. Immediately on the heels of that thought, he remembered her remark about her stipend. The implication that another man was trying to control her made him stiffen with outrage.

"Who's Edgar?" At his sharply edged question, Ophelia's eyes widened in surprise before her shoulders rolled in a movement that barely passed for a shrug.

"George's son. He controls the bulk of the estate."

"Controls?" At his question, he saw her hesitate before she looked out the carriage window.

"George left the majority of my share of the estate in Edgar's control. But I have an allowance to do with as I wish."

Her expression almost concealed her emotions, but he saw anger in the set line of her mouth. Something about her reply made him frown. When Ophelia had protested the expense of Sabine's work, he'd realized her clothing budget was more than likely to be much smaller than most of Sabine's customers.

The well-worn appearance of her parlor had further emphasized her finances were not as deep as most of his friend's clients, which included members of the royal family. It was why he'd ask Sabine to charge Ophelia what a far less skilled dressmaker would then bill him for the remainder of the charges.

When he'd instructed Sabine not to mention their financial arrangement to Ophelia, his friend had been far from happy about his request. He'd argued with the dressmaker for several minutes until she was convinced he had no ulterior motives for keeping the truth from Ophelia. He'd simply assumed Ophelia's clothing allowance didn't allow her to be extravagant. Now he wasn't so sure she even had a clothing allowance.

"Exactly how much is your stipend, Ophelia?" This time his question caused her entire body to straighten into a rigid position as she eyed him haughtily.

"I believe it's considered quite rude to ask such an indelicate question."

"Rude or not, I expect an answer." The image of the worn furniture in her parlor and her father's gambling made him determined to have the truth from her. She appeared ready to defy him, and he leaned forward slightly in what he knew was an intimidating manner. His eyes narrowed when she didn't answer him.

"How? Much?"

"Two hundred pounds."

"Two…monthly, I presume," he murmured, knowing he was wrong. But Mathias could hardly believe even Havenstock, for all his boorish ways, would want anyone to think he'd not left his wife well-cared for. As he stared at Ophelia in stunned disbelief, she flinched before bowing her head.

"I receive two-hundred pounds annually."

"*Sweet Jesus*," he bit out quietly.

"I don't want your pity." Her words were sharp as she jerked her head up to glare at him. "I can manage quite well on what George provided me with."

"I don't pity you," he said quietly. "But I don't understand why you were desperate enough to offer yourself in exchange for a piece of property when your stepson could have settled your father's debt."

"I told you, I wanted my home back."

"That's not an answer. Why offer yourself in exchange for Marymont if all you needed to do was ask Havenstock's son for the necessary funds?"

"I refuse to ask Edgar for any money."

Although she didn't say it, Mathias was certain she was regretting the agreement she'd made with him this morning. As much as he wanted to know more about her situation, he also knew it was the wrong time to pursue the topic further. She clearly didn't want to discuss Havenstock's son, and pushing her for more information could easily make her break their agreement.

That was the last thing he wanted to happen. He was enjoying Ophelia's company far more than he realized. He liked the sound of her voice and how she often put him in this place without restraining her amusement.

The realization set off fire alarms in the back of his head, but he shoved them aside. There was no harm in befriending her. He'd become good friends with Louisa over the years. It would be no different with him and Ophelia. A voice in the back of his head snorted with laughter at the comparison of his friendship with Louisa Rockwood and the sensations Ophelia aroused in him. The mocking voice in the back of his head whispered words he refused to listen to. Instead, he attempted to end the discord between them.

"I have no wish to argue with you, so let us dispense with our disagreement of opinion."

"Agreed," she said in the same crisp tone he would expect of a schoolmarm. "If you would, please take me home. I've lost my appetite for dinner."

Regret lashed into him at the thought of ending their evening at cross purposes. The idea of parting with her on such a sour note made him grimace. He'd done little this evening to keep things light-hearted between them, which had been his intention from the moment she'd agreed to become his student in the art of seducing a man. But for a second time in the space of minutes, he knew better than to try persuading her otherwise. With an abrupt nod, he tapped the ceiling of the carriage and quietly gave orders to return to Ophelia's home.

In a few short minutes, the carriage had rolled to a stop, and Jacobs was opening the door for them. Mathias quickly exited the vehicle, then turned to offer his hand to Ophelia. Without saying a word, she allowed him to escort her up the steps to the front door of her townhouse. As she pulled her key from her drawstring purse and inserted it into the lock, Mathias reached out to cover her hand.

"I regret upsetting you with my questions about Havenstock, but I did so out of concern for your well-being."

"I am quite capable of managing my well-being *without* assistance from you or anyone else, Mr. Gilchrist." The formal way she addressed him was irritating, but he refrained from commenting.

"Nonetheless, I'm sorry for causing you any distress." At his quiet reply, she looked at him with a small smile as her expression softened.

"Thank you for your concern, Mathias, but I truly am capable of looking out for myself."

"A trait you've emphasized quite well over the last few minutes," he said with a smile. "I stand suitably chastised."

"Suitably?" she mocked him with a soft laugh. "I find it difficult to believe you've ever thought you've done something worthy of a reprimand."

"Being reprimanded by you, my sweet Ophelia, is as pleasurable as it is painful." Mathias caught her hand and raised it to his lips to kiss her hand. "Say you'll ride with me in the morning."

"I'm not—"

"Of course, I could leave you to deal with Merrick, as I'm relatively certain he'll call on you at the first moment possible."

"You're a beast for saying such a thing."

"But an honest one no less," he teased as he winked her and kissed her hand again. "I'll bring a horse for you when I come in the morning."

"What time?"

"Eight o'clock. We'll avoid the masses who are interested only in being seen."

"Thank you. I prefer avoiding the crowds."

"Until tomorrow," he murmured as he released her hand and returned to the carriage. He paused briefly at the door of the vehicle to look back. The door to the townhouse was already closing behind Ophelia, and he launched himself into the carriage. With a sharp command for Jacobs to take him home, Mathias reclined back in his seat, determined to ignore the disappointment he was experiencing now that she was no longer in his presence.

Ophelia heard the soft sound of the front doorbell in her room and turned back toward the mirror to study her appearance. She winced slightly as she remembered the bill that had accompanied her new clothes. While the charge had been much smaller than she'd expected, it would take several months to pay off the account.

A wave of anger rolled over her at the necessity to curtail expenditures for the next six months. George had to have known the size of her annual stipend would barely cover normal living expenses. It made her wonder if he'd thought to continue his abasement of her by forcing her to deal with Edgar's advances. Despite the stipulations of her late husband's will, she'd learned how to economize and gone without to ensure Lizzie was dressed well.

She'd managed to make the few evening gowns she owned look new by adding different lace or making other alterations, so it appeared she had new dresses. That they were sedate in nature they had allowed her to remain quiet and obscure in the background wherever she chaperoned Lizzie.

Now, as she studied herself in the standing mirror, she marveled at how different she looked in the new riding habit she'd bought from Madame Sabine. It was a rich, dark red that softened her features. The riding habit was a clear example of why the dressmaker's talent was worth every bit of coin she charged. It was impossible to deny the amount of feminine pleasure it gave her when she wore one of her new gowns.

A sudden surge of confidence sped through her as she studied her appearance. It was an emotion she'd not felt since she had married George. Unwilling to appear too eager or hesitant to greet Mathias, she made one last adjustment to the black hat that matched the braided trim on her habit. Satisfied with her appearance, she dragged in a deep breath and made her way downstairs.

As much as she tried to slow her pace, she found it difficult to do so. She tried to tell herself that her eagerness was simply because she'd not ridden for some time. But in the back of her head, a small voice chided her for the lie. The sound of Lizzie's laughter made her relax slightly.

It was unlikely her father was awake at this hour, but if he was, her sister would prove a sufficient buffer between the baron and Mathias. At the foot of the stairs, Mathias's voice echoed out into the foyer. The sound of it sent a frisson skimming across her skin. She faltered slightly at the physical sensation, and trepidation made her stomach lurch. If she wasn't careful, she might actually find her heart in danger.

With a barely audible sound of irony, she dismissed the thought. Such a thing wasn't possible. Feeling passion was beyond her grasp, which meant she was incapable of falling in love with Mathias. Somewhere in the back of her mind, a mocking laugh taunted her as she walked into the parlor.

Lizzie was sitting on the settee drinking her morning cup of tea, but Mathias was the person in the room she saw. He looked devastating this morning in his black riding coat, tan breeches, and shiny black boots. His attention was on Lizzie, but almost as if Mathias could hear the frantic beat of her heart, he turned his head toward her. The smile he directed at her only increased the rate of her agitated pulse.

Suddenly breathless, she fought to control her breathing as she moved forward. Mathias crossed the floor to meet her and lifted her hand to his lips. The fire flashing in his eyes made Ophelia's cheeks burn as she realized she enjoyed the way he looked at her. It was an unusual sensation. No man had ever made her feel so self-conscious in such a pleasant manner as Mathias did. Throughout her marriage, she'd tried hard to fade into the background to avoid being the butt of George's cruel remarks.

It was the difference between night and day when Mathias spoke her name or looked at her. Was it possible he was right? Could it be she merely lacked confidence when it came to experiencing genuine passion? It contradicted everything she'd just dismissed as impossible a moment ago. Unwilling to contemplate the possibility, she greeted Mathias with a smile.

"Good morning," she said softly. His mouth lingered over her hand as he studied her intently and with what she thought was appreciation.

"If possible, you look even more enchanting this morning than you did last night."

"Another lesson in how to accept a compliment?" she murmured, all too aware of her sister's avid interest. Her amusement was greeted with a look of surprise before Mathias shook his head and grinned.

"It was an honest observation, but since you've broached the subject, I believe a reply is required."

"Thank you." Her quiet reply sparked a gleam of mischief in his eyes as he bent his head toward her slightly.

"A circumspect response given our present company."

"Whatever are the two of you whispering about?" Lizzie huffed with exasperation, clearly irritated that she could not hear their conversation. Mathias turned toward her sister and grinned with boyish charm.

"I was saying how lovely Ophelia looked, and she was attempting to disagree."

"She does look beautiful, doesn't she?" Lizzie said with a genuine smile of delight. "Whatever inspiration Mrs. Smithers has acquired, I think it's splendid."

"Mrs. Smithers?" Mathias's puzzlement made Ophelia's heart skip a beat.

"Our dressmaker," she said as she lightly touched his arm. "A subject few men find fascinating. However, I believe horses are a different matter."

"I'll not argue the point," he said with a wicked smile of amusement. "And since you've mentioned the subject, why don't I show you the horse I've selected for you."

With a quick goodbye to Lizzie, Mathias ushered Ophelia out of the house and down the steps to where a young groom held the reins of two horses. One was a large, dark chestnut with an air of majestic power and strength. The animal tossed his head in a definite test of the groom's strength. Although the young man was of a slender build, he controlled the horse with only a small amount of difficulty. The other animal was dark black with white stockings and a star on its forehead. Mathias gestured toward the horse.

"This is Storm. She's gentle-natured but can keep pace with Titan here. Since you mentioned riding at Melton Park, I assumed you were skilled enough to manage her easily."

Ophelia smiled with pleasure as she stepped forward to stroke the mare's neck. The horse turned its head slightly and blew out a soft breath of greeting.

"She's lovely," she said as she glanced over her shoulder at Mathias. Obviously pleased by her compliment, he smiled with satisfaction.

"Rufus, help her ladyship to mount, please." The command startled her slightly as she'd half expected Mathias to assist her. As he leaned around her to take the reins of his horse, his breath warmed her cheek as he whispered in her ear. "I'm afraid if I helped you mount, it would be difficult to resist caressing a shapely leg or imagining another type of mount you should ride."

The words echoed with wicked amusement, and Ophelia sucked in a sharp breath of shocked surprise. The moment she jerked her head toward him, she wanted to press her body into his. The smile curving his sensual mouth was enough to make any woman's heart flutter. But it was the sinful invitation in his green eyes that made her heart pound wildly in her breast. Unsettled by her reaction to his flirtation, she quickly turned away and mounted Storm, using the groom's cupped hands as a makeshift step.

In seconds, she was seated in the mare's saddle, one leg nestled securely between the top and lower pommels while Rufus helped slide her foot into the stirrup. Excitement slid through her as they trotted toward Hyde Park. Carriage Drive was sparsely populated with early morning riders, and they increased their pace to a canter. Rotten Row was almost completely devoid of riders, and Mathias pulled Titan to a halt. Amusement glittered in his eyes as he arched an eyebrow at her.

"Shall we race?"

"Although you said Storm is capable of keeping up, I think a race might be somewhat of a challenge when it comes to winning."

"So you're not up to the possibility of losing." The wicked smile curving his mouth blatantly sought to provoke her.

"You enjoy taunting me entirely too much," she laughed and shook her head. "Very well, a race. To the end of the run?"

"Agreed. Shall I give you a head start?"

"*Absolutely not*," she exclaimed. "If I am to win, I shall do so on my own merit."

"Then I shall afford you the courtesy of starting the race."

"All right. *Go.*"

Applying a sudden pressure of her leg to Storm's side, she made the horse leap forward in a gallop. She was more than a length in front of Mathias in two seconds. She glanced over her shoulder and laughed at his surprise. His startled expression became one of determination as he urged Titan forward. Ophelia turned her attention back to the track in front of her. Behind her the sound of hoof beats pounding the ground grew stronger, but she didn't look over her shoulder.

Instead, she nudged the mare again in an effort to increase the animal's speed. The two horses were soon neck-and-neck and remained that way almost to the end of the riding track when Titan surged ahead to win the race by almost a half a length. As the two horses slowed to a halt, Mathias turned around and rode up alongside her.

"For someone who didn't want a head start, you managed to gain the upper hand in the beginning."

"I can hardly be faulted for your lack of readiness," she murmured with a smile. His startled look swiftly changed to one of amusement, and he laughed heartily. A wicked gleam in his green eyes, he leaned forward until his mouth was close to hers.

"*You* are a minx, Lady Havenstock. I wonder what punishment would be suitable for your irreverent behavior."

"If you're asking me to suggest something, I'm afraid you'll be disappointed. I'm learning that irreverence is a necessity where you're concerned." She laughed at the dumfounded look on his features.

Almost instantly, he recovered from his amazement and reached out to capture her hand in his. Slowly raising it to his mouth, he pressed his lips firmly against her riding gloves while his thumb slid between the soft kid leather and the sleeve of her habit. In a gentle movement, he stroked the underside of her wrist. The touch sent an electric shock up her arm that made her pulse skitter out of control. She drew in a sharp breath as an unfamiliar sensation swept through her.

Mathias' eyes met hers as his mouth lingered on her fingers. The caress burned its way through her glove, spreading heat across her skin. His eyes narrowed as he gradually released her hand. The thunder of her heartbeat echoed in her ears while the sensation of hundreds of butterflies frantically fluttering in her stomach made breathing ragged.

"I think your lessons are proceeding faster than I anticipated, Lady Havenstock. I think you've been lying to yourself that you're incapable of a flirtation."

There was a rough edge to Mathias's words as his gaze darkened with an emotion she found difficult to name. She barely had time to consider the thought before she suddenly grasped the fact she'd been flirting with Mathias. It was an unexpected revelation, and the air left her lungs for a brief moment as she stared at him in mute astonishment. Mathias dropped her hand abruptly and straightened in his saddle with a jerk.

"You are an excellent teacher," she murmured. He bobbed his head sharply at her words.

"Come, we should walk the horses to cool them off."

A dark expression clouded Mathias' features, and Ophelia wondered what she'd done to displease him. She deliberately ignored the thought that she wanted to please him at all. With a gentle tug of the reins, she turned Storm around to catch up with him as he'd already urged Titan forward at a slow pace.

"You're angry," she said with confusion. "Why?"

He didn't answer her for a long moment, his attention fixed on the dirt track stretching out in front of them. When he finally looked at her, a wry grin twisted his sensual mouth.

"I'm not angry."

"You look as though you are."

"Trust me, Ophelia. I'm not angry. Disappointed perhaps, but not angry."

"I've disappointed you?" she said in dismay.

"Hardly." The wry twist of his lips gave way to a smile that could almost be labeled as tender. "It's simply that I remembered a ten o'clock appointment I'd scheduled, which means we'll need to end our ride sooner than I'd like."

"Oh. I see."

The fact that their ride was to be cut short made her feel as though someone had just dashed her hopes of receiving a present. She immediately cast the sensation aside, reminding herself that their agreement was for Mathias to change her from an ugly duckling into a swan so she could experience passion. Something she still questioned she was capable of, but she'd agreed to let him at least attempt to do so. Nonetheless, disappointment spiraled through her despite all her efforts to dismiss it.

"At least I can see you're equally disappointed at the idea of cutting our ride short." The roguish smile on his lips made her laugh.

"You are a rogue to suggest such a thing, Mathias Gilchrist."

He grinned at her reply but didn't respond, and Ophelia found his silence slightly nerve-racking. Whatever the man was thinking, she knew it was most likely to be a new lesson. An unexpected shiver of anticipation sailed through her. It was dangerous to be on tenterhooks where Mathias was concerned, but at this point, she would allow herself the small pleasure. All too soon, they'd part ways forever, and despite her better judgment, she'd intended to enjoy his company for as long as possible.

Chapter 7

Male laughter echoed through the air, and unable to help himself, Mathias's attention swung to the head of the large dining table where he saw the Earl of Chelmsford leaning toward Ophelia. The man suddenly pulled away from her to tilt his head backward and release a shout of laughter.

A moment later, the man seated to her left leaned toward her and said something, which made Chelmsford laugh even harder at whatever Ophelia's reply was. Seated to his left, the Countess of Lyndham laughed softly. Mathias quickly turned his head toward Constance and scowled at her.

"You find something amusing, Constance?" The sharp note in his voice made his friend's smile widened.

"I do," she murmured. "I think you're unhappy that Chelmsford and Davenport are enjoying Ophelia's company so much."

"Actually, I'm quite pleased they're intrigued with her." His reply made Constance release an unladylike snort.

"You might be able to fool someone else with that cavalier reply, but you forget how long we've been friends."

"And Percy's right. The Rockwood women like to meddle in the personal affairs of others."

"I hope he said we do so with splendid success," Constance said with a sly smile.

"No, he did not. But that's irrelevant where I'm concerned. I feel responsible for Lady Havenstock.

Chelmsford has a reputation for breaking hearts, and I have no wish to see Ophelia hurt."

"I seriously doubt Chelmsford will break her heart," Constance said quietly as she glanced toward the head of the table. "I think if anyone's heart is in danger, it's the Earl."

"What the devil makes you say that?"

"Ophelia's marriage to Havenstock was a nightmare for her. It would surprise me if she were to ever marry again."

"Are you saying the man beat her?" he growled softly as he stiffened in his chair and focused his attention on Constance.

"Not that I know of, but the man delighted in publicly humiliating her. Then there was the manner in which…" Her voice trailed away, and a soft pink flush crested in her cheeks. "You would need to ask Percy or Lucien about the man's behavior while not in the company of women."

Mathias frowned and picked up his wineglass to study its contents. Last night, when Ophelia had said she'd never marry again, he'd not believed her. Now Constance was saying the same thing. But his friend wasn't in Ophelia's situation. An annual stipend of two hundred pounds was barely enough to keep food on the table.

It was one thing to reject the idea of marriage, another thing entirely if she wished to avoid becoming impoverished. Although Mathias had only known Ophelia for a short time, he'd already come to realize how strong she could be when confronted by adversity. But he was certain she would choose the less painful of two evils in order to survive. His gaze drifted back to the opposite end of the table, where he watched Ophelia take a drink of her wine.

Almost as if she sensed him looking at her, Ophelia turned her head in his direction. The moment their eyes met, she smiled, then looked away as the earl captured her attention again. Something visceral lashed at Mathias's insides as he watched Chelmsford wield his considerable charm. If the man broke her heart—Mathias's thoughts came to an abrupt halt. What in God's name was wrong with him? He'd promised to transform Ophelia, and he was doing precisely that.

"You look positively grim, Mr. Gilchrist," the older woman beside him said quietly.

Aware he had been less than courteous in not engaging the Duchess of Trowbridge in conversation until now, Mathias smiled at the woman. In her younger years, the woman must have been a great beauty as she still possessed a regal bearing, and there was a youthful sparkle in her pale blue eyes.

"Forgive my poor manners, your grace. I've been ignoring you."

"She's quite lovely."

"I beg your pardon, ma'am." Mathias feigned ignorance at the older woman's comment.

"Lady Havenstock."

"Yes," he murmured, all too aware of the duchess's eye on him. "Yes, she is."

"Chelmsford seems quite taken with her. You will have to guard your territory if that man has anything to do with it."

"Lady Havenstock and I are simply good friends."

"Are you indeed?" The duchess arched her eyebrows as her amused chuckle mocked his reply. "My dear young man. I've lived a long, happy life, which included a wonderfully joyous marriage. I'm well acquainted with the mannerisms of a man besotted with a woman."

Mathias stiffened at the duchess's amused dismissal of his explanation of his relationship with Ophelia. He looked down the length of the table again to study the attentive manner Chelmsford was showing toward Ophelia. Another chuckle echoed in his ear.

"As I said, Mr. Gilchrist. I know the signs of a man besotted." The duchess's obvious amusement made him grimace in disagreement.

"I've been besotted only once in my life, ma'am, and that was a mistake, just as becoming besotted with Lady Havenstock would also be a mistake." Mathias managed to keep his voice light-hearted and even as he looked back at the older woman. The duchess's light brown eyes darkened with sympathy, and she shook her head.

"Whoever she was, the woman who hurt you clearly didn't see the goodness in you." This time it was Mathias's turn to laugh at the woman's words, but with cynicism, not amusement.

"I can assure you, ma'am, I've proved my lack of gentlemanly conduct on more than one occasion."

He picked up his wine glass to study the claret as he remembered his treatment of Ophelia the night they'd first met. She'd thought he was Charles, and he'd allowed her to abase herself before he'd revealed his identity. His behavior had been reprehensible. That she'd agreed to his counteroffer had surprised him a great deal. She'd said she would never marry again, so why would she have accepted the proposal they'd agreed to? Frowning, he took a deep drink of the claret. A gentle touch on his arm made him shift his gaze toward the duchess again as he set his glass down.

"Somehow, I think the lady in question is more than capable of determining that your good qualities far outweigh your irredeemable ones."

"Since my relationship with Lady Havenstock is one of mutual admiration and nothing more, the point is moot."

Determined to end their conversation about Ophelia, Mathias returned to his meal, ignoring the duchess's softly muttered comment about the stubbornness of men. For the remainder of the dinner, he divided his attention between Constance and the duchess, ensuring the discussions revolved on safer topics. Mathias also controlled his urge to glance in Ophelia's direction. By the end of dinner, he was pleased with the results of his efforts. When the women retired to the salon and left the men to their cognac, Chelmsford made his way across the room to Mathias's side.

"Gilchrist." The earl nodded his head in a quiet greeting. "What do you think of my cognac?"

"It's excellent, my lord."

"Tell me, how long have you known, Lady Havenstock?" The question scraped across Mathias's insides like a jackal gnawing at his insides. Quickly crushing the response, he shrugged slightly.

"Not long."

"So there is not an understanding between the two of you?"

"No."

It took every ounce of willpower for Mathias not to snarl his reply. What the devil was wrong with him? He should be pleased the earl was asking the question. This was the precise goal he'd intended to achieve. The fact it was happening so quickly was what startled him.

"Then you would not be offended if I were to call upon the lady in question?" Although he'd expected the question, he was unprepared for his reaction to it. Suppressing his sudden desire to pound the man into the ground, Mathias shook his head.

"Not at all. Ophelia is free to indulge in whatever liaison she wishes," Mathias said with as much indifference as possible. The earl nodded, and he frowned slightly as he stared down into his brandy.

"Actually, I can see Lady Havenstock as something much more than a liaison. She's intelligent, gracious, and warm-hearted. My mother has been parading a host of potential brides in front of me for the past year. None of whom intrigue me quite the way Ophelia does."

Mathias's muscles tightened until they were taut as a coiled spring waiting to be released with each word the man spoke. The earl seemed completely unaware of Mathias's reaction as the other man eyed the cheroot he rolled in his fingers.

"I should perhaps warn you that Ophelia has indicated she has no intention of marrying again," Mathias said with a sense of triumph.

"So she said this evening when I remarked I was surprised she'd not remarried after Havenstock's death."

Chelmsford met Mathias's eyes and smiled. "She was quite adamant in her reply, but I believe the right man could convince her to risk her heart again."

"There, I will have to disagree." Mathias smiled with conviction. "Even though our acquaintance has been relatively short, I've already learned she can be incredibly stubborn."

"I enjoy a challenge and can be quite persuasive when I wish to be. Ophelia seems well worth the effort." The earl pulled out his pocket watch and flipped the gold lid upward. He snapped the watch shut and swallowed the last drop of his cognac. "I believe it's time we join the ladies. We will need to leave for Markham's affair within the half-hour."

Chelmsford offered Mathias a cheerful smile before proceeding to direct his male guests toward the salon. Mathias slowly set his brandy snifter on the table and turned toward the door leading out into the main hall as he watched his host walk away. Outside the salon doorway, he inhaled a deep breath as he struggled to understand his reaction to the earl's observations about Ophelia.

It wasn't as if they had an understanding. In fact, he was pleased the earl was already infatuated with her. Chelmsford's attention would give her confidence a much-needed boost. She was only willing to accept his reassurances to a certain extent. As several of the men emerged from the dining room, Mathias followed them into the salon. It took him only a second to find Ophelia, and as he took a step in her direction, Chelmsford entered the salon was at her side in several quick strides.

Once again, his body tensed with an emotion he didn't want to feel, and he had the urge to simply leave the house, knowing Chelmsford would be more than happy to take over Mathias's duties as her companion for the evening. Ophelia laughed at something the earl said, and when the Duchess of Trowbridge suddenly diverted Chelmsford's attention, Ophelia's gaze swept across the room to meet Mathias's. The moment she smiled at him, it was as if someone had punched him in the stomach.

The sensation was one he was fast becoming familiar with where she was concerned. He bowed slightly in response to her smile, which he saw falter slightly before she turned to the duchess and the earl who drew her into their conversation. Mathias turned away from the scene to begin a conversation with Viscountess Warfield. The topics were inane and forgettable, and when Chelmsford suggested they leave for Markham's soiree, Mathias breathed a sigh of relief at having to forego another minute in the viscountess's company.

In a few short moments, he'd assisted Ophelia into his carriage and flung himself into the squabs of his seat. The silence inside the vehicle stretched between them as if a fissure in the ground had opened up. His entire body ached with the tension holding his muscles taut.

"You look decidedly grim, Mathias." The sound of his name rolling off her lips made his mouth go dry. He jerked at the observation before he rolled his shoulders in a nonchalant shrug.

"Do I?"

"Yes, I've not seen you smile once this evening." Puzzlement furrowed her brow as she eyed him intently.

"I wasn't aware smiling was a requirement for escorting you into the wolf's den." He heard the harsh note in his voice, and she leaned forward in a quick movement to touch his hand. The moment her fingers brushed against his, electricity zigzagged its way through his blood.

"Whatever is the matter with you this evening, and why are you suggesting you led me into the wolf's den? If you're referring to the earl, I'd hardly call the man a wolf."

"Don't tell me you're that naïve, Ophelia."

"For heaven's sake, I'm not in danger of losing my heart to the man."

"I believe the man is on the verge of losing his to you." At his sharp response, she quickly jerked away from him as if he'd bitten her. The sudden image of nibbling her neck filled his head as he studied her from the shadows of his seat. The image was followed by another and then another, each more explicit than the last.

"What on earth are you talking about?" she exclaimed with exasperation.

"The man asked if we had an understanding, and when I said no, he mentioned his mother is encouraging him to marry, and you're the first woman he's met that he's been willing to consider for the role of the next Countess of Chelmsford."

"Don't be absurd." Ophelia shook her head vigorously, clearly appalled. "The earl was pleasant company at dinner, but the man did nothing that suggested he was so infatuated as to propose marriage. And we *both* know how I would respond to such a proposal."

"Chelmsford's annual worth is nothing to dismiss so easily, Ophelia."

"Money can never be a substitute for my freedom to do as I please."

"You sound remarkably sure of that position."

"Question my resolve all you wish, but I will not change my position in the matter. And compared to the earl, you are acting exceedingly unpleasant," she snapped with irritation. "I was thoroughly enjoying myself this evening until you decided to be a curmudgeon."

Mathias frowned as he contemplated her words. He *was* acting exceedingly unpleasant, and he didn't have the slightest inkling as to why he was being such an ass. A cackling erupted deep in the recesses of his brain, but Mathias quickly crushed the sound and the notion that accompanied it. Instead of arguing with her more, he chose to remain silent.

The remainder of the ride to the Markham affair was filled with a tension Mathias knew he'd instigated but didn't know how to resolve. Another laugh echoed in the back of his head, but he stifled the sound as quickly as he had the first time. When the carriage rolled to a halt, he exited the vehicle, then offered his hand to Ophelia.

She accepted his assistance, but once she was out of the carriage, she quickly pulled her hand from his and left his side without a backward glance. With a quiet noise of anger, he followed her into the brightly lit Markham House. By the time he'd handed off his hat to the footman at the entrance, Ophelia had already been joined by Merrick and Viscount Margate, as well as another gentleman he recognized as Thomas Wilford. The sight of her surrounded by men who were clearly infatuated with her only irritated him all the more.

Margate offered Ophelia his arm as he said something that made Merrick glower at the nobleman. Ophelia hesitated slightly and glanced over her shoulder at Mathias. As she did so, a bewildered hesitancy crossed her features. It vanished quickly as she returned her attention to Margate and nodded at something the man said. A second later, she entwined her arm with the viscount's and allowed him to lead her into the ballroom. Merrick scowled after them before following along like a puppy unwilling to be left behind.

As Mathias watched the trio enter the ballroom, he experienced the need to be in the boxing ring at his club. Following at a discreet distance, he entered the ballroom to see Ophelia surrounded by a growing crowd of suitors. Instead of joining them to lay claim to her company, Mathias moved to stand next to one of the four columns situated at each corner of the room. One shoulder pressed into the marble pillar, he watched as Chelmsford joined the group circling Ophelia.

The tableau made him bite down on the inside of his cheek as he remembered another woman surrounded by a group of eager suitors. The past quickly rolled over him, and his body tightened at the painful humiliation Miriam had inflicted on him.

With hair the pale gold color of hay just before it was cut and blue eyes that could incite a man's lust just by staring into them, Miriam had been beautiful. She still held the reputation as one of the professional beauties the painter Frank Miles had captured on canvas beginning with Lillie Langtry. Miriam had had a bevy of suitors vying for her attention and had turned down several marriage proposals. He should have known better when she'd allowed him to call on her.

Despite his best intentions not to, he'd become enamored with her just as other men who sought her attention had. That she'd rejected proposals from titled men, as well as merchants, had made Mathias believe she was holding out for love. It was why he had dared to think he might be able to win her heart.

Over several months, they'd become the couple every hostess in the Marlborough Set sought to add to their guest lists. Mathias had been on the verge of proposing when he'd learned the real reason Miriam had appeared to have chosen him above all others.

As if it were yesterday, the memory of Miriam lying naked in his brother's bed filled him with the same fury he'd experience that night. His rage had been so fierce he'd almost dragged the woman out of Thornbury House to leave her on the street in the state of déshabille he'd found her.

Miriam had been after a title all along, and not just an ordinary title. She'd been determined to marry a title with great wealth. Charles was the prize she'd set her sight on, and she had exploited Mathias to achieve her goal. Just as it had that night, a wave of brutal anger lashed at every part of him as he remembered the evening's events.

He'd left Charles and his friends at the club, knowing his brother would no doubt spend the night there as he was already foxed. When he'd arrived home, Baxter had met him at the front door and notified him a young woman was waiting for Charles in the drawing-room.

Normally the butler would never have admitted the woman into the house, but it had been raining, and Baxter had believed no harm would be done to let her wait in the salon. When their unexpected guest was nowhere to be found, it had taken only seconds for Mathias to conclude the woman was intent on trapping Charles into marriage.

With the butler in tow, Mathias had entered his brother's room, expecting to oust an impoverished ingénue attempting to move up the social ladder. Instead, he'd been privy to the decadent sight of Miriam lying in wait for his brother. The woman had even arranged for her father to arrive after a pre-determined time, demanding to know where his daughter was. It had been a pointless exercise on the man's part as Mathias had already tossed Miriam out of Thornbury House.

Miriam's plan might well have worked if Charles had been the one who'd come home instead of Mathias. While his brother was rarely drunk, that night had been one of those rare occasions. Another situation Miriam had staged by enlisting several suitors to encourage Charles to imbibe a great deal of wine, then send him home quite inebriated.

He had no idea what story the woman had used to accomplish her goal, but if not for several of Charles's friends who'd arrived at the club, his brother might have actually fallen into Miriam's well-laid trap. That night had been a turning point for Mathias. He'd already been looking after his brother's business affairs for some time, but Miriam's treachery had made him vigilant in protecting his brother from any scandal as well. The sudden pressure of a strong male hand grasping his shoulder made him jerk in surprise as the images of the past receded.

"Good God, man, you look as though you wanted to rip something…or someone apart." Percy Rockwood chuckled as Mathias met his friend's gaze. "If I didn't know better, I'd say you were ready to have a go at Chelmsford in the ring."

"As usual, you exaggerate, Rockwood."

"Indeed," Percy murmured with raised eyebrows at the formal manner in which Mathias addressed him. The mockery in his friend's smile made Mathias grunt with disgust, but his churlish mood didn't abate.

He turned away from Percy and saw Chelmsford reach for Ophelia's dance card. The man scribbled something on the small square of paper, then returned it to Ophelia. She glanced at the card, then jerked her head up to stare at the man in surprise. The earl smiled and offered his hand as the small orchestra began playing a waltz. As Chelmsford pulled Ophelia into his arms and swung her out onto the floor, Mathias mumbled an oath.

The expletive flying past his lips earned him a look of outrage from an older woman who was passing by. Percy cleared his throat in a wordless rebuke, and Mathias muttered a sharp apology. Barely glancing at his friend, who was studying him with a look of puzzlement, Mathias focused his attention on Chelmsford dancing with Ophelia. The earl's attentive manner illustrated the man's determination to do as he'd suggested after dinner. The thought only deepened Mathias's morose state.

"No matter how much you glower at Chelmsford, it's unlikely the man will drop dead on the spot." At Percy's amused comment, Mathias turned and glared at the man.

"Where is your lovely wife?" he asked in a concerted effort to change the subject.

"She's with Constance." The Earl of Lyndham answered the question before Percy could as the other man joined them. Ruefully, Lucien glanced over his shoulder, then smiled. "The two of them were waylaid by Baroness Kimbolton. I imagine we'll have to rescue them shortly. Otherwise, there will be hell to pay later. Constance sent a warning glance in my direction when I left her and Rhea with the woman."

"Just a warning glance?"

Mathias laughed as his mood lightened. He'd liked Lyndham from the first moment Constance had introduced them. That the man adored his wife was evident every time he looked at her. There was a wicked glint of humor in the earl's eyes as he chuckled.

"Yes, and it was decidedly unpleasant."

"I'm sure my plight is certain to be the same as yours." With a wide grin, Percy nodded. "The Rockwood women know how to extract their pound in the flesh."

"True. But our journey to hell where we pay our retribution eventually transports us to a heaven that is always resplendent."

Lucien's expression of amusement changed to one of great love as he looked back to where Constance stood, nodding her head as an older woman chattered with animation in front of her. Clearly sensing her husband was watching her, Constance turned her head to look at him. Her gaze narrowed in obvious annoyance before she smiled at him in a manner that said her husband was definitely not in good standing with his wife.

"Oh, you're definitely going to pay tonight, Lucien." With a laugh, Mathias grinned at the earl. The man shrugged slightly and smiled as he looked back at his wife once more.

"I'll gladly pay whatever penalty I must where Constance is concerned."

A twinge of envy twisted its way through Mathias as he heard the note of deep love in the earl's voice. Almost without thought, he turned his head to search the room for Ophelia. It didn't take long to find her, as Chelmsford seemed to have attached himself to her side. In a split second, Mathias's mood darkened once more.

"You seem preoccupied, Mathias. Are you having problems with the female sex tonight as well?" Curiosity and a small touch of amusement filtered its way through Lucien's voice.

"Not at all." Mathias turned his head toward the earl who was studying him with interest.

"Lady Havenstock has bloomed of late, don't you think, Lucien?" Percy glanced at his brother-in-law before he nodded toward Ophelia surrounded by Chelmsford and several other men. "Now that Havenstock isn't around to deride her, she's coming into her own."

"I mentioned the same thing to Constance after dinner this evening. She believes you're responsible for the woman's newfound confidence, Mathias." Lucien's comment made Mathias shrug his shoulders.

"Constance exaggerates the influence I have over Lady Havenstock."

"Indeed." Lucien's response mimicked Percy's earlier observation, and Mathias's stiffened at the implications behind the word. Before he could respond, the Rockwood women reached their small circle.

"You, my lord, are a brute." Constance scowled at her husband. "You know how tedious Lady Kimbolton can be."

"My darling wife, we both know the poor woman doesn't have many friends, and she's told me on numerous occasions how much she enjoys your company."

At the gentle scolding, Constance's appeared completely chastened as she glanced over her shoulder to where the lady in question had seated herself in one of the chairs lining the wall of the ballroom. Inspiration suddenly lit up Constance's face, and the moment her husband saw his wife's expression, he immediately shook his head.

"Absolutely not, Lady Lyndham. Between you and Patience, there's been more than enough match-making in recent months."

"Nonsense. Can you deny how successful the Rockwood women have been in their *meddling*, as you and Percy call it?"

"I, for one, am delighted they meddled," Rhea said as she slipped her arm through her husband's smiling up at him.

"As am I, my sweet," Percy said softly as her returned his wife's smile.

Mathias's gaze swept across the faces of both couples before he turned away to study the dancers moving about on the floor. Although he was glad his friends had found great happiness, he knew he wasn't destined to enjoy the same outcome in his life. Miriam had ensured that.

"I believe you promised to dance with me all night, Lord Lyndham," Constance teased her husband before she reached out to touch Mathias's arm. "Of course, if you prefer to stand this one out, I'm sure I could call on Mathias to—"

Constance's light touch became a painful grip as her fingers dug into Mathias's arm. Startled, he jerked his head in her direction to see her hazel eyes had become glazed and transfixed. It was an expression Mathias remembered vividly from childhood. Lucien had already stepped forward to support his wife and pressed her into his side as a steadying influence. His childhood friend was in the throes of what the Rockwoods called the *an dara sealladh*. The incident lasted little more than a minute before the spell-bound look disappeared from Constance's features. Compassion filled her gaze as her grip on his arm slowly relaxed.

"Let go of the past, Mathias." Her tone gentle, his friend shook her head slightly. "If you don't, you could easily miss the opportunity for great happiness."

Mathias went rigid at Constance's words. Muscles taut with tension, he experienced a sinking feeling in the pit of his stomach. Whatever she'd seen, it had been enough to make her see some, if not all, of the secrets he'd never shared with anyone. The silence filling the space between him and his friend only hardened his muscles more until every inch of him ached from the strain of it. When he didn't reply, Constance lightly touched his arm, then turned to her husband.

"Lucien, instead of dancing, could we take in some fresh air?"

At her quiet request, the earl raised her hand to his lips, then pulled her arm through his and led her away without a word. Mathias glanced at Percy, who was eying him with concern. He appeared about to say something when Mathias saw Rhea reach for her husband's hand.

"Percy, dance with me. If you don't, I shall be forced to ask Mathias to risk injuring his feet. You know how often I step on your toes." Despite Rhea's request, his friend hesitated, and Mathias forced a smile to his lips.

"As much as I like your wife, Percy, I confess I'd prefer not to limp around the ballroom for the remainder of the evening." Mathias's reply made Percy chuckle as he nodded.

"Then we shall catch up with you a little later this evening."

"Certainly," Mathias said.

As Percy led his wife away, Mathias clasped his hands behind his back and turned to watch the couple as they reached the floor. His gaze lingered on them for a moment before he looked around the room, instinctively searching for Ophelia's tall, voluptuous figure. When he didn't see her, Mathias frowned. Across the room he saw Chelmsford looking around the ballroom with a frown of disgruntlement. The sight sent a small surge of satisfaction through Mathias.

Clearly, the earl was discovering Ophelia was not quite so easy a conquest as the man had expected if he didn't know where she was. Mathias continued to look around the room, but when he failed to see Ophelia's lushly curved figure, his frustration became concern. Where the devil was she? No sooner had he asked himself the question, he saw Ophelia hurry back into the ballroom through the open doorway that led out to the gardens. A tall, gaunt man was close on her heels. The man caught Ophelia's arm as she tried to walk away.

Even from afar, Mathias could see the tension holding Ophelia rigid as she refused to look at the man. Spurred into action, Mathias made his way quickly around the edge of the ballroom, ignoring the greetings thrown his way. He was only a few feet away from Ophelia when he heard the man laugh. It wasn't a pleasant sound.

"You have little choice, Ophelia. We both know you cannot live off of such a pittance of an annual stipend."

"I would rather go to the workhouse than be beholden to you." Anger filled her voice, but there was a touch of fear layered beneath her words.

The man was clearly threatening her, and a raw fury swept through Mathias at the realization. As if suddenly aware of his presence, Ophelia turned her head in his direction. Although her features didn't reflect any relief, he caught the flash of it in her large brown eyes. He closed the last few feet between them.

"Lady Havenstock. I believe you promised this dance to me."

Mathias ignored the man at her side as he offered his hand to her. Without a moment's hesitation, she placed her hand in his. The fact she was trembling, and her hand was like ice in his, startled Mathias. He directed a cool, polite nod to the man standing close to Ophelia before he led her out onto the dance floor.

She didn't speak, and her tremors continued to vibrate from her body into his. Something told him talking was the last thing she wanted to do at the moment, and he remained silent as he whirled her around the dance floor. They were more than halfway through the waltz before her trembling ebbed away. When she looked at him, there was a haunted look about her that aroused a need to protect her.

"Do you want to tell me who that man was?" he asked quietly. She stared at something over his shoulder, her expression guarded.

"George's son, Edgar." Her answer didn't surprise him, but the growing strength of the protective instinct it aroused inside him did.

"What did he want?" His question made her jerk her head up to meet his gaze before she quickly looked away.

"He was being unpleasant as always."

"Why do I think it was more than that?" He studied her closely, but she continued to avoid his gaze.

"I don't know. Why would you?"

"Because I think the man was threatening you." At his quiet observation, Ophelia's mouth thinned with anger.

"Must we continue this discussion? The man is repulsive, and I find it disgusting even thinking about him."

Ophelia glared up at him, her brown eyes dark with an emotion that troubled him. It was easy to conclude her confrontation with the new Viscount Havenstock had upset her, despite her frail composure. Edgar was apparently cut from the same cloth as his father. It was the only explanation that could account for Ophelia's obvious distress. They danced in silence until the final chords of the waltz died away. His hand under her elbow, Mathias guided her off the floor.

"Would you care to——" He didn't have the chance to finish his sentence as Chelmsford appeared in front of them.

"I believe this next dance is mine, my lady." The earl offered Ophelia his arm, and when she hesitated, he smiled. "I promise not to bore you with my predilection for gardening."

Ophelia released a small laugh as she met Chelmsford's gaze. His smile broadened as she nodded and slipped her arm through his.

"I don't mind you discussing your passion, my lord."

"I am finding that there are other things that I could be passionate about as well."

Chelmsford's earnest look sent a razor-edged blade slicing through Mathias. Damnation, the man had been deadly serious about setting his cap for Ophelia. His gaze jumped from Chelmsford to Ophelia, who smiled at the earl with a bemused expression.

Something deep inside Mathias clawed at him with vicious glee. Ophelia had expressed her distaste for marriage, yet at this moment, she appeared completely enthralled by Chelmsford. The anger that had assaulted him earlier returned anew.

"If you will excuse me, my lady," he bit out coldly as he bowed to her and then the earl. "Chelmsford."

As Mathias turned away, he thought he saw Ophelia's hand reach out to him, but he didn't bother to look in her direction. Instead, he simply walked away.

Chapter 8

Should I be jealous?" The earl's voice echoed with quiet curiosity, startling Ophelia. She turned away from Mathias's departing figure to meet Chelmsford's studious gaze.

"Jealous, my lord?"

"Gilchrist led me to believe there was nothing between the two of you."

"There isn't," she replied as her heart twisted slightly in her breast. She ignored the sharp pain and smiled at the earl. "Mathias is a friend. Nothing more."

"A friend who seems quite unhappy that I claimed another dance." Chelmsford pulled her into his arms and guided her out onto the dance floor.

"Mathias's attitude has little to do with whom I dance. We've argued twice this evening, and as a result, he's become quite ill-tempered."

"His behavior appears to be that of a frustrated suitor more than a man who's argued with a friend."

Chelmsford's eyebrows arched upward as he met Ophelia's gaze. The statement aroused a sudden wish for the earl to be right. The unexpected thought made her heart skip a beat, and she quickly dismissed it. Her relationship with Mathias was no more than that of a student to a tutor. He'd said he would teach her how to seduce a man. While Ophelia was still dubious as to her ability to feel passion, whenever she was with Mathias, she experienced emotions she'd never felt before. She shook her head and smiled despite the despondency suddenly spiraling through her.

"Mathias has a tendency to badger me until I share my thoughts."

"And did he?"

"Persuade me to share my thoughts?" She smiled slightly. "No. I can be rather stubborn. It's a trait Mathias finds annoying."

"And these thoughts you refused to share with him. Dare I hope they were about me?" There was a teasing note in the earl's voice, but the assessment in his gray eyes made her stare at him in surprise. He laughed softly. "I see I've caught you unprepared to answer."

"Not so much unprepared as startled, my lord."

"My name is Gideon, and I would like for you to address me as such, Ophelia."

"I'm not sure that's appropriate given our brief acquaintance, my lord."

"I rarely do anything appropriate, Ophelia." A wicked look of mischief glittered in his gray eyes, and she couldn't help but laugh at his reply.

"Clearly, I shall have to guard my words with you, my—" The earl scowled at her, and she quickly adjusted her reply. "Gideon."

"Now that has a decidedly pleasant ring to it."

"What does?"

"The way you say, Gideon. I would enjoy hearing that on a consistent basis," he murmured as he whirled her around in two quick circles to dodge a collision with another couple. The earl's choice of words made her gulp in a quick breath.

"As I said, we barely know one another, my—Gideon," she said and saw the earl's disappointment.

"A fact I intend to change. And I am confident of the outcome as well."

The man's certainty in Gideon's voice made Ophelia's heart sink. Perhaps Mathias had been right after all. The earl seemed far more interested in her than she'd realized.

Bemused by the realization, Ophelia looked over the earl's shoulder to see Mathias speaking with Percy and Rhea. He glanced in her direction, and their eyes met for a brief instant. In the blink of an eye, Mathias's expression hardened, and he turned his attention away from her. The manner in which he'd dismissed her made her experience a jolt of emotion she didn't know how to define.

"Come riding with me in the park tomorrow." The invitation made her shake her head.

"That's not possible," she said as she remembered riding Mathias's horse.

"You'll have to do better than that, Ophelia." Eyebrows arched in an arrogant but playful manner, he smiled. "Shall we say nine o'clock?"

"I'm not sure who likes to have their way more, you or Mathias." With a rueful shake of her head, Ophelia smiled. "As I said, it's not possible."

"If you insist on saying no, I'll need a much better reason than the one you've given me."

Once more, a hot flush warmed her cheeks. It was one thing for Mathias to loan her the use of a horse, but with the earl, it would be different. She didn't quite understand why. Perhaps it was pride preventing her from telling the earl she didn't own a horse.

If that were the case, why hadn't it bothered her when Mathias had loaned her Storm? As the music ended with a flourish of notes, the earl slowly released from his arms before cupping her elbow and guiding her out onto the dimly lit patio.

It was the second time she'd been here this evening, but at least she didn't find the earl's company unpleasant. In fact, she liked him. He had a pleasant sense of humor and was quite intelligent. As he guided her toward the balustrade, the earl pulled to a stop and met her gaze with a determined glint in his eye.

"I'll call for you at nine o'clock." The unyielding note in Chelmsford's voice made Ophelia slowly shake her head.

"I am sorry, my—Gideon, but I'm unable to join you as I have a previous commitment."

"Indeed." His eyes narrowed as he studied her intently. "And would this commitment involve Gilchrist?"

Startled by the irritation in his voice, Ophelia stared at him in surprise. The earl's expression was immediately rueful. With a shrug, the earl suddenly eyed her as if surprised by a sudden revelation.

"I suppose I haven't made my intentions clear, Ophelia. I'm a man who usually takes a great deal of time making decisions. I consider all my options." Gideon bent his head toward her in an obvious effort to keep his words between the two of them. "And although we've only spent a short time in each other's company, I believe we would do quite well together."

"Together?" She inhaled a sharp breath as she realized exactly what the man was saying. A small smile tilted the corners of his mouth as he nodded.

"You seem surprised."

"I'm not sure what to say," she murmured. "I've never…a liaison isn't—"

"Actually, I was thinking of something more permanent." At his amused expression, Ophelia took a quick step backward and shook her head.

"We hardly know each other," she choked out as she struggled with comprehending the strong possibility the earl was proposing marriage. "And surely you need an heir, I am…I do not believe I…"

"While I would welcome a son, my nephew is more than suitable to inherit my title. Until you, I'd not met a woman I was willing to look at across the breakfast table every morning for the rest of my life." His lips twisted in wry amusement as he met her gaze. "But the thought of hearing your voice every morning is a pleasant one, and I believe affection would grow between us over time."

"I am…I am flattered," she whispered as she tried to find the words to reject him without injuring his pride.

Despite liking him, she could never agree to marry the earl. "I'm sorry, but I could never marry again."

"I see." Arms folded against his chest, he eyed her with obvious amusement. "And is the thought of marrying me such an abhorrent one?"

"No, it's not…" When she hesitated, the earl's amusement dissolved into a look of inquisitive puzzlement as she shook her head in an attempt to soften her rejection. "Please, you must understand. I'm truly flattered, but the thought of marrying *any* man…I could never…it's impossible."

At the vehemence in her voice, Gideon studied her gravely for a long moment, then turned to stare out over the moonlit garden. He remained silent for a moment before he cleared his throat.

"Was Havenstock as much of a brute as I suspect he was?" he asked quietly as he continued to keep his eyes focused on shadows and the moonlight.

"I don't…" Her words faded away into silence as she noticed how hard the earl's profile had become. Her heart skipped a beat as a sense of doom spiraled through her.

"It was no secret the man had a propensity for indulging in the darker intimacies between a man and woman. I can only imagine the pain he must have caused you."

"Oh dear God," she gasped in horror. The earl quickly turned to her and grimaced with genuine remorse. Gently taking her hands in his, he shook his head with regret.

"Forgive me, Ophelia. I should never have questioned you in such a manner. I never heard the man mention your name, only the pleasure he derived from certain activities. Acts that no decent man would ever do with *any* woman. Your obvious determination not to marry again and my knowledge of the man's depravity is why I believe the man had to have been a brutish husband."

A cloud of anger swept across Gideon's face before his gray eyes met hers with a gentle understanding. Ophelia struggled to control her humiliation and find her voice to form a coherent reply. The earl shook his head with a look of frustration.

"I'm simply trying to say, and in clearly an awkward fashion, that I can understand why you might not wish to marry again. But I swear to you that I would never treat you with anything but kindness and respect."

Still stunned by Gideon's observations, Ophelia closed her eyes as she imagined all the gossip George's behavior had created, or perhaps even how he'd bedded her. The idea of being pitied by others was far more distressing than being a laughingstock. With a jerk, she pulled her hands free of the earl's.

"Please...I would like to go back in now." Ophelia heard the tremor in her voice, and Gideon grimaced with regret.

"Of course," the earl said with a small sound of self-disgust. Offering her his arm, he gently tucked it inside his. "Will you forgive me, my dear? I've clearly caused you pain, which was never my intent."

At the sincere note of remorse in his voice, Ophelia forced a small smile to her lips. She swallowed the knot in her throat as she met his gaze. The regret she saw in his eyes was profound, and the deep embarrassment inside Ophelia eased somewhat. With a brief squeeze of his arm, she nodded.

"You are forgiven. You simply confirmed what I have suspected all these years. I've simply never allowed myself to admit it before." Her quiet words caused relief to settle on his handsome features.

"Then there's hope for me yet." The gentle note in his voice was accompanied by a reassuring smile. "Which leads me back to my invitation that you ride with me in the morning."

Gideon's manner was oddly comforting, and she laughed softly. His sympathetic demeanor and genuine remorse eased some of her embarrassment. In a small way, she was grateful the earl had revealed his knowledge of George's depravity. A second later, she realized that if

Gideon knew of George's depravity, then others in the Marlborough Set no doubt knew as well.

The thought she might be an object of pity was far worse than any humiliation George's behavior had inflicted on her. Her mortification would only be amplified if Gideon were to learn of Edgar's attempts to coerce her into a liaison in exchange for what was rightfully hers. It made her even more unwilling to reveal that her limited funds didn't allow her to stable a horse. She shook her head.

"I am sorry, but—"

"But you've already made a commitment to Gilchrist." Gideon frowned with irritation, and she didn't correct his assumption. "I'm beginning to think I might have a rival for your attention, my dear."

"I'm certain you do not. I think Mathias would find marital bliss as confining as I do."

"Very well, I'll not press you on the matter any further, but I give you fair warning that I shall do my best to convince you that we would be good for one another."

"And I shall remind you it is unlikely I'll change my mind."

"*Ah ha*, you've now given me hope. You didn't say you wouldn't. You said unlikely, which means my chances of persuading you otherwise are not beyond the realm of possibility." The cheerful grin on his features made her laugh. Perhaps he was right. Maybe they would be good for each other. She immediately rejected the idea. Marriage was out of the question for her.

"You're quite incorrigible."

"Indeed," the earl said with satisfaction as he guided her back into the ballroom.

Ophelia glanced at Mathias's stoic expression as she accepted his hand and climbed into the carriage. He quickly followed her, closing the door behind him before tapping the roof of the vehicle signaling the driver to move on. The dimly lit interior of the small carriage made it difficult to see Mathias, but his icy demeanor was almost tangible. Irritated by his behavior throughout the evening, she leaned forward so she could see his him clearly. His sharp, angular profile was impassive, but a fiery emotion flared in his green eyes before his gaze became as unreadable as his features.

"Was tonight a test of some sort, Mathias?" Her soft question made Mathias jerk slightly as he narrowed his eyes at her.

"A test?"

"Yes." Ophelia tipped her head slightly in his direction. "Was I supposed to have spent the majority of the evening with you? Keep Chelmsford and others at a distance to encourage their efforts in seeking my attention?"

"No."

It was a curt answer that said he would not expand on his answer. Frustration made Ophelia frown in annoyance. She wasn't sure if the man was being deliberately aggravating or if something else was bothering him. With a sigh, Ophelia leaned back into her seat. The silence in the carriage was becoming more oppressive by the second, and she realized she didn't enjoy arguing with him. Even though he could infuriate her at times, Ophelia enjoyed his company. Leaning forward once more, she brushed her fingers over the masculine hand resting on his knee. He immediately jerked at the light touch but didn't pull away.

"Please, Mathias. I don't want to argue with you. You're angry with me, and I would like to know why."

"I am not angry." Despite the quiet, emotionless reply, something in his eyes flared as his gaze met hers. What the devil was wrong with the man?

"I find that difficult to believe. You've been ill-humored ever since we sat down to dinner. In fact, you glared at me throughout the meal."

"I didn't glare, Ophelia. I simply watched you charm Chelmsford over dinner."

"Isn't that what you wanted me to do?" she exclaimed with exasperation. "Did you, or did you not, convince me to be tutored by you in the art of seducing a man?"

"Yes, and you are an excellent student."

The soft, even reply held a note of hard steel. It was as if Mathias were holding something back. Something he didn't want her to see—to know. Frustrated by his cold, unresponsive manner, she eyed him with growing irritation. While his gaze remained unreadable, his mouth thinned slightly, and the strong hand beneath hers hardened with tension.

Blast the man. He'd commended her on being an excellent student, and yet she still felt as though she'd failed to meet his expectations in some way. Ophelia ignored the voice nagging her to answer why Mathias's approval was so important to her. Determined to end the discord between them, one idea after another fluttered through her head as she tried to think of a way to achieve her goal.

Each one was summarily discarded until the word honey popped into her head. Ophelia was certain he hadn't meant the lesson to be used on him except as an exercise, but if she'd done something to anger him, she wanted to know so that she could make amends. A shiver streaked down her spine as she closed the distance between them even more. If she hadn't been so close to him, she might have missed the almost indiscernible sound of him sucking in a quick breath.

"I don't know why you're upset with me, but I'm sorry for whatever my transgression is," she whispered as she drank in the warm male scent of him.

The scent of pine and leather filled her senses, and she lightly touched his cheek with her hand. Beneath her fingertips, his facial muscles twitched slightly. When he didn't respond, she sighed and brushed her mouth across his cheek. There was the faint hint of stubble scraping across her lips. The tingling sensation created an image of him lying in bed, unshaven, and with his hair tousled. Her breath caught in her throat at the pictures flooding through her head.

"I like the way you smell, Mathias," she murmured. "It's fresh and clean. Like a forest."

She allowed her lips to nibble at his ear as she cupped his cheek with her hand. A soft noise rumbled low in his throat, and she relished the sound. Ophelia's mouth slid downward to trace the line of Mathias's jaw in a feather-light caress. The moment her lips touched the corner of his mouth, she sensed a sudden change in him. She couldn't tell what had changed, she could only sense the taut tension between had strengthened to an incendiary emotion. It had a combustible quality, and the moment it flared to life, she knew it could consume her.

Ophelia's heartbeat skidded out of control as she realized how much she wanted to experience that fire. Experience the scorching passion she knew he could easily ignite in her. In a tentative, light caress, she brushed her lips over his. Although he didn't move, the heat of his mouth sent a fiery pulse sliding through her as if she'd been shocked. With increasing persistence, she pressed her lips against his before her tongue slid along the seam of his mouth.

Whiskey teased the tip of her tongue as a drop of coffee might. The tantalizing taste made her heart jump in her breast as she gently sought to part his mouth beneath hers. Another sound rumbled out of him, and a small wave of triumph swept through her at his reaction. In the next instant, his lips parted, and her tongue slipped into his mouth to savor the fire of the whiskey and its caramelized coffee taste.

A part of her half expected him to take control of the kiss, but he held himself rigid against her while yielding slightly to her caress. She swirled her tongue around his in a warm dance that teased her senses. Although he still held back, the tension holding him rigid eased a small fraction. A liquid fire streaked through her until her heart pounded frantically in her chest. From somewhere deep inside her, a wild need spread its way through every muscle in her body.

The need became a powerful longing. Without thought, she shifted her body until she was in his lap with her arms wrapped around his neck. A low growl rumbled in his chest as his fingers wrapped around the nape of her neck, and he took control of the heated caress. A white-hot heat singed every inch of her until the urge to have nothing between them made her tug at his necktie. She was already unbuttoning his shirt when he shuddered against her.

In a flash of movement, Mathias wrapped his fingers around her wrists and pressed her hands into his chest. He jerked his head away from her to press it into the leather squabs behind him. His eyes closed, his throat bobbed as he swallowed hard. A second later, his gaze met hers, and the fire blazing in his green eyes made her breathing hitch slightly.

"Are you trying to seduce me, Ophelia?"

His voice sounded as though he was being strangled, and she tipped her head to one side as she studied him for a moment. The dark emotion flaring in his gaze made her realize the power had shifted between them somehow. She wasn't sure how or why, but it had.

A sense of triumph, anticipation, and excitement skimmed through her body. Mathias wanted her. She was certain of it. She'd succeeded in arousing a man's desire. The knowledge caused her mouth to go dry. Ophelia dampened her lips with the tip of her tongue as she nodded.

"Yes, and I believe I succeeded."

The moment her quiet reply echoed between them, he stiffened as his mouth thinned with an emotion she couldn't decipher. In a sharp, rough jerk of his body, Mathias lifted her off his lap and set her down on the seat opposite him. She murmured a soft protest and bit down on her bottom lip as she stared at him in surprise.

Startled and confused by his reaction, she frowned in puzzlement. What on earth was wrong with the man? He'd been nothing but a curmudgeon all evening. She had yet to understand why, and now he was angry at her attempt to incite his desire. No, her success in arousing him.

Despite her bewilderment, the knowledge sent another rush of triumph through her. She'd actually succeeded in exciting Mathias Gilchrist. A man she was certain was always in control of his emotions when it came to any liaisons he entered into. As she studied him in silence, he grimaced, then looked away from her.

"I must be insane," he muttered. The terse comment made Ophelia stiffen as her confidence in her success wavered.

"I don't understand."

"I'm saying, I'm a madman for having allowed things to go this far." Mathias pinched the bridge of his nose.

"This far?" The relief that she'd not misjudged her success in arousing him was a short-lived emotion. Exasperated by his reaction when she knew he wanted her, she narrowed her gaze at him. "One would think you coerced me into doing something I had no inclination to do."

"Can you deny that if it weren't for our arrangement, you would never have kissed me the way you just did?"

"No. I cannot. But then I never *had* to agree to *our arrangement* in the first place."

"As I recall, I was quite persuasive in my efforts to secure your agreement to do so."

Anger surged through her at his conceit. The man actually thought she was incapable of resisting him.

"You, Mr. Gilchrist, are an arrogant jackass." Her sharp words made him jerk in surprise. "I am not some weak-minded female unable to resist *you* or misunderstand the proposition you made. One *I* originally proposed, and as I just said, I *agreed* to."

"That's not what I meant," he growled, and she wasn't sure whether his anger was directed at himself or her. He looked away from her once more. "I'm saying I provoked you into accepting my offer. Your original proposition was made under duress to regain your home. *My* proposition was an entirely different one, and it's an agreement I am revoking as of this moment."

"An excellent decision," she snapped.

Mathias's gaze swung back to her as he rapped viciously on the small wooden window just above his head. The small hinged door swung open almost immediately.

"Thomas, drop me off at the house my brother uses on occasion, then take Lady Havenstock home."

"Yes, sir," the driver replied before closing the small conversation window.

A stoic expression hardening his handsome features, Mathias sat rigidly across from her. Frustrated by his behavior, Ophelia glared at him, but he simply stared back at her with an unreadable expression. Even his gaze was unreadable. She exhaled a breath of irritation before looking out the window. The soft gaslight of the pole lamps lining the street allowed her to recognize Battersea Park before the carriage turned off onto a side street. Moments later, the vehicle rolled to a stop, and Mathias hastily exited the vehicle. About to close the door, he paused to look at her, his expression still unreadable, but she saw a tic flex the muscle in his cheek.

"Goodbye, Ophelia. Chelmsford is a good man. He'll treat you well."

With those parting words, Mathias closed the carriage door. Stunned by his assumption she intended to become intimately involved with the earl, she watched him stride up the steps of a small townhouse. With the same vicious knock he'd used on the carriage's small driver conversation window moments ago, she saw him pound on the front door of the house. A moment later, it opened, and light spilled out onto the steps.

It illuminated his tall figure, and his profile was no longer unreadable. What Ophelia thought had been anger was more like an expression of self-disgust. She barely had time to register the fact before Mathias disappeared through the door and the carriage rolled away. Ophelia sank back into the leather cushions of her seat, trying to comprehend what had just transpired between the two of them.

Was it possible Mathias had rejected her silent offer to enter into a liaison with him out of a sense of misguided guilt? He wanted her. She knew that. But their original agreement had been for her to become his pupil, nothing more. Mathias might think he'd coaxed her into being his student, but she knew better.

The man would never have been able to convince her to accept his proposition if she'd not wanted to do so. From the moment of George's death, Ophelia had been determined to make her own choices and choose her own path going forward. Mathias had been right. What she'd lacked had been the confidence to believe her husband was wrong about her.

George's constant criticism and physical abuse had drained her of anything but the belief she was exactly what her husband had said she was—a woman unable to arouse a man's desire or be excited by a man's touch. George might have stolen her confidence day by day throughout their marriage, but his death had freed her of his domination.

His demise had also given her the right to never give a man power over her again. But the most important thing she'd just realized was that George had been wrong. Very wrong. She *was* capable of passion and desire. It was a sensation that made her realize how much she wanted Mathias to touch her in the most intimate way possible.

Leaning forward, Ophelia rapped on the wood conversation panel. It was opened immediately, and she ordered the driver to take her back to where Mathias was. As the small window closed, she smiled. Mathias Gilchrist might think he'd coerced her into their agreement for him to transform her, but going to him now was solely her decision.

It was a choice she made not because of a need to test the skills Mathias had taught her when it came to intriguing men. The decision to go to him was simply because she wanted to feel the passion Mathias had said was inside her. A passion she wanted to experience in his arms. The knowledge that she was capable of something her husband said she wasn't made her even more determined to make Mathias listen to her. Ophelia would make him understand her decision to enter his bed was of her own volition, and the thought of what she would experience tonight sent a multitude of emotions flooding through her body. Sensations she knew would explode inside her with pleasure the moment Mathias touched her.

Chapter 9

Ophelia watched from the carriage window as the driver knocked on the front door Mathias had passed through. The driver had indicated that once the door opened, she would be able to enter the house quickly, thus diminishing the possibility of her being seen.

The door opened, and Ophelia watched him exchange a few words with the servant who'd been inside. With a nod, the driver hurried back down the steps and opened the carriage door.

"Anytime someone is visiting the house, my lady, a carriage is waiting in the mews," the man said as he extended his hand to her. "Just ask anyone to point you to the back door."

"Thank you," she murmured as the man helped her out of the vehicle and quickly guided her up the steps to the door. As the door closed behind her, Ophelia's heartbeat began to race.

The man who answered the door silently offered to take her shawl. As she handed it to him, she glanced around the small foyer. It was clearly meant for discreet, intimate encounters.

"Where is Mr. Gilchrist?"

"He's in his bed chambers, my lady. Would you like me—"

"No. I wish to surprise him," Ophelia said with a shake of her head. "If you'll simply tell me which way."

"The third door on the left at the top of the stairs, my lady." The man gave her directions without any surprise or disapproval. His reaction was that of a servant clearly accustomed to late-night arrivals such as hers. Based on Mathias's instructions to the carriage driver, she'd already realized it was the house Lord Thornbury used for assignations with his current lady of choice.

As she climbed the steps to the second floor, she wondered if Mathias used the house for his own liaisons. The thought made her stomach lurch. She dismissed the idea immediately. It didn't matter if Mathias did or didn't. All that mattered at the moment was that she was here and intent on following through with her plan.

The carpeted hall at the top of the stairs muffled the sound of her evening gown as she moved toward Mathias's door. She hesitated slightly as she faced the closed barrier standing between the two of them. With a quiet knock, she waited for him to answer the door.

"Enter." Harsh, abrupt, and filled with suppressed violence, the command made her hesitate a mere fraction of a second before she opened the door and stepped into the room.

Mathias stood with his back to her, one hand resting on the mantle of a small fireplace. He was shirtless, and the muscles of his back were like cords of supple steel. Tension radiated off his body as if he was battling inner demons. Excitement and a good measure of trepidation spread its way through Ophelia as she pressed her hand into her stomach. It was a pointless gesture to calm her suddenly unsteady nerves.

"What is it, Shipton?" he snarled before he finished off the glass of liquor in his hand.

He continued to stare into the fire, and Ophelia moved forward quietly. As if realizing she wasn't a servant, he turned around. The moment he saw her, Mathias jerked in surprise. Clearly stunned by her appearance, he didn't move or say a word. He simply stared at her in disbelief. Ophelia closed the distance between them and reached out to touch the hard muscles of his chest. The warmth of him skimmed its way across her skin until it engulfed her.

"What are you doing here, Ophelia?" he choked out, his expression still one of stupefied amazement.

"I think you know why, Mathias." Her reply made him take a step back, and the warmth of him vanished. She held his gaze steadily. "Do you intend to refuse me?"

"You're damn right I do," he growled.

"Why?" The question seemed to startle him before his jaw became a hard, inflexible line.

"Because our agreement didn't include sharing my bed."

"Only someone else's? Chelmsford, perhaps?"

"Yes, God damn it. I promised I'd turn you into a swan, and I have. I was wrong to insist on a month-long arrangement. As you said, a week would have been quite sufficient."

Mathias brushed past her and walked toward a small chest of drawers, where a decanter of liquor sat on a silver tray. As he passed her, the fresh, woodsy scent emanating from him filled her senses. Dear Lord, the man smelled delicious. She closed her eyes for a moment before focusing her gaze on him once more. In a vicious gesture, he splashed more alcohol into his glass. He took a swig before he turned back to her.

"I'll see you to the back door so Thomas can take you home."

He emptied his glass with another long drink and headed toward the door. Determined not to let him throw her out, Ophelia reached behind her, and with a hard tug, she yanked at the back of her dress to pull it apart.

The sound of more than a dozen buttons hitting the floor as they were ripped from the gown made Mathias come to a halt. He whirled around to stare at her with a look of shock that equaled his reaction when she'd entered his room. She tugged hard on the back of her dress again, and another round of popping filled the air.

Small, round-top buttons flew in every direction and further away this time. Ophelia didn't care where they landed. All that mattered was ensuring Mathias understood she would not leave. Slowly, Ophelia pushed the gown off her shoulders and down over her hips. It pooled at her feet, and she stepped out of the dress.

"I'm not leaving, Mathias."

His dazed stare emphasized how much her actions had stunned him, and it was clear he was uncertain how to react. She undid her garters, then placed her foot on a nearby chair to roll the silk hose off first one leg and then the other. Tossing the silk garments aside, she undid the laces holding her combination in place.

A hoarse sound echoed out of Mathias's throat, and it increased her confidence as she pulled her combination off, then dropped it to the floor. With nothing more than her chemise covering her, she slowly walked toward him. Reaching up to her breasts, she lightly touched her nipples beneath the thin lawn material.

"I believe you said I was to touch my nipples when I was alone and imagine your mouth was on me, your tongue flicking over them."

"*Christ Jesus,*" he ground out the moment she stroked her nipples. Desire flashed in his green eyes as his throat bobbed as he swallowed hard. "Damn it to hell, Ophelia. You need to leave—"

"Why? I've yet to hear you give me one good reason why I shouldn't share your bed." The tension in him was palpable, and she heard the unsteady sound of his breathing as she halted in front of him. "Well, Mathias? I'm waiting."

"Because Chelmsford won't like it," he grounded out between clenched teeth.

"You must be privy to information I'm not," she murmured as she lightly touched his chest. "I'm unaware that Lord Chelmsford has any say in what I do, where I go…or whose bed I share."

Ophelia trailed her fingers along the line of a hard shoulder, and he shuddered beneath her touch. Boldly, she leaned forward to kiss the rounded edge of his shoulder, then nibbled her way inward toward his neck. When she reached his throat, Mathias dragged in a deep, sharp breath. Strong hands grasped her arms as he forced her away from him.

"Enough," he mumbled fiercely as he put space between them. An undefinable emotion hardened his mouth, while alarm warred with desire in his jade-green eyes. Ophelia narrowed the space between them again to lightly stroke his cheek.

"What are you afraid of, Mathias?"

"*I'm* not afraid," he growled, low and deep in his throat. "I'm afraid *for you*."

"For me?" Startled, Ophelia jerked her head back slightly to stare at Mathias in bewilderment.

"Havenstock was a bastard. I don't want to frighten you, and I'm quite apt to do just that. Because right now, my willpower where you're concerned is almost non-existent," Mathias's words were frayed with a raw passion that made her heart skip a beat.

"I won't break, Mathias," she whispered as she met his gaze steadily. "I trust you not to hurt me."

He studied her for a long moment, his entire body as rigid as one of the oak trees at Marymont. Suddenly blowing out a harsh breath, he tugged her against him and kissed her. The heat of the caress wrapped its way around her until her body was on fire. Every inch of her seemed consumed with the white-hot feel of him against her body, but it wasn't enough. She wanted to feel her skin against his.

Her hands reached for her chemise, and with his lips still crushing hers, she tugged the fine lawn upward. She broke away from him just long enough to pull the chemise over her head. The garment fluttered to the floor, forgotten as she was in his arms again. As he kissed her, his hands pulled the pins from her hair until it fell over her shoulders. Long fingers slid through the fallen tresses to grasp the nape of her neck and pull her even closer.

The strong flavor of whiskey brushed across her tongue as it mated with his. Everything about him flooded her senses with a multitude of sensations. His mouth left hers and skimmed its way down her throat to the curve where her neck and shoulder met. A shudder rippled through her, and she gasped as his hands cupped one breast, and his mouth singed the rounded top portion.

A wild tremor rocked its way through her, and she arched backward with a silent prayer that he would take her in his mouth. She gasped as his tongue flicked across her nipple. It sent another shudder rippling its way through her. The instant his mouth closed around the rigid peak, a moan of delight blew past her lips.

Her fingers spiked through his dark hair, and when he bit gently on the stiff nipple, she cried out from the pleasure of it. He repeated the sweet torment on the other breast. With each flick of his tongue, the intensity of the wild sensations stirring her blood made her ache for something more.

The world shifted beneath her feet as he swung her up into his arms and carried her to the bed. As the mattress gave way beneath her, she stared up into his green eyes. They glittered with passion as he studied her for a long moment. At his hesitation, she reached out to touch a hard thigh.

"I want this, Mathias. I want *you* to show me how it should be between a man and a woman. All I experienced in my marriage was humiliation." Her fingers slid up his muscular thigh to caress his hip. "But when you touch me, all I feel is pleasure. A pleasure I don't want to end."

An emotion she couldn't define swept across his face as he nodded his understanding. Despite her reassuring words, there was a visible restraint in his movements as he removed the rest of his clothing. When he'd tossed them aside, she tried to keep breathing.

Everywhere she looked was lean, hard muscle. The sheer magnificence of him made her heart skip a beat before it began to race with excitement. As he sat down beside her on the bed, she reached up to touch his shoulder in a gentle caress. Slowly, as if savoring the moment, his gaze swept down the length of her, then upwards until their eyes locked once more.

"I don't think I've ever seen a more beautiful sight in my life." Heat burned her cheeks at the compliment, and his mouth tipped upward slightly. "It's true, sweetheart. You're exquisite."

The words were a soft breeze against her throat as he lowered his head to burn a steady, leisurely path downward with his mouth. Every touch of his lips on her skin sent invisible flames streaking across her body. They burned hot on her flesh as his mouth explored the curve of her waist, then her hip. The moment his mouth nibbled at the inside of her thigh, she gasped in surprise and trepidation.

Fear of humiliation, born of the past, made her instinctively shift her body away from his touch in an attempt to escape. Panicked at the thought she'd made a mistake where he was concerned, she trembled with apprehension. A powerful hand grasped her hip in a gentle hold to still her movement as he lifted his head to meet her wide-eyed gaze. His fingers stroked her skin as he soothed her in an obvious effort to ease her trembling.

"Close your eyes, and trust me," he said softly.

The silent promise in his green eyes that he'd do nothing to hurt her slowly eased her fear, and her trembling subsided. She swallowed what was left of her apprehension to do as he'd ordered and allowed her head to fall back into the soft mattress. When his mouth caressed the inside of her leg a moment later, she stiffened as her fear of degradation returned.

In response, his fingers massaged her hip and waist in a soundless gesture of reassurance. A split second later, his tongue slid into her and swirled around the sensitive spot between her legs. Shocked, she cried out in surprise before the air left her lungs.

The instant her body jerked against his mouth, his hands caught her hips in an inflexible grip and prevented her from retreating. With each stroke of his tongue, her senses sparked to life in a way she'd never known. Everything was heightened to a new pitch of awareness. The warm, masculine fragrance of him brushing against her nose, the small gasps of air she heard as they escaped her mouth, and every jolt of pleasure as her body responded to each stroke of his tongue.

Even the strength of his hands on her hips as he held her firmly in place was emphasized all the more acutely. Her skin tingled with pleasure as each of her nerve endings hummed a message of intense excitement to her brain. She barely had time to comprehend the strength of her heightened senses when his teeth scraped across the most sensitive part of her.

Unexpected pleasure streaked through her, and a cry of surprised delight flew past her lips. In response, his tongue circled the now almost unbearably sensitive spot before his teeth tugged at her again. Dear God, not even in the dark of her own room when she'd touched herself had she ever experienced such intense delight. She had thought it impossible to know—feel passion, but she'd been wrong. This was beyond anything she'd ever imagined was possible to feel or experience.

Intermingled with the pleasure of his epicurean touch was an unfamiliar sensation. It was an exquisite pressure that spread across her stomach and down to where his mouth was teasing and pleasuring her. The only thing her mind could describe it as was fiery sensation need. Another cry escaped her as his teeth nipped at sensitive flesh, followed by the soothing stroke of his tongue. The need taking hold of her was becoming almost unbearable. It made her tremble with an excitement she'd never experienced before.

Everything about the sensations rolling over her drove a rising need inside her for something she couldn't define. It pulsated through her, pressing her to give herself up to the deliciously new and powerful urges building inside her. Her hips twisted against his intimate touch, and he tightened his grip on her. The strength of his grasp was unyielding as he continued to nibble and caress her with his mouth.

Relentless and steady, he wove a web of pleasure around her that pulled small whimpers from her throat. The beat of her heart pounding wildly in her chest echoed in her ears as his every touch heated her blood. Flames licked their way through her veins until she burned not only on the outside, but on the inside as well.

The aching need consuming her intensified and grew exponentially with incredible speed until it exploded inside her. With a small scream, her back arched up off the bed in a fierce reaction to the physical release cresting over her like a wave that drowned her in pleasure. It sent one spasm after another flowing through her with an intensity that made her sob from the fiery heat engulfing her.

Lost in mindless ecstasy, her body writhed on the bed as she sobbed with delight at the sensations assaulting her senses. Slowly, her tremors subsided, and a warm lethargy settled in her limbs. Utterly spent from the experience, she shuddered as his mouth worked up over her body at a leisurely pace.

"Are you glad you trusted me?" Mathias's voice blew a warm breath of air across her breast as he stopped to tease a still rigid nipple. She immediately gasped.

"Oh please, no. Not yet. I don't think I could bear it again so soon." Her eyes opened to find him hovering over her, a gleam of satisfaction in his green eyes.

"Well?" The single word demanded a reply, and Ophelia smiled.

"It was wonderful," she whispered before a warm heat filled her cheeks. "I never dream it possible…possible to feel something like that."

With one hand, he brushed a lock of hair off her cheek. It was a lover's touch that warmed her heart as well as her body. He lowered his head and kissed her deeply. Her essence was still on his lips, and a shudder rocked her body as she remembered the pleasure he'd just aroused in her. When he lifted his head, a roguish smile tilted his mouth.

"As you've just learned, not every pleasure is solely for a man. Although I thoroughly enjoyed your reaction." He chuckled softly. "As I said before, the passion you thought you lacked has been laying just beneath the surface all along."

Startled by his words, Ophelia frowned slightly in concentration as she considered his words. Mathias was right. She wasn't the passionless creature her husband had declared her to be. The sensation of Mathias's hand sliding down to cup her breast brought her out of her thoughts as she focused her attention on him again. A wicked look darkened his eyes as their gazes locked.

"I think it's time for another lesson. One that will give both of us immense satisfaction."

Sinful and rich, the seductive note in his voice made her heart skip a beat. A tremor shook its way through her as his hand moved downward until his fingers touched her where his mouth had been a short time ago. Almost as if it had been waiting for his touch, her body jerked upward in reaction to the caress.

Passion flared in his gaze, and she sucked in a sharp breath as his thumb rubbed and pressed down on her. She moaned softly, and he smiled as he lowered his head to kiss her. Eagerly, she welcomed the heat of him as their tongues mated in a hot, fierce dance of passion.

A heady excitement swept over her as fire stirred in her body again. The ache he'd appeased moments before had returned, but this time it was far more intense. Anticipation flowed through her as his lips grazed her cheek and moved downward to the side of her neck. The solid warmth of him seeped into her pores as his body covered hers. As his hard erection brushed against her thigh, she stiffened. He lifted his head to stare down into her eyes.

"I promise this will be equally pleasurable, sweetheart."

The soothing, confident note in his voice made her nod her head slightly in acquiescence. He kissed her again. This time it was more insistent and demanding. There was a heat to it that reminded her of what she'd already experienced with him, but it was somehow different. This time he was demanding where before he'd simply given. His tongue danced with hers, tugging a response from her that was wild and unrestrained.

Lost in the heady taste of him, she gasped as, with one slow stroke, he filled her completely. He paused for a brief second, then retreated from her in an unhurried manner before sliding into her again. Every time he retreated from her, her insides tightened around him, but she was powerless to stop him from pulling away. As his body mated with hers, a sharp pitch of desire rose inside her. It stirred a now familiar sensation in her. Sweet heaven, she wanted—no, she could never label this as want. This was a craving. It was a sharp, fiery need that stirred a hunger inside her until she was blinded to everything but him.

A small jolt rocked its way through her body and into his the moment he buried himself inside her slick heat. He didn't move for a moment as he enjoyed the sensation of being so deeply connected to her. The sweet blend of citrus and vanilla wafting off her skin tantalized him as he inhaled and savored the scent of her. Even her mouth was a delicious warmth as his tongue swirled around hers.

Warm and succulent, the taste of her increased his desire as the champagne she'd had earlier this evening danced its way off her lips into his mouth. Her quiet whimper of need instantly tightened his cock. It throbbed inside her with a hard demand for its release. In a determined effort to extend the delight and pleasure for them both, he ignored the message his body was sending.

One hand braced against the mattress, he explored the voluptuous curve of her with his other. She was soft and feminine everywhere, with a heady scent of desire. He cupped the fullness of her breast, enjoying the warmth of her in his hand. Beneath his touch, her skin warmed his palm, but it was nothing compared to the fire of her body wrapped around his cock.

Christ Jesus, she was enough to drive a man mad. The picture she'd painted of herself when they first met couldn't have been any less accurate. She wasn't a passionless ice-queen, unable to give or experience pleasure. The ease with which she ignited a fiery need in his body was proof enough. The intensity of his hunger for her set off an alarm in the back of his mind, but he barely heard the sound. The only thing he was aware of was the intense pleasure assaulting him with each stroke of his body into hers.

The hot friction between them intensified his cock's demand for release, but he was unwilling to relinquish so quickly the sensation of her wrapped around him. He ignored his body's need for satisfaction and deepened their kiss. The distraction was temporary as her muscles contracted around him in an urgent summons for her release, which heightened his body's demand to be satiated.

Despite the loud calls for a release, he was determined to enjoy the pleasure her body gave him for as long as possible. He focused his mind on exploring the softness of her shoulder with his lips. The warm scent of her desire engulfed his senses as her quiet moan echoed in his ear. Her hands suddenly gripped his hips as she pressed her curves up into his in a silent demand for him to increase the speed of his thrusts.

Instantly, he tried once again to control the rising urges of his own body, but the moment her fingers dug hard into his hips, he was lost. Unable to deny his craving for satisfaction, he surrendered to her demand. With hard, rapid thrusts, his body shouted its pleasure at the way she responded to him. That she met pounding rhythm eagerly and fiercely as his own only increased the desire surging through him.

The hunger she aroused in him roared through his blood, and he increased the pace of his body moving against hers. Seconds later, a cry of abandon escaped her beautiful mouth, and her contractions gripped him hard and tight. It was as if a tight vise surrounded his cock to create an acute pleasure that bordered just on the edge of pain.

With every spasm of her body, the heat of her clutched around him until it unleashed a raging storm inside him. It blinded him to everything but her and the control she possessed over his body. The intensity of the desire raging through him rose swiftly until his body jerked against her slick, tight heat. In the next instant, he released his seed with a shout of pleasure.

Only their ragged breathing broke the silence between them. Mathias pressed his forehead against hers as his body continued to shudder a moment longer. As the aftershock of his body's release vanished, he slowly eased himself down into her soft body. He didn't pull away from her. The need to maintain his physical connection to her was something he didn't understand, but he accepted it without question.

The thud of his heartbeat in his ears subsided to a quiet beat as he enjoyed the way her warmth blended with his own. He couldn't remember the last time he'd been so satiated in a woman's arms. The sudden lazy movements of her fingers stroking his back made him murmur a sound of pleasurable satisfaction. There was something warm and comforting about her touch.

Her soft laugh brushed across his neck like a sultry breeze in the middle of summer. It emphasized the contentment he was feeling. The sound of her quiet sigh made him lift his head to stare down at her. Her eyes were closed, and there was a small smile on her tempting lips.

"I take it you approve of lesson two this evening?" he said with amusement. Her eyes fluttered open, and her smile broadened.

"Yes, I heartily approve, and I would like to do it again, please." The teasing look she gave him highlighted the golden flecks in her brown eyes.

"I consider myself equal to the task of pleasuring your body with mine on a regular basis, my sweet, but there are limits even to my own ability for a repeat performance so quickly." He laughed. "But, I promise you, I intend to spend the rest of the night enjoying the pleasures of your body and emphasizing just how intoxicating you are."

An odd light flickered in her gaze, and with a gentle push, she made him roll off her onto his back, then sat up to hover over him. Brown hair spilled over her breasts, hiding them from view, while the smile on her dark pink mouth had vanished. Despite her seriousness, she was temptation personified. Already she had his body responding to her on the most base of levels. When her sober look didn't disappear, he narrowed his gaze at her. As if sensing his perplexed reaction, she shook her head.

"I cannot possibly spend the night, Mathias. While it's highly doubtful my father will note my absence, Lizzie will." She nibbled on her lip. "I should leave now."

"Not yet. Stay an hour or two more. I'll make certain Thomas sees you safely into your house through the back door." Indecision darkened her beautiful brown eyes, and he caught her hand to pull her forefinger into his mouth. "I'm not ready to part with you yet, especially when I can promise you'll enjoy our next few lessons."

"You truly are a rogue, Mathias Gilchrist," she whispered as desire darkened her eyes. He grinned with satisfaction that she'd silently agreed to stay awhile longer.

"You have *no* idea how much of a rogue I am, Lady Havenstock." Mathias's hand slid around her neck to pull her down to him. As he kissed her gently, he murmured against her mouth. "You have no idea at all."

⤲⤳

Ophelia woke to the warmth of a masculine arm draped across her stomach. For a moment, she wasn't sure where she was. Slowly turning her head, she saw Mathias sleeping soundly beside her. Almost immediately, her heart skipped a beat. Awake, he was strong, handsome, and virile. But asleep, he looked much younger, almost boyish. She lightly touched his cheek with the back of her hand, but he didn't wake. He simply shifted his head in a small movement.

As she stared at him, Ophelia remembered the pleasure he'd given her. With every touch and stroke of his hand or body, he'd driven every perverse, unpalatable moment of her marriage out of her head. It was a gift she could never repay. Last night she'd discovered what it was like to hold sway over a man and demand he make love to her. But what she hadn't expected was how much pleasure there was to be had in a man's arms. No, Mathias's arms. She wasn't sure she would ever be able to share another man's bed as she had shared Mathias's last night.

She grew still at the thought. *Dear Lord*, had she fallen in love with the man? She immediately dismissed the possibility. No, she might be capable of passion and desire, but love wasn't something she would ever allow herself to feel. Her determination never to marry again was a guarantee against surrendering her independence, but falling in love would make her a slave to her feelings and the man she loved. She'd spoken the truth when she'd told Mathias a liaison wasn't possible for her, any more than marriage was.

Last night had been nothing more than a pleasurable interlude. With each caress, Mathias had taught she was more than capable of receiving pleasure and giving it. He'd also helped banish the self-doubt George had relentlessly cultivated in her throughout their marriage. Mathias had helped destroy the demons of her past, and for that she would be eternally grateful.

Certain he would protest her leaving, she carefully slid out from under the weight of his arm. When she was free of his grasp, Ophelia quietly gathered her clothes and began to dress. When she picked up her gown, she eyed it and its lack of buttons with a grimace. She'd been so determined to make Mathias let her stay, she'd failed to consider the ramifications of keeping a gown on without buttons to hold it in place.

The short shawl she'd worn last night wouldn't cover up the state of the dress. She would have to ask for a cloak to hide its disheveled state. When she was dressed, Ophelia quietly left the room and made her way downstairs. Almost as if she was expected, the servant who'd answered the door the night before emerged from the back of the house. Embarrassment made her cheeks burn as she met the polite gaze of the man.

"Thomas said he would be waiting for me."

"Of course, my lady, please follow me." The man quickly moved to where her shawl hung on a coat rack, clearly intent on covering her shoulders. She shook her head in protest as she tugged the shawl from the man's hands.

"If you don't mind…I…I require a cloak."

As if it were the most natural of requests, the servant bowed slightly and hurried into a room off the small foyer. When he returned, he made a move to drape it over her shoulders. With a shake of her head, she took the cape from him and hastily swung it around her to cover her back. The servant headed toward the back of the house with a polite gesture to follow him.

"Ophelia. Stop."

Startled, she jerked her gaze upward to see Mathias hurrying down the steps in his pants and nothing more. The sight of him made her heart skip a beat. When he reached the bottom of the steps, he caught her hand in his.

"You're leaving without saying goodbye." The irritation in his voice made her smile.

"You were sleeping. I didn't want to wake you."

"Don't do it again." The firmly spoken command made her stiffen. As much as she wanted to tell him there wouldn't be another time, something told her to remain silent. He narrowed his gaze at her. "I shall call on you tomorrow for a ride in the park."

"I doubt I'll be up that early," she murmured as she glanced at the grandmother clock over his shoulder. "It's almost five o'clock now."

"Then lunch at Rules."

"I don't—"

"You have to eat, Ophelia." The almost belligerent tone of his voice made her nod.

"Very well. Lunch at Rules." Her acquiescence made him smile with satisfaction.

"I'll call for you at eleven-thirty."

Mathias carried her hand up to his mouth to kiss her fingertips. A quiver streaked through her at the caress. She turned away, then stopped.

"Mathias…I want to thank you."

"Thank me?" A look of astonishment sent his eyebrows upward. She touched his cheek. Beneath her fingers, his early morning stubble was rough against them. It emphasized his maleness and made her ache to have him carry her back to his bed. Ophelia swallowed the need that had suddenly erupted inside her and forced herself to continue.

"Yes. Last night was wonderful. I can never repay you for what you did." Her words of gratitude made him narrow his gaze at her.

"Explain."

"Until last night, I didn't understand what it was like to feel pleasure. You made me see I wasn't the woman I believed myself to be. I have you to thank for that."

At her quiet reply, Mathias pulled her into his arms. His mouth moved gently over hers. It was a kiss of tenderness, and although she didn't understand why, she suddenly felt like weeping. When he lifted his head, she met his gaze steadily, determined not to reveal the feelings he'd stirred in her with the gentle kiss. A strange emotion flashed in his eyes, but it was impossible to determine what he was thinking. He kissed her brow and turned his head toward the servant who had been standing a discreet distance away.

"See her ladyship to the carriage, Shipton, and make sure Thomas understands he's to personally escort her to the back door of her house and see her safely inside."

"Yes, Mr. Gilchrist." The man turned and walked toward the back of the house. Mathias kissed her with an urgency that surprised her, and he took a quick step back when he released her.

"Go, while I'm still able to let you do so. If I escort you out of the house, there is a high probability I'll simply keep you from leaving."

The moment he growled his command, she knew he was contemplating doing just that. Her heart crashed into her chest as she realized how much she wanted to stay with him. The moment the dangerous thought pierced her consciousness a chill swept across her skin. She was on the brink of giving him the power to control her completely, and the thought terrified her.

Without giving him a chance to reconsider and impulsively seduce her into staying, she hurried after Shipton. As she walked quickly down the hall, her back burned as she sensed Mathias's gaze following her. What would he have done if he'd known she had no intention of ever returning? It was a question she didn't want to answer.

Chapter 10

The sound of her bedroom door opening made Ophelia look over her shoulder. When her younger sister returned her smile of greeting with a frown of worry, Ophelia quickly moved forward to draw her sister deeper into her room.

"Something's upset you. What is it? Has father become embroiled in another scandal? Is it Mr. Nickens?"

"No, it's nothing like that."

Lizzie bit down on her bottom lip as if trying to think of a way to broach an unpleasant topic. Immediately, Ophelia's heart sank in fear. Had Lizzie seen her returning to the house so late? No, that wasn't possible. She'd checked on her sister early this morning before going to bed.

"What is it then, dearest?"

"Did someone take advantage of you last night, Ophelia?" Lizzie blurted out.

"Why on earth would you ask a question like that?" Startled by the question, she eyed her sister with amazement.

"Alice just showed me the dress you wore last night. Did Mr. Gilchrist hurt you?"

The note of fear in her sister's voice made her take Lizzie's hand in hers and pull her over to the bed. As she sat down next to her sister, Ophelia studied her for a long moment.

"No, he didn't," she said softly. "In fact, Mathias helped me see that everything George made me believe about myself was a lie."

"I don't understand."

"I wouldn't expect you to, and I'm certain your Mr. Nickens would never do anything to you that would enable you to understand." Ophelia sighed. "George was a brute, Lizzie. There is no other way to describe him."

"Oh dear Lord, but you never said…you never told us…"

"How could I, and what would you have done?" Ophelia shook her head, then smiled at her sister. "The past is dead, and I will no longer let it define me."

Lizzie stared at her for a moment, then in a spontaneous gesture, enveloped Ophelia in a tight hug.

"I'm so sorry, Ophelia. I'm so sorry." As Lizzie slowly released her, she frowned. "But it still doesn't explain your dress."

"*I* ripped it," she said quietly, knowing her best defense was to tell the truth without disclosing everything.

"*You* did?" Lizzie met her gaze with a perplexed look. "Why would you deliberately tear your dress, Ophelia?"

"I wanted to go to bed, and it was difficult to get out of it on my own." She eyed her sister sternly. "Now enough with the questions. Weren't you going to walk in the park with Mr. Nickens?"

"Yes, he's waiting for me downstairs, but I—"

"Then why, in heaven's name, aren't you downstairs with him?" Ophelia stood up and pulled Lizzie with her.

"Paul—Mr. Nickens—knew I was worried about you. He insisted I come to check on you."

"Well, now you have, and I think it's time you stop making the man wait." Ophelia pulled her sister toward the door. "I'll go with you, so he can see your fears were groundless."

Without waiting for Lizzie to protest any further, Ophelia quickly ushered her sister downstairs and into the parlor. Paul Nickens's face brightened the moment he saw them.

"Lady Havenstock. I'm delighted to see you are well. Eliza—Miss Sheffield was quite worried about you."

"She had no reason to be," Ophelia said with a smile. "I think it's high time I warn you that Lizzie is quite often a mother hen who wants all her chicks to be happy."

"That I learned shortly after we met. She chastised me as to my not eating on a regular basis." Amusement danced in the young man's eyes as he shifted his gaze to Lizzie. A blush rose in Lizzie's cheeks as she scowled at her suitor, then puffed out a breath of exasperation.

"The two of you are making sport of me," she huffed. Immediately, Paul Nickens reached for her hand. Brushing her fingertips with his mouth, he shook his head at Lizzie.

"Never, my dear. I would never mock you. Tease you perhaps, but nothing more."

There young man's repentant look as he looked down into Lizzie's eyes made her sister's expression softened as she smiled at him. The silent communication between the two of them made Ophelia suddenly feel as though she were an interloper. It also aroused a twinge of envy at her sister's obvious happiness. She immediately squashed the emotion. Lizzie was happy, and that was all that mattered.

"Didn't the two of you have plans to walk in the park?" Ophelia said with a smile.

"We did. I promised Miss Sheffield that we would buy some breadcrumbs with which to feed the swans." Paul Nickens said cheerfully. "Perhaps you would like to join us, my lady."

"Oh yes, please do, Ophelia. The weather is most agreeable today."

"Thank you, no. I have correspondence that needs attention."

With a wave of her hand, she urged the couple out of the room. As the two left, Ophelia returned to the parlor. She stared around the room, noting how small it looked with Lizzie's piano and the other pieces of furniture that had come with the townhome. An image of Marymont's large rooms and high ceilings filled her head. It filled her with a longing to go home.

It would have to wait until Paul Nickens proposed to Lizzie, and from the way the man had looked at her sister this morning, she was certain that moment was imminent. With finances being what they were, a small wedding would be a necessity. But then, knowing Lizzie as she did, she was certain her sister would want to be married in the small church they attended while at Marymont. The only real extravagance would be Lizzie's trousseau and wedding gown. A smile touched her lips as she imagined the excitement of a wedding. On the heels of that thought was the knowledge she would never know the happiness she was certain her sister would. A small noise of self-disgust blew past her lips. She would be perfectly happy at Marymont, where she would be free of the dictates of any man. The sound of her stomach growling reminded her she hadn't eaten since dinner at Chelmsford House. She rang for Taggert, then moved to the small secretaire in the corner of the room. The name of a men's tailor on one of the bills lying on the desk made her heart sink. For the second time in a month, her father had apparently ordered a new coat.

"Good morning, my lady." Ophelia looked up from the bill and greeted the butler with a smile.

"I'd like some tea and toast, Taggert."

"Of course, my lady." The butler turned away but stopped when Ophelia called to him.

"Oh, and is my father home?"

"No, my lady. He sent word last night that he would spend the night at his club and return later this afternoon."

At the man's explanation, Ophelia frowned with bitter resentment. No doubt her father had been playing cards somewhere free of any scrutiny and had most likely lost money they didn't have. At least he couldn't wager Marymont again. She suddenly realized the butler was still waiting patiently for further instructions.

"Thank you, Taggert. I'll take my tea here."

"Of course, my lady."

Ophelia turned back to the secretaire as the butler left the room. A weary sigh escaped her lips as she turned to the task of settling the accounts she could and setting aside those that could wait until the next month. She'd barely finished when she heard a low male voice coming from the entryway. Engrossed in her work, she'd not even heard the doorbell chime. A quick glance at the clock said it was well past eleven.

The memory of Mathias saying he would call for her at the half-hour made her heart skip a beat. She'd completely forgotten her agreement to dine with him at Rules, and he was early. Frantically, she tried to think of some excuse not to go with him, but failed.

Worse, she'd yet to think of a way to break with him completely. The consequences of a more permanent liaison with Mathias were far too dangerous. Last night had convinced her how easily she could lose her heart to the man. It was why she had no intention of entering his bed again.

As Ophelia stood up and turned toward the door, shock froze her muscles as she saw Edgar enter the room. There was a slight twist to his thin lips that was so reminiscent of his father it made her stomach roil. Ice scraped its way down her back. It caused her to shiver slightly.

Edgar could almost be considered handsome if it weren't for his personality, but she could already see the signs that heavy drinking had caused around the eyes and nose. She sincerely doubted the man would be a jovial drunk. No, Edgar would be just like his father—cruel, heartless, and brutal.

Obviously aware of her discomfort, her stepson smiled slowly. Striding forward, he stopped less than a foot away from her. The moment he took her hand in his, he carried it upward to brush his lips over her knuckles. When his mouth lingered over her hand, she jerked it free of his grasp.

"Why are you here, Edgar?"

"To apologize for upsetting you yesterday evening."

"I find that difficult to believe."

"You wound me, Ophelia. I'm not a heartless man."

"No? I think you're just as much of a brute as your father was."

"My father was a fool to not recognize the jewel he possessed."

"Possessed?" she said bitterly. "Yes, I suppose he did, and I have no intention of ever being a man's personal property again."

"And you shouldn't be, Ophelia. You were meant to be treasured, showered in jewels, and cared for as one would a piece of art."

At the man's lavish compliment, she stared at him in amazement before she laughed with true amusement. Edgar's surprise at her reaction made him eye her with puzzlement before he realized she was laughing at him. Eyes narrowing to thin slits, he studied her in silence until her laughter faded. Ophelia dismissed his embellished words with a shake of her head.

"A leopard can no more change spots than you could change your manipulative, controlling nature, Edgar. You are cut from the same cloth as your father, and I want nothing to do with you."

"You do me a grave injustice, Ophelia." Although his voice was well-controlled and devoid of anger. She saw the glint of outrage in his dark eyes. "I am not the cruel, perverse, impotent man my father was. In fact, I am quite certain you would find bedroom sport with me quite enjoyable. I also have no doubt of your ability to perform acts many married women refuse to do."

Appalled by his comments, she took a step back from him. *Dear God*, had George actually confessed to his son the most intimate of details of their marriage? Her stomach lurched as she remembered the substance of her conversation with the Earl of Chelmsford last night. If Gideon had heard rumors about George's displeasure with her ability to arouse him, it was more than likely her husband had told Edgar the same thing.

The difference was that she was certain George had done so in far greater detail. Humiliation rolled over her in the same way a enormous wave would. It threatened to pull her out to sea with no hope of any mooring to save her.

"Do not look so dismayed, my dear." Edgar closed the distance between them until the heavy scent of poorly rolled cigars permeated her senses. The smell made her stomach churn. "It's not as if you didn't suspect my father would express his displeasure at your performance."

"Get out, Edgar."

"I wouldn't be so hasty in that command, sweet Ophelia." The calculating gleam in his eyes made her heart slam into her chest. "You see, I took the liberty of paying off a few of your father's debts. Naturally, I did this out of the goodness of my heart, but you can hardly expect me not to ask for a few concessions."

"You know damn well, you're the one who controls the money your father left to me. No doubt you paid my father's debts using *my* money."

"Tch, tch, such language from a lady of your standing. While it's true I have control of your finances, I know you'll find me more than generous when it comes to returning control of those monies to you."

"And what am I to do to be the recipient of your generosity?"

"I think you know the answer to that."

The sly smile curling his lips made Ophelia quickly sidestep him to move out of reach, but she wasn't quick enough. Edgar's fingers dug into her arm as he tugged her into his chest.

"Let me go," she snapped.

"You really have no choice, my pet." The moment his mouth sought hers, she turned her head away. Edgar's lips made their way across her cheek to her ear. "I like a woman with spirit, Ophelia. I will enjoy our tussles in the bedroom."

The moment his hand clawed at her breast, she summoned every bit of her strength and broke free of his grasp. She managed to put several feet between them as she glared at him with loathing.

"I'll not tell you again, Edgar. I have no intention of marrying you. Now *Get. Out.*" Despite the vehemence in her voice, it was obvious it hadn't fazed him at all.

"Did I mention marriage?" Cold amusement glittered in his beady eyes. Startled, by his reply, her skin grew cold as his gaze roamed over her in a way that alarmed her. His smile one of disdain, he shook his head slightly. "Yes, I suppose I did. I actually gave you the choice of marriage or simply being my mistress."

"And I refused you on every occasion you've made those vile propositions."

"Yes, you did. But things change, and I believe I'm in a far better position than Gilchrist to meet any financial arrangement you've made with him."

"I beg your pardon," she exclaimed angrily as she ignored the fear spreading a layer of ice over her skin.

"Come now, Ophelia. We both know you've been sharing Mathias Gilchrist's bed.

"I don't know what you're talking about." Grateful that her voice echoed with cold outrage, she struggled to hide her fear from him.

"Don't you?" There was a triumphant gleam in Edgar's eyes as he started walking toward her. "I have it on good authority from a pretty little seamstress in Madame Sabine's shop that one Mathias Gilchrist paid the balance of your bill for your most recent dress order."

"You're lying," she retorted in an icy voice. "I paid an installment on my bill from Madame Sabine yesterday."

"Are you really that naïve, Ophelia?" he asked in amazement. A moment later, he shook his head. "It appears you are. I shall enjoy making you far worldlier, my dear."

Edgar moved too fast for her to avoid being caught in his arms. The moment his mouth covered hers, she wanted to retch. She shoved at him with a strength born of anger but was unable to break free of his clutches. Her hand groped behind her in search of some weapon with which to save herself. The cool feel of porcelain against her fingers made her grab the fairly large-sized clock off the table.

With every ounce of strength she possessed, she slammed the time piece against Edgar's head. Instantly, he slumped into her. Ophelia shoved his heavy weight off of her, and he slid to the floor. Trembling with a mixture of horror and fear, Ophelia stared down at Edgar's still form. There was an angry cut on his head, and a trickle of blood meandered its way down over his cheek. Had she killed him? The thought made her stomach roil as she quickly crossed the room and tugged hard several times on the bell cord. Taggert was in the room almost immediately. Concern furrowed her butler's brow as he looked at the man.

"Is he dead?" she rasped in fear. The butler moved quickly to Edgar's side and bent over him.

"He's still breathing, my lady."

"Thank God," she whispered, and her breathing slowed to a more manageable rate. "Have his driver help you remove him. I don't *ever* want him to enter this house, or Marymont, again. Is that understood?"

"Yes, my lady. I'll gladly see to it."

A soft groan drifted up from the floor, and Ophelia pressed her hand into her stomach in a fruitless attempt to calm her fears. Taggert immediately slipped his hands under the man's arms to drag him out into the hall. When Edgar was out of sight, Ophelia stumbled to a nearby chair.

Grateful for something steady to support her, she sank down into the stiff, oval-backed seat. Her fingers gripped the chair's wooden arm as she leaned over it in an attempt to end the dizziness assaulting her. She'd drawn blood. It wasn't something Edgar would forgive or forget. The man would make her pay a steep price, and she was convinced it wouldn't be with demands for her to share his bed. Her stepson excelled in spreading gossip.

While she doubted it would affect Lizzie's future happiness, her own humiliation would be excruciating.

Mathias had lied to her. He'd said Madame Sabine was a friend and would reduce her bill for the dresses. Instead, he'd underhandedly paid the balance despite her insistence she wouldn't allow him to treat her as he would a mistress.

She'd been a fool. She'd known the dressmaker's bill was far too low and hadn't questioned it. Even now, she was forced to admit how quickly she'd allowed herself to believe the woman's generosity was simply a matter of friendship with Mathias. A friendship she'd always known had more to do with the bedchamber than anything else.

The realization twisted something inside her so painful she gasped from the strength of it. A small voice offered up an explanation for the pain, but she refused to listen or accept what it was telling her.

"Ophelia."

Mathias's voice echoed from the foyer into the parlor, and she jerked up right in her chair. When he appeared in the doorway, the fear and pain assaulting her became a blistering anger that raced through her veins. He'd lied to her, and in doing so, he'd given Edgar the ammunition with which to humiliate her anew.

Mathias stared at Taggert and another man as they lifted Viscount Havenstock into the carriage. The man had a healthy gash on his temple, and had apparently been knocked unconscious by a blow to the head. Instantly, his insides tightened with fear. Had the bastard hurt Ophelia?

"Taggert?"

"Her ladyship is all right, sir. Shaken, but unharmed." At the man's reassurances, Mathias ran up the steps into the townhouse.

"Ophelia."

Even to his ears, the fear and panic in his cry was evident. He covered the short distance into the parlor in two long strides. The sight of her slumped over the side of a chair made his heart crash viciously into his chest before anger beat a steady drum in his head. If Havenstock hurt her, he would beat the man to within an inch of his worthless life.

Ophelia looked up as he charged into the room and quickly sprang to her feet. He took two steps toward her before she waved her hand at him to stop. The pallor of her complexion worried him, and he took another step toward her.

"He tried to force himself on you, didn't he?" he bit out through clenched teeth.

The sharp nod of her head was her only answer. It sent a dark rage speeding through his body. He'd see to it the bastard would never touch her again. He ached to pull her into his arms and comfort her, but the fragility of her demeanor warned him not to. "Did he hurt you?"

"No. I am uninjured."

"The same cannot be said for Havenstock." Mathias allowed a small smile of vicious satisfaction to touch his lips as he remembered the viscount being lifted into his carriage. She clearly had the heart of a lion to fight the man off and win.

"Why are you here, Mathias?"

"We'd agreed I would take you to Rules for lunch, but given—"

"That is out of the question." The curt, abrupt statement as she interrupted him made Mathias frown.

"I understand, which is why I was about to say we'd have our lunch here."

"No. I won't eat lunch or do anything else in your company." There was a harsh finality in her words that made his heart slam into his chest. A jolt of fear knotted his stomach.

"Might I ask why?"

"You said yourself last night that our agreement is at an end, and I completely agree."

"I see. And what prompted this sudden decision?"

Mathias eyed her calmly, despite the dread slithering its way through his body. Something had happened in the hours since she'd left him. The differences between the woman in front of him and the woman he'd kissed goodbye just a few short hours ago were subtle, but they were there.

He'd known she'd been embarrassed this morning when she'd stolen so quietly out of his room, but he'd thought he'd reassured her that last night had been more than a brief interlude and exchange of pleasure. In fact, every moment he'd spent in her company emphasized it would be a long time before he was willing to part with her.

"Suffice it to say, I have no desire to be associated with a liar."

The accusation made his muscles grow rock hard with tension as he met her stony gaze. Havenstock had said something to make her label him as deceitful. The strong possibility it involved Sabine made Mathias's heart sink as he narrowed his gaze at her.

"A liar?"

"You lied to me about Madame Sabine. Edgar told me *you* paid for my gowns. How much did you pay?"

"It was an insignificant amount," he replied quietly. While he knew it was an insignificant sum to him, he knew Ophelia would find the sum far from trivial. It was almost a quarter of her annual allowance.

"As you once asked me, *how much?*" The gleam of outrage in her brown eyes made him hesitate, and she narrowed her gaze at him. "*How much, Mathias?*"

"Thirty-six pounds," he murmured as his gut twisted viciously.

"*Thirty-six…*" The color that had been returning to her face faded almost instantly. He took a step forward, only to halt beneath her look of fury and contempt. "Even though I *refused* to let you pay—*refused* to be your mistress—you ignored my express wishes."

The bitterly cold condemnation made his jaw tighten hard with anger. The next time he saw the new Viscount Havenstock, the man would rue the day he'd been born. Mathias had no idea how the bastard had learned of his agreement with Sabine, but he was certain someone would have to hold him back to prevent him from doing considerable harm to Havenstock.

"I said I would ask Sabine to give you every consideration, and I did that."

"But you paid the lion's share of the bill like any man would for his mistress."

"I won't deny telling Sabine to send me a bill for any balance you were unable to pay. And if I'd known the *full extent* of your financial status, which *borders on the edge* of *poverty*, I would have convinced you to let me pay *the entire damn bill*," he snapped.

The moment she stiffened, he closed his eyes and drew in a deep breath. Losing his temper was a mistake. She was right. He'd bought her new wardrobe as if she were his mistress. He'd gone against her wishes without her knowledge, and he understood why she was so angry. Ophelia's cold fury made him realize if she'd been a man, they would have come to blows. She glared at him.

"I told you I wouldn't be your mistress, and yet you proceeded to treat me as if I were."

The contemptuous arch of her brow made him clench his jaw to avoid saying something that would only make matters worse. He hesitated for a long moment before clearing his throat before he met her gaze steadily.

"It was not my intent to do so," he said, struggling not to sound angry.

"And yet you did—something I'm certain you planned from the start."

"As I recall, I delivered the deed to Marymont and was on my way out the front door when you stopped me. Hardly the actions of a man intent on weaving a web of deceit to make you his mistress," he snarled. He immediately regretted his fierce response when she grew still as a statue. Slowly, she tilted her chin upward as she looked at him coldly.

"And it was a terrible mistake to invite a spider back into my parlor."

"A spider who remembered your desperation when you came to me with your original proposition." Mathias took a step toward her, expecting her to shy away, but she didn't. There was still a cast of pallor to her skin, but her anger had begun to restore a hint of color in her cheeks. "I wanted to prove to you that Havenstock was wrong, and I did that. As we discovered last night, you are capable of great passion."

"Last night was an error in judgment." Her acerbic words made his muscles knot with anger underlined with a sense of foreboding.

"An error—tell me, Ophelia, is this really about my contribution to your new wardrobe, or are you experiencing fear."

"Fear of what? Entering your bed again?"

"No, the fear of being human enough to experience— to want—something more than passion. The fear that you might actually consider it possible to marry…again."

Christ, what the hell was he doing mentioning the possibility she might marry someone? She flinched at his quiet words, and there was an air of vulnerability about her that aroused an urgent need to take her into his arms and comfort her. He buried the urge, knowing it would be a mistake to touch her. Instead, he clasped his hands behind his back as they balled up into tight fists.

It was bad enough he'd almost mentioned Chelmsford's name as a potential husband. The last thing he was going to do was push her in that direction. The thought triggered something in the back of his head while a voice cried out for him to stop speaking and simply leave.

"And I told you I had no intention of ever marrying again," she snapped bitterly.

"Your father's behavior might leave you with little choice…or worse, being forced to do something far more humiliating." Angered by her stubbornness, his words were brutal, almost cruel.

Ophelia immediately jerked her head back in fearful surprise. As he watched a multitude of emotions sweep across her lovely features, he experienced the urge to close the distance between them and shake her hard before pulling her into his arms. It was obvious she'd not contemplated the possibility of finding herself forced to deal with a man who might not be a gentleman. Scornful laughter echoed in the back of his head at the idea he was any more of a gentleman where she was concerned.

"Is that your way of suggesting I become your mistress?"

"I'm not suggesting anything. But I'll not deny I'd hoped we might enjoy each other's company going forward."

"I suppose that's not an unreasonable assumption considering how much I owe you," she said bitterly. "Exactly how many times am I expected to share your bed before my debt has been worked off?"

"I don't know. Why don't you tell me what you think you're worth?" Mathias snarled at the insinuation he was demanding payment in the form of bedding her. But it was the savagery of his words that made him mutter an oath as her entire body jerked as if he'd slapped her. *Christ Jesus*, what the hell was wrong with him.

"Get out, Mathias." The flat note in her voice caused a vise to tighten around his chest until he found it almost impossible to breathe. He pulled in a deep breath before bowing slightly in her direction.

"As you wish."

A moment later, he was striding out of the house and cursing himself for having coerced her into their bargain. He should have simply courted her as any other gentleman would have done—as Chelmsford would do. Anger pounded its way into his blood at the thought of the earl catering to Ophelia's every whim. He'd see the man in hell first.

The thought pulled him up short as he reached the sidewalk outside her door. Frozen in place, he tried to comprehend what his brain was telling him. It wasn't possible. He knew better than to become enthralled with any woman, let alone come to care for her.

With a snort of self-disgust, he moved forward. A round of exercise at the club would clear his head and put an end to this nonsense. It wasn't possible for him to care for Ophelia, let alone any woman for that matter. The mocking laughter in his mind at the thought sent despair crashing through him. Exercise might not work after all.

Chapter 11

Mathias stepped through the front door of Brooks, and with a curt nod at the clerk behind the desk, made his way through the club toward the Common Room. He couldn't remember ever having been in such a foul mood. He'd spent the last week sending a daily note to Ophelia, asking to see her, but she'd not replied to a single one. Her refusal to respond emphasized the depth of her outrage.

He didn't know what irritated him the most, his error in having ignored her wishes or her refusal to accept his remorse at injuring her. Not even Miriam had ever aroused such an intense frustration in him. Perhaps worst of all was the sense of desperation taking hold of him. It was an emotion he'd never experienced with any woman, and he didn't like it. He didn't like it at all.

The entire situation was wearing on him to the point that even Charles had noticed how brusque his manner had become. His friends had learned even more quickly how to avoid any mention of Ophelia. Despite their silence, the amusement on their faces, especially those who were married, was another trial he'd been forced to endure.

Of all his friends, Percy and Constance had restrained their amusement the most. The Rockwood siblings had even discretely informed him when they knew of an event Ophelia would be attending. Last night, he'd specifically attended the Beaumont event after Percy had mentioned Ophelia would be present.

When she'd arrived on the arm of Chelmsford last night, Mathias's reaction had not been one he enjoyed. As he'd watched the earl's attentive, almost possessive manner with Ophelia, a raw fury had assaulted him. Every time the earl had pulled her away from the numerous suitors gathering around her, Mathias's anger had grown. Percy and Rhea had been at the affair, and Percy had quietly urged him to approach her.

When he'd finally taken his friend's advice, the result had been a humiliating one. The moment her gaze had met his, her icy contempt had made him turn and walk away. As if his humiliation wasn't enough, the incident had resulted in his insides being twisted into painful knots. It was as if a sparring partner had knocked him to the mat with a sharp jab to his stomach.

Tonight he'd tried once more to have a moment alone with her, but Chelmsford had made every effort to occupy her attention whenever the man saw him approach Ophelia. He was convinced she'd enlisted the earl's help in keeping him at bay. When an opportunity finally did open for him to ask her to dance, Ophelia's icy gaze had barely met his before she simply turned her back on him.

This time his humiliation had been observed by several members of the Set, and it had been one of the most unpleasant experiences of his life. Not because others had witnessed Ophelia's snub, but because her reaction had filled him with a level of despair, he'd never known before.

Until now, he'd thought it would simply be a matter of days before he could heal the breach between them. After tonight, he was no longer so optimistic. His actions had done more damage than he'd ever thought possible. He'd not been thinking at all when he'd paid the balance of Ophelia's bill. Now he was suffering the fires of hell because of his arrogance and refusal to heed Ophelia's wishes.

His suffering was made even worse whenever he saw Ophelia smiling up at Chelmsford. The man was working hard to win her. The fact wasn't lost on him that the earl might succeed in his quest before Mathias could convince Ophelia to forgive him. The knowledge deepened his dark mood this evening. The woman would no doubt take pleasure in knowing he was pining after her. At the thought, Mathias drew up short and came to an abrupt halt. Damnation. He *wasn't* pining for the woman. He was lusting after her. It wasn't anything more than that.

A cackling laugh echoed in the back of his head, and he exhaled a loud breath of air at the thoughts trying to push their way forward into his consciousness. Ignoring the whispers deep in the back of his mind, he continued along the hall toward the Common Room. He'd failed to have Baxter order a bottle of his favorite cognac at Thornbury House and had been forced to come to the club for a snifter.

As he approached the billiards room, loud laughter spilled out into the hall. He glanced into the room as he passed the door, but didn't stop. His cursory glance didn't fully sink in until he was several steps further down the hall and drew up short. A member who had been following him nodded a silent greeting as Mathias retraced his steps to the door of the billiards room.

Four men were gathered around the green worst-covered billiard table, good-naturedly taunting a man lining up to take a shot. His gaze settled on one man, standing slightly back from the other men. What the devil was Havenstock doing at Brooks? He knew the man wasn't a member, as he'd checked several days ago in his effort to seek the man out.

Baron Lansdale leaned his head back slightly to say something to Havenstock, who laughed at whatever the baron had said. Mathias narrowed his gaze at the two men. Lansdale wasn't known for being all that bright when it came to the company he kept, and tonight made that obvious. Until now, Mathias failed to find Havenstock in a somewhat secluded venue, short of going to the man's home. He'd not wanted to create an incident that dozens of people would be privy too. But he also knew enough about Havenstock to know it would be best to have one or two witnesses to any exchange in the event the viscount tried to cause trouble.

The clack of a billiard ball being hit echoed in the room, and the man who'd taken the shot straightened upright. Mathias immediately recognized Viscount Beaumont. On numerous occasions, the man had visited Charles at Thornbury House to discuss legislation proposed in Parliament. Slowly entering the room, he saw Beaumont glance his way then looked back with a welcoming grin.

"Gilchrist, how are you? Have you come to see Harrows here put my skills to shame at billiards?"

At the friendly greeting, Mathias moved around the table to shake Beaumont's hand in greeting. Beside the man, Viscount Harrows smiled his greeting as he extended his hand.

"Hello, Gilchrist. It's been a while." As Lord Harrows shook his hand, Mathias nodded.

"Do you know everyone here, Gilchrist?" Beaumont asked as he waved his hand in the direction of the other men. "Timothy Longwood, a finer solicitor you'll not find in the city. Lord Lansdale and Lord Havenstock."

All three men stepped forward to shake his hand. Havenstock was the last to extend his hand, but Mathias ignored it as he tilted his head to look at the wound on the viscount's head.

"That's quite a nasty bruise you have there," Mathias said as he nodded toward the man's head. "How did it happen?"

His hand still extended, Havenstock flushed slightly when Mathias continued to ignore his offer of greeting. The man's lips thinned with anger, and he glared at Mathias.

"I had a slight accident."

"It must have been quite a fall. It's almost a week old, isn't it?" Slowly moving his gaze from Havenstock's injury to meet the man's gaze, Mathias eyed the man coldly. The jovial atmosphere in the room had changed dramatically as the small group shifted uncomfortably at his open antipathy for Havenstock.

"It was."

"As I understand it, Viscountess Havenstock used a clock to administer the blow." At the sardonic amusement in his voice, the viscount stiffened and glared at him in outrage.

"What lies has that woman been spreading?"

"I'm unaware of any lies the lady in question has been sharing."

"Clearly, she has, or you wouldn't have insulted me."

"As I said, Lady Havenstock has not been spreading lies. In fact, you owe her a debt of gratitude for remaining silent about your assaulting her," Mathias said in a soft, icy voice.

The air in the room changed again as the demeanor of the men in the room expressed growing disapproval. To Lansdale's credit, he'd stepped away from Havenstock.

"I think Lady Havenstock has been overly dramatic in whatever she's told you, sir."

"No, I don't think so." Mathias narrowed his gaze at the man. "In fact, I happen to know that you've been trying to take advantage of the lady for quite some time."

"That's absurd," Havenstock huffed.

"Just as it's absurd not to believe Lady Havenstock hit you upside the head with a clock." Mathias arched his eyebrow at the man, who, despite a flash of fear in his gaze, snorted with laughter.

"Now you truly are indulging in fantasy, sir."

"I don't invest my time in fairy tales, Havenstock. I believe in facts. The lady rejected your advances with a clock to the side of your head, rendering you unconscious." Mathias nodded toward Havenstock's head wound. "It's also a fact I arrived moments after she'd done so, and you were being loaded into your carriage like a heavy sack of flour."

The viscount flinched and looked around at the faces of the men watching the argument. Mathias didn't have to see their faces to know Havenstock was being silently condemned for his behavior. The man's throat bobbed in an obvious effort to find his voice, but Mathias didn't allow him to speak.

"I've also discovered several things about you, Havenstock, that I don't like. You've abused your fiduciary control of the monies your father left Lady Havenstock."

"That's a lie. I've done everything in my power to ensure Ophelia's investments are monitored closely and that her financial situation is sound."

"Oh, I'm not questioning your management of her finances. I'm referring to the fact that you've refused to give her access to any of the funds that rightfully belong to her."

"You don't know what you're talking about, Gilchrist. Ophelia simply has to ask, and I'm happy to provide her with whatever monies she needs."

"As long as she agrees to share your bed, correct?" Mathias said softly. Behind him, Harrows uttered an oath of disapproval, and he saw Lansdale put even more distance between him and Havenstock.

"Take care, Gilchrist," the man snarled. "I'll not have my good name sullied by the likes of you."

"You seem to forget who my brother is, Havenstock."

"I know who your brother is, but you've no right to say things that aren't true."

"So, Lady Havenstock simply hit you with that porcelain clock for no reason at all." The man's mouth moved as he tried to respond. Mathias narrowed his gaze at him. "I'm going to say this one time only, Havenstock. Give Ophelia complete control over her finances immediately and *without* any conditions, or I'll see to it you're run out of polite society. Is that clear?"

Fury tightened Havenstock's mouth in a hard line, but Mathias saw the fearful resignation in the man's eyes. The viscount's only response was a nod of compliance. Satisfied he'd made his case, Mathias said goodbye to the other men in the room and headed toward the door. He paused just inside the room and turned around.

"Oh, and Havenstock. If you ever go near Ophelia again, I'll make you wish you'd never been born. I won't kill you, but I'll make you wish I had."

Despite his fury, Havenstock still blanched. As Mathias waited, the man sharply jerked his head in understanding. Satisfied he'd made his point clear, Mathias nodded at the rest of the small party and walked back out into the hall to continue his way toward the Common Room.

Satisfaction barreled through him as he remembered how his parting words had made the color drain from Havenstock's face. He'd have the family solicitor check into Havenstock's finances in a few days to ensure the man returned control of Ophelia's monies to her.

Only a few members were sitting in the Common Room, and Mathias noted the time on the grandfather clock standing near the fireplace. It wasn't even nine o'clock, which meant the club's ranks wouldn't expand until much later in the evening. The moment he took a seat in a large wing-back chair, a footman was at his side.

"Good evening, Mr. Gilchrist. Would you like me to bring you something?"

"Napoleon cognac."

"Certainly, sir."

As the footman walked away, Mathias leaned back into the chair and closed his eyes. No sooner had he done so than an image of Ophelia filled his head. The memory of her cries of delight when he'd made love to her was enough to stir his cock to life. His eyes opened quickly as he pushed aside the memory of her silky skin against his. The footman returned with a snifter of cognac, and he accepted the glass with a nod of thanks.

He took a slow drink of the amber liquid and enjoyed the subtle hints of cinnamon and vanilla mixed with the taste of dried fruits. The expensive liquor was one of his few vices, and he savored the cognac as it danced across his tongue almost as sweetly as the taste of Ophelia's mouth when she'd kissed him so passionately the other night.

Mathias released a grunt of disgust at the fanciful thought. Ophelia's lips weren't the first woman's he'd ever tasted, and they wouldn't be the last. A voice in the back of his head shouted a harsh denial that Mathias immediately crushed into silence. Instead of taking a second sip of his cognac, he tossed the whole thing down his throat in one gulp.

He knew connoisseurs would view it as an insult to the richness of the brandy, but he'd lost his appetite for savoring the expensive drink. With a sharp gesture at the footman, he ordered a bottle of whiskey instead. When it arrived less than a minute later, he poured himself more than two fingers of the Scotch into his glass. If it was the last thing he did tonight, he'd drink himself blind until every thought of Ophelia was obliterated from his memory.

"It's the truth." Percy Rockwood barely contained his laughter as he met his friend's amazed expression. When it was obvious he'd completely hoodwinked the other man, he grinned. "When are you going to learn to always question what I tell you, Charles?"

The Earl of Thornbury scowled at his friend before a good-natured smile lightened his handsome features.

"You're a master at spinning tales and exploiting the gullibility of people, Percy." At the compliment, Percy grinned, but before he could reply, Charles shook his head. "But we both know I'm rarely one of your victims. Your story was believable because the lady in question has a reputation for bawdy bedroom skills, or so I've heard."

"You say that as if you know more than you're willing to admit. "

"A gentleman never speaks out of turn where a lady is involved."

"And in this case?

"As I said, a gentleman—"

"Never speaks out of turn." Percy's cheerful irreverence made Charles grin broadly as he clapped Percy on the shoulder.

"Come along. I know a bottle of good cognac is waiting for us in the Common Room."

Percy followed his friend through the club in the direction of the main gathering place, where members discussed politics, among other things. Most of the club's membership was rooted in the Whig Party before the political organization had transformed itself into the Liberal Unionist Party. As they entered the room with its grouping of chairs forming small conversation areas, a loud, belligerent voice exploded in the air, demanding more whiskey.

Charles came to an abrupt halt at the shout, and Percy's forward momentum sent him crashing into his friend's back. The force of the impact made Charles stagger forward a few steps before he regained his balance. Without a glance over his shoulder, the earl crossed the floor to where a pair of legs were stretched out in a haphazard sprawl.

"What the devil are you bellowing about?" Charles stood glaring down at Mathias, who was slouched in his chair. His younger brother looked up and narrowed his gaze at Charles.

"I aaked them for another bottle of whiskey."

"*Christ almighty.*" Charles's eyes widened with dismayed surprise. "You're drunk, little brother."

"Yerrr, riight, I am." Mathias raised an empty glass at his brother in a drunken gesture. "Where the devil is my whiskey?"

At his brother's bellow, Charles directed a look of disbelief and amazement at Percy. Uncertain what to do, Percy shrugged and threw his hands up in the air in a silent gesture of helpless bewilderment. Mathias bellowed for his whiskey again, and Charles jerked his head back to look down at his brother.

"That's quite enough, Mathias." Charles's tone was harsh and authoritative.

Percy found himself straightening his back at his friend's command. Mathias met his brother's gaze, then looked away with a grunt.

"Go away, Charles." The slurred speech made the earl's lips thin with anger.

"I'm taking you home." The earl raised his hand as Mathias started to protest. "Not another word. Whatever her name is, she's not worth this."

Mathias was out of his chair in a flash of movement to stand swaying in front of his brother. Percy immediately leaped forward to keep the man from doing something he'd regret in the morning. As he gripped Mathias's arm, Percy jerked slightly as a small wave of the *an dara sealladh* swept over him. It lasted only a split second, but it was enough to fill his head with an image of Mathias, half-dressed, kissing Ophelia with great passion.

As the picture faded from his head, Percy breathed a silent sigh of relief. The last thing he wanted was to be privy to any intimate moments between the man and Ophelia. Percy arched his eyebrow at Mathias, who was glaring at his brother over Percy's shoulder. All too aware of Charles's intense displeasure, Percy patted Mathias on the back.

"Come on, old man. Let Charles and me take you home. You can drink in your bedroom if you like and fall asleep there."

Mathias continued to glare at his brother before his head bobbed in an abrupt jerk. With a drunken lurch, the younger man turned around to grab his coat and the tie he'd removed and flung over the arm of his chair. The moment Mathias bent forward to gather his things, he almost fell.

Hesitant to touch his arm again, Percy looked at his friend and tipped his head at Charles's brother with a shake of his head. Gray eyes widening slightly, the earl quickly moved to the other side of his younger brother. In an affectionate gesture, he squeezed Mathias's shoulder and gently took the clothing out of his brother's hand.

"It will be all right, Mathias."

At his brother's quiet words, the younger man stared down at the floor for a long moment, and Percy recognized that look of despair. The man was in love with Ophelia. Sympathetic to the man's pain, he watched in silence as Mathias staggered forward. Charles immediately grabbed his brother's arm to keep him from falling, and Percy half expected Mathias to jerk away. To his surprise, Mathias allowed his brother to guide him out of the room and through the building to the establishment's front door.

"She won't see me, Charles," Mathias muttered in a voice filled with pain.

"We'll talk about it tomorrow. For the moment, you need to be in bed."

Certain the earl could deal with Mathias's drunken stagger, Percy quickly walked ahead of them to the exit to ensure Charles's carriage was waiting for them. In less than five minutes, they were on their way to Thornbury House. When they reached the residence, Percy summoned a footman to assist Charles in helping his brother up the stairs to his room. As Percy watched his friend skillfully maneuver and guide his brother up to the second floor, Charles glanced over his shoulder.

"There's some brandy in the study. Pour yourself a drink. I'll be down in a few minutes."

Percy followed his friend's instructions, and true to his word, Charles strode into the study a short time later. He made his way toward the liquor cart to pour himself a drink. Never one to hedge his questions, Charles turned to meet Percy's gaze.

"You saw something." It was an emphatic statement.

Percy winced slightly at the unspoken demand for what he'd seen. Outside of his family, only his close friends knew the extent of his true ability when it came to the *an dara sealladh*. Charles was one of them. As roommates at Eton, his friend had been privy to several episodes Percy had experienced at school.

The first one had been particularly debilitating as the vision had occurred at the time of his father's death. If not for Charles, he might have injured himself falling down a flight of stairs. As a result, he'd been forced to take Charles into his confidence, and his friend had guarded his secret throughout their school years and even beyond.

"Not much, just a glimpse of Mathias with Ophelia." Percy deliberately omitted the full details. But Charles intuitively understood more than Percy realized, as his friend sighed.

"This is as bad as when Miriam betrayed him." Charles frowned. "Actually, worse. Mathias rarely drinks. The only other time I've seen him this drunk was when he found Miriam in my bed several years ago."

"He said Ophelia won't see him. Did he tell you why?"

"Something about Sabine and a bill. The only thing I could make heads or tails of was a bargain he made with the lady in question. Apparently, he had a secret arrangement with Madame Sabine to pay a major portion of Lady Havenstock's dress bill.

"*Christ Jesus.*" Percy stared at his friend in shocked disbelief. "No wonder she won't see him. Although she's closest to Louisa, the family is quite fond of her, and we've known her since childhood. Ophelia isn't the type of woman who would accept anything from a man unless he was her husband."

"The question now is how does he make amends?" Charles looked down into his glass with intense concentration on his dark, brooding features.

"I highly advise *against* interfering in this whole thing. Trust me. I learned that lesson with Patience."

Percy shook his head vigorously as he remembered how Patience had backed him into a corner when he'd fallen in love with Rhea. His sister had gained the upper hand in that particular argument. Not that he minded because he'd won Rhea's heart in the end.

"There are things we can do to nudge the matter in the right direction." Charles shrugged his shoulders.

"Oh, there's no *we* in this conversation at all." Percy waved his hand in a negative gesture. "I've learned that interfering in the love interests of others will only bring you headaches."

"I'm not talking about *you* interfering." Charles raised his head with a sly smile. It made him look a great deal like the boy Percy had roomed with years ago. "Actually, I'm thinking about your sisters."

"Why do I have a feeling you're going to have me ask them to interfere?"

"I would never suggest that. However, making your sisters think it was *their* idea…"

"In other words, tell them about the situation and tell them not to interfere."

"Precisely. If there's one thing I know about your sisters, it's that the minute you tell them *not* to do something, they invariably do exactly that." Charles grinned at him.

"I cannot deny that," Percy said with a chuckle. "I'll mention Mathias's drinking bout tomorrow to Louisa. She'll find a way to address the situation."

"Excellent." Charles grinned as he took another drink of his brandy.

"Speaking of interference, have you heard the latest about Lady Beatrice?" Percy asked quietly.

"No."

The short, sharp reply made Percy grimace. Charles finished the rest of his drink in one gulp, then turned to refill his glass. When he turned around, his expression was neutral, almost disinterested.

"Gossip from America, I presume."

Despite the lazy drawl in Charles's voice, Percy knew his friend well. Whatever had happened between the couple, their relationship had ended with Beatrice sailing off to

America on the arm of a steel magnate. He cleared his throat softly and shook his head.

"It seems her husband died suddenly, and Beatrice came home a wealthy woman. I just remembered the two of you seemed quite close at one time." Percy rolled his shoulders in a nonchalant gesture.

"As I recall, I escorted her to one or two soirees, but it was never anything to remark upon." Charles took another sip of his brandy without any display of emotion other than disinterest.

"She has a son." Percy looked down at his drink. "He reminds me of you when we were first at Eaton."

With a gentle motion of his hand, Percy swirled the whiskey in his glass before he raised his head to meet his friend's unreadable gaze. The sharp, angular planes of Charles's profile were frozen as if he were a statue. Despite his inability to read his friend's thoughts, Percy the tension holding his friend rigid was quite visible. Charles clearly hadn't known about Beatrice's son. Aware that he'd pried into a matter he shouldn't have, Percy quickly finished his drink and rose from his chair.

"I should be going. Rhea is certain to be home by now from that new play at the Lyceum." The statement made Percy's friend nod with understanding before he grimaced and turned to stare down at the liquor sideboard.

"I envy you, Percy."

Startled by his friend's quietly worded statement, Percy tipped his head to one side in puzzlement.

"What the devil do you have to be envious of?"

"You found a wife who adores you and doesn't protest when you go out with your friends."

"Actually, I think Rhea deliberately attends parties or events she knows I'll detest so she can encourage me to spend an evening with friends while she's out of the house."

Percy smiled as an image of his wife filled his head. Charles was right. He was a man to be envied. His friend abruptly set his glass on top of the liquor cart and turned back to him. Charles's cheerful smile made it appear as if he didn't have a care in the world.

"As I said, I envy you. Rhea is an exception to the rule when it comes to wives. A situation I have no intention of exploring anytime soon."

"I thought the same thing, but look how things turned out for me." At the amused note in Percy's voice, his friend arched an eyebrow as if to say Percy had lost all use of his faculties.

"And here I thought your sisters were the only matchmakers in your family."

"I lack the superb skill my sisters possess. Give them the word, and they'll work hard to weave their magic."

"Then, if there should be any sly comments regarding my lack of a countess, the next time I see any of your sisters, I can guarantee you will *not* enjoy our next exercise in the boxing ring at the club."

"After the sound beating I took the other morning, I'll heed your warning quite diligently." Percy raised his hands in a muted form of surrender as he laughed, then stepped forward to shake his friend's hand. "I'll see you soon. And I'll be certain to drop some subtle hints to Constance and Louisa. I think they'll put a plan of action into motion within hours of my dropping hints."

Charles nodded his head as he shook Percy's hand. While his friend's expression was one of amusement, Percy could tell there were turbulent emotions running deep beneath the surface. Emotions that centered on Lady Beatrice, and something told Percy that the woman wouldn't be happy to see Charles headed her way.

Mathias suppressed a groan as he entered the breakfast room to see Charles at the breakfast table. He had a miserable headache, and he was in no mood to talk. In fact, he'd hoped his brother would have left already for his usual morning ride. Last night was mostly a blur, and Mathias wasn't eager to be subjected to a round of questions this morning. As Mathias sat down at the table, his stomach lurched in protest as his brother added haddock to his plate.

"Jeremey, would you ask Mrs. Harper to fix me some tea, please?" Mathias said as he looked in the footman's direction.

The servant nodded and hastened out of the room. Trying to breathe through his mouth to avoid the smell of his brother's fish, he reached for a piece of toast and the butter. Determined to overcome the nausea the haddock was causing, Mathias concentrated on the warm smell of the piece of toast he was spreading with butter. Charles was reading the newspaper as he ate.

"You look like you found the wrong side of the bottle last night, little brother." Charles didn't look up from his paper.

"I'm fine," Mathias mumbled as he took a bite of his toast.

"Really? Then your constitution is quite remarkable given the amount of drink you must have consumed last night." Charles slowly lowered the newspaper to narrow his gaze on Mathias. "Do you recall bellowing for more whiskey at the club as if you were in an East End pub?"

"Vaguely," he lied as he tried to remember how loud he'd been.

"Drowning your sorrows in a bottle is the last thing you should do, Mathias." The quiet words made him stiffen. How much had he told his brother last night?

"I wasn't drowning my sorrows," he snapped, instantly regretting the harsh sound of his voice as it made his head pound even more.

"I see."

Charles returned to his paper, and Mathias gratefully accepted the tea the footman had brought him. He added a small amount of sugar and milk before he took a drink of the hot brew.

"What are you going to do about it?" Charles's voice echoed out from behind the newspaper, and Mathias froze in the middle of lowering his cup to its saucer. It took him several seconds to slowly set the cup down.

"Do about what?" The pounding in his head increased as he sought to head off the conversation his brother seemed on the verge of starting.

"I'm not in the mood to play games with you this morning, Mathias." The paper slowly dropped to reveal Charles's scowl of irritation. "I asked you a question. What are you going to do about it?"

"Nothing."

"Nothing?"

Charles carefully folded his paper and dropped it on the table next to his place setting. He leaned back in his chair, allowing the armrest to support his elbow as he rubbed his chin in a contemplative manner. Ignoring his brother's stare, Mathias took another bite of his toast and stared down at his plate.

"Do you love her?"

The quiet question made Mathias jerk his head toward his brother, who was studying him with curiosity. For days now, he'd refused to believe he was in love with Ophelia. Now his brother was forcing him to accept the truth. Mathias met his brother's gaze as the harsh reality of his situation crashed over him with the strength of an angry wave in a stormy sea. The understanding in Charles's blue eyes was sympathetic as the earl nodded.

"It appears you've just had a revelation as to your feelings for the lady in question."

His brother's quiet observation made Mathias jerk his head in the affirmative. Closing his eyes, he slouched back in his chair and struggled with the magnitude of what he'd done. Not once since Miriam's betrayal had Mathias allowed himself to become emotionally attached to any woman. He indulged in pleasant liaisons, but he'd always walked away without looking back. But Ophelia had slipped past all the barriers he'd erected over the years.

"Then you have one of two choices, little brother. Either take action or forget her." The challenge in his brother's harsh words sliced through the raw emotions rising to the surface.

"It's not that simple," he bit out between clenched teeth as he ignored the pounding in his head.

"It *is* that simple, Mathias." The confidence in his brother's voice made him sit up and glare at his brother.

"Do you honestly think I'd be sitting here if I knew of a way to make things right between us?"

"*Christ Jesus.* For a man who always has an answer when it comes to solving *my* problems, one would think you'd be able to solve one of your own," Charles said in a disgusted voice. "Fight for her, *damn it.*"

"Who the hell are you to give me advice? As I recall, I tried to convince you to go after Beatrice, but you refused," he said in a savagely bitter voice. "All I'm doing is following in your footsteps."

Charles's features hardened into a stony façade. The steely glint of fury in his brother's eyes warned Mathias there would be hell to pay if he said one more word. His brother's mouth thinned with anger as he narrowed his gaze at Mathias.

"This conversation isn't about my past. It's about how you resolve the situation between you and Lady Havenstock." Charles's voice was flat and emotionless as he met Mathias's gaze.

With a jerk, his brother shoved his chair out from under him to stand up, then make his way to the door. Charles paused for a moment in the doorway of the dining room and looked over his shoulder.

"The choice is yours, Mathias. Don't make one you might regret." It was his brother's final parting shot as he left the breakfast room, leaving Mathias to consider his own future.

Chapter 12

We had to carry the man out of Brooks." Percy dropped his gaze at the appalled expressions on his sisters' faces. It was all he could do not to laugh.

When Charles had suggested Percy might be able to help Mathias reconcile with Ophelia, it had been an emphatic no to meddling in the affair. But the moment Charles had suggested he casually mention the incident to his sisters, Percy knew it was a task he'd be all too happy to place at his sisters' feet. The Rockwood women were far more skilled when it came to match-making than he would ever be. And if it helped Ophelia find some happiness, all the better.

"Percy, are you listening to us?" Clearly exasperated, Louisa glared at him when he looked up from the book he'd been reading when Rhea and his sisters had entered the salon.

"What?" He met his youngest sister's gaze with feigned puzzlement.

"Mathias never drinks to the extreme. What in heaven's—"

The moment Louisa halted in mid-sentence, he quirked an eyebrow at her, but she waved her hand at him in a dismissive gesture before she turned away from him to look at Constance and Patience. He returned his gaze back to his book, merely pretending to read as he surreptitiously watched the small plotting session begin.

"He's in love with Ophelia," Louisa exclaimed with confidence.

"How on earth do you know that?" While there was a dubious note in Constance's voice at the youngest of the Rockwoods statement, Percy knew she was already partially convinced Louisa was right in her declaration.

"Because the only time he's ever imbibed to the point of needing to be carried out of any establishment was when Miriam…oh what is her name…she led Mathias on just to throw her cup at Charles." Louisa turned back to Percy, and he quickly turned the page of his book as if he was completely impervious to the conversation.

"What was that woman's name, Percy?" At Louisa's question, he kept his eyes focused on the book he'd not read a word of since his sisters had entered the room.

"Hmm?" he said without looking up.

"I asked you the name of the woman who broke Mathias's heart several years ago." Louisa rolled her eyes at him as she waited for an answer. As if pondering the question, he feigned a puzzled frown.

"Miriam…Miriam Wadsworth?"

"Yes, her," Louisa exclaimed with triumphant contempt. "She married some poor viscount not long afterward, and just in time, it seemed as she was enceinte not long afterward."

"Are you talking about Lady Liddle?" Patience asked as she entered the parlor during his reply to Louisa.

"Yes, Lady Liddle," Louisa said with disgust. "I never did like her, but when she broke Mathias's heart, I wanted to push her head into a bowl of punch."

It was a struggle, but Percy managed not to make a sound as he swallowed his laughter. As always, his youngest sister was a fierce champion of those she cared about. Louisa had always had a soft spot for Mathias, and in the past, he'd often wondered if Louisa had ever thought herself in love with the man. If she had, it was a shame she'd married Devin. The thought of his brother-in-law made his mouth tighten with suppressed anger.

Despite the rest of the family's opinion, he was certain he was the only one of his siblings who knew the truth about Louisa's marriage. He'd always like Devin, but a few weeks before the fire at Westbrook Farms, the an dara sealladh had shown him images of Devin with another woman. Rhea was the only one he'd told about what he'd seen, and she'd been a wise counsel.

Every time he'd debated whether to confront the man or speak to his sister, his thoughtful, compassionate wife had told him not to. But the images he'd seen had made it difficult for him to treat his brother-in-law as if he'd seen nothing. His vision had made him believe the man had betrayed his sister at some point in their marriage. It was a betrayal he was certain Louisa was oblivious to until shortly before the fire that claimed Devin's life and his brother Caleb.

After Devin's death, he'd been grateful he'd not shared his suspicions with Louisa. The grief that had consumed her for more than two years now demonstrated how much she'd loved her husband. It would have been cruel to tell her of Devin's betrayal. In the end, he'd been thankful for Rhea's threats of banishment from their bedroom if he breathed even one word to either his sister or her husband.

"Oh, I don't think we should, Louisa." The uncertainty in Patience's voice pulled him out of his contemplation, and he looked up from his book to see his sisters huddled together.

"Of course we should," Louisa exclaimed as she dismissed her sister's doubts. "Don't you agree, Constance?"

"But what if she doesn't love him, Louisa?" The middle of his three sisters expressed her doubts as well. "While I agree with you that Mathias cares for Ophelia, won't it make it harder for him if she doesn't return his affections?"

"Possibly, but I know Ophelia. She's blossomed recently, and that's Mathias's doing. You didn't see the way she looked at him that night at the opera. If she wasn't in love with him then, she was on the verge of it."

"But hasn't she been seen with the Earl of Chelmsford for the past week? I heard just the other day that the man was seriously considering offering for her."

"Oh dear lord, then we must move quickly. I'm convinced Ophelia's in love with Mathias, and whatever falling out the two of them have had, I'm certain it can be overcome." Louisa eyed her sisters with an obvious determination to enlist their help in reuniting the two estranged lovers. With a slow nod of her head, Constance agreed. Patience, however, shook her head with regret.

"I cannot, Louisa. I've promised Julian I'd not meddle anymore when he found out I'd helped Constance with the arrangements for Lady Kimbolton to visit the orphanage, at the same time Lord Hubbard and the rest of the board of directors were there for their monthly meeting."

"Do nae tell me ye are interfering in someone else's affairs, Patience MacTavish," the displeasure in her husband's voice made his sister wince. The tall Scotsman towered over his wife as he eyed her with irritation.

"I promised you I wouldn't, and I was refusing to do so." Her hand touched her husband's arm in reassurance. Satisfied with his wife's reply, his brother-in-law's nodded. Julian's complacency disappeared a second later as Patience met his gaze with an impish smile. "After all, I seem to recall you made a promise to me as well."

"Aye," he said with a grimace before he grinned down at her. "But ye will have to think of something else tae make me promise after tonight, m'eudail."

At the blush rising in his sister's cheek, Percy experienced a small wave of the an dara sealladh sweep through him, and an image of Patience heavy with child made him grin as he studied his sister. Almost as if she'd read his mind, his sister's gaze suddenly met his. Percy quickly nodded his understanding not to reveal what he'd seen. Instead, he simply beamed at her with pleasure.

"What are you looking so happy about, Percy Rockwood?" A suspicious note in Louisa's voice made him look at his sister as he caught Rhea entering the room.

"The fact that my wife has finally arrived," he quipped as he set his book aside and rose to meet Rhea halfway across the room. "Can a man not be happy to see the woman he adores?"

As he kissed his wife's cheek, he saw Louisa frown slightly before her suspicion was replaced with a haunted look that made him want to hug her tight. The instant she realized he was watching her, Louisa's pain vanished. Rhea's hand squeezed his arm, and as he met her questioning gaze, he simply smiled.

The sound of children's voices filled the air as the youngest members of the Rockwood family swept into the room, followed by his aunt. A brief instant later, Sebastian and Helen arrived, and the Rockwood clan was complete. Over the cacophony of voices, Julian cleared his throat loudly. It took several more times for the Scotsman to gain everyone's attention. When everyone had turned toward them, he carried Patience's hand to his mouth.

"I believe Patience has something she'd like to say." Julian smiled down at his wife with a look of pride and happiness. His obvious adoration made Patience's cheeks filled with color as she returned his smile. Still smiling, she turned her head toward the rest of the family.

"Julian and I intend to expand the Rockwood family ranks sometime next spring."

For a moment, everyone stared at the beaming couple in astonishment before the room erupted with cries of happiness and excitement. The family quickly gathered around the couple, exchanging hugs and Sebastian shaking Julian's hand. When he didn't react with surprise, Rhea glanced at him with amusement.

"You knew already, didn't you?" At her question, he shrugged slightly and grinned.

"Actually, not until a few moments ago." His words made Rhea shake her head as she kissed his cheek. With her hand in his, she pulled him toward the happy couple.

Ophelia looked up from her needlepoint at the sound of voices in the hall. A moment later, her friends, Viscountess Westbrook and the Countess of Lyndham entered the room. Although their visit was unexpected, she was delighted to see her friends. Louisa's smile was cheerful as she moved forward to greet her with a hug. Constance quickly followed suit. As her friends seated themselves, Ophelia quietly asked Taggert to bring tea.

"Oh, no, we can't stay long. We have an appointment at Madame Sabine's, and I don't want to be late." Louisa waved her hand slightly as she rejected the offer. "Although I know Sebastian will chide me for the expense.

The mention of Sabine made Ophelia stiffen as she met her friend's gaze. Louisa smiled at her pleasantly and gave no sign that to make Ophelia think the viscountess knew anything about Mathias's actions. Seated across from her sister, Constance laughed.

"I highly doubt that. Sebastian isn't about to scold you as it's been a long time since you visited Sabine."

"Sebastian worries too much. All of you do," Louisa said with a laugh, but the warmth in her gaze as she looked at her sister said she appreciated how much her family cared for her. "Actually, I'm a bit worried Sabine will protest my lack of ball gowns, but I only require one for when Aunt Matilda hosts the gathering of the clans at the first of the year."

"When are you leaving for Callendar Abbey?"

"Saturday, I hope. It will depend on Madame Sabine and how quickly she can have my new dresses ready. I only intend to order a few things, but I have a feeling she'll insist on one or two more gowns than I really need, which the woman will know I'll not be able to refuse."

Ophelia smiled at Louisa's rueful confession. Although it had only been a week since she'd seen her friend, the relaxed, spirited demeanor of the youngest member of the Rockwood clan's reflected the Louisa of their childhood. It delighted her to see her friend's grief slowly lifting off of her.

"I think it unlikely Madame Sabine will override any objections you have, Louisa."

"I agree," Constance said with an unladylike snort of laughter. "Even as a child, you rarely allowed any of us to hold rule over you."

"Am I really that bad?" Louisa made a pretense of looking aghast before she laughed. "Yes, I suppose I am."

"Lucien and I are attending the Sherrington affair this evening," Constance said as she looked at Ophelia. "Will we see you there?"

"I had thought I'd stay home this evening, but Gid— Lord Chelmsford insisted I attend with him as my escort."

"Constance tells me the man is quite enthralled with you. She says he's always at your side." Louisa tipped her head to one side and pinned Ophelia with a look of assessment. "He's considered quite the catch."

"I have no interest in catching anyone," she said firmly as she met her friend's curious gaze.

"I have a feeling Chelmsford might have something to say about that subject, Ophelia." The teasing note in Constance's voice made her smile.

"Lord Chelmsford is very charming, but as I've mentioned in the past, I'll not marry again."

"What about Mathias?"

Louisa's question threw her off-balance, even though she should have known his name would eventually come up in their conversation. Since that terrible day Edgar had assaulted her, she'd done everything she could to forget Mathias. A part of her understood his motives had been well-intentioned, even considerate. Every day he sent a note asking for her forgiveness. The first of his notes had been autocratic in tone, but the missives had grown more somber in his request for forgiveness with each passing day. Most of all, his words had seemed heartfelt and sincere.

But it was impossible to trust the sincerity of his words when he'd betrayed her trust so easily. She'd thought herself free of any obligation to Mathias, but she'd been wrong. It made the one night in his bed far more painful than she'd thought possible. She'd discovered her ability to give and receive passion in his arms, only to find those few hours cheapened by his actions.

Uncertain how to frame her reply to Louisa's question, Ophelia wished she had the tea service in front of her. It would have been easy to offer her friends a fresh cup before diverting the conversation in a different direction. Although she knew full well, it would only be a temporary distraction, as Louisa could be quite tenacious. Her friend arched her eyebrow at her when Ophelia didn't answer the question. Slightly flustered, she shook her head.

"What do you mean? I haven't seen Mathias for some time now." Her response made Louisa roll her eyes.

"It means exactly that. How could you possibly choose Chelmsford over Mathias?"

"I haven't chosen anyone over Mathias. To say such a thing would mean Mathias and I had some sort of understanding." Ophelia frowned as she remembered the agreement they'd made, but it wasn't the same thing.

"Well, whatever has caused a rift between you, it's made Mathias excessively morose. In fact, just the other night, the man drank himself into a stupor, leaving Percy and Charles to carry him home," Louisa sniffed with irritation as she glared at Ophelia. "There's only been one other time Mathias has ever done such a thing, and that was when Miriam Wadsworth betrayed him."

"Are you suggesting I'm the reason Mathias imbibed too freely?" Ophelia eyed her friend in amazement.

"I am, and I—"

"What Louisa is saying, and quite poorly, I might add." Constance glared at her younger sister as she interrupted the flow of conversation. "While we know this is truly a private matter, we care about Mathias and you. Not only because you're both dear friends of the family, but because we think—"

"We think Mathias has feelings for you, Ophelia. Actually, I'm fairly certain he does," Louisa blurted out as she reclaimed control of the conversation. Stunned by her friend's declaration, Ophelia stared at Louisa as she tried to comprehend the other woman's words.

"Louisa."

The disapproval in Constance's voice made the younger woman wince. With a look of concern, Constance leaned forward to touch Ophelia's arm in a comforting, sympathetic manner.

"As always, the reckless trait so prevalent in the Rockwoods has caused you embarrassment. Forgive us."

At Constance's apology, Ophelia shook her head as she met the other woman's gaze before she turned her head toward Louisa. Confusion quickly merged with her astonishment as she studied her friend, searching for any sign that her friend's outlandish statement was the result of her special gift. What could possibly have made Louisa think Mathias harbored any feelings for her?

"Why would you say such a thing, Louisa?" she asked quietly.

"Because we've known Mathias for years. In fact, I'm actually surprised the two of you have never met at one of the family parties, which is neither here nor there. But what is obvious to the family is that he's in pain."

"Louisa Rockwood Morehouse." A frown of disapproval furrowed Constance's brow as she tried to silence her younger sister. As always, Louisa ignored any warnings when it came to ensuring her family or her friends' happiness.

"Forgive me for being so blunt, Ophelia. I know it's unbelievably rude and inappropriate to broach the subject."

Regret darkened Louisa's eyes as she apologized. "But I can hardly stand by and watch two of my dearest friends at odds with one another, especially where their hearts are concerned."

By the time her friend had finished speaking, the shock of Louisa's revelation had ebbed away. With a shake of her head, Ophelia dismissed her friend's speculation. Mathias was no more in love with her than Gideon was.

"I'm certain you're wrong, Louisa."

"Despite my sister's impulsive rush to share her suspicions, Ophelia. I must agree with her." Constance said in a quiet voice. "I've seen the way Mathias looks at you, my dear. He doesn't realize it, but his feelings for you are quite evident to those of us who know him well. The real question is, how do you feel about him?"

Ophelia jerked her head back to Constance. Over the past week, she'd not dared to ask such a question of herself for fear of the answer. Now that her friends had asked the one thing she'd been reluctant to ask herself, she didn't know how to respond. No, that wasn't true. Ophelia knew the answer. She'd given Mathias Gilchrist more than her body. She'd given him her heart as well. The realization made Ophelia's stomach lurch.

Until this moment, she'd been content to view Mathias's mistake as a betrayal simply to avoid admitting the truth. She knew it would have been impossible for him to predict a shop girl's loose tongue or Edgar's use of that knowledge to renew his efforts to coerce her into his bed. What had angered her hadn't been Mathias's blunder. It had been something far worse.

When he'd declared that prior knowledge of her financial situation would have made him insist on paying Madam Sabine's entire bill, an icy finger had scraped down her spine. The wintry, invisible touch had penetrated her skin and chilled every inch of her. Not once since the reading of George's will had she accepted charity of any kind from anyone.

But Mathias's words had changed all that. The idea that he might see her as a charity case had been devastating. Not even if she'd been stripped bare and thrown out into the cold could she have felt so cold and vulnerable. It was for that reason she'd refused to admit the truth.

Loving Mathias was a weakness she couldn't afford. Edgar would exploit the knowledge the minute he learned she'd lost her heart to Mathias. Her stepson would threaten to make the knowledge public, and she'd be faced with a terrible choice. Submit to Edgar's demands or suffer the ultimate humiliation of Mathias knowing he'd captured the heart of a woman he pitied.

The thought sent horror slithering through her limbs until her body was rigid with tension. Determined not to reveal the true measure of her heart or the fear that accompanied the depth of her feelings, Ophelia rejected her friend's suggestion with a shake of her head.

"I'm certain you're reading far too much into Mathias's behavior. It's a fanciful notion to believe his actions are proof of feelings for me."

Her heart skipped a beat as a small voice in the back of her head urged her to believe the impossible. Another voice immediately warned her to dismiss the possibility. Hope would only bring about her downfall where Mathias was concerned.

Determined not to act the fool, she swallowed hard and looked first at Louisa and then Constance before her gaze focused on Louisa again. The certainty on both their faces alarmed her. They truly believed Mathias—she immediately stopped the thought from completing itself. Louisa leaned forward.

"You didn't answer Constance, Ophelia. Are you in love with Mathias?" The resolve in Louisa's voice said she wouldn't leave without an answer. Her throat tight with emotion, Ophelia shook her head.

"No. I'm not," Ophelia lied firmly. Louisa arched an eyebrow in disbelief. It stated emphatically that Louisa didn't believe her. Desperately, Ophelia struggled to hide her feelings from her childhood friend. The light touch of Constance's hand on her arm made Ophelia jerk.

"I'm sorry we broached the subject with you, Ophelia. Will you forgive our reckless impudence?"

"Of course. I'm grateful Mathias and I have friends who care so deeply about our happiness." She was amazed at how serene her voice sounded. Inside, she was frantically fighting the urge to race up to her bedroom and hide from the world.

"We should go," Constance said quietly as she rose to her feet.

Louisa looked at her sister for a moment, then nodded. Constance moved to hug Ophelia, and Louisa followed suit. The young widow pressed her cheek against Ophelia's and whispered in her ear.

"Don't let the horror of a terrible marriage prevent you from finding happiness now, dearest. I know you love Mathias. I can see it in your eyes."

Ophelia flinched at her friend's words. As if sensing her bemused state, Louisa smiled reassuringly at her as she released Ophelia from the warm hug. Forcing a smile to her lips, she escorted her friends to the front door. Constance paused in the open doorway and kissed Ophelia's cheek.

"Lucien and I will look for you and Lord Chelmsford this evening at the Sherringtons."

All too aware of how shaky her voice would be if she spoke, Ophelia remained silent. Instead, she forced another smile to her lips and nodded as if she was looking forward to the event. With a small chorus of farewells, the sisters left the house, and Ophelia closed the door behind them. The instant she was alone, she sagged against the door and pressed her forehead against the wood.

How could she have been so foolish? She should never have made her bargain with Mathias. No. Her first mistake had been to offer herself in exchange for Marymont. But desperation made people do foolish things, and she was no different. Her real folly was that she'd given her heart to him.

It was the most foolish thing she'd ever done. It explained why she'd entered his bed without hesitation.

Ophelia pushed herself away from the door and made her way back into the parlor. Slowly sinking down into the nearest chair, she leaned back and closed her eyes. What if Louisa and Constance were correct? Was it really possible Mathias had deep feelings for her? No, she couldn't allow herself to even consider the possibility. Ever since the day Edgar attacked her, Mathias had sent a daily note. After opening the first one, she'd thrown all the others away.

The chime of the front doorbell echoed into the salon, and she jerked upright in the chair. She heard Taggert open the front door, and a male voice drifted through the air. Mathias. A jolt of anticipation followed by fear spiraled through her, and she quickly rose to her feet. The sight of Taggert in the salon doorway with a short man behind made her heart sink.

"A Mr. Smythe to see you, my lady."

The butler stepped aside to allow the man to step into the parlor. Ophelia frowned as she recognized George's, and now Edgar's, solicitor. Smythe moved toward her with an obsequious smile.

"My lady, such a pleasure to see you again. I hope you're well." Smythe's voice was filled with ingratiating warmth. She tightened her lips at the man's lascivious gaze. The solicitor had always made her feel uncomfortable, and today was no different.

"Mr. Smythe. Your arrival is quite unexpected."

Her cool greeting made the man frown slightly, and he glanced at the sofa as if expecting her to ask him to sit down. She had no intention of doing so. The man cleared his throat as he realized she had no intention of inviting him to stay long. With a slight frown of irritation, the solicitor pulled a briefcase from under his arm. With a nod toward the secretaire, he gestured to the case.

"If I may, my lady, I've brought documents for you to sign."

"What sort of documents?"

"Lord Havenstock has informed me that he is releasing control of all the monies and investments his father left for you in his will. He instructed me to deliver the necessary paperwork for your signature."

"I beg your pardon?" Ophelia stared at the solicitor in amazement. "Edgar is giving me control of the monies my husband left me?"

"Yes, my lady." Smythe shook his head in disapproval as he laid several papers on the lid of the secretaire. "I did try to convince Lord Havenstock to maintain a small interest in your financial affairs as few women have a strong sense of business, but he was quite insistent that full control of your assets be returned to you."

"Everything?" Still stunned, she ignored the man's disparaging opinion as to a woman's intelligence.

"Yes, my lady. Of course, properties and certain funds that are part of the entailment belong to his lordship, but he is relinquishing all control of everything left to you by the late Lord Havenstock." The solicitor gestured to papers he'd spread out on the small desk. "If you would, my lady. I require several signatures that will allow you to handle future transactions. Naturally, I assume you'll require my services to help guide you in the direction and care of your finances."

Ophelia moved forward to sign the documents. With each stroke of the pen, she felt a heavy weight slowly falling off her shoulders. It was a tangible sensation. When Smythe began to gather the documents, she raised her hand to stop him.

"You may leave the papers with me, Mr. Smythe."

"But my lady, I'll need to keep these in a safe place. I'll require access to them to attend to any matters that need attention."

"Your involvement in my financial matters is no longer required, Mr. Smythe."

"But, my lady…you'll require someone to handle various aspects of financial transactions," the man sputtered.

"I'll find another solicitor to assist me, Mr. Smythe. I have no intention of using the services of a man who thinks me incapable of managing my finances. A skill I've learned quite well since my husband's death and the pauper's funds I've received annually since that time."

"I don't understand, my lady." Smythe continued to protest. "Lord Havenstock told me himself that he was more than willing to provide you funds from the monies he controlled, and all you need do was to ask."

"I'm sure he did," Ophelia said coldly, and her mouth tightened with anger. "I'll bid you a good day, sir, and thank you for your assistance in restoring my control over my money."

The man stared at her in disbelief as his mouth flopped open like a dead fish. For a moment, Ophelia almost laughed at his expression before she remembered his disdain. She narrowed her gaze at him, and the man's features clouded with angry contempt.

"As you wish, my lady. I only hope you don't fall victim to a solicitor whose character will cost you a great deal should your financial holdings be mismanaged."

Ophelia didn't answer him. She merely tipped her head in the direction of the hall and front door. Still outraged, the man turned and stalked his way out of the parlor, muttering about the female sex and their incapacity to manage their own finances. The man disappeared from the room, and seconds later, she heard the front door open and close behind the man.

Slowly sinking down into the chair at the secretaire, Ophelia stared at the papers in front of her. What in heaven's name had possessed Edgar to change his mind? The day he'd attacked her in the parlor, he'd made it quite clear he would restore her monies to her only if she became his mistress.

Bile rose in her throat as she remembered the way he'd slumped to the floor when she'd hit him with the clock. She knew her stepson well enough to know he did nothing without a reason. Did he assume she was left with little choice but to accept his offer? The thought made her stomach roil.

Confused and worried by her stepson's behavior, Ophelia touched the papers in front of her. Despite her trepidation, the documents beneath her fingertips were real. A rush of elation sped through her. For the first time in her life, she was truly independent.

She could finally pay Mrs. Barstow and Taggert the back wages they'd insisted they didn't need. Lizzie would have a wonderful new trousseau with a lovely wedding. There would be money to restore Marymont to its former beauty. There was also no longer a need to worry about her father offering her or Lizzie in marriage in exchange for the payment of his debts.

And the first thing she would do was repay Mathias the monies he'd paid Madame Sabine on her behalf. An image of Mathias's handsome features fluttered through her head, but she pushed it aside. Her gaze fell back on the documents Smythe had delivered.

The monies George had left her were quite substantial if she was reading the paperwork correctly. Although she still couldn't fathom a reason for Edgar's sudden change of heart, she refused to question it. Nonetheless, she needed to quickly acquire the services of a reputable solicitor to ensure Edgar hadn't laid a trap of some form or another. Why had he suddenly been willing to relinquish his control over her? There was no logic to it at all, unless someone had intervened—Mathias.

Her heart skipped a beat. Had Mathias forced Edgar's hand about her finances? He'd been infuriated when he'd learned the amount of her stipend. But why would he have bothered to interfere when they'd parted company so unpleasantly?

Hope swept through her. Were Louisa and Constance right? Was it possible Mathias actually cared for her? She closed her eyes as she suddenly realized what such a possibility meant if it was true. If Mathias did have feelings for her, he would want something more than her love. Despite his roguish manner at the start of their bargain, she'd come to see him as an honorable man.

Something deep inside said he'd insist on the permanent state of marriage, and that she couldn't do. Even if Mathias declared his love for her, it would be impossible for her to give up her freedom. She could never surrender her independence to a man again, no matter how much she loved him, and she loved Mathias with every part of her being.

Even if he pledged never to restrict her freedom or not. It was impossible for her to take such a leap of faith. Her love was all she could give—nothing more. A devastating hopelessness wrapped its cold arms around Ophelia as she shuddered and closed her eyes. A tear forced its way past her closed eyelid and rolled down her cheek.

How could she have done something so foolish as fallen in love with Mathias? The reality of her situation caused a tight, invisible band to wrap itself around her chest. It made it difficult to breathe, and she gasped softly at the physical pain it invoked. Another tear rolled down her cheek as she accepted the truth. It left her bereft of all hope, and with a sob of anguish, she buried her face in her hands to cry for a love and passion that would never be.

Chapter 13

If she won't reply to my letters, what makes you think she'll even talk to me this evening? If she even comes tonight." Mathias scowled as he searched the crowded room for Ophelia.

"She's here," Percy said with confidence. "Constance saw her a short time ago."

"On Chelmsford's arm, no doubt."

"Did you think it would be easy, little brother?" Charles's dark voice floated over Mathias's shoulder as the earl joined him and Percy on the edge of the dance floor.

"No," he bit out through clenched teeth.

"Look. Over there." Percy nodded toward the doors leading out onto the terrace. Mathias immediately shifted his gaze in the direction Percy had indicated.

Ophelia stood just inside the doorway, speaking with her sister. She laughed at something Lizzie said and nodded. The fan she held stirred the air in front of her in a leisurely motion, and a soft look crossed her features as she looked at someone over her sister's shoulder.

Pain ripped through his body as he followed her gaze, expecting Chelmsford to be approaching her. When he didn't see the earl, his gaze shifted back to Ophelia. A young man had stopped in front of them and bowed to both Ophelia and Lizzie. Whatever his greeting had been, it made wild color rise in Lizzie's cheeks. A moment later, he watched the man lead Ophelia's sister out onto the dance floor.

"Now's your chance, Mathias," his brother murmured. "It might be your only one tonight."

Mathias jerked his head in understanding and quickly made his way through the crowd that lined the space between the wall and the dance floor. He kept his eye on Ophelia, and when he saw her move out onto the terrace, Mathias experienced a small taste of elation. He'd be able to talk to her alone without people listening to their conversation.

The weather had become chilly a few days ago, but compared to the heat of the crowded room, the terrace's cool air wouldn't feel cold. Rather than making his way to the opposite side of the room, Mathias reached the patio from a doorway three doors down from where Ophelia had walked through. As he stepped outside, he saw her standing at the balustrade looking up at the clouds partially covering the moon. Mathias had taken several steps forward when Chelmsford appeared on the small patio. Without hesitating, Mathias quickly stepped out of the light to stand in the shadows.

"My dear, you'll catch a cold out here."

"You worry too much, Gideon. I'm fine," Ophelia said with a smile as she turned toward the earl. Chelmsford took her hands in his and carried them to his lips.

"I wouldn't want to see you fall ill."

"So you don't like women who sniffle and have red noses." The laughter in her voice made Chelmsford chuckle.

"I think a wife would be an exception." The earl's words assaulted him as if they were physical blows. Chelmsford smiled affectionately at Ophelia and tucked her arm inside his. "Now ease my concern for your health and return to the ballroom with me."

"Only if you promise to save me from Lord Boult this evening. My feet suffered the last time he led me onto the floor."

"I'll not deny you anything, my dear."

Frozen in disbelief, Mathias didn't move from his place in the shadows as they left the terrace. The bastard had proposed, and she'd accepted. She'd accepted Chelmsford's offer of marriage. Anger flowed through his veins. Her claims she would never marry again had been tossed aside the minute Chelmsford had made an offer. The fact he'd actually believed her when she'd emphatically stated she would never marry again only angered him more.

Slowly stepping out of the shadows, he walked to the doorway Ophelia had passed through on the arm of Chelmsford only a few seconds ago. She was already in the earl's arms as he swung her out onto the dance floor. Something cold and bitter settled in Mathias's chest as he saw her look up at Chelmsford and laugh. As the man turned her around on the floor, Ophelia glanced in his direction.

The moment she met his gaze, she stumbled slightly, forcing the earl to quickly adjust his step. With a fierce growl of disgust at the scene, he made his way back to where he'd left Percy and Charles. As he approached the spot, he saw Percy escorting Constance off the floor. Out of the corner of his eye, he saw Lyndham guiding Rhea around the floor in a waltz.

He came to a halt, deliberately keeping his back to the dance floor. The prospect of seeing Ophelia in Chelmsford's arms a second time would only enrage him more before he spiraled in the depths of despair. Constance frowned as she met his gaze, but was distracted by a friend who captured her attention. Tension latched onto his muscles as Percy arched an eyebrow at him in curiosity.

"Well, what did she say," his friend asked quietly.

"She's to marry Chelmsford."

"What?" Percy's mouth sagged as he stared at Mathias in disbelief. "Did she actually tell you that?"

"She didn't have to. I heard Chelmsford refer to her agreement to marry him."

"I don't believe it. Louisa and Constance were convinced…" Percy stopped speaking as his sister turned back to them.

"What were we convinced of?"

The suspicion in the Countess of Lyndham's gaze made Percy shrug as if mystified by her question. Constance narrowed her gaze at him for a long moment, and beneath her intent stare, Percy flushed with guilt. His sister's expression darkened with irritation.

"You were meddling. You deliberately mentioned…"

Constance's words trailed off into silence, as if suddenly remembering Mathias was within earshot. Her gaze shifted in his direction, and she tipped her head to one side as she studied him intently for a moment before sighing quietly.

"What's happened between you and Ophelia? I know she's positively miserable about whatever argument the two of you had."

Mathias's jaw tightened as he scowled at Constance. He wasn't about to reveal how he'd betrayed Ophelia's trust and been responsible for her stepson's belief her favors were for sale.

"That's between Ophelia and me," he snapped. Unruffled at his brusque response, Constance returned his glare.

"Well, whatever it is, it's up to you to fix it."

"It is an irreparable situation," he said with the bitterness that had already taken root inside him. With a final glare at the siblings, Mathias spun about and strode toward the exit.

Damn the Rockwoods to hell. It was now quite obvious Percy and Constance had meddled in his affairs, and most assuredly under Charles's guidance. Unlike other times when his friends meddled in affairs of the heart with others, the situation between him and Ophelia had not ended happily. In fact, if not for Chelmsford's timely arrival on the patio, it would have been a debacle beyond his comprehension.

Tonight he'd narrowly escaped a humiliation that would have far outweighed anything he'd experienced at Miriam's hand. His feelings for Ophelia were of a far greater substance and depth than anything he'd ever felt for Miriam. As much as he hated the earl at the moment, he was grateful the man had appeared on the terrace when he did.

It had saved him the embarrassment of acting like a love-sick schoolboy. Ophelia would have been as scathing in her rejection as Miriam had been the night Mathias had found her in Charles's bed. He should never have allowed Charles and Percy to convince him to come here tonight. The best thing to do at the moment was leave. He wasn't about to cause a scene and allow Ophelia to even think his behavior could be attributed to her refusal to see him. He'd verbally eviscerate Percy in the near future. As for Charles, he was certain he would most likely come to blows with his brother.

A firm hand gripped his arm and tugged him to a halt. With a vicious sound of fury, he spun around, expecting to see Percy with more advice. Instead, he found himself staring into the Earl of Lyndham's narrowed gaze. Mathias's surprise didn't last long as he glanced over Lucien's shoulder to see Percy and his sister watching them. At the moment, he was too angry to be pleasant, and he eyed the man with antipathy.

"What do you want, Lyndham?"

"I'm simply passing on a message," Lucien said with a look of startled puzzlement as he released his grip on Mathias's arm. "Your brother asked me to have you meet him in Meacham's library."

"What the devil would he be doing in the library?" Mathias scowled at the man in front of him.

"Something about Meacham and a special brandy the man is reluctant to put in the smoking room. Apparently, our host reserves it for special guests."

The earl's explanation made Mathias give the other man an abrupt nod before he turned and continued to make his way out of the ballroom. For the briefest of moments, he thought about stopping to see where Ophelia was in the room, then crushed the temptation.

From this moment forward, he would obliterate every thought of her whenever one dared to enter his head. He would wipe his soul clean of the woman until he never thought of her again. In the back of his head, scornful laughter echoed in his head, but he ignored the sound. As he reached the library, he frowned at the silence emanating from the room. Had Meacham simply left his brother to taste the brandy on his own?

The possibility seemed unlikely as the viscount was intimately involved in decisions concerning his guests' enjoyment. The library door opened with a slight whisper as he entered the softly lit room. Charles's tall figure wasn't in sight, nor Meacham's short, stocky build. Lyndham must have misunderstood his brother's request. Mathias turned to leave when he heard a faint sound echo near the wall furthest from the door. A quick glance over his shoulder revealed Ophelia staring at him in bewilderment.

"What are you doing here?" he snarled.

Ophelia jumped slightly as the anger in his voice, and looked at him as if he'd suddenly grown two heads. Despite his efforts not to be moved by her, he couldn't deny how beautiful she was in the firelight that reflected the sweetness of her features, fullness of her breasts while reminding him how lushly curved the rest of her was beneath her skirt.

"I…your brother sent word…he asked to speak with me."

"More likely, you asked to speak with him." Mathias eyed her with angry contempt. "Although I confess to being puzzled as to why. Charles's financial worth is far less than Chelmsford's."

"What on earth are you talking about?" she snapped as anger flashed across her lovely face.

The display of indignation shot a bolt of fury through him. The intimate scene he'd witnessed between her and Chelmsford on the terrace only made the affront she displayed now ring false.

"As you can see, my brother isn't here. So I suggest you run back to Chelmsford."

An odd expression crossed her features, but he couldn't determine whether it was scorn or something else. It didn't matter. As always, he was the one standing between Charles and a scheming woman intent on climbing the social ladder by becoming the Countess of Thornbury. He had no intention of allowing Ophelia to sink her claws into his brother. She'd already deceived him. He refused to let her calculating schemes injure Charles.

Ophelia stared at him for a long moment before she nodded and headed toward the door. The tilt of her head suggested he'd injured her in some way. She passed him, and he breathed in the scent of citrus and vanilla. The smell made him close his eyes for a brief second. Christ Jesus, what if he was wrong? What if Charles had deliberately set up this meeting so they could resolve the discord between them?

Without thinking, he moved quickly and caught her by the arm just as her fingers wrapped around the doorknob. One hand braced against the door to hold it closed he tugged on her arm until she was forced to turn around. Brown eyes large in her face, he hated himself for remembering how they'd flashed with desire more than a week ago. Now all he saw was anger.

"Let me go, Mathias," she said in an icy voice.

The frost-covered words belied the heat inside her. A scorching fire he'd experienced first-hand. He narrowed his gaze as he searched her features for some sign he was right— hoping for a flicker of emotion that would reveal she'd come to the library hoping to find him, not Charles. Disappointment lashed out at him as he saw nothing but cold anger. Not even her gaze revealed any emotion that gave him hope, yet he couldn't let her go without knowing the truth.

"Why did you really come to the library, Ophelia?"

"I told you why. Your brother asked me to meet him here."

The stubborn tilt of her chin pulled a growl of anger out of his chest. She didn't flinch at the sound, but he heard the soft intake of air into her lungs. The sharp breath echoed with trepidation, and it made him doubt her words. Jaw clenched with determination, he lowered his head and closed the small space between them until the warmth of her breath brushed across his skin.

"Very well, for the sake of argument, let us assume my brother did invite you to meet him here." Mathias watched her carefully as he spoke. "It still doesn't explain why you came here."

"I came because I thought…" Her voice faded away as a look of fear widened her eyes. Ophelia turned her head away for a moment before she glared at him with a defiant arch of her delicate eyebrows. "I came because it was a summons, not a request."

"Why do I think you're lying? Why do I think you were the one to instigate a meeting?"

"I am not a liar, and you have no right to question my comings and goings," she snapped as she tried to break free of his grasp.

"When it comes to protecting my brother's honor, I have every right to question you," he snarled. "Whatever plot you've devised, I can assure you it will not come to fruition."

"If I were plotting anything, it would be your downfall." The scorn in her eyes as her gaze raked over him was like taking bitter medicine.

"My downfall? For what reason," he snarled.

"For lying to me. For making—" Ophelia's angry reply ended suddenly as she sucked in a sharp breath of air and grew pale.

"For making you what, Ophelia?"

At his question, vulnerability darkened her eyes, and she turned her head away. The fragile air about her softened his anger. Had she really come to the library hoping he'd used Charles's name to summon her here? He almost laughed out loud at the thought. She'd accepted Chelmsford's proposal, which made him a fool for thinking otherwise. But where Ophelia was concerned, he was a fool. A fool deeply in love. He grasped her chin with his fingers and forced her to look at him.

"Tell me, Ophelia. What have I done to make you wish for my downfall?"

"You lied to me."

"And I've expressed deep remorse for my mistake, several times in fact, and yet not once have you accepted my apology."

"I don't want your apologies," she snapped as he saw fear flash in her eyes. "I simply want to forget I ever met you."

"Why?" he murmured. Something in her gaze caused his heart to slam into his chest. Had Charles and his friends been right? Was it possible Ophelia actually cared for him, or was he imagining her reaction in the desperate hope she cared for him?

"This conversation is pointless. Let me go. I wish to return to the ballroom." Her voice was icy, and every muscle in his body hardened at the reason for her desire to return to the party.

"Return to Chelmsford's side, you mean," he bit out through clenched teeth. Her only answer was a defiant tilt of her head.

Her refusal to respond to his accusation caused a vivid image of her in the earl's arms to fill Mathias's head. The emotion it aroused in him was one he'd never experienced before. He could only identify it as jealousy. It was a sensation he didn't like one bit. Even worse was the desperate need not to let her go. His gaze fell down to her mouth.

"Tell me, Ophelia. Do you expect to find the same passion in Chelmsford's arms you found in mine?" The question made her gasp softly, and her eyes widened in surprised bewilderment before she quickly narrowed her gaze at him.

"You don't seriously expect me to answer that, do you?"

Despite the note of anger in Ophelia's haughty response, he heard the small catch in her voice. It was a sound he knew well. It meant she was avoiding the question. He bent his head to nip at her earlobe. The small mewl that escaped her sent a rush of exhilaration surging through him. She'd made a similar sound the night he'd made love to her. Mathias lifted his head, and she quickly averted her gaze from his.

"Are you afraid of what your answer would be?" he growled as his finger lazily trailed the edge of her bodice.

Ophelia shuddered beneath his touch. A bitter triumph swept through him. She might have agreed to marry Chelmsford, but she trembled beneath his touch. His gaze fell on the sweet curve of her lips. Full and succulent, Ophelia's mouth was slightly parted, and her ragged breathing whispered in his ear.

Desire charged its way through him at the sound. To hell with Chelmsford. To hell with it all. With a growl, he captured her mouth in a hard kiss. A sound of surprise escaped her before she opened her mouth to him.

Light and bubbly, the taste of champagne danced off her tongue onto his while the warmth of her penetrated his body. Every muscle in his body ached for her. She was intoxicating in a way no amount of brandy could ever match. His mouth slid off her lips and moved downward to nibble at the side of her neck.

The silky touch of her hand caressed his skin as she pulled him closer, then gently thrust her hips forward into his. Need surged through him at her silent invitation. He wanted to inhale the very essence of her so he'd never forget the scent of her skin, the sweet taste of her lips, or her gasps of pleasure at his touch.

Their one night together and the memory of this moment would be all he had when she became Chelmsford's wife and entered the earl's bed. Anger and pain accompanied the fleeting thought, but he shoved them aside. The here and now was all that mattered. His hand brushed over her breast, and frustration barreled through him that he couldn't touch her soft, satin-like skin.

"Oh please, Mathias…I need…"

The passionate plea in her soft whisper intensified his own desire, and his cock jumped at the husky sound. Desire and love crashed through him and held him hostage to her. He sought her mouth again as a stark hunger blistered its way into his body. Oblivious to everything but her, his body shouted its craving for the satisfaction he knew only she could ever give him.

A quiet moan echoed out of her as she shifted her hips against his in a sign of her own need and frustration. With her body pinned between him and the door, he quickly freed his cock and tugged her skirts upward until his hands were gripping soft, lush thighs. Lost in the sweet essence of her scent and taste, his hands cupped her buttocks firmly. The small sound she made at his touch vibrated against his lips. Her small cry of pleasure made him lift his head. His breathing ragged, he saw her eyes flutter open in surprise.

"Tell me how much you need me." His command made her jerk slightly, and his cock protested the delay.

"Oh dear god, Mathias. Please don't make me beg," she whispered as frustrated desire darkened her lovely countenance.

"Say it," he ground out as his body ached with unfilled desire.

Every inch of him roared a protest as he waited for her response. He ignored the sensation. His body might need physical fulfillment, but his heart demanded some small concession on her part. Even if her reply was only a temporary surrender to him, he needed to hear her admit this moment of passion was something she wanted as badly as he did. She hesitated for a brief second before her brushed across his mouth.

"I need you. Can't you see how much I need you?" Her voice echoed with the same hunger gripping his body.

Triumph stormed through him as her mouth met his in a fervent display of passion. As her tongue mated eagerly with his, he lifted her up off her feet to thrust his cock into her.

God, but she felt good. The white-hot heat of her made him jerk from the pleasure of being a part of her once more.

Although he tried to savor the sweetness of the moment, he could not restrain his need for her. With a hard thrust, he rocked his body into hers. A strangled cry escaped her as her body responded to his with each stroke, and her body contracted and tightened around him like a vise.

Her hands cupped his face as she sought his lips in a kiss that made him drive into her harder. In the back of his head, a bell sounded. He might be in heaven now, but his world was about to become a living hell the moment he walked away from her tonight. She could never know how much he loved her—how much his body loved worshiping hers. He could never let her see what this moment in time meant to him. He couldn't let her see how her marrying Chelmsford would destroy him.

Mathias's body filled hers completely, and her heart sang with joy. Eagerly, Ophelia sought his mouth in her need to drink every part of him into her body and soul. The tip of her tongue laced his lips until they parted, and her tongue danced with his in the same way his body mated with hers.

This wasn't like the other night. This was hot, passionate, forbidden, and completely unrestrained. Her body tightened around his, trying to keep him from retreating. She failed, only to have fire skim through her as his hips thrust forward again. He was hot male against her tongue, and his body burned hers with every stroke. Every inch of her was sensitive to the heat of him as he aroused and stimulated her senses until she had to bite back his name for fear someone would hear her wild cry.

Instead, she released a soft sob of pleasure as her hips worked against his in a moment of blissful intensity.

Oblivious to everything except this moment, her body welcomed him with each fiery stroke. His mouth broke away from hers to sear her skin as he lowered his head to kiss the tops of her breasts.

As his tongue slid into the valley between her breasts, her body shuddered against his. The blazing heat of him engulfed her like a bonfire flaring up into the sky. Sensation after sensation pulsed through her, and she wanted to weep from the pleasure of each hot stroke and kiss. The pace of his thrusts increased, and her forehead grazed his as she reveled in his possession.

Their harsh breaths echoed loudly in the quiet room. The sound emphasized the heat, passion, and intense need pulsating through her. A now familiar force filled her body. It pressed its way down to the most sensitive part of her. The strength of the sensation sped through her at a hard, fast pace, until it erupted in one swift blur of pleasure.

Instantly, her body jerked against his, then arched upward in his arms to shudder hard. Fingers digging in his shoulders, she clung to him as tremor after tremor rocked her body. In response to her climax, he thrust into her with a blistering speed that heightened and intensified her pleasure even more than she'd ever dreamed possible. Seconds later, he buried his cry of release against her breasts as he throbbed inside her.

Slowly, his hands eased off her buttocks to glide over her thighs as he allowed her to slide downward against his chest until her feet were on the floor. His face was pressed against her neck, and she rested her head against the door. Eyes closed, she felt fully satiated. As the pleasure slowly eased out of her, the memory of their sharp words filtered their way into her mind.

Was it possible his anger and the references to his brother and Gideon meant he was jealous? Louisa and Constance had said he cared for her. But was it love, or was it simply him coveting what he thought another man possessed? She wasn't sure which would be worse, his coveting her simply because she seemed out of reach or his pity.

Mathias released her completely, and turning his back on her, he put several feet between them as he adjusted his clothing. Ophelia followed suit. As she shook her skirts out, the heat of him continued to burn her skin in a manner that made her ache for him all over again. Her eyes focused on Mathias standing motionless in front of her.

He held himself so rigidly it sent an icy thread of fear wrapping its way around her. She took a hesitant step forward. The instant her hand touched his shoulder, he jerked violently. Her heart in her mouth, she trembled as she drew her hand away from him.

"Mathias?" At the question in her soft voice, he slowly turned around. The moment she saw his stoic expression, her stomach lurched with sickening dread.

"I thank you for that delightful interlude, my lady," he said with a nonchalance that sent a rush of fear through her. "You've been an extraordinary student. I shall miss sampling your wares in the future."

Interlude? Wares? Ophelia stared at him in bewilderment and confusion. The air between them was still thick with the heat of their passion, but something else began to fill the space between them. Dark and painful, it tore at her senses as the weight of his cruelty pushed its way into her conscious stream of thought.

The words hadn't simply been an insult. They'd been deliberately designed to humiliate her. Louisa and Constance had been wrong. Mathias found her to be little more than a common street whore. The realization had the same effect as if he'd struck her with a whip. She swayed slightly, but he didn't move to steady her. If anything, his sharply defined features hardened further.

"I...I don't understand."

"Then allow me to clarify, my lady. I enjoyed our little fuck, and regret your marriage will not allow us to repeat the pleasure in the future."

Stunned by the crude savagery of his words, Ophelia felt the air leave her lungs as she stared up at him in shock. It was as if she was standing in front of George again, hearing words meant to debase and debilitate her. Mathias's handsome profile was unreadable as she took a stumbling step backward.

Pain pierced every part of her as Ophelia's brain sluggishly tried to comprehend what was happening. How could she have been so wrong about him? No, she hadn't been wrong. He'd shown his true colors when he'd betrayed her trust. He'd made a fool of her then, just as he had a moment ago.

But she refused to let him see what his actions and words had done to her. Years of humiliation at George's hand gave her the strength and wherewithal to bury her pain. Despite her desire to flee the room, Ophelia straightened her shoulders and lifted her head to steadily met Mathias's gaze.

"You said that with great flair, Mathias," she said, satisfied her voice rang with all the quiet dignity she could muster. "Unfortunately, your attempt to degrade me lacked the finesse my husband perfected during our marriage. But I commend you for your effort."

He jerked slightly at her words, but his expression didn't change. Ophelia met his gaze unflinchingly, and she saw something undefinable darken his eyes. If she didn't know better, she might have thought it was anguish. The silence between them was taut with tension until he bowed slightly.

"I shall bid you good evening, my lady. And please accept my best wishes on the occasion of your forthcoming marriage."

Ophelia didn't move as he stepped around her and walked out of the library. The hard thud of the door closing behind Mathias made her jump. The sound echoed loudly in her ears as her heart shattered. A shiver rippled through her. The icy chill coating her skin made her hug herself in an effort to warm her arms.

She'd allowed Louisa and Constance to make her believe Mathias cared for her. She'd been a fool to even consider the possibility, and it was a mistake that had cost her dearly. Behind her, the soft click of the door opening made her draw in a sharp breath. He'd come back. Ophelia whirled around to see Gideon walk into the library with a look of concern.

"Are you all right, my dear?"

"Yes." She turned away again as tears of disappointment welled in her eyes.

"Why am I not convinced of that?" The somber note in his voice was as gentle as his touch as he forced her to face him. He drew in a sharp hiss of air and muttered an incoherent oath. "I'm going to make the man pay for this."

"What do you mean?" Startled, Ophelia stared up at him in alarm.

"Gilchrist."

"Oh no, Gideon, please." At her soft plea, the earl's mouth twisted in a wry grimace of disgust.

"He doesn't deserve your love, Ophelia."

The statement made her gasp in horror. Was her love for Mathias that evident? Could people see it on her face? Dear God, did Mathias realize the extent of her feelings? The thought made her body grow as cold as if she'd was standing naked in a bitter winter wind. Her humiliation and pain would far surpass anything George had ever done to her if Mathias knew the truth. Another sound of regret escaped Gideon.

"Other than your friends and me, no one else has any suspicion of your feelings, my dear." Gideon pressed a light kiss to her forehead and pulled her into a kind, comforting embrace. "Everything will be all right, Ophelia. As time passes, the pain will ease."

Something in his voice said he'd lost at love with the same depth of pain she was experiencing now. Closing her eyes, she pressed her cheek into his chest. Whomever the woman was who'd broken Gideon's heart had turned her back on a good man. A quiet sound whispered in the room, and her eyes fluttered open as the library door slowly swung open to reveal Mathias's tall figure.

The sight of him in the doorway made her stiffen in horror as she realized how it must look to be in Gideon's embrace. For a fleeting moment, Mathias's expression reflected what she thought was anguish. It vanished too quickly for her to be certain, and an icy mask of contempt hardened his features into a façade of chiseled stone.

Their gazes locked, and the scorn in his eyes sliced through her as if it were a sharp blade splaying her open in one vicious blow. With one last sweeping look of condemnation, Mathias turned and disappeared from sight. A soft moan of despair escaped her as her body went numb, and she sagged against the earl.

"Ophelia," Gideon exclaimed softly as he bore the weight of her against him. Struggling to contain the cry of anguish ripping through her, Ophelia pressed her forehead into his shoulder.

"Please take me home, Gideon."

At her strangled request, he bent over her slightly and lifted her head to study her face for several seconds. He turned his head to look at the empty doorway, then back to her. Ophelia averted her gaze from the questioning look on Gideon's face. After a brief second, he murmured his acquiescence and linked her arm with his to lead her out of the room.

Chapter 14

Ophelia ran her finger over the list of accounts in the journal in front of her. Ever since George's death, she'd learned to be frugal, and restoring Marymont to its original beauty had been nothing more than a dream.

It was a dream no longer. Even with the extensive restoration costs, her father's debts, and the almost certain need of a wedding trousseau for Lizzie, there would be more than enough money to live quite comfortably in the country.

Closing her eyes, she rubbed her fingers against her temple. It had been almost a month since the Meacham affair, and her pain had not lessened. In truth, it had only deepened. By the time Gideon had escorted her to her front door that night, she'd become numb to everything around her except her pain. For two days, she'd retreated to her room to nurse her wounds in the way an injured animal might.

Even despite her broken heart, every time the front doorbell rang, hope would spring to life inside her only to have it wither and die when it wasn't Mathias on the doorstep. One day rolled into the next, and hope gave way to despondency, then resignation. Not even Gideon's quiet reassurances that time would ease her suffering allowed her to refute the reality of her situation.

It had taken her even longer to remember Mathias's words alluding to her relationship with Gideon. In the end, she'd been grateful he believed she was to marry. It had afforded her the time to put her finances in order and prepare to leave London. The sooner she returned to the country, the sooner her heartache would ease. She ignored the scoffing laugh in the back of her mind and forced herself to bring forth a picture of Marymont.

The effort only caused her to close her eyes in pain before she looked down at the ledger on the secretaire. As much as she loved her home, she knew it would take her away from London and any hope of ever seeing Mathias again.

On the few occasions Lizzie or Gideon had been able to gently bully her into attending the theater or a social affair, she'd done so only in the hope of catching a glimpse of Mathias. The two or three times she'd caught sight of him had merely been a brief glimpse of his profile.

Only once had their eyes met. The contempt and loathing on Mathias's face before he'd turned his back on her left her reeling. She'd been thrown back to that moment in the library at Meacham House when she'd seen him in the doorway as Gideon had been comforting her.

Ophelia shivered at the painful memory, and her body grew cold. She turned to look at the elaborately decorated coal stove that had been installed recently. Through the thin grates, she could see the fiery glow of coal. It was clearly not the room, only her body reacting to her memories.

At the sound of the front doorbell, Ophelia closed the journal, placed it in the secretaire's drawer, and locked it. The sound of Gideon's voice made her smile as she rose to greet him. As he strode into the room, Ophelia stretched out her hands to welcome him. Gideon kissed both her cheeks, then with his hands on her upper arms, he pushed her away from him to study her gravely. Seconds later, his features lightened with relief.

"You look better today than I've seen you look in weeks."

"If that is what you call a compliment, I would hate to hear one of your insults." She laughed, and Gideon grinned unapologetically.

"Making you laugh is always my first goal, no matter how skeptical you are of my words of admiration." His cheerful reply made Ophelia shake her head with amusement as she gestured toward the room's small settee and chairs.

"Shall I call for tea?" she asked as she sank down into the cushions of the settee.

"No, I can't stay for long as I have another appointment. I simply wanted to tell you that I paid the last of your father's debts from the monies you gave me." Satisfaction crossed his face as he smiled. "I've also discreetly made it known he has no money with which to gamble, and that I will not cover any debt he incurs in the future."

"I cannot express enough my gratitude for what you've done, Gideon. If Father were to learn I'd regained control of my money, his gambling would have been out of control."

"Are you aware he came to visit me a few days ago?" The question startled Ophelia, and she stared at her friend in open-mouth dismay.

"Oh dear Lord, surely he didn't ask you for money." Embarrassment caused her cheeks to burn.

"He didn't ask me for money." Gideon's gaze narrowed on her. "He asked when we intended to marry."

"Merciful heaven. I hope you explained we're simply friends."

"I did." Gideon nodded as his mouth twisted wryly. "It will ease your mind to know that he thanked me for settling his debts, which is the reason he broached the subject with me."

"At least he had the good graces to express his gratitude." Ophelia didn't bother to hide her anger at her father's behavior. Gideon was all too aware of her feelings about her father's lack of decorum.

"Sometimes I think you're too hard on him, Ophelia. He has a problem, but he obviously cares about you. He's noticed how unhappy you are, and he said I could make you happy. I would have to agree."

"Please, Gideon, don't…"

"I know you're not in love with me any more than I am with you, Ophelia. We both know our affection for one another is nothing more than friendship."

"We've had this conversation before, and my answer hasn't changed."

"Have you no desire for companionship in the years ahead, Ophelia?" The puzzlement in Gideon's voice brought a small smile of sadness to her lips.

"Companionship?" Ophelia dragged in a deep breath, held it for a moment, and then slowly released it. "Not at your expense or that of my freedom. I could—"

"Are you telling me that if Gilchrist suddenly appeared on your front step with an offer of marriage, you would turn him away?"

The amazement on his face made Ophelia hesitate to reply, and she looked away from her friend. Only in the deepest part of her heart had she considered the possibility of being Mathias's wife. Even though she'd accepted that there would never be such an offer made, what would she have done if Mathias had proposed to her?

Would she have actually been able to refuse him? The question was moot. Mathias didn't love her, and the depth of his contempt for her solidified her belief the question was one she would never have to answer. But despite that knowledge, it did nothing to change her own feelings. She looked back at Gideon and shook her head.

"I will love Mathias until I breathe my last breath, but it's a question I'll never have to answer."

"You do the man a disservice to think him capable of locking you in a gilded cage." There was a slight hint of rebuke in her friend's voice. Ophelia rolled her shoulders in a small shrug.

"It's still pointless to contemplate what my answer would be." There was a slight bitterness to her reply, and Gideon frowned.

"And is that why you refuse my proposal? Do you believe I would try to control you—restrain you in any instance?"

"No, I don't think that at all," she said with a small sigh. "But I refuse to restrict your freedom either. What would you do if you were to meet someone, and you were tied to me? Then you would know the depth of my misery."

"As I've said before, I'm a realist when it comes to love."

"A point of view that your—" Ophelia stopped in mid-sentence as she remembered her promise not to mention the dowager's visit.

The Dowager Countess of Chelmsford was determined to see her son married and had called on Ophelia yesterday morning. The woman had come straight to the point of her visit. She'd gently but firmly demanded to know why Ophelia was refusing to marry her son. Startled by the woman's question, Ophelia hadn't been able to form a reply.

The dowager had quickly apologized for speaking out of turn, but it didn't hinder the woman's objective to persuade Ophelia to accept Gideon's offer. The countess had reassured Ophelia that she would welcome her as a daughter-in-law and never interfere in their marriage. It had been impossible not to like the woman's pleasant, forthright nature or her efforts to emphasize all of her son's excellent qualities. It illustrated how deeply the woman loved her son, and a tiny part of her regretted her inability to marry Gideon.

"You were saying?"

Her friend narrowed his gaze at her as he waited for her to continue. When she remained silent, Gideon eyed her with puzzlement. A brief moment later, his handsome face darkened with annoyance as his gray eyes flashed with anger. "Has my mother been to visit you?"

"Only once," she said in a placating tone of voice.

"Once too many. She should not have interfered," Gideon muttered fiercely.

"She loves you, Gideon. She only wants your happiness." At her quiet words, her friend shook his head.

"My mother is a hopeless romantic. I learned a long time ago not to indulge in whimsical fantasy."

"Whether you believe in whimsical fantasy or not, it doesn't change the fact that a marriage between us would be a mistake." The resolute statement made Gideon attempt to protest, but Ophelia stopped him with a wave of her hand. "You know I'm right, and I value our friendship too much to jeopardize it by marrying you."

Gideon stared at her in silence for a long moment before he nodded. In the hall, the clock chimed the half-hour, and he grimaced.

"I've stayed longer than I should. I have a meeting with the Lord Admiral on the hour." As he stood, he took her hand and kissed it. "Are you still standing firm on your decision not to attend the Melton dinner party next week?"

"Yes. I cannot risk Louisa or Constance meddling again by inviting Mathias."

Gideon nodded his understanding, and with a tender kiss to her brow, he left the house. Her friend had barely been gone five minutes when the front door opened with a loud bang. Alarmed by the sound, Ophelia jumped nervously, then relaxed as she heard Lizzie calling her name with great excitement. As her younger sister hurried into the room, Ophelia saw Paul Nickens following close behind. Lizzie rushed forward to hug her enthusiastically.

"Father said yes, Ophelia. Father told Paul we could marry."

Happiness swept through Ophelia for the first time in weeks. She returned her sister's hug before kissing her cheek. As she released Lizzie, she turned to her future brother-in-law.

"I couldn't be more delighted by this news," she said with a smile as she moved forward to kiss the young man's cheek. The bright flush of color rising in his face made her smile.

"Thank you, my lady, I—"

"Please, call me Ophelia, and I shall call you Paul. After all, we are to be family." At her gentle command, Paul's face deepened with color, and Lizzie quickly moved to his side and kissed his cheek.

"I told you Ophelia would be happy for us. She knew precisely when I fell in love with you." Lizzie looked over her shoulder. "Didn't you, Ophelia?"

"Yes, I remember exactly how moonstruck you were."

"We want to be married right away, Ophelia," Lizzie said firmly. Surprised by her sister's declaration, she shook her head in dismay.

"But there are things to do. We need to order you a wedding trousseau, and plan for a wedding and reception."

"No." Lizzie shook her head vehemently. "I know we have no money for any of those things. I'm quite content to be Paul's wife. We can go home to Marymont and have Vicar Blackburn marry us."

"There are more than enough funds for a lovely wedding and your trousseau, Lizzie."

"I know better, Ophelia. We barely have enough to scrape two pots against, let alone everything that comes with a wedding."

"Money is no longer an object for us," she said with a smile.

"I don't understand." Puzzlement furrowed Lizzie's brow.

"Edgar returned control of my funds to me."

"What?" A gasp parted Lizzie's lips as she stared at Ophelia in shock. "He gave you control of the monies George left to you?"

"Yes." She smiled and nodded at her sister. "It happened a few weeks ago. I didn't want to say anything until I was certain the monies were mine to do with as I wished."

"What did you say to Edgar to make him relinquish control?" Lizzie stared at her in wide-eyed amazement.

"I didn't say anything."

Ophelia's throat tightened as she remembered the last time she'd seen her stepson. Even when he'd been carried out of the house after his assault, she'd thought for certain he would be back. She knew he wouldn't let her act of self-defense go unanswered. He was too much like his father, and George had never allowed her to go unpunished for even the smallest offense. The knowledge made Edgar's change of heart astounding. His absence even more so. If not for the bank's confirmation that all funds and investments had been safely transferred into her name, she would have found it impossible to believe.

"But surely he must have given a reason for his sudden change of heart."

"The solicitor gave me no reason for his decision to return control to me, and I have no desire to seek Edgar out to ask why." Ophelia pressed a hand into her stomach. She never wanted to see the man ever again, not even from a distance.

"I still find it quite remarkable, but I am so glad you no longer have to worry about finances."

"None of us will, and you're not to say a word to Father about our good fortune. Is that understood?"

"I understand. He'll only gamble more freely." Her sister sighed with resignation, and Ophelia released a breath of relief.

"Thank you. It's been difficult enough preventing Father from discovering I'm the one paying his debts."

"And it was Lord Chelmsford who paid father's debts in your stead?" There was a troubled note in her sister's voice, and Ophelia eyed her in puzzlement.

"The earl was kind enough to make it appear he was the one responsible for seeing to Father's debts, but he did so with my money."

"Then what they're saying is true?"

"That I'm going to marry Lord Chelmsford? No, I am not going to marry Gideon."

At the reply, Lizzie bit down on her lip and bent her head. Confused by her sister's reaction, Ophelia glanced at her future brother-in-law, who quickly looked away from her, and she returned her gaze to her sister.

"What exactly are people saying, Lizzie?"

"Nothing," her sister said too hastily as the silence in the room became uncomfortable. Ophelia stared at Lizzie for a long moment before she gasped in horror.

"They think Gideon is paying Papa's debts because they think I'm...?"

Unable to complete the sentence, Ophelia stared at the couple in horror. Their distraught expressions made her press one hand into her stomach in an effort to stop it from churning as bile rose in her throat.

Dear God, what would Mathias think? The moment the question filled her head, she declared herself a fool for even thinking about Mathias and his reaction. Had Gideon heard the rumors? Was that why he'd proposed again this afternoon? She swayed slightly, and Lizzie quickly stepped forward to steady her.

"It's only gossip, Ophelia. People talk. It's of no consequence." When Ophelia didn't reply, Lizzie squeezed her arm. "He couldn't possibly think ill of you, Ophelia."

"Who?" she rasped. "Gideon?"

"No. Mr. Gilchrist. Isn't that who you were..." At Lizzie's reply, Ophelia froze as she met her sister's look of sympathy and concern. Although it took every bit of willpower and perseverance she possessed, she straightened her spine and eyed her sister sternly.

"Mr. Gilchrist's opinion of me is of no consequence, and I have no wish to discuss him, now or in the future. Is that clear?"

Ophelia's sharp words made Lizzie stare at her in amazement before she nodded her agreement to obey Ophelia's command. Eager to flee the room and avoid any other potentially dangerous questions, she forced a smile to her lips.

"If the two of you will forgive me, I have things I must attend to." She looked at her sister's fiancé and lightly touched his arm. "I truly am delighted to welcome you into the family, Paul. My sister is a lucky woman."

"Thank you, my—Ophelia. But I'm the lucky one. I promise you I'll do everything in my power to make her happy and to keep her out of trouble."

The last words of the young man's declaration made Lizzie sputter with indignation, and Paul smiled cheerfully at the sound. As her sister began to protest, Ophelia quietly walked around the couple and left the parlor. At the foot of the stairs, she braced herself with one hand on the wall in an attempt to will away the nausea swirling in her stomach. Eyes closed, she fought to hold back the bile rising in her throat.

Tongues had been wagging for the past month as to what had happened between her and Mathias. He'd not openly declared his contempt for her, but it was easily discernible by others. It was clear in the way he'd politely excused himself and walked away before being forced to greet her. His scorn was difficult enough to bear, but how much of his contempt was due to the gossip about her and Gideon?

Tears blurred her sight, and she stumbled her way upstairs. When she reached the safe haven of her room, she locked the door behind her. A quiet sob escaped her as she sank to the floor, and her body shuddered with heartfelt anguish.

Ophelia didn't know how long she sat there crying, but as her sobs slowly ebbed away, she rubbed her cheeks dry. Her back pressed into the door behind her, Ophelia closed her eyes. She'd never been so weary in her entire life. But she couldn't rest, at least not until she was home at Marymont.

Whether the repairs at Marymont were complete or not, she would insist they return home as quickly as their affairs could be settled here in town. She would take Lizzie to be fitted for a trousseau tomorrow. Everything could be delivered to Marymont. If things went smoothly, she could be home in less than a week. The thought gave her the strength to rise to her feet. It was impossible to change the past, and she needed to focus on the future. In time her heart would mend, and she would be happy again. In the back of her mind, she heard a cry of despair, but she chose to ignore the sound and its meaning.

Chapter 15

Mathias glared at Charles seated across from him in the carriage. His brother simply arched an eyebrow in amused disgust. With a quiet sound of irritation, Mathias looked out the carriage window.

He should have known better last night than to be lulled into thinking he had a winning hand. Charles was renowned for his skill at cards, and like a fool, he'd played right into his brother's hands.

Certain of the cards he held, Mathias hadn't hesitated to wager his agreement to accompany Charles to dinner tonight. He'd lost the hand, and it wasn't until his brother informed him where they were going this evening that Mathias realized what a fool he'd been. He'd allowed himself to be placed in a situation where he'd be forced to watch Ophelia and Chelmsford together.

"Scowl all you want, Mathias. It won't change the fact that you lost the hand." The exasperation in his brother's voice made Mathias jerk his gaze back to his brother.

"And it doesn't change the fact that you knew I would never have agreed to the wager if I'd known we'd be attending a dinner party with the Rockwoods this evening."

"You make it sound as if I'd condemned you to hell."

"There will come a time, Charles, when you'll try to win Beatrice back, and you'll be condemned into this hell with me. When that happens, I'll remind you of this moment," he snarled viciously.

Charles didn't answer him, but his brother's features had become a stony façade that said Mathias had struck a nerve. The regret he experienced at taunting his brother evaporated as the carriage rolled to a halt in front of Melton House. His brother had interfered in his life again, despite Mathias's warning. As the vehicle's door opened, Charles didn't move. Instead, he gestured toward the open door.

"After you."

"Afraid I might not honor our wager, brother?" Mathias said sardonically.

"Shall we just say the thought had crossed my mind?"

Mathias muttered an oath and quickly stepped down onto the sidewalk. Not bothering to wait on Charles, he strode up the steps to the front door of Melton House. Before he could knock, the door swung open as Madison, the earl's butler, greeted him and Charles.

"Good evening, Mr. Gilchrist. Lord Thornbury."

Mathias silently acknowledged the older man's greeting with a jerk of his head as he handed the butler his hat. The quiet hum of conversation flowing out of the main salon into the foyer made his muscles tighten as Percy emerged from the salon with a broad smile on his face.

"Charles. Mathias. Welcome."

"Percy." Mathias bit out his greeting as he shook hands with his friend. As he watched Percy shake Charles's hand, the two men exchanged a look that made Mathias realize his brother might have had help ensuring he was in attendance tonight. He narrowed his gaze at Charles, whose eyebrows arched up as if daring Mathias to question his justification. Percy turned back to Mathias and frowned.

"Christ Jesus, man. You look as though you've just been given a prison sentence."

"Do I?" Mathias said with a heavy dose of sarcasm, his jaw taut with tension.

"I've considered throwing him out of Thornbury Place." Charles released a quiet noise of unsympathetic brotherly disgust. "He's been snarling like a wounded lion for the past month."

Mathias knew better than to refute his brother's observation. It would be a lie to do so. He knew he'd been far from pleasant since the Meacham affair. When he'd confronted Charles about his role in sending Ophelia to the library, his brother had reluctantly confessed to arranging the meeting.

His reaction had surprised both of them when Charles had landed on the floor from a strong right-hand punch to the jaw. Mathias hadn't bothered to apologize or help his brother to his feet. Instead, he'd coldly ordered Charles not to interfere in his affairs again. It was beginning to look as if his brother had disregarded the warning. A firm hand patted his shoulder, and he met Percy's sympathetic gaze.

"She's not here, Mathias."

The quiet words made him jerk slightly with relief, followed by a disappointment that was as sharp as it was bitter. He immediately berated himself for feeling anything for Ophelia at all. In the next instant, he grasped the fact that Percy's words were an open confession he'd conspired with Charles to ensure he came tonight.

The sudden urge to drop his brother to the floor again made him turn sharply toward Charles. His brother took a quick step back, but didn't bother to hide his complicit behavior. An irritable frown settled on his brother's brow.

"Can you blame me? Your ill-temper has wreaked havoc with the staff, and I don't enjoy being your punching bag. Something I'm certain you wish I were at this exact moment."

"What are the three of you doing out here?"

Louisa stood in the salon doorway, eyeing them with an innocent expression that he knew wasn't innocent at all. Christ Jesus, was there no one in the Rockwood family who hadn't aided his brother in this hellish conspiracy? Louisa had either been privy to, if not the mastermind of the plot to drag him here tonight. With a last glare at his brother and Percy, he stepped forward to kiss Louisa's cheek.

"We just arrived a moment ago," Mathias said with a grim smile as the youngest Rockwood hugged him tight for a brief second. If he'd wanted confirmation of her involvement in the conspiracy, her warm greeting confirmed it.

"Well, come join everyone else. We'll be dining shortly, and I have two ladies who'll need an escort into dinner." Louisa tucked her arm in Mathias's and pulled him toward the salon.

As Mathias walked into the salon with Louisa, he instinctively searched the room for Ophelia. Although Percy had said she wasn't here, it was impossible not to look for her as much as he hated himself for doing so. The moment his gaze fell on the Earl of Chelmsford, Mathias grew rigid. Almost as if Louisa could read his mind, she touched his arm.

"You're wrong about him. The earl is a good man."

"Forgive me for disagreeing," he said in a low voice.

"You're a stubborn man, Mathias Gilchrist."

From across the room, Chelmsford met his gaze, and the two of them acknowledged each other's presence with a brusque nod. Anything more than that, and Mathias would not have wanted to be held accountable for his behavior. Louisa looked over her shoulder at his brother with a smile.

"Oh, Charles, I almost forgot. An old friend of yours is here tonight. Constance asked Beatrice Wiltshire to join us since she's about to retire to the country at the end of the week."

Mathias didn't have to look at Charles to feel the tension suddenly bouncing off his brother. His gaze quickly swept across the room until he found Beatrice in a lively conversation with their host, the Earl of Melton. Sebastian laughed at something she said, and a soft sound behind him indicated Charles had seen her smiling at their host in a flirtatious manner.

If Louisa was aware of his brother's discomfort, there was nothing in her expression to suggest she'd planned a reunion between Charles and Beatrice. Despite that, Mathias wouldn't have been surprised to learn that either she or

Constance had arranged the chance meeting. For the next half hour, Louisa worked hard to coax Mathias out of his dour mood.

Although she didn't admit it, her efforts only deepened his belief she'd been privy to, if not the mastermind of the plot to drag him here tonight. It also made him believe her determination to entertain him was a silent apology for any role she'd played in the plot.

By the time dinner was announced, she'd managed to make him laugh more than once. Something he'd not done in weeks. He didn't know why he was startled to find himself escorting Beatrice into the dining room. Deep inside, he'd assumed Louisa would have seated her next to Charles.

Perhaps he'd been wrong about the youngest Rockwood's intention of meddling in Charles's personal affairs. From several places down the table, he saw his brother glance in his direction. It was barely a cursory look, but the moment he saw Beatrice seated next to him, Charles's features looked as if they'd been chiseled out of marble. For a fleeting moment, he experienced sympathy for his brother before a cold satisfaction swept through him. Tonight, he wouldn't be the only one in hell. His brother would be joining him.

"You look well, Mathias." At Beatrice's quiet words, he turned his head and smiled at her. He'd always liked Beatrice. The biggest mistake his brother had ever made was letting her go to America as another man's wife.

"Flattery from a beautiful woman is always a pleasant thing to hear." At her blush, he chuckled. "When did you return from America?"

"Almost two weeks ago. My father has been ill, and the possibility…the possibility of him never meeting Nathanial made me decide to come home."

"Nathanial?" Although Mathias was certain she was referring to the son he'd heard others mention, the child's name startled him. It was Charles's middle name, and he wondered if Beatrice had chosen the boy's name with his brother in mind.

"So, seeing his grandson played a role in your father's recovery?"

"Yes, I think our arrival was all he needed to recover," she sighed with relief before a pensive look crossed her lovely features. "Perhaps I should have come home sooner, but there were many things to do after Barnabas's death."

"Forgive me. I was remiss in offering you my condolences on the loss of your husband," Mathias said with a wince at his oversight.

"Thank you," she murmured as she bowed her head slightly and avoided his gaze. "Barnabas was a kind and generous man."

"Then you were happy?"

Mathias didn't know why he pressed her on the matter, but something in her voice made him think her marriage might not have been as idyllic as many had been led to believe. She didn't answer him for a long moment, and she gave off the impression of a gazelle ready to flee a predator.

"Barnabas worked a great deal, but I had Nathanial. I was lonely more than anything else."

"Surely you had friends." Mathias eyed her in puzzlement.

"A few, but New York society is far more…restrictive than here at home." A smile tugged at her lips. "I know there were many mothers who found it difficult to open their doors to me. Barnabas was one of the most eligible bachelors in the city before he married me."

"Louisa mentioned you were leaving for the country in a few days. I'm assuming you'll be returning to Ravenswood." At the curiosity in his voice, she hesitated before she nodded.

"Yes. Nathanial will be off to school in a few years, and I'd like him to enjoy his childhood in the country. Father will also benefit from the fresh air."

Mathias nodded his understanding as Beatrice's attention was pulled away from him by the gentleman on her left.

On his right, the Duchess of Trowbridge was engaged in a lively conversation with the man seated beside her. The older woman was a friend of Lady Stewart's, the current chief of the Callendar Stewarts clan. A frequent dinner guest at Melton House, he always enjoyed his conversations with the duchess, but at the moment, he was content to consider Beatrice's relationship with Charles.

Her return to London had clearly been precipitated by her father's illness. While he understood Beatrice's reasons for retiring to the country, he couldn't help wondering if Charles had played a role in her decision. Ravenswood Hall was less than three miles across the pastures from Thornbury Hall. Was she leaving town to avoid Charles, or was she hoping he'd follow her to the country as he once had to London?

Even before he'd inherited his title, Charles had always had a natural tendency to enjoy life without thought of consequences. When their father died, Charles had simply delegated most of his financial and estate management responsibilities to Mathias. It was at one of the house parties he'd hosted at Thornbury Hall when he'd met Beatrice.

She'd just returned to Ravenswood from finishing school in France, and the two had met while out riding. His brother had been the Earl of Thornbury for little more than two years at the time and had earned a reputation for breaking hearts when he'd met Beatrice. When Charles had followed Beatrice to London, Mathias had hoped it was a sign his brother was ready to fulfill his duties. He'd been wrong.

Beatrice had sailed for New York with her new husband, and his brother's enjoyment in life took a reckless turn. Charles had constantly put himself at risk until a near-fatal horseback accident had made his brother change course. Mathias glanced toward the end of the table and met his brother's gaze. The emotion flashing across Charles's face was undefinable, and Mathias frowned with irritation. He'd never met a more stubborn person in his life. A voice protested in the back of his head, but he ignored the sound.

For the remainder of the meal, Beatrice managed to avoid any more personal conversations with him. Whenever they spoke, she quickly changed the subject by replying to his questions with a question of her own. Throughout the meal, he continued to study Charles down the length of the table. His brother acted as if he were enjoying himself immensely, and it made him wonder if he'd read more into Charles's reaction to Beatrice than he should have.

After the meal's last course, the women left the dining room while the men remained behind to enjoy a glass of cognac. Mathias leaned back in his chair to study the amber liquid in his glass. He moved his hand in a gentle motion and watched as the brandy swirled around in the crystal glass. Across the room, Mathias saw Percy speaking with Chelmsford. The foul mood he'd been in earlier returned. He was tired of polite conversation.

As soon as it was respectable to do so, he'd leave. There was a decanter of whisky waiting for him at home. In the past month, alcohol had been the only way to drown out his pain. It deadened the ache in his body and suppressed the thoughts of Ophelia that haunted his every waking moment. He took a swig of his brandy before setting it on the table.

That night at the club had been the last time he'd drank to excess in public. He'd confined his drunken stupors to his bedroom. If he were to have imbibed too freely at the club, the gossips would have ensured Ophelia heard of his excessive drinking. He wasn't about to give the woman any satisfaction as to how her betrayal had affected him.

"Might I have a word with you, Gilchrist?"

Startled out of his thoughts, Mathias stiffened in his chair as Chelmsford sat down in the chair next to him. His resolve not to drink too heavily in public vanished as he reached for his brandy. He took a deep drink of the cognac, not bothering to savor the dried fruit flavor mixed with citrus zest. Afraid he would thrash the man if he looked at him, Mathias focused his gaze on his glass.

"What do you want, Chelmsford?"

"Actually, I think it's more a question of what you want." At the earl's odd reply, Mathias jerked his head toward the man.

"Cryptic conversations hold no appeal for me, my lord. Say what you have to say, then get the hell away from me."

"As you wish." The earl shrugged slightly. "I'd like to know what happened between you and Ophelia the night of the Meacham affair."

"Nothing," Mathias lied as he eyed his empty brandy snifter instead of looking Chelmsford in the eye.

A great deal had happened that night. There had been his anguish when he'd discovered Ophelia had accepted Chelmsford's proposal. The moment he'd been unable to let her leave the study. The memory of her passionate response to him flooded through Mathias, followed by an image of her humiliation when he'd brutally insulted her.

The final blow that night had been the agony he'd suffered when he'd returned to Meacham's study, intent on begging her forgiveness, only to find her in Chelmsford's arms. Mathias's chest constricted as if a band of metal had suddenly been wrapped tightly around him, and it was difficult to breathe.

"Why don't I believe you?"

"I don't give a fuck what you believe, Chelmsford," Mathias said quietly, yet forcefully, as he turned his head and eyed the earl with antipathy. "As I said, say what you came over here to say, then get the hell away from me."

"Do you love Lady Havenstock?"

The earl's question stunned Mathias, and he stared at the man in open-mouthed astonishment. His amazement vanished a second later as he narrowed his gaze at Chelmsford, and intense dislike surged through him. He'd like nothing better than to challenge the man to a boxing match, but he knew he'd be at a disadvantage. The earl was well known for his exemplary pugilistic skills.

"Whatever game you're playing, Chelmsford, I suggest you play it with someone else," Mathias growled.

"It's a simple question, Gilchrist. Are you in love with Ophelia?" This time, the question didn't surprise him. Leaning back in his chair, Mathias eyed the man coldly for a moment before he shook his head.

"I seem to recall you asking me a short time ago if Lady Havenstock and I had an understanding," Mathias said as he eyed the other man coldly. "I told you at that time we did not and that the lady was free to indulge in whatever liaison she wished."

"Rockwood said you were stubborn."

"Percy is hardly an authority on the subject." Mathias looked at his empty glass and wished he hadn't swallowed the cognac so quickly. "But since you've mentioned Lady Havenstock, I understand congratulations are in order."

"Congratulations?" A bewildered frown creased Chelmsford's forehead.

"I understand Lady Havenstock has agreed to your offer of marriage."

This time it was the earl's turn to look astonished. Mathias almost released a bitter laugh at the man's expression, but he was far from being in a laughing mood. With a sharp movement, he shoved himself out of his chair.

"If you'll excuse me, Chelmsford, this conversation has become boring." He'd taken only two steps when he heard the earl's snort of mocking laughter.

"You aren't just stubborn. You're a blind fool as well."

Mathias remained still for a moment as he struggled to control the rage surging through him. He'd never wanted to pummel anyone as much as he did this man. It took several seconds to curb his anger before he slowly turned around.

"I'm well aware of your skill in the ring, Chelmsford, but at the moment, your insults are making it difficult for me not to challenge you."

"The truth is never an insult, Gilchrist. You're as stubborn as you are blind. What would you say if I said Ophelia will not be the next Countess of Chelmsford?"

The earl's words took a moment to sink in as Mathias stared at his enemy in bewildered silence. Ophelia wasn't going to marry Chelmsford. But why? With a look of annoyed disgust, Chelmsford narrowed his gaze as he stood up.

"Do you love her or not?" The earl bit out his question in a display of impatient exasperation.

"Yes." The word was a guttural sound as Mathias met the man's gaze.

"Good. If you'd said no, I think I would have been the one challenging you to a bout in the ring," Chelmsford said sharply. "I'm quite fond of Ophelia, but she refuses to marry a man she doesn't love."

"She said she would never marry again," Mathias bit out between clenched teeth as he remembered how emphatic Ophelia had been on the topic.

"And so when you thought she'd agreed to marry me, you assumed the worst about her and her character." The earl's gaze hardened as he studied Mathias. "I've no idea why she loves you, Gilchrist, but she does."

Mathias jerked at the man's statement, his head not quite comprehending everything that had occurred in the past few moments. Was it possible? Did Ophelia really love him, or was Chelmsford mistaken? His questions must have been visible on his face as the earl eyed him with extreme annoyance.

"For God's sake, man, I've no reason to lie to you."

"Where is she?" Mathias growled as his mind grappled with the revelation Chelmsford had just shared. "Why isn't she here tonight?"

"She refused to come because whatever you said to her the night of the Meacham affair nearly destroyed her."

The sharp words filled Mathias with a pang of deeply stark guilt. He'd been a bastard. He'd treated her with the same contempt her husband had, simply because he'd not had the courage to ask her if she'd agreed to marry Chelmsford. The only question now was whether she loved him enough to forgive him.

"You don't deserve her, you know." Chelmsford's quiet words made Mathias meet the man's judgmental gaze, and he nodded.

"You're right. I don't. But I'll do everything in my power to be a man who does."

"See to it that you do, unless you want to meet me in the ring, and I can assure you, I'll be quite unforgiving."

The threat tugged a small smile to Mathias's lips. With a nod of understanding, he turned away and headed for the main hall. Behind him, Chelmsford said something, but he didn't pay any attention. When he reached the hall, he waited impatiently for Madison to summon a hack for him. Louisa emerged from the parlor to stare at him in surprise.

"You're leaving?"

"Yes, I've something to do."

"If your errand is what I think it is, she's not there," Louisa said quietly.

"What do you mean?" Mathias's muscles grew taut as he waited for the youngest Rockwood to answer his question. Sympathy flashed in his friend's eyes.

"She left London almost a week ago."

"Where are you going, Mathias?" The quiet sound of his brother's voice echoed behind him, and he looked over his shoulder to see Charles and Percy moving toward him.

"He's going after Ophelia, and I can only say it's about time," Louisa said with a note of pleased satisfaction before her expression dimmed slightly. "Unfortunately, he won't see her tonight."

"What in heaven's name are the lot of you doing in the foyer?" Constance exclaimed as she stepped out into the hall. The moment she saw Mathias with his hat in hand, she narrowed her gaze at him. "You're leaving, Mathias?"

"He's finally come to his senses and is leaving to go after Ophelia." Her sister's proclamation made Constance smile with happiness. She didn't have a chance to respond as Lady Stewart's voice echoed out from the doorway of the parlor.

"Ach, now, what in the name of all the Stewarts is going on out here?"

Lady Stewart stepped into the hallway as curious dinner guests gathered in the salon's open doorway. Mathias experienced a sudden sensation of being cornered, and the sound of Madison's quiet voice announcing a hack was waiting at the curb made Mathias expel a harsh sigh of relief. He caught Louisa's hand and kissed it quickly.

"Please convey my thanks to the earl and countess for a delightful meal and a…most enlightening evening," he said as he saw the Earl of Chelmsford walk out of the dining room, followed by Sebastian.

Unwilling to answer any more questions, Mathias nodded at the earl as their eyes met across the distance before he hurried out the front door. He had just reached the sidewalk when he remembered Louisa saying Ophelia had left London. Had she gone back to Marymont or somewhere else?

"Mathias. Wait." At the sound of his name, he turned to see Louisa hurrying down the front steps of Melton House. She halted in front of him as she shook her head in amusement. "Don't you want to know where to find her?"

"Where is she?" he demanded in a no-nonsense tone.

"She's gone to Marymont. Leave town as you would if you were going to Melton Park. When you reach the road leading to the family estate, take the right fork. Marymont is about five miles from there. You'll be able to see the house from the road." Louisa kissed him on the cheek, and gratitude surged through him.

"Thank you," he said softly. Without waiting for his friend's reply, Mathias climbed into the hack and ordered the driver to take him to Thornbury Place. He had plans to make if he was to leave town at dawn.

Chapter 16

Mathias reined Titan to a halt and stared at the house that was less than a half-mile away. There was a quiet elegance to Marymont that its owner also possessed. Now that he was here, his confidence in his ability to convince Ophelia how much he loved her had diminished significantly.

The gray, forbidding sky overhead had a sobering effect on him. It was a representation of his overall mood these past weeks. He'd be fortunate if Ophelia even agreed to speak to him, let alone listen. The memory of those last moments in the Meacham library made his chest constrict painfully.

He hadn't been just a bastard. He'd been unbelievably cruel. He'd known the instant his offensive, cutting words had passed his lips, he'd gone too far. Ophelia's look of humiliation and devastation in those few seconds had ripped him apart inside. It didn't matter that anger, jealousy, and the knowledge he'd lost her to the earl had been the driving force behind his ruthless behavior.

Not even his need to hide his love for her could absolve him of his words. Even if she had accepted Chelmsford, she wasn't the social climber Miriam had been. Deep inside, he'd known she would never change her mind about marriage unless there was a good reason. When she'd compared him to her late husband, her quiet dignity had eviscerated him in a way her anger could not.

But it had been the dark anguish in her lovely eyes that had gutted him as he'd considered the possibility he'd been wrong about her. It was why he'd returned to the library several minutes later, only to find her in Chelmsford's arms.

The memory of that terrible moment and the conclusion he'd reached made him jerk slightly as he remembered Chelmsford's revelation last night. The man was convinced Ophelia loved him, and he prayed the earl wasn't mistaken. The façade of the comfortable-looking house, such a short distance away, came into focus once more.

An unfamiliar sensation twisted his gut. Fear wasn't something he'd experienced a great deal of in his life, but then his life rarely hung in the balance as it did now. If Ophelia refused to forgive him, the hellish existence he'd been living for the past month would become permanent. His jaw tightened with tension as he nudged Titan forward.

The stallion covered the distance to the house in a shorter span of time than Mathias would have liked. He was still struggling to find the best way to convince Ophelia to forgive him as Titan pranced to a halt in front of the house. Mathias slowly dismounted, then froze for a moment as uncertainty snaked its way through him. As if the horse could sense his hesitation, Titan's large head dipped downward to toss restlessly against his arm.

He grimaced slightly at the notion the horse recognized his fear. Would Ophelia see it in him as well? Not waiting for the animal to nudge him again, Mathias moved toward the front door. The knocker echoed harshly in his ears as he waited for it to open. It was no more than a minute before the door swung open, but it seemed an eternity. Taggert's gaze met his, and the butler frowned. Mathias couldn't tell if it was an expression of disapproval or concern.

"Taggert." He jerked his head in an abrupt greeting. "Is Lady Havenstock at home?"

"She went for a walk, sir."

"Where?" When the butler hesitated, Mathias met the man's gaze steadily. "My intentions are honorable ones, Taggert."

"She mentioned walking to the pond near the north pasture, Mr. Gilchrist." The man hesitated slightly before pointing in the direction of Melton Park. "If you ride toward the earl's estate, you'll see a small orchard. The pond is beyond that."

"Thank you."

Mathias didn't wait for a reply as he strode back to Titan and quickly mounted the horse. With a gentle squeeze of his thighs, he urged the stallion in the direction Taggert had pointed. It didn't take long to find the orchard, and as he cleared the small group of trees, he saw the body of water. His gaze quickly found Ophelia. She was standing at the edge of the pond with her back to him. The sight of her made his heart slam into his chest.

Tension spread through Mathias as he dismounted and dropped the reins to the ground to ensure Titan remained where he was. With each step he took in Ophelia's direction, every muscle in his body grew taut. He was only a few feet away from her when he saw her reach up to touch the back of her neck.

Almost instantly, she whirled around. A brief flash of undefinable emotion crossed her lovely face before her expression became one of cold antipathy. For a moment, he remained silent and simply drank in the sight of her. She was the most beautiful woman he'd ever seen. Just looking at her made him happy. God help him if she refused to forgive him.

"Why are you here, Mr. Gilchrist?"

The formality of her question made his lungs constrict until it was difficult to breathe. How could he explain in words what she meant to him? When he hesitated, she narrowed her gaze at him.

"You had a great deal to say the last time we met, and I'm puzzled that you seem bereft of words now."

"Forgive me. You simply took my breath away," Mathias said, ignoring the reference to their last meeting.

Ophelia stared at him with dislike as she tugged the shawl draped around her shoulders until the material was taut. The weather was unseasonably warm for November, but the air still had a bite to it. It was impossible to determine if she was using the shawl to keep the temperature at bay or if she was using it as a shield against him.

"Your frivolous platitudes are a waste of time on me." The coldness of her reply made him wince.

"It's the truth," Mathias said as he searched her expression for a sign she might be willing to forgive him. "You're the most beautiful woman I've ever seen."

Her lovely mouth thinned as she dismissed him with a frosty glare. Without a word, she stepped around him and began to walk away. Mathias didn't think. He simply reacted. His hand reached out to halt her departure, and at his touch, she yanked herself free of his grip, only to stumble. To prevent her from falling, he pulled her into his arms. The warmth of her penetrated his clothing and made him ache to never let her go. A familiar citrus scent filled his nostrils as she pushed against his chest.

"Let me go." The outrage in her voice was accompanied by a slight shudder that pulsated its way into his body. Reluctantly, he released her, and she quickly put several feet between them. Brown eyes flashing with anger, her gaze traveled over him in a scathing look of contempt.

"I'll ask you again. Why are you here, Mr. Gilchrist?"

"Because I love you." At his quiet reply, Ophelia gasped, and the color drained from her cheeks.

"This is a new low, even for you, Mathias. But I should have expected no less from a man such as you." The contempt in her accusation made his body jerk as if she'd swung a sword and sliced him open. She didn't believe him. The optimism that had shored him up since last night vanished.

"It's the truth," he said with quiet firmness. "I love you, and I came to tell you that and ask your forgiveness."

"Then your journey was a waste of time." Ophelia's frigid words weren't anywhere as cold as her icy gaze was.

The finality in her tone sank deep into his bones. Christ almighty, had his words at the Meacham affair completely destroyed any hope of healing the breach between them. Fear dried his mouth as she turned and began to walk back to Marymont.

"Ophelia. Wait," he exclaimed as he stepped forward to catch her elbow then quickly released her. "At least hear me out."

"No," she snapped as she faced him. "You listen to me. I loathe you. There isn't a man I know, living or dead, that I despise more. There's nothing more you can add to what you've already said. Nothing."

"For God's sake, Ophelia, please," he said hoarsely. "I know I'm a bastard. I was wrong to ignore your wishes regarding Sabine. But that mistake pales in comparison to my behavior in Meacham's library. The words I spoke were cruel—unforgivable."

"And yet here you are, standing in front of me and having the temerity to ask for my forgiveness."

"Damn it, I'm doing more than asking you to forgive me. I'm asking you to believe I love you. God knows I don't deserve your forgiveness, let alone your heart, but I'm asking you to give me the chance to be worthy of you. I love you deeper than any words I can express. I want to marry you. Even if you refuse to be my wife, at least let me spend the rest of my life loving you and giving you as much of the world as I can."

As his voice died away, Mathias steadily met Ophelia's gaze looking for some small sign that she'd believed the depth of his remorse and his declaration of love. It was impossible to determine what she was thinking, and his heartbeat thundered in his ears like a herd of wild horses. After a long moment of silence, she shook her head.

"You ask for something I cannot give, Mathias." The soft words struck deep into his soul and sent pain crashing through him until his muscles were tied into knots.

"Cannot or will not?" His terse question made her narrow her gaze at him.

"Does it matter? You made your contempt for me quite clear that night in Lord Meacham's library."

"God help me, Ophelia, if I could take my words back, I would." Mathias paused slightly as he saw something flicker in her soft brown eyes. Was he reaching her? "I was out of my mind with jealousy and anger thinking you'd accepted Chelmsford's proposal."

"Proposal?" For a brief second, confusion made her frown before her eyes widened with amazement, then narrowed at him with an icy outrage. "You believed me capable of giving myself to you in a moment of passion, even if I'd pledged myself to Gideon?"

"I was too angry to think straight. You'd been so adamant you wouldn't marry again, and I believed the worst of you."

"Your arrogance in thinking I couldn't resist your touch is second only to your low opinion of me." Beneath her anger, he could see how deeply he'd injured her, and guilt hammered its way deep into him.

"The only low opinion I have of anyone is me. I knew better. But a man is capable of doing and saying terrible things when he's afraid of losing the woman he loves. I will never be truly worthy of you, Ophelia, but I will spend the rest of my life trying to be if you'll just let me love you."

His quiet reply caused her eyes to flash with an emotion he couldn't decipher, and his inability to determine what she was thinking sent fear crashing through him. Had he reached her? In the deep recesses of his mind, a bleak possibility pushed its way forward. What if he failed to earn her forgiveness, let alone her heart?

It had been a long time since he'd prayed, but now he silently begged the Almighty for help. The silence stretched out between them for a long moment as he waited for her to say something. He saw something that might have been regret darken Ophelia's eyes before she shook her head.

"I want you to leave, Mathias. I want you to leave and never come back here ever again."

The emotionless, quiet words were tangible blows to his body, and they inflicted a pain far greater than anything he'd ever experienced in his lifetime. He'd lost. The one thing in his life he needed as badly as the air he breathed was lost to him. Mathias stood frozen in place as he met her gaze. When he didn't move, she turned away.

"Goodbye, Mathias."

The soft words drifted over her shoulder as she walked away from him. It was only when she disappeared from sight that he realized he hadn't moved because he'd been hoping for a miracle. Chelmsford, Louisa, Percy, they'd all been convinced she loved him, but they'd been wrong. They'd been so very wrong. Ophelia didn't love him. Her words and deportment had illustrated far too well her opinion of him.

Ophelia despised him.

An invisible vise wrapped around Mathias's chest so tightly the pain almost drove him to his knees. A man bound for the gallows couldn't be more deeply immersed in hell than he was. But a condemned man never had long to wait before his torment ended. For Mathias, his torment would not end swiftly. His life would be nothing but a bleak, parched desert for years to come.

Ophelia stepped into the mudroom and closed the door behind her. A small shudder rippled through her, followed by another, and then another. The violence of her trembling forced her to sink down onto the roughly hewn bench next to the door. She leaned back and rested her head on the wall behind her. What had possessed Mathias to come to Marymont?

Although she tried to ignore it, his declaration of love echoed loudly in her head. All the way back to the house, a small voice had frantically urged Ophelia to turn around and run back to Mathias. Even if she had obeyed the voice and gone after him, how could she trust him again? How could she trust him never to treat her in the same way George had?

The voice in the back of her head chided her fiercely. Mathias was nothing like George. Except for the cruel words he'd spoken that night in the Meacham library, he'd always treated her honorably. Mathias had proven that the night she'd chosen to enter his bed and experience passion in his arms. Mathias had tried desperately to stop her from doing something he believed she would regret. Even when he'd paid the balance of her bill with Sabine, he'd done so for no other reason than simple generosity and an attempt to ease her financial worries.

The mere fact that he'd paid the bill without her knowledge demonstrated he'd had no ulterior motives or expectations as the result of his actions. Then there was Edgar suddenly returning control of her finances to her. She had no proof of Mathias's intervention, but she was certain he'd played a role in that as well. No. The only reason he could have had for coming to Marymont was precisely for the reason he'd said. He loved her.

She closed her eyes as her mind flitted back to that night in the library and the terrible moments following their wild moment of passion. Mathias's tension had been an almost tangible sensation when she'd stared at his back immediately afterwards. His brutal, icy demeanor had been in direct conflict with the emotional intensity she'd experienced with him during their lovemaking.

But there had been one emotion flowing out of him she'd been unable to define until now. There had been a desperate despondency to everything he'd said and done, leading up to the cruel words that had crushed her. Mathias said a man was capable of doing and saying terrible things when faced with the prospect of losing the woman he loved. She understood that now.

What she'd thought had been dismissive cruelty on his part had been something completely different. His confession only a few moments ago made her realize his words that night had been born out of pain. Humans were no different than any other animal when they were in pain or cornered. They lashed out. It was a defense mechanism, and she was no less susceptible to it either.

Her angry rejection of Mathias today illustrated that. Love and joy had engulfed her when she'd turned to see him standing in front of her. A split second later, fear had swallowed up those happy emotions. Instinct had reminded her how easily he could destroy her. Instead of listening, she'd greeted his pleas for love and forgiveness with scathing words and rejection.

Tears pushed at the back of Ophelia's eyelids, and she dragged in a deep breath. None of it mattered now. All hope of happiness had vanished the moment she'd walked away from Mathias. With the heel of her palm, she wiped the moisture away from the corners of her eyes. She had no desire to provoke any concern on Taggert's or Mrs. Barstow's part.

She made her way through the back of the house and hurried past the kitchen door, where she heard Mrs. Barstow gently chiding the kitchen maid for some slight error. Taggert's voice echoed from the back stairwell, and she darted along the hall toward the empty foyer. One foot on the first step of the main staircase, she froze at the sound of her father's voice behind her.

"Ophelia, my dear, might I have a word?" At the question, she slowly turned toward the baron.

"Of course, Father," she murmured politely as he gestured toward the small library doorway behind him. In silence, she moved past her father and entered the small room. Although things were still strained between them, her father had been making a visible effort to improve his behavior ever since they'd returned to Marymont. He restricted himself to wine at dinner and a glass of port in the evening.

His only form of entertainment was the chess games he enjoyed with the vicar several nights a week. She didn't know whether returning to Marymont was the reason for the sudden change, but she was grateful for it. Ophelia crossed the floor to one of the room's tall arched windows to stare out at the bleak weather. The sound of her father clearing his throat made her turn around. There was a guilty look on his face, and her heart sank.

"I'm afraid I have a confession to make, my dear."

"Who do you owe money to this time, Father?" At her question, the baron sighed. Regret twisted his lips in a grimace of regret.

"I understand why that would be your first question, my dear. I have not been the best of men since your mother died. You and Lizzie have suffered for it."

"Simply tell me who you owe money to, Father." She didn't bother to hide her angry disappointment.

"I have no debts that need to be paid. It's something else entirely. I've interfered in a matter that perhaps I shouldn't have."

"What matter?" she asked as tension slid through her. An image of Vicar Dobson filled her head. Dear God, had the two men been discussing her lack of a husband.

"My only defense is my desire for your happiness."

"Oh, Father, please tell me you've not been discussing my lack of a husband with the vicar."

"Dobson?" Baron Sheffield's eyes widen for a moment before he shook his head. "Heavens no, the man is quite pleasant, but I know your heart lies elsewhere."

"Elsewhere?"

"Actually, I believe directly across the hall in the salon." Confused by his words, Ophelia frowned. Had Gideon come to visit already? Her father had expressed he was in favor of her marrying the earl. While Gideon had promised to visit, it surprised her that he'd not sent word he was coming. The Baron's discomfort became more pronounced as a dark flush of color filled his face. "He was adamant you wanted nothing to do with him, but I managed to convince him—"

"Mathias." She barely breathed the word, but her father heard her.

"Yes."

The baron winced in obvious preparation for Ophelia to berate him for his interference. She stared at him for a brief heartbeat, then ran toward the door. Her father said something, but she didn't pause to listen. Ophelia slipped slightly on the foyer's marble floor as she raced toward the salon. She darted through the open doorway, and her gaze swept the room.

It was empty. Ophelia's heart twisted painfully in her chest. Mathias had simply waited for her father to leave him alone before quietly leaving the house. Ophelia whirled around and raced back into the hall toward the front door. As she flung the door open wide, she didn't see Mathias. Dear God, she'd not been in time to stop him.

Her heart in her mouth, she ran down the steps to stop on the pebbled driveway. Frantically, she looked in every direction in search of his tall figure astride Titan. A light rain had begun to fall, and she wasn't sure whether her cheeks were wet from her tears or raindrops.

Desperation sent her running down the drive in the hope of catching him. As she passed the corner of the house, she glanced toward the orchard and saw Mathias riding toward Melton Park.

"Mathias," she cried out as she ran after him. When he didn't stop, she screamed his name as loudly as she could. "Mathias."

For a brief second, she thought he'd paused, but when he didn't turn in his saddle, she lifted her skirts to race after him, calling out his name over and over again as loudly as she could. Her vision quickly became blurred as tears flowed down her cheeks. Her heart pounding with fear that he wouldn't hear her, she shrieked his name again.

Unable to see clearly, Ophelia tried to wipe the tears from her eyes as she ran and almost fell as she stumbled over an uneven spot on the ground. Her eyesight somewhat clearer, she ignored how her chest burned as she raced after Mathias. She tripped over another rough spot on the ground and screamed for him as she fell.

Staggering to her feet, she looked up to see he'd turned around. The moment he urged Titan forward in her direction, she ran toward him. In seconds, Mathias closed the distance between them. He dismounted and strode forward to catch her as she flung herself into his arms.

"I love you, Mathias," she sobbed. "I was wrong to send you away. I don't want you to go."

She shuddered as he roughly pulled her deeper into his embrace to hold her tight against him. The solid warmth of him enveloped her as she buried her face in the dampness of his jacket, and they stood silently in each other's arms. Cheeks still damp from her tears, Ophelia lifted her head to look at him.

"I love you, Mathias," she whispered.

"I thought I'd lost you." The hoarse words echoed with pain as his fingers lightly traced the curve of her cheek. "Can you forgive me, my darling?"

"Yes," she whispered as she brushed her lips against his. "I forgive you."

"Thank God." Mathias released a harsh breath of air as his mouth brushed across her forehead. The tender touch made her shiver at how close she'd come to losing him as well. Immediately, his embrace relaxed slightly as he glanced at their surroundings, then touched her hair, now completely wet from the drizzle.

"We need to get you indoors where you'll be dry and warm."

"I'm fine," she said with a shake of her head as her gaze met his. "Mathias…did you mean what you said about being willing to be with me…to love me, even if I didn't want to marry?"

Mathias stiffened against her, but he didn't push her away. If anything, his arms tightened around her. A sudden wave of fear rolled over her. What if he refused? She knew the answer. It would mean his love wasn't strong enough to let her go, and letting go meant relinquishing all control. The silence settling between them was fraught with tension before he sucked in a deep breath.

"I said I wanted to give you the world, and I meant it," he said quietly, but there were white lines at the corners of his mouth as if he were struggling not to protest. "I don't want to lose you, and I won't ask something of you that you can't give. I'll accept whatever terms you wish as long as it means I don't have to part with you."

Each word was heartfelt, even though she could hear the disappointment in his voice that he was desperately trying to hide. She closed her eyes for a moment at the knowledge he loved her enough to give her the freedom she asked of him. Deep inside her, she heard the sharp sound of a chain snapping.

There was a long pause before another shackle snapped. In rapid succession, the links that had made it impossible for her to trust easily broke away, leaving her with a sense of freedom she'd never experienced before. Tears formed in her eyes, and as they rolled down her cheeks, Mathias uttered a soft exclamation of alarm.

"Please don't cry, sweetheart. Don't cry. I'll never deny you the independence you need. I love you too much," he choked out in obvious concern as his fingers brushed away her tears with a tenderness that made her heart swell. His sincerity echoed in each light touch of his fingers against her cheek. "Your happiness means more to me than my own. If that means loving you outside of societal conventions, then so be it. My happiness is tied to yours."

Unable to restrain her sob, her hand wrapped around his neck to force his head down as she sought his lips in a passionate kiss. The moment she did so, it was as if a dam broke, and the raging waters swept her along in a wild and exhilarating river of sensation. Every part of her was on fire, and she ached to be a part of him—to be with him completely until she couldn't feel where she ended and he began.

A rumble in his chest vibrated against her fingers as he pulled her so tight into his body that if she'd been a fragile piece of china, she would have broken into a million pieces. Her mouth parted beneath his, and the moment his tongue swirled around hers, passion blinded her to everything but him. Eagerly, she met the demands of his mouth as he took control of their kiss. Need stirred in the center of her body, and she moaned her desire as she clung to him. A shudder shook his solid frame, and he broke their kiss to lift his head. The desire burning in his gaze sent heat coursing through her blood. With a grimace of what could have been pain, he shuddered again.

"God knows I want to show you how much I love you, sweetheart, but this is hardly the time or place." His mouth twisted in a small, wry smile. "You're soaked through and through."

"I could be standing in a downpour, and I wouldn't care because I'm with you. I need you as the earth needs the rain, Mathias. I'll always need you. I'll always love you."

The passion in his eyes darkened with another emotion, and she saw his throat bob as he swallowed hard. His only response was an abrupt nod, but the adoration in his green eyes told her everything she needed to know. A second later, she gasped in surprise as Mathias's embrace shifted, and he swept her off her feet. He carried her to where Titan was standing a few feet away, then set her in the saddle.

The horse's reins in hand, he gripped the horse's mane at the bottom of the animal's neck, then mounted the stallion to sit behind her. The strength of him flowed through her, and with a sigh, she leaned back into him. An overwhelming wave of happiness rolled over her, and the strength of it frightened her. Almost as if he could sense her reaction to the intensity of the emotion, Mathias lowered his head, and his mouth brushed the side of her temple.

"I love you, Ophelia."

The soft words warmed her skin, and this time the happiness sweeping over her didn't alarm her. Instead, she welcomed it with an open heart and a soft sigh of contentment

Epilogue

irelight was the only illumination in the bedroom Mrs. Barstow had prepared for him at Ophelia's request. Mathias had snuffed out the bedside candles a short time ago hoping to encourage sleep, but his mind was too active. Behind him, the flames cast shadows on the walls, and they danced to the soft snaps and pops of the burning wood in the hearth.

One shoulder pressed into the window frame, Mathias stared out the window. The rain had stopped after supper, and the clouds had begun to slowly roll away, so the moon was able to cast its light on the grounds.

In the space of hours, he'd been thrown into a hell beyond all imagining, only to be saved by the woman he loved calling out his name. He closed his eyes at the memory of Ophelia running through the rain to stop him from leaving. When he'd heard her cry out his name, he'd thought it had been his mind taunting him.

He'd called himself a fool for even stopping to turn his head toward the sound of her voice. It had taken him several seconds to realize his imagination hadn't conjured up the sight of her stumbling toward him. Even when she'd flung herself into his arms, it had still been hard to comprehend what was happening. It was only when she was trembling against him that he accepted the reality of it all. She loved him. She'd forgiven him. It was more than he'd dreamed possible.

When she'd ordered him to leave Marymont, he'd been desolate. The situation had been made even more impossible when he'd met Baron Sheffield on the drive. The man's persistent demand that he return to the house had been impossible to refuse without revealing why doing so would be so painful for Ophelia. The last thing he'd wanted was to cause her any further suffering. He'd inflicted far too much insult and injury on her that he knew would never be comparable to his own misery.

The finality of Ophelia's demeanor when she'd turned her back on him at the pond had nearly brought him to his knees. It had made him believe Baron Sheffield's invitation to return to the house was the universe's way of taunting him with the memory of that moment. When Ophelia had disappeared from view without looking back at him, he'd been forced to accept the final judgement she'd handed down.

There was no one to blame for the pit of despondency and guilt she'd condemned him to other than himself. It was a hell of his own making. The lifetime sentence had stripped him of any hope she'd ever have a change of heart, let alone forgive him in the span of a few short moments. But Baron Sheffield had been adamant in extending his invitation, and it had forced Mathias into a corner he couldn't escape without an explanation that might injure Ophelia further.

When he'd yielded to the baron's persistent demand, he'd done so with the condition the baron inform Ophelia in private that he'd returned. He'd known it would allow her to refuse to see him while providing him the opportunity to leave without any objection by the Baron. The possibility of clemency had never occurred to him until Ophelia had flung herself into his arms.

That moment had been one of overwhelming relief, no different from a man pardoned from the hangman's noose at the last possible moment. Even now, the relief he'd experienced in that instant had yet to evaporate. He wasn't sure it ever would. He'd almost lost everything he held dear in the world, and it was something he would never forget. It would ensure he strived every day to be a man worthy of Ophelia's love.

The hours following Ophelia flinging herself into his arms had been filled with the simplicity of being near each other. Supper had been a happy but quiet affair, and Baron Sheffield had enjoyed taking credit for being the catalyst of their reconciliation. While the man had stated his amazement at Ophelia following Mathias out into the rain, the baron didn't question the why of the matter.

The only awkward moment of the evening had been when Sheffield had posed the question of a wedding date. Mathias had forced a smile and allowed Ophelia to reply. She'd done so with a vague response that had satisfied the baron. For Mathias, it had been a confirmation of her desire that their future be unencumbered by the constraints of any marital bonds.

Mathias suppressed his yearning for a stronger commitment from her as he stared out at the grounds once more. The only question left to answer now was how best to handle their relationship's highly unconventional aspect. He was determined to protect her as much as possible from the Set's vitriol. Except for a few friends, Ophelia would be subjected to open contempt, and she'd be shunned in an open and caustic manner.

Flaunting society's norms was perfectly acceptable for men but not for women. Fortunately, he didn't think it would be difficult to convince her to spend as little time as possible in town. Ophelia loved Marymont, and although he knew she wouldn't be spared censure here in the country, it would be nothing compared to what she'd find in London. He grimaced at the knowledge of what lay in store for her.

There was little he could do except protect her as best he could. As much as he wished she would marry him, he refused to force her to choose either him or her freedom. His refusal to present her with such an ultimatum was more than just a desire to prove his love. The potential outcome of such a demand scared the hell out of him.

There was the distinct possibility she might walk away from him simply to safeguard her independence. Even if she surrendered to his demands, there was the very real possibility she would come to hate him for coercing her into giving up her freedom. Short of losing her, that terrified him the most. No matter what she asked of him, he'd do everything in his power to make her happy, even if it meant sacrificing his own hopes and desires.

The faint sound of a click made him turn his head, and his heart slammed against his chest at the sight of Ophelia closing the bedroom door. The firelight highlighted the vibrant blue of the silk robe she wore. The garment was parted slightly at the neck to reveal a sheer gown beneath the robe. She took his breath away as she moved toward him.

He'd hoped she would come, but he'd not expected it. There was the problem of her father they had yet to discuss. While the baron held no sway over his daughter, the man still deserved time to take in his daughter's decision to lead an unconventional lifestyle. When she came to a halt in front of him, she reached up to touch his cheek as a smile curved her sweet mouth.

"You're surprised I came?" The quiet question made him wince slightly.

"Yes."

"Why?" She tipped her head to one side as she studied him with obvious puzzlement.

"We've not yet explained the…the uniqueness of our relationship to your father. The man, at the very least, deserves some warning as to our arrangement."

"Hmm," she murmured, then nodded with a sang-froid that startled him. Her fingers traced a path along his jaw and downward to where his shirt was opened to the waist. The touch made him drag in a sharp breath, and she smiled up at him. "That's true, and it's why I made sure Mrs. Barstow gave you a room as far away from Father's as possible for the time being."

"For the time being?"

"At some point, he'll have to become accustomed to seeing you strolling out of my bedroom every morning." Her quiet words were filled with a confidence he wasn't sure how to respond to. With a shake of his head, he frowned.

"Perhaps, but it won't be easy for him…or for you."

"I think it will be easier than you think." The confidence in her voice seemed even stronger, and he released a soft groan of dismay.

"It will definitely be easier here at Marymont, but London is a different battlefield."

"Battlefield?" A hint of a smile touched her lips.

"Society is forgiving of a man who indulges in liaisons, but it eviscerates a woman for daring to do the same," he said quietly as he reached out to caress her cheek. "Here at Marymont, I'm better able to protect you from the cruelty of others."

"Does that mean you *want* to make an honest woman of me?" The soft words drifted through the space between them, and he swallowed hard.

"I've already told you I won't force you to make a choice between your independence or the bonds of matrimony. I love you too much to see you come to hate me for issuing such an ultimatum."

"So, you prefer that our relationship remain as it is."

"*Damn it, Ophelia.* Are you deliberately trying to back me into a corner on the subject?"

"No, I'm simply trying to discern whether you'll be happy when it comes to us living together openly."

What the hell was he supposed to say to that observation? Ophelia narrowed her gaze to study him intently. It was impossible to determine what she was thinking, and it was an unsettling sensation. He scowled as one gently curved eyebrow arched upward in a silent demand for his answer.

"I don't give a damn what others think. So my answer is yes. Yes, I'll be happy," Mathias ground out with more than a hint of irritation at her questioning.

"But not completely."

"What the hell does that mean?" Exasperated by the direction of their conversation, he scowled down at her.

"It means my happiness is contingent on your happiness."

"As mine is to yours," he said with a sense of relief that he'd reassured her as to his pledge not to restrain her freedom or independence.

"So we are at an impasse." The matter-of-fact note in her voice made his relief vanish in the blink of an eye.

"Impasse? How in God's name did you come to that conclusion?"

"Did you not just say you won't ask me to marry you?"

"*Yes.*" The abrupt response made her eyebrows arch again, and he exhaled a harsh breath. "If you're worried, I'll try to persuade you at any point in the future, I won't."

Despite his adamant reassurance, Mathias knew there would be times when it would take every bit of willpower he possessed not to plead with her to marry him. But he'd given his word, and he'd suppress any future moment of weakness to ask for something she couldn't give.

"So there is no chance you'll ever ask me to marry you."

"Didn't I just say that?" he said between clenched teeth. The woman was confounding him at the moment. "I won't risk you growing to hate me or, worse, walking away from me altogether."

"Does that mean you *don't* want to marry me?" She tipped her head to one side as something indefinable flickered in her gaze.

"*No.* That's *not* what I'm saying. I'm saying I *won't ask* you to marry me. I *won't ask* you to give up your independence, nor will I risk losing you by forcing the issue."

"Then you leave me with little choice." Her sigh was exaggerated as she eyed him with amused disgust. Mathias clenched his jaw at the sparkle of mischief in her gaze.

"What choice?" he snapped.

"To do what you are clearly determined not to do. Will you marry me, Mathias Gilchrist?"

Stunned by her quiet question, he stared down at her in disbelief. The amusement in her eyes suddenly vanished, and hesitation flitted across her face when he didn't answer the question. Mathias swallowed hard and drew in a deep breath. He was afraid his imagination was running amuck again.

"Did I hear you correctly?" he rasped.

"Yes. Will you…*do you* want to marry me?" The vulnerability in her whispered question made Mathias caress her cheek and kiss her gently.

"Yes, my love. There's nothing that would make me happier than to make you my wife." His muscles knotted with tension as he stared down into her eyes. "But are you certain it's what you want? I never want you to regret marrying me."

"I won't," Ophelia whispered as her lips softly brushed over his. "I love you, Mathias. I want to be your wife. I want everyone to know you're mine, and I'm yours."

"I've been yours from the moment you made that reckless proposal." Mathias pulled her close and pressed his lips to her temple. "You're the other half of my soul, Ophelia. I'll never treat you as anything less than the best part of myself."

Relief and happiness lightened her sweet features as she tipped her head back to look up at him. Her expression compelled him to kiss her again. If she were ever to think she'd surrendered her freedom and independence to him, she'd be wrong. In asking to be his wife, she'd done the exact opposite. The moment she'd entrusted him with her heart, she'd bound him to her in a way nothing else could. It was a gift of love he would never betray.

With a soft sound, she pressed her body into his and responded to his caress with a fervency that made his heart slam hard into his chest. The instant she tugged his shirt out of his trousers, he jerked his head up to look down at her.

"*Christ almighty*, Ophelia," he muttered as her hands caressed his chest. "This isn't Charles's love nest. You still have a reputation for me to protect."

"Your body doesn't seem too concerned as to whether we act circumspectly." Laughter threaded its way through her words as her hand stroked his erection with a confidence she'd never displayed before.

"*Damn it to hell, Ophelia*," Mathias growled as he jerked at the erotic touch. Muscles knotted with tension, he sucked in a sharp breath as she stroked him again. "I'm trying desperately to be a gentleman here, not the rogue who made you an offer."

"I'll always prefer the rogue in you over the gentleman." The sultry note of seduction in her voice made him drag in another harsh breath as she smiled. "You offered to give me the world, Mathias, and I expect you to make good on that promise right now."

"You don't intend to give one quarter, do you," he rasped.

"When it comes to loving you, never."

The depth of emotion shimmering in her lovely eyes made his heart slam into his chest. A second later, she pulled his head down to kiss him, and he knew there was little he would ever refuse her.

Thank You!

Thank you for reading Mathias's and Ophelia's story. I hope you enjoyed it. I chose to start *The Reluctant Rogues* series because I couldn't completely let go of my Reckless Rockwoods. They've become my book family. As part of the **Reckless Rockwoods Novel series**, the Reluctant Rogues means I can give new heroes their happily ever after with Rockwood family members as pivotal supporting characters.

I also am doing research for the world of the next generation of Reckless Rockwoods as the younger members of the family strike out to find their own HEA.

In closing, I'd like to ask a favor of you. Please share your thoughts on the vendor's website about *The Rogue's Offer*. Whether you loved, hated, or just felt meh about the story, you, the reader, have the power to make or break a book simply by sharing a sentence or two on the vendor's website.

Reviews play an important role in how often the book is shown to other readers in searches and recommendations. The more reviews, the more often the book shows up in searches

Again, thank you so much for reading *The Rogue's Offer*. I hope you enjoyed a couple of hours of escape reading the book. I love hearing from readers, so drop me a line and let me know what you think about the story. Happy Reading,

The Rogue's Countess

May 1895

Moonlight draped a pale shroud over the garden landscape as Phoebe descended the wide stone stairs leading into Lord Montjoy's gardens. Behind her, the music spilled out of the ballroom. It followed her as she moved deeper into the large decorative gardens that extended away from the mansion.

The further away from the house, the softer the music became until it faded to a mere whisper. Despite the heat of the day lingering in the garden, it was a welcome respite from the crowded ballroom and its stifling heat.

She had deliberately waited until Alfred was engrossed in conversation with his latest mistress and several of his friends before she'd dared to venture out into the garden. If Alfred had realized what she was planning, he would have stopped her, which meant her efforts to save her dearest friend would fail. Failure meant Lawrence would pay a far greater price than any humiliation or pain Alfred could inflict on her.

In the almost six years they'd been married, her senses had become dulled to Alfred's drinking, philandering, and cruelty. She'd learned to step outside of herself when he rutted on top of her, but it was much harder to insulate herself from his verbal tirades. Those she tried to avoid at all costs. It was so much easier if she didn't incite his anger.

Tonight had been one of those rare moments when she'd failed to keep her wits about her. It had been a long time since she'd spoken without thinking in Alfred's presence. Instinctively, Phoebe's hand reached up to touch the back of her head. Her scalp still stung from where Alfred had pulled viciously on her hair earlier this evening.

From the beginning of their marriage, her husband had never shown her kindness, and her inability to give him an heir had made things worse. After her second miscarriage, Alfred accused her of having taken steps to rid herself of a child. It was the farthest thing from the truth, A child would have made life more bearable, and his cruel words had made her lose her tongue.

Alfred had become enraged when she'd declared he might be the one responsible in the matter as well. She'd pointed to his drinking, which usually made him impotent when he shared her bed. The moment the back of his hand had hit her cheek, she'd learned a hard lesson. It was the first and only time he'd actually hit her, but Phoebe had never made the same mistake again until tonight.

It was only when Alfred was between mistresses that Phoebe ever had to dread him entering her bedroom to demand his conjugal rights. It was why she'd been surprised to see him enter her room earlier. He had only recently taken up with his latest paramour, and she'd been too bewildered to think twice. Before she could stop herself, she'd questioned his reason for being in her rooms. Normally, Alfred inflicted pain with cruel words. In his inebriated state, he'd tried to slap her. When she'd darted out of the way, the only thing he'd been able to grab hold of was her hair. She winced again as the memory seemed to make her scalp sting worse.

The garden path darkened as the row of trees lining the pebbled walkway blocked the night sky. Ahead of her, she could see where the path broke outward to encircle a small fountain illuminated by the moon. As she left the trees' shadows, she sat down on one of the white marble benches situated around the ornamental structure to wait. Lawrence would be here soon.

Soft voices echoed nearby as other guests sought a more intimate setting. It wouldn't be difficult for her and Lawrence to convince someone that they were having an affair. Rumors of a liaison would simply be seen as the result of a longtime friendship. Alfred would most likely beat her for daring to cuckold him, but it didn't matter. News of her alleged affair would save Lawrence from prosecution. Phoebe frowned as she recalled how frantic her friend had been when he'd visited her that morning.

Phoebe had just finished pouring a cup of tea when Lawrence had called on her. Although clearly upset, her friend had managed to wait until the door had closed behind Bateman before speaking.

"I'm done for, my pet," Lawrence exclaimed in a hoarse voice as he kissed her cheeks in greeting, then turned away to pace the floor like a caged animal. Her friend was rarely rattled, but his manner was that of a hunted man.

"What's wrong?" she exclaimed softly.

"I was careless." One hand shoving its way through his blond, wavy hair, her friend prowled the room with a dark and grim expression. "I wouldn't be in this damnable position if I had simply used my head."

Even despite his obvious fear, Lawrence still struck a dashing figure. With his firm, full mouth, long, sooty eyelashes, and crystal blue eyes, women in the Set always vied for her friend's attention. It wasn't simply his looks that caused a stir. He was witty, charming, and kind. Although, as far as mothers were concerned, it was her friend's title and money that was the true attraction. Already wealthy in his own right, as the future Earl of Linshal, Lawrence stood to inherit a great deal more once his father was gone.

Yet, none of those things were what made Phoebe adore her friend. As an American heiress, her father had bought her a title. It wasn't something she'd ever asked for or wanted. In fact, she would have preferred to simply wait to fall in love with a man who loved her as well. But her father had been adamant that only a husband with a title was good enough for his daughter.

Worse, he had made no effort to be discreet about the fact he was hunting for a husband suitable for his daughter. While her dowry had not been something to sneer at, it had been less than substantial to secure her a duke or earl. Her father's blatant and often uncouth efforts to gain her a title were why many of the Marlborough Set had always viewed her with disdain. Alfred's bombastic, often drunken behavior only exacerbated the situation. Nor did her husband's low standing on the social ladder in terms of land and wealth.

The first few social events she'd attended after her wedding had been nothing but haughty condescension and outright snubs. It was at one of those affairs that Lawrence had witnessed several women snub her. He'd immediately charged to her rescue and introduced her to members of the Set who had willingly included her in their circle.

From that moment forward, she and Lawrence had been best friends, and over the years, the bond they had formed was akin to that of brother and sister. Although Alfred disliked Lawrence, her husband knew Phoebe's friend opened doors all the way up to the Prince of Wales himself. Doors that would have remained closed to them without her friendship with Lawrence.

It was a social power Alfred was keenly aware of, and she was certain it was the only reason he'd never forbidden her to discontinue her friendship with Lawrence. It was a fact for which she was grateful as Lawrence was the only person she could confide in completely. Her friend had placed his trust in her as well.

"Come sit down and tell me what's happened." Phoebe patted the cushion beside her on the settee. Like an obedient child, Lawrence sat down next to her.

"It's Coombs. He saw Anthony and me leaving the Boulders club together," her friend rasped. "He's denounced me as a sodomite to several of his friends."

"Dear lord." Phoebe stared at him in heartfelt dismay.

Almost from the beginning, Phoebe had known Lawrence was different from other men. It didn't make her love him any less. She'd always believed Lawrence was who he was simply because it was the way God and nature had made him. Now he might be punished for the fact, and the thought horrified her.

"Ever since the bastard lost all that money to me when my mare beat his stallion at Newmarket, he's had it in for me." One hand rubbing his forehead, Lawrence leaned forward to stare at the rug beneath his feet and shook his head. "Now he's determined to ruin me, or worse, have me locked away."

"Are you certain he saw you with Anthony?"

"Yes," her friend said with a dark note of dismay in his voice. "He didn't say a word. He just smiled, and I knew he wouldn't simply turn his head away as someone else might have." A shudder ripped through her friend, and Phoebe wrapped her arm around his shoulder.

"Surely there's something we can do to discredit Coombs so others think he's simply trying to make trouble."

"I've been up all night trying to think of something. Anthony has already left for France, and I can't think of any other alternative for myself."

"No, there has to be another way." Phoebe shook her head in protest at the thought of losing her closest friend.

"I don't see how, my pet." Her friend released a harsh breath. "My money might keep me out of Newgate, but the scandal…Father's unwell, and it will devastate him."

"We will not let it come to that. We're going to find a way to stop Coombs," Phoebe said with a firmness she didn't feel. "And I find it reprehensible that Anthony deserted you so easily."

"He didn't desert me." Lawrence rebuked her with a gentle glare before standing up to pace the floor again. "He pleaded with me to come with him."

"And you chose not to leave because of your father."

"If the scandal doesn't kill him, Phoebe, learning the truth from someone other than me would."

"Then you're going to tell him?"

She eyed her friend with sympathy. For years, Lawrence had debated whether to reveal his lifestyle to his father. The two men were close, and the thought of his secret destroying that relationship tormented her friend. On more than one occasion, Phoebe had encouraged her friend to tell his father the truth.

She'd suspected the old earl already knew his son's intimate relationships were not with those of the female persuasion. The fact that Lawrence's father never pushed his son to marry made Phoebe believe he already suspected the truth. Her friend jerked his head in a positive response.

"I have no choice," he said grimly. "Coombs would take great pleasure in telling Father if I don't tell him myself."

"He loves you, Lawrence. That won't change when you tell him the truth."

"Perhaps. But he will be devastated, nonetheless."

Phoebe nibbled at her lip as she contemplated her friend's predicament. He was right. Even if Lawrence's father had already guessed his son's secret, the earl would most likely still be upset by the news. It was one thing to ignore the possibility of a truth and something altogether different to be confronted with the reality of it.

No matter who told the earl that his son's lifestyle was outside society's boundaries, it would still distress the old man. She liked Lord Linshal a great deal and despised the thought of him being hurt by scandal. Phoebe released a soft sigh.

"If only fate had been kinder to us both. If you'd not been in France for all those months, Father was prowling London in search of a title for me, things might have been different," she said wistfully.

"Husband and wife." A look of sadness crossed his handsome features as his mouth twisted in a slight grimace.

"It would have been the perfect solution for both of us, would it not?"

"Yes."

Phoebe nodded in agreement. It wasn't the first time she'd thought of what might have been. If they had been married—she drew in a sharp breath at the idea that flitted through her head. There would be a price, but she would willingly pay it to save her friend.

"You don't have to tell your father. No one has to know," Phoebe said in a resolute voice. "There is a way to make Coombs look like he simply wants to cause trouble."

In quick succession, puzzlement, hope, and protest swept across Lawrence's face as she'd laid out her plan. He'd immediately dismissed the idea, stating no one would believe what she was proposing. Unfaltering in her determination to help her dearest friend and protect his father, Phoebe countered all of Lawrence's arguments until he'd reluctantly agreed that it might work. It took her only a few minutes more to convince him that tonight was as good a chance as any to stop Coombs.

The only drawback to her scheme was Alfred's reaction. She knew her husband would be furious at the thought of being cuckolded, but a part of her wanted a moment of vengeful satisfaction for all Alfred had put her through since they'd been married.

Water splashed quietly into the stone basin from the fountainhead behind her as a shrill, feminine laugh nearby made Phoebe tremble with trepidation. Where was Lawrence? She'd dropped several hints to Lady Lydia that she had an assignation in the garden. The woman was an infernal gossip, and Phoebe knew the woman would be watching her like a hawk to learn who her lover was. If they were to be caught in each other's arms when Lady Lydia stumbled upon them, Lawrence needed to arrive soon.

Had he rethought his decision and decided not to follow through with her idea? If Lawrence thought for even an instant that Phoebe would suffer Alfred's wrath, her friend wouldn't meet her as they'd arranged. No sooner had the question slipped through her mind than a heavy tread on the gravel path made her jerk her head toward the sound.

Relief swept through her at the sight of the tall, masculine figure walking through the shadows in her direction. Only a short distance away, she heard another couple talking. When he hesitated, Phoebe leapt to her feet. She refused to let Lawrence rethink her proposition, and the presence of another couple nearby would help propagate the notion that they were involved.

"You came," she exclaimed, making her voice loud enough to carry, but still inviting as if she were greeting her lover. Rushing forward, she launched herself into her friend's arms and pressed her lips to his. It took only a split second for her to realize her mistake.

The body she'd flung herself against was hard and solid. Lawrence was not a weakling, but this man was a rock by comparison. Stunned, Phoebe stood braced against him and struggled to comprehend the error she'd made. The stranger's lips held the warmth of sunshine on a summer's day as his mouth moved gently against hers. Still disoriented, Phoebe didn't pull away as his kiss sent a pulse of heat through her.

Unlike Alfred, this man didn't crush her mouth beneath his. He made no attempt to dominate. Instead, the stranger's lips teased and cajoled a response from her with disturbing ease. Dear Lord, she needed to stop this insanity. She was a married woman.

Laughter drifted through her head with bitter mockery. A financial arrangement was not a marriage. She was nothing more than chattel. A pound of flesh for Alfred to rut with like a common whore when he was without a mistress or a whipping boy when he was angry.

The warmth of the stranger's mouth was a tantalizing caress that sent her senses reeling. Unable to move, her protest died in her throat as muscular arms pulled her deeper into his embrace, and a hot tongue gently pushed its way into her mouth. Despite the fire in his kiss, the stranger's touch was gentle, tender, almost.

His fingers stroked her cheek in a way that made her feel as though she were a beautiful jewel. No one had ever kissed her like this before. This was a sweet seduction that offered a promise of pleasure, not a cold, painful act of humiliation. With a shudder, she jerked her head backward and away from his incredibly sensual lips.

"Forgive me," she choked out as she stared up into gray eyes that were almost silver in the moonlight. "I thought…thought you were someone else."

"A mistake I'm happy to forgive." The words were a sinful, velvety caress across her senses, and she trembled as his fingers trailed their way along the curve of her exposed shoulder to the edge of her sleeve.

"Perhaps…if you would release me."

"Is that what you really want?" The quiet question sent another tremor rippling through her.

"I don't understand."

Phoebe's heart fluttered like a frantic bird in her breast as something foreign swept over her. She could tell he felt it too. It was a fierce and fiery sensation that she knew was desire. Incapable of pulling away from him, she tried to keep breathing as his fingers caught her by the chin, and his thumb rubbed across her lower lip in the lightest of caresses.

Every inch of her was on fire, unlike anything she'd experienced before, and she realized she wanted more of his touch. The thought made her suck in a sharp breath of surprise and trepidation. This man was dangerous not only to her senses, but to everything she'd come to accept as her lot in her life with Alfred.

"Most women would have protested quite vigorously the moment they realized their mistake." The silken whisper layered her skin with a frisson. He lowered his head and brushed her ear with her lips. "And yet, you seemed quite content to remain in my arms."

"That's not true."

It was a lie. She knew she should have put several feet between them the moment she'd realized he wasn't Lawrence and certainly when he'd returned her kiss. She didn't know why she hadn't done so already.

"You're not a very good liar," he murmured with obvious amusement as he bent his head to tease her lips in a hot kiss. "You're still in my arms."

Wild excitement washed over Phoebe at the playful caress. Quivering, she closed her eyes and breathed in his masculine scent. Brandy, leather, and pine poured over her senses as his mouth nipped at hers. It was a heady sensation. Tantalizing.

"I am not about to struggle with you like a damsel in the arms of a cad," she snapped as she saw his amusement. "I am waiting for you to release me."

"Another lie?" he chuckled. It was a pleasant laugh, unlike Alfred's malicious one. The stranger's gentle humor declared he was teasing her. "I think you enjoyed kissing me, and I think you'd like me to do so again."

"I would not," Phoebe gasped as she stared up at him in dismay. Another lie, but she could hardly admit the truth.

"Very well then," he said with a wicked smile. "I won't stop you from fleeing."

In the next instant, his arms were no longer wrapped around her, and he took a small step backward. The loss of his warmth stunned Phoebe. It was as if she'd been abruptly thrust out into a cold and bitter winter day. She didn't move. She couldn't. When she didn't try to escape, he reached out to stroke her cheek with his forefinger.

"I wonder if you know how lovely you are," he murmured as his finger grazed its way across her bottom lip once more in a sensual stroke.

Phoebe flushed at his compliment. She knew she should run back to the sanctuary of the ballroom as fast as she could, but logic was swiftly overruled by her desire to stay. His kiss was the first intimate touch she'd ever experienced that hadn't involved some form of cold humiliation. It was impossible to deny his touch had stirred a longing deep inside her. A yearning for something more in her life, if only for the briefest of moments.

"I…" She shook her head as she struggled to describe what she was feeling.

He closed the narrow space between them once more, but didn't touch her. Instead, he bent his head, his warm breath feathering its way across her ear lobe.

"Have you never been properly kissed, sweetheart?"

"I don't know what you mean," she said with a catch in her voice. His mouth nibbled at her ear. The sensation sent shock waves rippling through her.

"Your kiss is reticent, almost innocent," he murmured with the merest hint of puzzlement. "It's as if you've never been kissed before."

The stranger's observation made her throat close up with emotion. What he'd said was true. Phoebe couldn't recall a single instance when her husband had kissed her as this stranger had done. Alfred's touch had always been a cold, painful assault on her mouth. It had always created a sickening feeling in the pit of her stomach. This man's kiss was the first taste of pleasure she'd ever known.

"I am no stranger to a man's bed, if that's what you mean," she said in a tight voice as images of Alfred rutting over her like a pig filled her head.

"Then it was a poor lover who left your mouth tasting so delectably untouched." His mouth singed hers for the briefest second as he kissed her lightly. "You might be acquainted with a man's bed, but whoever he was, it's obvious he left you longing for something more."

She drew in a sharp breath at the way he'd seen into her soul so easily. He kissed her again. The caress sent her heartbeat skidding out of control. Pleasure tingled its way down her spine as she leaned into him and reveled in the fire of his touch. Everything faded away as she experienced something she'd only dreamed about.

The stranger pulled her close once more, and her mind reeled as her mouth eagerly parted for him. His kiss connected her to him in a way that made her forget everything, but the way his touch heightened her longing for something that had never been within her reach until now. Common sense tried to push its way through the mist of pleasure enveloping her, but it was smothered by the honeyed languor flowing through her limbs.

From deep inside, the years of longing for a lover's gentle caress welled up to engulf her. Held hostage to the sensations gripping her, she willingly allowed herself to drown in a whirlpool of arousal and need. Blinded to everything but the taste of him, she explored his mouth with a fervor that stunned her. In response, his lips broke away from her mouth and down the side of her neck.

White heat skimmed over her skin, and her head fell back as his mouth nipped at the side of her neck and moved downward. A fraction of a second later, his tongue slid hot and wet into the valley between her breasts. It was a decadent caress that pulled a low moan of pleasure from her. It made her crave something even more intense and intimate.

Desire washed over her at a frightening speed as somewhere in the back of her mind, she realized exactly what she'd been missing from her marriage bed. Wild and erratic, her heartbeat pounded loudly in her ears as molten heat streamed its way through her belly, down to the sensitive spot between her legs. The rush of warmth there tugged a small cry from her as she shuddered against him.

"Oh, please, I…please. I want…" she gasped.

In a bold move that made her heart thud violently, she stroked him through his trousers. He jerked at her caress, then pulled her tighter, trapping her hand between them until his erection pressed deeply into her palm. A shudder rippled through her at the thought of him inside her while a small voice cried out a warning. Desire silenced the soft cry. A dark growl rumbled in his chest. The sound reverberated against her lips before he lifted his head to stare down at her.

"I think it best I let you return to the ballroom before I lose control completely," he rasped.

Desire blazed in the depths of his gray eyes as he stared down at her. It was clear he was attempting to be a gentleman, despite the heated caresses that had already passed between them. The fact that he was unwilling to push his advantage said a great deal about the kind of man he was—a man who was honorable enough to forego acting on his carnal needs.

This was a man who would be a considerate lover. He would never take without giving in return. The knowledge sent a pulse of stark need streaking through her. If only for this singular moment in time, she wanted to experience a lover's touch without revulsion or dread.

"I don't want to return to the ballroom," she whispered and impulsively tugged her head down to his.

All she wanted was to feel alive—to revel in an ecstasy she'd never experienced in her life. His mouth spoke of passion, but his touch was gentle as he stroked his fingers along the curve of her neck.

There would never be another moment such as this, and every second was a gift she would cherish. This brief interlude would be a memory she would summon whenever she was faced with the harsh reality of her daily life. It would remind her that someone had once touched her gently and passionately. She would remember that for a few brief moments she had been more than an object used to satisfy the base physical needs of a man.

The spicy scent of him filled her nostrils. He smelled clean, strong, and powerful. Every part of him overwhelmed her senses until desire violently stripped her of all reason. She didn't protest as he guided her off the path into the darkness of the foliage that lined the path. Instead, she went willingly, frantically as her body demanded something she'd never experienced before, but she still recognized it. The cool night air nipped at her thigh before a large hand seared her skin. From deep within her, an unexpected passion rose inside her until her mouth was clinging to his. Long fingers tangled with hers as they worked the buttons on his trousers free.

Seconds later, his heavy weight was in her palm, and with inexperienced fingers, she ran her hand over his thick, hard length. The touch made him groan before his hand slid up her thigh to reach the heat of her center. He rubbed lightly against her sex, and she jerked. Her breaths hot and rapid, she thrust her hips forward.

"Oh, please. Now. I need to feel…" Her words trailed off into a low moan as he increased the pressure to the small nub of flesh between her legs.

There was no right or wrong, only this moment of human connection that promised to fulfill her in ways she'd yet to realize. His hand forced her to wrap her leg around his waist, and in the next breath, he filled her with a mind-numbing thrust that pushed her over the edge of an abyss.

Almost as if he knew what her reaction would be, his mouth swallowed her cry of intense pleasure. Hard and fast, he stroked her body with his. A pitched sensation grasped her insides until she felt her body tighten around him. Her spasm drew a dark growl from him as he increased the speed of his thrusts.

Suddenly, a wave of fire engulfed her, then skimmed its way across her skin and downward to the apex of her thighs. White-hot heat raced through her blood until it tightened her insides and convulsed with an intensity unlike anything she'd ever experienced.

Her cry of ecstasy was silenced by a passionate kiss. Beneath her hand, his heartbeat pounded a fierce rhythm against her palm as he possessed her at a blistering pace. A second later, he buried himself deep inside her and throbbed against her with a ferocity that matched her own climax. Ever so slowly, the rasp of his harsh breaths and Phoebe's frantic ones slowed to normal.

Reluctant to give up the power, warmth, and comfort of his touch, she clung to him. She wanted this moment to never end. She didn't want to leave the tenderness of his embrace or give up the brief moment of contact that said she was alive inside. This stranger had pulled her deepest desires up from the depths of her soul until she'd been blind to everything except the sensations holding her prisoner.

Gray eyes smoky with the remnants of desire met hers, and she wanted to drown in the warm steel of them. Strong and rugged, his features spoke of a strength that was as much physical as it was emotional. It was impossible to tell if his hair was black or dark brown in the dim light, but it was his gaze that hypnotized her. It was the first time she'd consciously studied his face. She'd been so consumed by an overwhelming need to connect with another soul, it wasn't until now that she'd truly looked at him.

His mouth twisted in a slight smile, almost as if he could read her thoughts. With obvious reluctance, he retreated from her. The tip of his finger traced the curve of her bottom lip in a sensual invitation. It made her ache for him all over again. What would it be like to spend one night after another in this man's bed? Phoebe drew in a sharp breath.

Dear God, what had she just done? Horror held her rigid as the full extent of her folly took shape in her mind. She'd lowered her personal standards to that of her husband. Not once during her marriage had she ever contemplated having a liaison with any man. The thought had been unthinkable. Not because she feared Alfred, but because she possessed little except her self-respect. Something she'd surrendered to a stranger in a few brief moments.

It didn't matter that Alfred meant nothing to her, that he was cruel to her, or that he had a string of mistresses. She'd lowered her standards to that of her husband. Guilt and shame lashed through her with a violent shudder. Phoebe avoided looking at stranger, and quickly stepped aside to shake out her skirts. With trembling fingers, she tried to restore her appearance, all too aware of the lock of hair brushing her shoulder that would be difficult to pin up.

"Here, let me," he said in a deep, husky voice.

Phoebe stiffened as he turned her around and proceeded to repair her hairstyle and brush off the back of her gown. Somewhere in the back of her mind, she experienced gratitude for the fact her dress was a midnight blue. The color would hide any dirt left behind from her wild, rash behavior.

When he'd finished, the hands glided across her shoulder and down her arm while his mouth nibbled at the curve of her neck. It was a lover's caress, and she struggled to fight the powerful urge to lean back into him, but guilt held her in check. With a jerk, she pulled away from his touch and spun around struggling desperately not to give in and stay.

"I…I must go," she breathed.

"First, tell me why." It was a gentle command, but a command nonetheless.

"Why?" Phoebe pressed her hand against the base of her throat as if she didn't understand his question. It was a pointless gesture. She knew precisely what he was asking. She shook her head with a sense of helplessness. "I…needed to feel…"

"Desirable." He finished her statement, but it wasn't the right word.

"No," she whispered. "I needed to feel human. To feel alive."

He stared at her for a long moment, and his intense scrutiny made her look away in embarrassment. A warm hand stroked her cheek, and somewhere in her tumbled thoughts, she ached at the thought she would never feel alive again. The knowledge jolted painfully through her, and she fought to stave off tears of self-pity.

"And do you feel alive now?" The soft question made Phoebe draw in a deep breath as she looked up at him.

"Yes." *So alive that I shall never forget you.* Her throat tightened as she remembered the reality she had to return to.

"I want to see you again."

His soft words made Phoebe jump, and her heart stopped for a full beat before it resumed. For a fleeting moment, she almost said yes. She wanted to feel him touching her once more. She wanted to feel alive over and over again. Shame washed over Phoebe at the thought. In one swift stroke, she'd failed to save Lawrence as well as sacrificing her principles.

Where was Lawrence? He should have been here by now. Phoebe peered into the shadows of the garden path, willing her friend to appear. When he didn't, she looked back at the stranger. An odd glint flashed in the silvery gray of his eyes as he lightly touched her cheek. A knot formed in her throat. How could her plan to help her dearest friend have gone so terribly wrong with something that felt so right?

Chapter 2

I want to see you again."

Gideon ran his thumb across her lower lip. There was something fragile and vulnerable about her. It was an emotion he was certain she rarely showed to anyone. Hesitation swept across her beautiful features, and he thought she was about to say yes. Intense disappointment sailed through him when she shook her head vehemently.

"No. It's impossible."

"Nothing's impossible," he said firmly as he caught the faint hint of another accent threading its way under her English accent. It was undefinable, but he ignored the thought. "Tell me why you won't let me see you again. Are you married?"

The moment the question passed his lips, a voice in the back of his head clanged as loudly as the bells on a fire wagon. Gideon had made it a rule never to indulge in liaisons with married women. He'd restricted himself to widows and courtesans. Now, for the first time in his life, he was considering setting aside his principles to see this woman again. A powerful surge of emotion pumped its way through his blood and told him to do whatever it took not to let her go.

"Tell me."

Instantly, she retreated a step at his softly spoken command. As she darted backward, Gideon quickly reached out and caught her arms in a gentle grasp to keep her from fleeing. A shudder rocked its way through her body and into his. Christ Jesus, she was terrified. He jerked away from her. The last thing he wanted to do was frighten her. Was her husband a brute? Was that why she kept glancing over her shoulder as if terrified someone would find them together?

Shame made her turn away and nodded. Gideon's heart sank as she confirmed the truth. He'd been desperately hoping she was a widow, even though instinct had told him otherwise. Gideon knew he should simply walk away, but he couldn't. Instead, he caught her chin in his fingers and tipped her head upward.

"Does he beat you?" he demanded roughly. Surprise made her flinch before she shook her head.

"I have learned not to give him any reason to do so," she whispered. Again, Gideon noted the muted rhythm of something foreign in her voice that made him wonder if English was her natural language. He dismissed the thought as he focused on her. She pulled free of his light hold of her chin and turned her head away. Fury flooded his limbs at the thought of someone hitting her. A man who hit a woman deserved to be beaten until they were one breath away from death.

"Please, you must let me go."

"Let me help you." For a split second, Gideon saw her waver as she debated his offer, then shook her head.

"You cannot," she whispered.

"I don't believe that."

Frustration sailed through him as he watched several emotions flash across her features. Confusion, dismay, shame, and fear. It was the fear that gnawed at his gut. Gently, he cupped her cheeks and forced her to look at him once more. She stood frozen in front of him before she pulled away with a sharp movement. Gideon saw her swallow hard as if something had lodged in her throat.

"What happened….it was a mistake," she whispered.

"You're wrong."

Although he spoke softly, there was a ferocity in his voice that made her draw in a sharp breath. She denied his statement with a shake of her head, but the anguish he saw in her convinced him that she'd experienced the same bewildering connection between them that he had. Loud cries echoed in Gideon's head, demanding he prevent her from leaving. He had no explanation for his reaction to her or why it was so imperative he should not allow her to leave.

Silence filled the space between them, and he released a harsh breath of frustration. She suddenly took a step back and extended her hand as her expression became polite yet distant. It was as if she'd crawled into a shell where no one could see anything except a woman of serene composure.

"I must go before…I trust the remainder of your evening will be an agreeable one." There was an absurdity to her words that angered him.

"Damn it to hell," he muttered as he caught her smaller hand in his. "At least tell me your name."

"It's best we remain strangers. What happened here was a moment of madness," she said firmly, but he could see the despair engulfing her despite her matter-of-fact manner. In the shadows, her beautiful eyes were soft and luminous, and a grunt of frustration made him tighten his fingers on hers.

"And if we meet in the future?"

"We will act as if we've never met before."

"Do you really think it possible either of us can forget what passed between us?" he said tersely.

"We must, and if we should meet again, I'll have your word as a gentleman. You'll act as though we've never met." When he hesitated, a look of determination made her lips thin with resolve. "Your word."

Gideon shook his head in protest at the sharply spoken demand. At his silent objection, she grew still as a small animal facing danger. It was impossible to tell if it was a fear of him refusing to abide by her demand or something else that caused her to remain unmoving in front of him. The urge to pull her close and simply hold her until her fear receded twisted his gut.

"Don't ask me to—"

"Your word," she demanded.

One idea after another crashed through his head with a desperation he didn't understand. Every possible argument he could think of to make her change her mind was useless. The moment her lovely mouth thinned with determination, Gideon accepted the fact there was nothing he could do except agree to her request.

Resignation slid through him as he slowly turned her hand over in his and pressed his mouth to the inside of her wrist. A small shudder rippled through her at the touch, and Gideon breathed in the soft, sweet smell of roses. It was as if she'd picked the most fragrant of the flowers in his garden and brushed them across her skin. He slowly lifted his head, and their gazes locked as, with great reluctance, he nodded.

"You have my word," he bit out.

The air between them vibrated with raw tension. Relief flared in her gaze before guilt and shame replaced the stark emotion. Her vulnerability returned as she tugged her hand out of his to take two quick steps away from him. Without thinking, Gideon immediately followed, then stopped as she stretched out her hand as if to hold him at bay.

"Please, please don't make this even more difficult for me than it already is." The plea in her voice sent a bolt of awareness through him. She was as reluctant to leave him as he was to let her go. His throat closed, and it became difficult to breathe.

"If you have need of me in the future—"

"I shall not," she said with resolve, despite the bleakness reflected in her voice.

Then, with a sharp inhalation of breath, she spun around and hurried back along the garden path leading to the ballroom. Gideon took two strides forward as he started to run after her, but his mind brought him to an abrupt halt. He'd given his word to her. To break it would only cause her pain.

The moment his mysterious enchantress disappeared around the bend in the path, his anger and frustration exploded in a vicious gesture. As the side of his fist slammed into the rough bark of a nearby tree, he grunted at the lack of satisfaction the resulting pain gave him. It was doubtful he would find someone at this late hour to join him in the ring. Even if he did, it still wouldn't be enough. He needed a brawl.

What the devil had just happened to him? One minute he'd been on his way to meet Lady Westerly for a brief moment of pleasure, and in the next, he'd found a passion unlike anything he'd ever experienced in the past. From the first moment she'd thrown herself into his arms, it had been difficult to let her go. Who had she come out to the garden to meet? A lover?

Gideon found that difficult to believe, even though she'd flung herself into his arms with a breathless greeting. While the note of relief in her voice had been distinct and poignant, almost as if she'd been greeting a friend and not a lover. He was also certain it was the first time she'd ever come close to having a liaison. It had been easy to see her horrified reaction as the reality of what had happened registered with her. She'd lost all her inhibitions in his arms, and her shocked dismay convinced him that he was the first man who'd touched other than her husband.

Every visible emotion she'd displayed told him she'd been appalled at having lost control of her senses. Yet despite her obvious shock of having made love to a stranger, he firmly believed she'd not wanted to leave him any more than he wanted to let her go. With every caress and touch of his hand, she'd responded to his touch like a violin did at the hands of a virtuoso. She'd held nothing back, and neither had he.

The realization stunned him. It was the first time since he'd been witness to Edith's shallowness that he'd broken his vow. An oath he'd made to never let another woman cause him to lose his head. But the bewitching creature he'd held in his arms for just a short time had done exactly that. All of his liaisons had been physically satisfying, but not once had he allowed himself to feel anything more than gratification and pleasure in a lover's arms.

The moment a woman indicated she wanted more from him, Gideon ended the relationship. Although he'd remained friends with one or two of his past lovers, his feelings for them were that of friendship and nothing more. All of that had changed moments ago. Not only had he broken his firm rule never to cuckold another man, but he'd also broken the promise he'd made to himself. Not since Edith had he forgotten everything but the woman in his arms.

Still dazed by his lack of discipline where his sweet enchantress was concerned. Gideon headed back toward the ballroom. Gideon knew he should at least seek out Lady Westerly and express his regrets, but he was in no mood to pander to the woman after what he'd just experienced. Everything about his mysterious temptress had thrown him off balance. Something Edith had never done where he was concerned.

Gideon's stride was long and fast as he returned to the house. He'd agreed not to recognize her if they met again, but she'd not extracted his promise not to search for her. In the back of his head, he heard a voice reminding him that she was married. If he'd known that before he'd made love to her, would it have made a difference? The resounding no echoing through his head emphasized how deeply his mystery lover had affected him.

As he strode up the steps leading onto the patio outside the ballroom, Gideon paused outside the doorway to study the guests from his position in the shadows. Despite his hunger to catch another glimpse of her, the sea of people made it impossible to find her among the throng. Resigned as to his ability to find her easily, he muttered a vicious oath beneath his breath.

The heat of the ballroom pressed into him as he walked through the French doors leading into the house. No matter which direction he turned, he still couldn't see her. Had she left the ball to avoid meeting him again? A low chuckle on his left caught his attention, and he jerked his head toward the sound.

The sight of Sebastian Rockwood, Earl of Melton, smiling at him renewed Gideon's hopes he could be able to find her. Sebastian was someone everyone sought to know. The Reckless Rockwoods, as the Set called them, knew almost everyone in polite society. An introduction would at least give him the opportunity to enjoy her company, even if he never had the chance to feel her in his arms again.

"You look extremely frustrated, Gideon. Who is she?" His long-time friend arched an eyebrow at him as the two of them shook hands.

"I don't know." At his reply, Sebastian's eyebrow rose higher. A small smile touched the Earl of Melton's lips.

"Perhaps she's all too aware of your reputation where the ladies are concerned."

"No," he snarled at his friend's jest. "We've never met before tonight."

"Are you certain?" Sebastian frowned in confusion. "That's highly unusual. What is her name?"

"I don't know. She wouldn't tell me," Gideon ground out his reply between clenched teeth as he looked around the room, searching for his mysterious enchantress. "But there was something different about her voice."

"Something different? If I didn't know better, I'd say you were beyond enamored with this mystery woman." There was a touch of amusement in his friend's voice, and Gideon shot a fierce glance in Sebastian's direction. A somber look immediately darkened his friend's features.

"What does she look like?" Sebastian asked in an apologetic voice. "I'll help you find her."

Gideon quickly described his elusive enchantress, and with a nod, Sebastian joined him in the search. The two of them studied the room in silence for several moments before a soft feminine laugh floated through the air toward them.

"The two of you look as though you were searching for something that's impossible to see." At the light-hearted teasing in the Countess of Melton's voice, Gideon turned to greet Sebastian's wife. With great effort, he forced a smile to his lips while he carried the hand Helen offered him to his mouth to brush the air over her fingertips.

"Good evening, Helen. How are you?"

"Quite well, thank you." The countess tipped her head to one side and eyed him with curiosity as he resumed his search of the crowded ballroom. "Are you looking for someone?"

Gideon didn't answer Helen as he saw the woman he was so desperately wanted to see again. Indecision barreled through him. Now, what was he to do? A man he vaguely recognized suddenly appeared at her side, and she took his arm as he guided her toward the exit. Gideon jerked his head in the couple's direction.

"There, Sebastian. At the main entrance to the ballroom. Do you know her?"

"No, I'm afraid not." The earl turned his head toward his wife. "Helen, are you familiar with the lady standing close to Lady Montjoy?."

"The pretty woman in the midnight blue gown?" Helen asked quietly. A quick glance in her direction revealed the Countess of Melton's perplexed look. Gideon jerked his attention back to the man and woman at the ballroom exit.

"Yes," he said in a tight voice.

"That's Viscountess Helstone."

"The woman just about to go out the door?" Gideon bit out as he watched his enchantress.

"Yes," Helen said with a nod. "She's one of the American heiresses that took London by storm last year. I believe she married the viscount a few months after she arrived."

"Are you certain?" Gideon asked with a growl as his gut suddenly tightened. "She sounds as if she's from the Continent and grew up with an English governess."

"That is most likely the result of her attending Le Manoir. I imagine they did their best to remove any trace of her American accent," Helen said with a sympathetic note in her voice. "The school is renowned for their students marrying well."

Gideon grew rigid at Helen's explanation, but his attention never wavered from Lady Helstone. It wasn't simply his failure to recognize the faint hint of an American accent beneath the aristocratic notes of the viscountess's sultry voice that angered him. What enraged him the most was that she'd married a title. The anger crashing through him made his muscles knot painfully throughout his body. For a second time, he'd played the fool to a woman who'd married for social position.

"I've heard that it's a very unhappy marriage," Helen said with a note of sympathy in her voice.

"No doubt." Gideon turned away from the woman he'd broken his own rules for and to see Sebastian's eyebrows arched in puzzlement. With a shake of his head, Gideon's jaw locked with tension as he bowed in Helen's direction.

"Helen. Sebastian. If you'll excuse me, I'll bid you goodnight."

Before his friends could say a word, Gideon turned away and made his way to the exit. There was a brawl with his name on it somewhere in town.

Chapter 3

"Y ou look lovely, dearest."

Constance Rockwood Blakemore, Countess of Lyndham, forced a smile to her lips as she met her baby sister's gaze in the full-length mirror. Louisa's dismay was obvious as she stared at her reflection in the cheval glass mirror inside Madame Sabine's shop.

"Doesn't she look lovely, Helen? Patience?" At Constance's silent urging, Helen Rockwood, the Countess of Melton, quickly nodded her head.

"You look beautiful as always, Louisa," Helen said with a smile despite the hesitant note in her voice.

Standing to the left of her sister-in-law, Patience released a small noise, and Constance wasn't sure whether it was suppressed laughter or a sound of disagreement. Louisa tipped her head slightly to see the reflection of the Mistress of Cairnlarich in the mirror. The hat Patience wore had a netted veil she'd pulled down to cover her scars. It made it almost impossible to determine what she was thinking. When their middle sister remained silent, Louisa whirled around and frowned at her sister.

"Well, Patience?"

"*You* are beautiful, but all those flowers, ruffles, and bows make you look like a wedding cake, and *you*, dearest, are the bride, *not* the cake," Patience said firmly. "If you wear that gown, you're quite likely to appear as a figure of fun in Currer's next serial installment."

Patience's words made Louisa stiffen in horror as she spun about on her heel to study her appearance in the mirror once more. Her younger sister's mention of the Currer Chronicles made Constance start slightly. The biweekly serial had turned the Set on its ear in recent months as P. Currer had slyly taken aim at various members of the peerage by including them in his stories.

A work of fiction, the author's characters were based on actual members of the Marlborough Set. Although names were changed, there was little left to doubt in the reader's mind as to who the author was poking fun at. The skill and precision with which Currer lampooned the antics, scandals, and behaviors of the peerage was an amusing read until one was on the receiving end of the author's mighty sword of ink. With a brief glare in Patience's direction, Constance turned her head toward her baby sister, a placating smile on her lips.

"I find it highly unlikely Mr. Currer would mention a wedding dress," Constance said firmly with a shake of her head in her attempt to reassure Louisa. "The man has a great deal of fodder to draw from, given the recent antics of Lord Barrington and his latest mistress."

"We are *not* the Reckless Rockwoods without justification, Constance. I truly think we're living on borrowed time in escaping evisceration by the man's wicked pen."

Patience defiantly tilted her head as she disagreed with the eldest of the three sisters. It was impossible to read Patience's features through the netted veil, but the Mistress of Crianlarich's bearing emphasized her irritation. Constance knew her sister's dissent was not without merit. The Rockwoods *had* been lucky to date when it came to being singled out in Currer's serial.

"It's true. I had fully expected Currer to target Percy for threatening to thrash Lord Sproats last week." Louisa lent her voice of support to Patience. At the mention of the viscount, Patience's posture became one of fierce anger.

"Our brother was well within his right to dress down the man. Sproats's comments were crude and deeply insulting to Rhea," Patience snapped. "It's a small wonder Percy didn't pound the man into the ground, and he would have without any trouble at all."

"And if Rhea hadn't displayed such grace under pressure, our brother might easily have found himself in Newgate." Constance glared at her middle sister before she sighed. "But I agree. Percy was well within his right to threaten the man for his insulting advances toward Rhea. I'm simply grateful she insisted on returning to Green Hill House the next day."

"Well, *we* might remain untouched by Currer's caricature of the Set, but some of our friends have not." Anger flared tightened Louisa's mouth. "Look at how Gideon has been taken to task in recent months."

"For heaven's sake, he's a grown man," Constance bit out through clenched teeth. "His reputation for breaking hearts is well-established."

Currer's droll, doubled-edged word-play had recently made the Rockwood family friend, Gideon Lethbridge, Earl of Chelmsford, the latest character in the Currer Chronicles. As one of the Set's most eligible, yet elusive, bachelors, the earl had been mocked in the latest serial. Now, Patience had dumped oil onto the fire by suggesting Louisa might be mentioned in the next edition of the satire. As Louisa stared at her image in dismay. Constance quickly stepped forward to wrap an arm around her younger sister's shoulder.

"We'll have Madame Sabine find a way to fix the dress."

"The wedding is in two weeks, and she hasn't finished half of my trousseau," Louisa said in a voice filled with panic. Mortification caused her to shake her head as she was obviously struggling not to cry. "Patience is *right*. I *do* look like a wedding cake."

"You could walk down the aisle in rags, and Ewan would still find it impossible to look at another woman. The man is blinded by his love for you." Constance smiled with encouragement. "I'm certain Madame Sabine can fix this gown. We *all* know the woman will move heaven and earth to keep her most devoted *and lucrative* client happy."

"I agree wholeheartedly. Madame Sabine would fight the hounds of hell to ensure you're happy." Helen, who'd remained silent until now, smiled with confidence at her youngest sister-in-law. "I know how high your dressmaker bills are. Sebastian is constantly muttering his frustration every time he sees the latest bill from Madame Sabine."

"But it's not *his* money he's spending," Louisa replied as a cheerful grin replaced her dismay.

"A fact I remind him of whenever he expresses his disgust and outrage at what your dresses cost," Helen replied with a laugh. "That and the fact he promised never to begrudge you a dress bill again for helping him rescue me from Lord Templeton."

The mention of those frightening events more than ten years ago caused a shadow to sweep across the countess's face. Louisa quickly stepped forward to clasp her sister-in-law's hands and kiss Helen's cheek with great affection.

"My brother is fortunate to have a wife who patiently listens to his complaints." Then, in the next second, a mischievous smile curved Louisa's lips. "*But* even if he had listened to me to begin with, he still would have been forced not to begrudge my fashion vice."

Laughter followed Louisa's mischievous remark. Satisfied things were on an even keel for the moment, Constance turned away, intent on finding Madam Sabine. The seamstress could weave magical gowns that almost equaled Monsieur Worth but at far less a cost. If Sebastian knew how much a gown by Worth costs, he would be appalled.

Constance's dressmaker bills were rarely as high as her younger sister's. In fact, Lucien had remarked on more than one occasion he was glad she didn't have her sister's extravagant tastes. But the bill from Monsieur Worth last year had put Lucien in a state of shock. It had been an impulsive purchase, but the moment she'd seen the gown, it had been impossible to resist.

She'd excused her extravagant purchase based on needing a new gown for Helen's and Sebastian's anniversary ball. She'd also been seven months pregnant with Isabel, and

Monsieur Worth's creation had emphasized all her best features while cleverly hiding the true size of her expanding girth. She bit back a smile as she remembered her husband's outrage when the bill had arrived.

His anger had been short-lived when she'd modeled the gown that had arrived with the invoice. Instinctively, he'd realized she'd been feeling like a large cow, and the dress had bolstered her spirits. Her husband had then demonstrated he would always find her beautiful.

The soft swish of the curtains that hid the inner confines of Madame Sabine's workshop pulled Constance out of her musings. A woman emerged from the back of the shop carrying several bolts of material with her chin pressed into the one on top to manage her load better. As the clerk set the material down on the counter, Constance stepped forward to capture her attention.

"Pardon me, would you please tell Madame Sabine that Lady Westbrook needs to speak with her about her wedding dress?" The moment the woman looked at her, Constance stiffened with surprise. "*Lady Helstone.*"

The woman flinched at Constance's soft exclamation before she shook her head vehemently. Cheeks flooded with a rosy color, the woman cast a furtive glance around the shop.

"I'm sorry, my lady, but my name is Mrs. Hodges."

At the woman's denial, Constance stared at her in disbelief and tipped her head to one side to study the woman's features more closely. A sliver of doubt made Constance frown. It had been over two years since she'd last seen Lady Helstone. The viscountess had disappeared from society after her husband had been shot and killed by his mistress.

Even with the spectacles the woman wore and her hair pulled back in a severe bun, Constance would have wagered a heavy sum that the woman was Lady Helstone. Every physical attribute was still visible despite the severity of the woman's appearance. The only thing that seemed off was the woman's cultured English accent. There wasn't even a hint of the American dialect, but then several years at boarding school and time in the company of the Marlborough Set could be the reason for that.

"Forgive me, but the resemblance is uncanny." At Constance's observation, a wry smile tilted the woman's lips upward as if she were enjoying a private joke.

"So I've been told, my lady. Even Lady Helstone has remarked on our similar likeness." The woman's ironic amusement vanished as Mrs. Hodges glanced over her shoulder at the curtain, hiding the workshop behind her. It was almost as if the woman was frightened someone might hear their conversation. "Let me find Madame Sabine for you, my lady."

Constance frowned as the woman vanished through the curtains in search of the dressmaker. The woman was lying. She was certain of it. Even though the woman's quiet voice held no trace of an American accent, Constance knew an excellent finishing school would have seen to that. The more she thought about it, the stronger her conviction became that Mrs. Hodges and the Viscountess Helstone were one and the same. But why? What in heaven's name would make Viscountess Helstone deny who she was, let alone work in a dressmaker's shop?

Constance paid little attention to gossip, but news of Lord Helstone being shot and killed by his mistress during a lover's quarrel wasn't a tidbit one quickly forgot. Even though it had been more than two years ago, the scandal had been in the news for months. The trial had been a spectacle, with Helstone's mistress pleading self-defense and subsequently being acquitted. Constance's focus drifted toward the bolts of cloth the woman had set down on the counter.

With just one touch, the *an dara sealladh* might tell her something about Mrs. Hodges. The gift of sight and royal blood of the Stewarts had flowed in her mother's veins, making Constance and her siblings far more unique than most people realized. Except for her brother Sebastian, all of her siblings had varying strengths of the *an dara sealladh*, but it wasn't something they openly put on display.

While Lucien supported her assisting those who actually came to her for help, he objected strongly to Constance taking it upon herself to help people who didn't ask for her assistance. She winced. Lucien didn't just object to her interfering without someone's permission. He was vehemently opposed to her meddling in the affairs of others, particularly when it involved matters of the heart. If he were here now, he would drag her out of the shop to prevent her from satisfying her curiosity. They seldom argued, but when they did, it made her feel awful.

Constance winced slightly as she remembered the argument they'd had two months ago in front of the family. The memory made her debate walking away from the counter, but a whisper in the back of her head protested strongly. Of course, the *an dara sealladh* might not even show her anything at all. This last thought ended her indecisiveness.

In a leisurely fashion, Constance walked along the counter and stopped in front of the material Mrs. Hodges had brought out from the back of the shop. As if she were merely examining the bolt of silk, Constance ran her hand over the spot that still bore the slight indentation from Mrs. Hodges's chin.

Constance drew in a deep breath and waited. After more than a minute, she released a sigh of frustration. It seemed she would have to accept Mrs. Hodges's story, after all. Constance slowly turned away from the counter and saw Madame Sabine at Louisa's side, exclaiming with horror at the dress. She was about to rejoin her sisters when the bell over the shop entrance jingled. Constance turned her head toward the door to see Lady Wrotham walk into the dressmaker's shop. The moment the marchioness saw Constance, a wide smile curved the older woman's mouth.

"My dear Constance, how lovely to see you." Lady Wrotham hurried forward to clasp Constance's hands in hers in a warm greeting.

"It's wonderful to see you as well, my lady," Constance said as she bussed the woman's cheek.

"How is the dowager? I heard she had taken ill a month ago."

"Grandmama is recovering nicely. We're fortunate she was in town when she became ill. She wanted to return to Lyndham Keep, but Lucien was adamant she remain here with us. He indulges her, *and me*, quite often, but this was one occasion when he refused to be swayed by Grandmama's protests."

"And how *is* that devilishly handsome husband of yours?"

Amusement sparkled in the older woman's gray eyes. The marchioness had been a friend of Aunt Matilda's for years, and Constance had accompanied her aunt to Lady Wrotham's house on numerous occasions. The woman had buried three husbands, and Constance had always marveled at the woman's indomitable spirit enduring so much grief over the years. She wasn't sure she would be able to find such strength to go on if anything happened to Lucien. An image of her husband filled her head, and she smiled at the marchioness's question.

"Other than experiencing frustration with me from time to time, Lucien is quite well. And you?"

"Desolate," Alva sighed with obvious frustration. "My secretary decided to run off to Gretna Green and marry a schoolteacher, so I decided a new dress would cheer me up."

"I'm so sorry. How long had she been with you?"

"Almost six years. It has come at a most unfortunate time too." The marchioness released another sigh. "The charity ball for St. Catherine's is little more than a month away, and Lydia's skill with numbers made her invaluable. I placed an advertisement in the Times this morning, but I fear finding a new secretary will prove quite difficult."

The marchioness's voice became a distant sound as the *an dara sealladh* pulled Constance down into a familiar darkness. Like a theater curtain being pulled open to reveal the stage, she found herself standing in a cold, uninviting room. A shiver skimmed through her as the chilly air slid across her skin. Twilight filtered through a small window, but it barely illuminated her surroundings.

Small fragments of charred wood were scattered about in the hearth, which made Constance believe there had not been a fire in the hearth for some time. The bed in one corner appeared less than sturdy, while a table was pressed against the opposite wall. A ladder-back chair was angled away from the table as if someone had left their place with great haste. Against another wall was a wardrobe. It was a bleak room filled with the weight of defeat.

The emotion eased slightly as a soft glow on top of the table caught her attention. The light surrounded a stack of papers, but it shone brightly on the name written on the top sheet. P. Currer. For some odd reason, the light engulfing the papers was as if a ray of hope had found its way into this grim, dreary room. Behind her, a door creaked open, and she turned toward the sound. She barely had time to register Mrs. Hodge's coming entering the small lodgings when she was hurtled forward into a well-lit room where smoke created a haze in the air.

Her brothers, Percy and Sebastian, were seated at a card table with their friend, the Earl of Chelmsford, and another man. Although she couldn't hear what they were saying, her brothers were grinning like cats who had swallowed a handful of canaries. In a split second, she was standing behind the patriarch of the Rockwoods. Sebastian pointed toward the pile of banknotes in the center of the table as Gideon shook his head in disgust.

A movement to her left caught Constance's attention. The sight of Mrs. Hodges moving to stand beside Gideon took her by surprise. As the woman reached out to touch his cheek, Mrs. Hodges's appeared overwhelm with confusion, longing, and another emotion that puzzled Constance. It was almost as if the woman were experiencing guilt.

Suddenly, she heard a quiet sound that she recognized as laughter. Constance jerked her head toward Percy, who was grinning with triumph as he reached toward the middle of the table to collect his winnings. As he did so, the bank notes dissolved into a mist to become a sheaf of papers.

Constance instantly recognized the papers as she watched the last sheet fall onto the stack with a soft light shining down on the author's name, P. Currer. With amused resignation, Gideon shrugged in defeat. With a wry twist of his lips, the earl dropped his cards onto the baize-covered tabletop. The cards fell downward in slow motion, and the *an dara sealladh* threw her back into the present.

The transition was more abrupt than usual, and she swayed on her feet. Immediately, a firm hand cupped her elbow, and she recognized Patience's soft voice expressing concern. Incapable of responding, Constance struggled to maintain her balance.

The *an dara sealladh* always left her drained emotionally and physically for a short period, but this time it was more debilitating than usual. Everyone in the family experienced different physical reactions when they emerged from their visions. They were all well-acquainted with the signs of the *an dara sealladh* as well as each other's unique type of after-effects from their visions.

Normally she was seated when she emerged from her visions, but this time she was deeply grateful for Patience's firm grip as her sister wrapped her arm around Constance's waist. If not for Patience, she was certain she would have collapsed to the floor. As the remnants of the *an dara sealladh* faded away, Constance opened her eyes to see Alva, her sisters, and Madame Sabine gathered around her with varying levels of concern and understanding on their faces.

"My lady, you must sit down," Sabine exclaimed in a low voice as she glanced at several customers in the shop. Constance rejected the suggestion with a small wave of her hand, but the dressmaker dismissed her silent response. "I insist. My office has a comfortable place for you to rest."

"I don't think—"

"You're going to sit down, Constance," Patience said quietly. "If you could see how pale you are, you wouldn't argue. Now come along."

Surrendering to Madame Sabine's and Patience's insistence, which Helen's and Louisa's quiet voices reinforced, Constance nodded her consent. In short order, she was seated in a comfortable chair in Madame Sabine's office in front of a cheery blaze in the fireplace. Once the dressmaker was satisfied Constance was comfortable, Sabine excused herself to resolve the problem of Louisa's horrendous wedding gown. Patience was about to sit down opposite her, but Constance waved her hand in protest.

"No, I'll be fine. Helen will need your support to help keep Louisa calm," she said with a small smile.

"All right," Patience nodded, then grimaced behind her veil evident. "The dress is most assuredly a disaster. It's nothing like what Louisa described."

"Well, for heaven's sake, do *not* mention the Currer Chronicles to her again." Constance eyed her sister sternly. "I have no doubt Sabine will manage to make that disaster of a dress into something superb, even if the woman has to make a completely new gown."

"I think it will be a new gown entirely," Patience said dryly before her demeanor changed, and she bent over to rub her hand over Constance's back in a soothing gesture. "But I'm not sure I should leave you alone. You were dreadfully pale. If I wasn't so certain you'd experienced the *an dara sealladh*, I would have thought you on the verge of morning sickness—"

"*Heaven forbid!* It's been less than seven months since I had Isabel," Constance exclaimed as she remembered how difficult her daughter's birth had been. "I'm not ready for another baby so soon, even though I know Lucien would like to have a son. He's not said so directly, and until he does, I have no intention of broaching the subject with him.."

"All right, but *do not move* from that chair. If you were to have another—"

"I doubt that will happen, but I promise not to move until I'm certain I'm fully recovered."

She smiled at Patience, who studied her for a moment from behind the veil hiding the burn scars she'd suffered during the deadly fire at Westbrook Farms three years ago. As if satisfied with Constance's answer, Patience gave her a quick hug and headed toward the door of the dressmaker's office. Her sister had almost reached the exit when Constance called out to her.

"Oh, Patience, I *would* love a cup of tea. Would you ask Mrs. Hodges to bring me a cup?"

"Of course."

"And Patience, see to it that it's *Mrs. Hodges* who brings me my tea."

"Mrs. Hodges?" Her sister stiffened slightly as she looked over her shoulder at Constance.

"Yes, Mrs. Hodges."

"If you're thinking of doing what I think you are, have you forgotten what happened two months ago when Lucien—"

"Go, Patience. I am already feeling much better, and I can only feign distress for a little while longer." Constance frowned and waved her hand at her sister.

Although she couldn't see her middle sister's arched eyebrows, she knew Patience was eyeing her with more than a hint of concern. The family had all been privy to her terrible argument with Lucien when he'd learned she had advised Lady Reigate to reconsider accepting Lord Shively's proposal. With a shake of her head, Constance glared at her sister for questioning her.

"I really *could* use that cup of tea, Patience."

With a sharp nod, her sister hurried out of the room. Left alone with her thoughts, Constance pushed the thought of Lucien's disapproval aside to contemplate her vision.

Whether Mrs. Hodges was Lady Helstone or not, the woman was living in squalid circumstances.

The conditions would be heart-wrenching for anyone, whether they were a member of the working class or the nobility. However, Constance knew such poverty for a noblewoman was highly unusual. What had reduced Lady Helstone to such a penniless state?

Constance remembered the woman had been one of the American Dollar Princesses who'd arrived in London seeking to marry a title. All of those brides had brought substantial dowries to their marriages. It made little sense as to how the woman could be penniless upon Helstone's death. She frowned as she contemplated what she'd seen in her vision.

As always, the *an dara sealladh* had revealed only bits and pieces of the story, and everything she'd seen was too jumbled to make much sense of it. The most puzzling thing was Lady Helstone appearing at Gideon's side. It was quite likely she'd met the earl, but the expressive emotions on her features as she'd reached out to Gideon indicated a relationship far closer than simply acquaintances or even friends.

There had been something intimate about the woman's manner that made Constance feel as if she'd intruded on something deeply personal. Despite its lack of clarity, the *an dara sealladh* had convinced her of two things. The woman calling herself Mrs. Hodges was living in squalid conditions. Two, the woman was also connected to P. Currer and Gideon somehow. Whatever had brought the woman to such circumstances, Constance was determined to help the woman if she could. She even had a solution to make it happen. The question was whether Mrs. Hodges and the marchioness would like each other.

The soft sound of china rattling outside the room broke through Constance's thoughts. As the soft clatter echoed through the air, Constance turned her head to see the woman calling herself Mrs. Hodges enter Madame Sabine's office with the tea Constance had asked for. As the woman set the tea tray on the side table on her left, she avoided looking at Constance.

"Do you require anything else, my lady?"

Instead of answering the woman's question, Constance reached out to pour a small amount of milk into her cup, then added tea. She didn't look up, but it was easy to sense the rising tension in the woman.

"Do you know who I am, Mrs. Hodges?" Constance took a sip of her tea as she looked up at the woman over the rim of the delicate teacup.

"Yes, my lady."

"And do you know anything about me?" When the woman didn't answer, Constance released a sigh and gestured toward the chair opposite her. "Please sit, Mrs. Hodges."

"I cannot, my lady, I have—"

"I insist," Constance's head tipped to one side in a silent demand the woman do as she'd asked. The woman was clearly ready to dart from the room, and Constance released a soft sound of exasperation. "Madame Sabine will not question you as I shall explain you did so under protest."

The woman didn't move, and Constance sighed. Setting her teacup and saucer on the tray, she shook her head.

"You leave me with no choice but to stand as well."

"*Oh no, my lady.*" The genuine concern in Mrs. Hodges's voice was reflected in her sudden look of dismay. Although she showed a distinct reluctance to do so, the woman sank down into the chair opposite Constance.

"Thank you. Now then, let me ask you again. Do you know anything about me other than my name?"

"I have…I have heard rumors."

"Would you please elaborate on that statement?"

Mrs. Hodges hesitated at the softly spoken command for a moment before she straightened in her chair and a worried frown her brow.

"It's rumored you can talk with the dead."

"The rumors are true, although my family and I are discreet about our abilities."

Constance winced at the half-truth. The Rockwoods had earned their reputation for impulsive behavior justly, and their unique talents had added to their sometimes reckless behavior. Pushing the thought aside, Constance picked up her teacup again.

"While there are a growing number of Rockwoods who possess the ability, I am the only one who does consultations with those seeking to reach out to lost loved ones. However, even those are by referral."

"If you have a message from beyond the veil you wish to share with me, I've no interest in hearing it."

Bitterness threaded its way through the woman's voice as her chin tipped slightly upward in defiant disdain. Startled by the woman's reaction, Constance took another sip of the beverage that was still hot.

"I received no message to pass along to you, but there's one thing the rumors appear to have left out. I also have the ability to see things from the past as well as what the future might hold."

"I don't understand." Mrs. Hodges drew in a sharp breath. Although her features were serene and unreadable, behind the spectacles she wore Constance saw the woman's trepidation.

"I sometimes see things about people I meet. People such as yourself."

"*Me?*" Although her countenance remained unreadable, the woman's body language conveyed her apprehension. Her back was ramrod straight as she sat rigidly in her chair while her hands were clasped tightly together in her lap. "I'm uncertain what your…experience might have revealed about me, but I doubt it was anything of significance."

"I confess my vision was confusing on several points, as is often the case." Constance shrugged her acceptance of how the *an dara sealladh* worked. "But I *do* know you're not Mrs. Hodges, are you, Lady Helstone?"

The observation was a gamble on Constance's part, but what little doubt she had was laid to rest at the woman's reaction. Dismay and resignation furrowed Lady Helstone's brow as turned her head away. It was only for a brief instant before the noblewoman lifted her head in a regal, almost defiant, movement to look at Constance without remorse.

"You are correct, my lady." Constance quickly set her teacup down on the tray at the woman's response and leaned forward in her chair.

"But why?" she asked with avid curiosity.

Anger darkened Lady Helstone's countenance, and Constance immediately regretted not holding her tongue. It had been a rude, impertinent question. Remorsefully, she reached out to touch the woman's hand. The woman quickly jerked away from the touch as anger and possibly even fear furrowed her brow. Clearly, the woman had heard a touch was enough to trigger the *an dara sealladh.*

"Forgive me. That was terribly rude," Constance said softly as she drew back from the woman. "In addition to our gift of sight, every Rockwood is somewhat reckless when it comes to acting or speaking without considering the ramifications."

The woman nodded sharply in response to Constance's apology. The cold anger on her oval-shaped features faded, but her outrage was still apparent. Constance winced with self-reproach.

"I truly am sorry, my lady. My curiosity was prompted out of concern for you and my desire to help." The remorse in Constance's voice made Lady Helstone relax slightly as she nodded.

"Your ladyship is kind, but I have no need of assistance, despite anything you…anything you might have seen."

"What I saw were lodgings with a fireplace that hasn't seen a fire in days. A bed that looks as if it will fall apart the moment someone lies in it, a small chifforobe, a table, and a chair," Constance exclaimed with indignation at the description. "It wasn't fit for the working class, let alone a noblewoman."

The woman paled slightly, but she reveal nothing as to what she was thinking. If anything, the woman exuded a quiet strength as she stiffened her shoulders in silent indignation.

"And once again, my tongue has given offense," Constance sighed quietly at her inability to guard her tongue. She was fortunate Lucien wasn't within earshot, or hellfire would rain down on her head. "Forgive me. It was not my intent to cause you discomfort. It's simply that my family is familiar with the hardship of others, and we always do our best to help those in need."

"If your rash nature is indicative of the rest of your family, then I understand why the Set refers to your family as they do."

A wry smile touched Lady Helstone's lips as she looked at Constance, and a small flash of amusement danced in the woman's gaze. Relieved the viscountess was willing to excuse her behavior, Constance released the breath she'd been holding.

"You are most gracious in forgiving my insulting manner, not once, but twice."

"Your comments reflect concern for my welfare, and I appreciate your kindness in doing so. However, as I've already said, I have no need of assistance."

Constance frowned with frustration. It was obvious the woman thought Constance was offering her charity. She needed to tread lightly if she wanted to ensure Lady Helstone understood it wasn't charity but an opportunity. Whether the noblewoman's decision to seize upon the chance to improve her living circumstances was her choice.

Based on her observation in the past few minutes, Constance was certain Lady Helstone would work well with the marchioness. The real question now was whether or not the woman possessed the skills the marchioness required. A quick glance at the woman's hands revealed she lacked the usual calluses on her fingers that most seamstresses had. So that begged the question as to what she did for Madame Sabine.

The question of why sent a dozen more questions thundering through Constance's head, but she managed to bite her tongue. As she took another drink of her tea, a soft laugh echoed out of Lady Helstone. The sound make Constance jerked her head toward the viscountess to see a small smile curving her lips.

"It truly is a struggle for you not to ask questions, isn't it?"

"I confess it is far more difficult than most people realize," she sighed with exasperation as the woman's smile of amusement broadened.

Constance smiled in return. She liked Lady Helstone. In fact, she was certain they would become great friends, especially if she was correct in thinking the viscountess was meant to be with Gideon.

"Then, I shall put you out of your misery and tell you that I do Madame Sabine's books."

"Her bookkeeper," Constance murmured as she remembered Lady Wrotham bemoaning the loss of her secretary and the woman's skill with figures.

"Such as it is."

"How long have you been working for her?" Deliberately, Constance turned her head away from Lady Helstone and reached for the teapot to freshen up her cooling tea.

"More than two years."

The response made Constance swallow a gasp of dismay as she remembered Lady Helstone's impoverished circumstances. The viscountess's words triggered several questions in Constance's head, which immediately triggered more. That meant the viscountess had been employed by Madame Sabine shortly after Lord Helstone had been shot and killed. The timing was not lost on Constance. What had happened to make the viscountess's finances so dire? Helstone had been a brute, but the viscount's death should not have changed Lady Helstone's financial situation. If anything, her husband's demise should have given the woman a great deal more freedom than most women enjoyed.

Images of the papers she'd seen in her vision popped into her head. As if the mental pictures were a puzzle falling into place, she drew in a quick breath. P. Currer. If she remembered correctly, Lady Helstone's first name was Phoebe. Given her vision, it was not much of a leap to think the woman was the Chronicles author. Working in Madame Sabine's shop was the perfect place for gathering the latest gossip that the woman could use in her satire. The question was, why? Without thinking, Constance tipped her head to one side and stared intently at the other woman.

"Tell me, Lady Helstone, are you acquainted with the Currer Chronicles?

Chapter 4

Phoebe struggled to control her rising panic as she stared at Lady Lyndham for a long moment. If anyone else had asked, Phoebe would have interpreted it as a simple query as to whether she was familiar with the Currer Chronicles. But this was the Countess of Lyndham, a member of the Rockwood family. A woman who could see what others could not.

As their gazes met, Phoebe saw the countess's astute expression. Whatever the woman had seen had convinced her that Phoebe was connected to Currer. It changed everything. This was precisely why she'd never mentioned any of the Reckless Rockwoods in her serial.

She'd heeded the rumors, and it had obviously been a wise decision on her part to avoid any mention of them. Not that the Rockwoods had actually done anything in recent memory that deserved to be scorned at the hand of her pen. Phoebe folded her hands in her lap and prayed her anxiety wasn't visible.

"I think everyone in London is well-acquainted with the Currer Chronicles, my lady."

"I meant, do you know the author personally?"

The question only strengthened Phoebe's conviction that the countess knew she was the author of the Currer Chronicles. At the time of Alfred's death, his heir had thrown her out of the house her dowry had bought. Her father's poor business sense had ensured all her money went to Jasper Wakefield. Although she knew her father had thought the money would pass onto his grandchildren, he'd failed to consider the possibility she might not have children. Perhaps worst of all, her father had failed to negotiate an annual stipend for her in the event of Alfred's premature death. The end result was that she'd lost her home with no annual stipend, which had left her penniless.

It was a harsh reality Phoebe had been forced to deal with the minute the new Viscount Helstone had ordered her out of the house that was now his. If Lady Lyndham had seen her current lodgings in her vision, then the countess had most likely seen something that suggested Phoebe was connected to the author of the chronicles.

She blew out a small breath of quiet resignation. It was pointless to deny her association with the serial. She could only hope the countess would keep Phoebe's involvement a secret.

"I know the author quite well. *I'm* P. Currer." Her quiet reply caused Lady Lyndham to jerk slightly as if Phoebe had surprised her with such a direct response. Unable to help herself, she smiled with amusement at the countess's astonishment. "Your reaction suggests you expected me to deny it."

"Well…yes," Lady Lyndham said with a light-hearted laugh while a frown of puzzlement furrowed her brow. "I did."

"I've learned over the last two years to choose my battles wisely. I know when to fight, when not to, and when to surrender."

"A wise woman, indeed," the countess said with another laugh as she set her teacup on her tray. "And quite clever, I might add. The entire Set hangs onto your every word while hoping they're not the ones being placed under the microscope next."

"Do you intend to out me as the author?" she asked with bated breath.

"*Of course not*! The repercussions would be quite severe." The countess exclaimed in an appalled voice as she shook her head vehemently. "If you chose to return to society, it would be a painful experience. The Set can be as vicious as a rabid dog. I would never subject you, or anyone else for that matter, to such a painful verbal flogging."

"I am well-acquainted with the Set's taste for blood, and I have no wish to reenter their midst so they may inflict more wounds." Phoebe bit out through clenched teeth as she remembered the people who'd been unkind to her from the moment she'd been introduced to London society.

"When it comes to the Marlborough Set drawing blood, we agree, which is precisely why I know already we shall become close friends."

"Friends, my lady?"

"Absolutely. I think you're quite clever, have a wonderful sense of humor, and you are kind. *That* I know from your willingness to forgive my transgressions earlier. In fact, I insist you call me Constance."

Stunned by the offer of friendship, she stared at the countess in amazement. Although Lawrence's women friends had welcomed her into their inner circle, none of them had ever made any effort to befriend her as Lady Lyndham was doing. Not only that, but the countess had said they would become close friends. The woman barely knew her. How could she possibly know that? A second later, Phoebe realized how ridiculous the question was given the woman's talent.

Still bemused by the countess's cheerful declaration, she couldn't think of a reply. Out of the corner of her eye, Phoebe saw a movement in the doorway. She turned her head to see the woman who had escorted Lady Lyndham into Madame Sabine's office. Tension flooded Phoebe's body. Had the woman heard her confession? As the woman walked toward them, the countess leaned forward and patted Phoebe's hand.

"You have nothing to fear. My sister, like my other siblings, might be reckless occasionally but would never betray a friend." The gentle reassurance in the countess's soft words made Phoebe relax slightly.

"Are you feeling better, Constance?"

A netted veil made it difficult to see the woman's features, and Phoebe suddenly realized Lady Lyndham's sister was the Rockwood who'd been badly burned in a terrible fire. She'd heard the tragic story about how the woman had barely survived the deadly blaze that had cost two family members their lives. Her heart went out to the woman.

"I am feeling much better," the countess replied as she waved her hand in Phoebe's direction. "Patience, have you met Lady Helstone? Phoebe, may I present my sister, Lady Patience MacTavish, Mistress of Cairnlarich."

"How do you do, my lady," Lady Patience nodded politely at Phoebe. For a fraction of a moment, Phoebe thought the woman was on the verge of saying something else before she turned toward Constance. "Madame Sabine says she intends to create a new gown for Louisa."

"A new gown?" Constance asked as she arched her eyebrows slightly.

"Apparently, Sabine assigned one of her new apprentice seamstresses to make the dress, and the woman mixed up two different patterns to create that monstrosity. Sabine was as horrified as we were."

"Oh dear, I hope the poor woman isn't dismissed."

"Louisa made it clear to Sabine that she would never shop here again if that happened."

"And will everything be ready in time for fittings?"

"Sabine said there was more than enough time to create a new dress and finish the rest of Louisa's trousseau. She's clearly not willing to lose a client as faithful as Louisa."

"Good, I was worried we would leave here with her in tears."

"Our little sister is all smiles at the moment, but she's quite eager to return to Melton House. Apparently, Ewan is arriving on the afternoon train from Stirling. But she asked that I make certain you're well enough to go home."

"I am completely recovered." Lady Lyndham smiled at her sister as she stood up, and Phoebe rose as well. "In fact, I was just about to invite Phoebe to tea tomorrow before you arrived."

Speechless once again at the countess's generous nature where she was concerned, Phoebe shook her head. She couldn't possibly accept the invitation. While she had no regrets that she was no longer a member of the Marlborough Set, accepting the offer of tea was foolish. Heaven only knew what would happen if Lady Lyndham had another vision. Not to mention the fact she had an obligation to Madame Sabine. Phoebe shook her head.

"That's very kind of you, my lady—"

"Constance, please." Lady Lyndham gently chastised her as she reached out to take Phoebe's hands in hers and squeezed them in a gesture of friendship. "I'll see to it that Madame Sabine does not object."

"I really don't—"

"I refuse to take no for an answer, Phoebe. Shall we say tomorrow at three o'clock? Lyndham House on Park Street in Mayfair." The countess smiled merrily and didn't give Phoebe the chance to express any objections. "I look forward to seeing you again."

Still smiling, Lady Lyndham slipped her arm through her sister's, and the two women walked out of the room before Phoebe could gather her wits and refuse the woman's invitation.

Other Titles by Monica Burns

THE RECKLESS ROCKWOODS SERIES

Obsession #1
Dangerous #2
The Highlander's Woman #3
Redemption #4
The Beastly Earl #5

THE RECKLESS ROCKWOODS NOVELS

The Rogue's Offer
The Rogue's Countess

SELF-MADE MEN SERIES

His To Command #1 (Novella)
His Mistress #2

STAND ALONE TITLES

Kismet
Mirage
Pleasure Me
Forever Mine
A Bluestocking Christmas
Love's Portrait
Love's Revenge

THE ORDER OF THE SICARI SERIES

Assassin's Honor #1
Assassin's Heart #2
Inferno's Kiss #3

About The Author

Monica Burns is a bestselling author of spicy historical and paranormal romance. She penned her first romance at the age of nine when she selected the pseudonym she uses today. Her historical book awards include the 2011 RT BookReviews Reviewers Choice Award and the 2012 Gayle Wilson Heart of Excellence Award for Pleasure Me.

She is also the recipient of the prestigious paranormal romance award, the 2011 PRISM Best of the Best award for Assassin's Heart. From the days when she hid her stories from her sisters to her first completed full-length manuscript, she always believed in her dream despite rejections and setbacks. A workaholic wife and mother, Monica is a survivor who believes every hero and heroine deserves a HEA (Happily Ever After), especially if she's writing the story.

Find all the ways you can connect with Monica on the next page.

Connect With Monica

Follow For New Release Alerts

Bookbub

Monicaburns.net/BBpage

Amazon

Monicaburns.net/Amazon

Social Media

Facebook

Monicaburns.net/readergroup

MeWe

Monicaburns.net/mewe
Monicaburns.net/readergroup2

Other Connections

Newsletter -Free Digital Book

Monicaburns.net/newsletter

Website

www.monicaburns.com

Email

monicaburns@monicaburns.com

www.ingramcontent.com/pod-product-compliance
Lightning Source LLC
Chambersburg PA
CBHW071130180726
48291CB00007B/2120